"Dad, Mum, you're not going to believe—"
He stopped.

They were sitting at the table, but it wasn't laid for dinner. In the middle of it lay a length of folded yellow cloth. It looked a bit like a scarf.

"This came for you," his father said.

He said it like someone had died. It was just some cloth. Oh, he thought. He took a step forward, picked it up and unfolded it. Not a scarf; a sash.

His mother had been crying. His father looked as though he'd woken up to find all the stock dead, and the wheat burned to the ground and the thatch blown off.

"I shot a possible," he said, but he knew it didn't matter.

His father frowned, as though he didn't understand the words. "That's good," he said, looking away; not at Teucer, not at the sash. "Well?" his father said suddenly. "Tell me about it."

"Later," Teucer said. He was looking at the sash. "When did this come?"

"Just after you went out. Two men, soldiers. Guess they're going round all the farms."

Well, of course. If they were raising the levy, they wouldn't make a special journey just for him. "Did they say when?"

"You got to be at the Long Ash cross, first light, day after tomorrow," his father said. "Kit and three days' rations. They're raising the whole hundred. That's all they'd say."

Praise for the novels of K. J. Parker

"I have reviewed books before that I thought might someday be found to have achieved greatness... K. J. Parker is writing work after work that demands to be placed in that category."

—Orson Scott Card on The Engineer Trilogy

"A richly textured and emotionally complex fantasy... Highly recommended."

—*Library Journal* on The Engineer Trilogy (starred review)

"[*Sharps*] is a ripping good adventure yarn, laced with frequent barbed witticisms and ace sword fighting... Parker's settings and characterizations never miss a beat, and the intricate political interplay of intrigue is suspenseful almost to the last page."

—*Publishers Weekly*

"This is another splendid offering from K. J. Parker, the British fantasist who seems incapable of writing in anything but top form."

—*Locus* on *Sharps*

"Well-crafted, powerful and downright unmissable."

—*SFX* on *The Company*

"Imagine *Lost* meets *The Italian Job*...a masterfully planned and executed book, one that builds on ever-revealing characterization and back-story, leading slowly yet inexorably to its final conclusion."

—SFFWorld.com on *The Company*

"Parker's intricately plotted and meticulously detailed book... moves as deliberately and precisely as an antique watch."

—*Entertainment Weekly* on *Devices and Desires*

"As efficient and well constructed as its protagonist's well-oiled machines."

—*Starburst* on *Devices and Desires*

By K. J. Parker

The Fencer trilogy
Colours in the Steel
The Belly of the Bow
The Proof House

The Scavenger trilogy
Shadow
Pattern
Memory

The Engineer trilogy
Devices and Desires
Evil for Evil
The Escapement

The Company

The Folding Knife

The Hammer
Sharps

The Two of Swords: Volume 1
The Two of Swords: Volume 2
The Two of Swords: Volume 3

By Tom Holt

Expecting Someone Taller
Who's Afraid of Beowulf?
Flying Dutch
Ye Gods!
Overtime
Here Comes the Sun
Grailblazers
Faust Among Equals
Odds and Gods
Djinn Rummy
My Hero
Paint Your Dragon
Open Sesame
Wish You Were Here
Only Human
Snow White and the Seven Samurai
Valhalla
Nothing But Blue Skies
Falling Sideways
Little People
The Portable Door

In Your Dreams
Earth, Air, Fire and Custard
You Don't Have to be Evil to Work Here, But It Helps
Someone Like Me
Barking
The Better Mousetrap
May Contain Traces of Magic
Blonde Bombshell
Life, Liberty and the Pursuit of Sausages
Doughnut
When It's A Jar
The Outsorcerer's Apprentice
The Good, the Bad and the Smug
The Management Style of the Supreme Beings

Dead Funny: Omnibus 1

Mightier Than the Sword: Omnibus 2
The Divine Comedies: Omnibus 3
For Two Nights Only: Omnibus 4
Tall Stories: Omnibus 5
Saints and Sinners: Omnibus 6
Fishy Wishes: Omnibus 7

The Walled Orchard
Alexander at the World's End
Olympiad
A Song for Nero
Meadowland

I, Margaret

Lucia Triumphant
Lucia in Wartime

TWO OF SWORDS

VOLUME ONE

K. J. PARKER

www.orbitbooks.net

Cover design by Lisa Marie Pompilio
Cover art by Trevillion

Orbit
Hachette Book Group
1290 Avenue of the Americas
New York, NY 10104
orbitbooks.net

Originally published as an ebook serial by Orbit in 2015
First Paperback Edition: October 2017

Orbit is an imprint of Hachette Book Group.
The Orbit name and logo are trademarks of Little, Brown Book Group Limited.

Library of Congress Control Number: 2017951010

ISBNs: 978-0-316-17772-6 (trade paperback), 978-0-316-21538-1 (ebook)

Printed in the United States of America

LSC-C

10 9 8 7 6 5 4 3 2 1

For David Barrett, with thanks

The Rules of the Game

Deal nine cards, face upwards.

The Stakes

Director Procopius of the Imperial Academy of Music and Performing Arts came by the scar when he was eighteen months old, on the day when his father, in a drunken rage, stabbed his mother sixteen times before turning the knife on his baby son and then himself. The scar, an inch wide, ran from his left eye to the right corner of his mouth, and he knew that for as long as he lived, regardless of what he achieved (and he had already achieved so much), it would always be the first thing people noticed about him and their most abiding impression. He knew that they would burn with curiosity to know how he'd got it, and would be far too polite or embarrassed to ask.

Just before the battle, General Moisa gave orders to strike camp, form columns and retreat. Immediately one of his junior officers stormed into his tent, forcing his way past the sentries. He was a good-looking young man with curly blond hair, rather a round face; stocky build, medium height. "Permission to speak freely," he said. His name was Senza Belot.

Moisa was putting his maps back in their case. He was a tidy man, who took care of his possessions. "Well?"

"With all due respect," Senza said, "are you out of your mind? Sir?" he added quickly. "We've got them pinned down, we're between them and the road, it's flat as a chessboard and they'll have the sun in their eyes. And you want to run away."

Moisa looked at him. He liked Senza. "We're outnumbered three to one," he said.

"Exactly," Senza replied. "There's a lot of them. Far too many. Unless they get control of the road, they'll have run out of food by this time tomorrow. They're desperate. We can slaughter them."

Moisa nodded, as though this was an exam and Senza had scored full marks. "We don't have any arrows," he said.

Senza had opened his mouth to make his next point. He stood there with it open for a couple of heartbeats. Then he said, "What?"

Moisa took out one of the maps, unrolled it carefully and weighted down the corners with four pebbles from the jar of corner-weighting-down pebbles he always had by him. "There." He prodded the map with a sausage-like finger. "Ten carts, a hundred thousand arrows, supposed to be here at first light today. Got washed away by a flash flood crossing the Euryphiale." He lifted two pebbles and let the map roll itself up again. "No arrows, no battle. Bloody shame, but there it is."

Senza looked at him, like an idiot staring straight into the sun. "Is that all?" he said.

Moisa smiled. "It'll do," he said.

Then came the first recorded instance of the Senza Far-Away Look, so familiar nowadays to audiences of cheap novels and market-square melodramas. Moisa later said he rolled his eyes, which isn't quite how the Look is portrayed in the classical tradition. "Permission to do something about it. Sir."

Moisa shrugged. "How long?"

"Hour." Senza frowned. "Maybe two. But after one hour you'll know I've succeeded."

Senza's elder brother Forza was reckoned to be the most promising soldier of his generation, already in command of a battalion at the age of twenty-one. It was a shame he was on the other side. "All right," Moisa said. "Talk to me."

Shortly after that, the retreat was called off, the army assumed the standard chest-and-horns formation against the enemy front, and six hundred of the elite Seventh heavy infantry advanced in a long double line, followed by two pike regiments in squares of five hundred, preceded by thirty of the great pavises that Moisa had prepared for the siege of Thrassa. The pavises were big shields, made of ox hides stitched together, about the size of a warship's sail, hung on square wooden frames and mounted on carts. They headed straight for the centre of the enemy line, which was mostly made up of archers covered by triangles of light infantry.

"He's going to try and punch through," said the enemy general (his name is not recorded). "He must be mad."

His aide, Colonel Forza Belot, grinned. "He hasn't got any arrows," he said.

The general frowned. "That's interesting," he said. "How did you know that?"

"Little bird told me. They all got washed away crossing some river. So, he's got two choices, go home or try and smash through. He can't break our heavy infantry, so he's going for the soft middle." He shrugged. "It's what I'd do, if I was desperate."

"We've got ten thousand archers in there," the general said. "It's crazy."

"Yes," Forza replied. "Sometimes you have to be."

The line advanced, the sails of the pavises billowing in the strong tailwind, until they came into medium range of the Western archers. "Well?" the general asked.

"Let 'em have it," Forza replied.

The archers loosed. They were levies from the northern hill country, trained from childhood to shoot fast and far. They let go twenty volleys in just over two minutes. The six hundred men-at-arms in the front two ranks were wiped out. The advance stopped dead and immediately withdrew, taking long-distance fire until they were out of range. The general, watching from the hilltop, grinned and turned to Colonel Forza. "Well," he said. "That's that."

"Maybe," Forza said.

The Easterners completed their withdrawal, and the front ranks parted to let them through. The pikemen resumed their positions in the line, but the pavise carts passed on to the rear, where Moisa and the archers were waiting.

"There you go," Senza said. "Arrows."

The archers scrambled up on to the carts and started pulling arrows out of the pavises. "Twenty volleys," Senza went on, "ten thousand archers, that's two hundred and forty thousand arrows. Say eighty thousand misses, five thousand hits on the Seventh, that's still—"

Moisa nodded. "Enough," he said. Then he added, "You didn't tell me about the Seventh."

Senza shrugged. "They had to have something to shoot at," he said, "and we don't need those men today. What we need is arrows, not heavy infantry." He smiled. "Plenty more where they came from."

Moisa now had enough arrows for ten volleys. In the event it only took him seven to win the battle, but he was unable to press home his advantage, mostly because of an inspired rearguard action by the Western Nineteenth Foot, under Colonel Forza Belot. The Westerners then cut across the marshes to reach the road, where they met their supply train. A week later, the situation was more or less exactly how it had been at the start of the campaign.

Six months later, the newly commissioned Colonel Senza Belot of the Eastern Fifth attended a reception at the Winter Palace, where he found himself talking to the widow of an officer of the Seventh. She gave him a polite smile over the rim of her wine glass and said, "I think you're the man who sent my husband to his death."

Senza put his glass down. "Permission to speak freely."

"Yes, why not? I'd be interested to hear what you've got to say to me."

Senza took a moment. "When I barged into Moisa's tent," he

said, "I had maybe three seconds to get his attention and sell him on a plan of action. In those three seconds I considered two options. One was to take our best men, the Seventh, your husband's unit, loop round a long way to the west into some dead ground I'd spotted, sneak up on the enemy baggage train and try and drive off a dozen or so carts full of arrows. It was a reasonable plan, I think. I'd had my eye on those arrow carts for about a week, on and off, while we were playing footsie with the Westerners up and down the Belsire river. I knew they'd be out back of the camp, and that their general probably hadn't figured out about the blind spot. But to get there without being seen would've taken an hour, during which time our army would've been standing about doing nothing, which would've looked very odd, which could've put the other side on notice we were planning some sort of prank. Also, if it had all gone wrong we'd have got a good smacking and no arrows; even if it all went just right, I'd have had to leave the Seventh behind to hold off pursuit while we got the arrows safely back to our lines, and they'd have been slaughtered by the Western lancers. The other alternative, which is what I actually did, was pretty well foolproof, and we were pulling arrows out of the pavises three quarters of an hour after it all started. Your husband would've died either way. He could have died fighting bravely against overwhelming odds, to give Moisa the seven shots he needed to win the day. As it was, he walked straight into an arrow storm and probably had no idea what hit him. That's really all there is to it."

The widow looked at him for a moment. "You thought all that in three seconds."

"That and other things. I've only told you the relevant bits."

She fidgeted with her glass. "But it all came to nothing anyway," she said. "There was a stalemate before the battle; there's the same stalemate now. Nothing's changed at all, except that a lot of men were killed, and you got your promotion."

"Yes," Senza said. "But at the moment, my job's winning

battles, not winning wars. If I'd been in Moisa's shoes, I'd have done what I originally intended, turned round and gone home. Really, he should've known better than to listen to me."

"I see," the widow said. "Thank you. Tell me, is there anything you care about other than your own career?"

Senza smiled gravely. "Yes," he said. "One thing."

"Go on."

"I want to find my brother Forza and cut his throat," Senza said. "Now, please excuse me, there's someone over there I need to talk to."

The Cards

1

The Crown Prince

The draw in Rhus is to the corner of the mouth; it says so in the Book, it's the law. In Overend, they draw to the ear; in the South, it's the middle of the lower lip—hence the expression, "archer's kiss." Why Imperial law recognises three different optimum draws, given that the bow and the arrow are supposedly standardised throughout the empire, nobody knows. In Rhus, of course, they'll tell you that the corner of the mouth is the only possible draw if you actually want to hit anything. Drawing to the ear messes up your sightline down the arrow, and the Southerners do the kiss because they're too feeble to draw a hundred pounds that extra inch.

Teucer had a lovely draw, everybody said so. Old men stood him drinks because it was so perfect, and the captain made him stand in front of the beginners and do it over and over again. His loose wasn't quite so good—he had a tendency to snatch, letting go of the string rather than allowing it to slide from his fingers—which cost him valuable points in matches. Today, however, for some reason he wished he could isolate, preserve in vinegar and bottle, he was loosing exactly right. The arrow left the string without any conscious action on his part—a thought, maybe:

round about now would be a good time, and then the arrow was in the air, bounding off to join its friends in the dead centre of the target, like a happy dog. The marker at the far end of the butts held up a yellow flag: a small one. Eight shots into the string, Teucer suddenly realised he'd shot eight inner golds, and was just two away from a possible.

He froze. In the long and glorious history of the Merebarton butts, only two possibles had ever been shot: one by a legendary figure called Old Shan, who may or may not have existed some time a hundred years ago, and one by Teucer's great-uncle Ree, who'd been a regular and served with Calojan. Nobody had had the heart to pull the arrows out of that target; it had stayed on the far right of the butts for twenty years, until the straw was completely rotten, and the rusty heads had fallen out into the nettles. Every good archer had shot a fifty. One or two in the village had shot fifty with eight or fifty with nine. A possible—fifty with ten, ten shots in the inner circle of the gold—was something completely different.

People were looking at him, and then at his target, and the line had gone quiet. A possible at one hundred yards is—well, possible; but extremely unlikely, because there's only just enough space in the inner ring for ten arrowheads. Usually what happens is that you drop in seven, maybe eight, and then the next one touches the stem of an arrow already in place on its way in and gets deflected; a quarter-inch into the outer gold if you're lucky, all the way out of the target and into the nettles if you're not. In a match, with beer or a chicken riding on it, the latter possibility tends to persuade the realistic competitor to shade his next shot just a little, to drop it safely into the outer gold and avoid the risk of a match-losing score-nought. Nobody in history anywhere had ever shot a possible in a match. But this was practice, nothing to play for except eternal glory, the chance for his name to be remembered a hundred years after his death; he had no option but to try for it. He squinted against the evening light, trying to figure out the lie of his eight shots, but the target was a hundred yards away: all he could see of the arrows was the yellow blaze of the fletchings. He considered calling hold, stopping the shoot while he walked up the range and took a closer look. That was allowed, even in a match, but to do so would be to acknowledge that he was trying for a possible, so that when he failed—

A voice in his head, which he'd never heard before, said quite clearly, *go and look*. No, I can't, he thought, and the voice didn't argue. Quite. Only an idiot argues with himself. Go and look. He took a deep breath and said, "Hold."

It came out loud, high and squeaky, but nobody laughed; instead, they laid their bows down on the grass and took a step back. Dead silence. Men he'd known all his life. Then, as he took his first stride up the range, someone whose voice he couldn't identify said, "Go on, Teuce." It was said like a prayer, as though addressed to a god—please send rain, please let my father get well. They *believed* in him. It made his stomach turn and his face go cold. He walked up the range as if to the gallows.

When he got there: not good. The marker (Pilad's uncle Sen; a quiet man, but they'd always got on well) gave him a look that said *sorry, son*, then turned away. Six arrows were grouped tight in the exact centre of the inner gold, one so close to the others that the shaft was actually flexed; God only knew how it had gone in true. The seventh was out centre-right, just cutting the line. The eighth was in clean, but high left. That meant he had to shoot two arrows into the bottom centre, into a half-moon about the size of his thumb, from a hundred yards away. He stared at it. Can't be done. It was, no pun intended, impossible.

Pilad's uncle Sen gave him a wan smile and said, "Good luck." He nodded, turned away and started back down the range.

Sen's nephew Pilad was his best friend, something he'd never quite been able to understand. Pilad was, beyond question, the glory of Merebarton. Not yet nineteen (he was three weeks older than Teucer) he was already the best stockman, the best reaper and mower, champion ploughman, best thatcher and hedge-layer; six feet tall, black-haired and brown-eyed, the only possible topic of conversation when three girls met, undisputed champion horse-breaker and second-best archer. And now consider Teucer, his best friend; shorter, ordinary-looking, awkward with girls, a good worker but a bit slow, you'd have trouble remembering him ten minutes after you'd met him, and the only man living to have shot a hundred-yard possible on Merebarton range—

He stopped, halfway between butts and firing point, and laughed. The hell with it, he thought.

Pilad was shooting second detail, so he was standing behind the line, in with a bunch of other fellows. As Teucer walked up, he noticed that Pilad was looking away, standing behind someone's shoulder, trying to make himself inconspicuous. Teucer reached the line, turned and faced the target; like the time he'd had to go and bring in the old white bull, and it had stood there glaring at him with mad eyes, daring him to take one more step. Even now he had no idea where the courage had come from that day; he'd opened the gate and gone in, a long stride directly towards certain death; on that day, the bull had come quietly, gentle as a lamb while he put the halter on, walking to heel like a good dog. Maybe, Teucer thought, when I was born Skyfather allotted me a certain number of good moments, five or six, maybe, to last me my whole life. If so, let this be one of them.

Someone handed him his bow. His fingers closed round it, and the feel of it was like coming home. He reached for the ninth arrow, stuck point first into the ground. He wasn't aware of nocking it, but it got on to the string somehow. *Just look at the target*: that voice again, and he didn't yet know it well enough to decide whether or not it could be trusted. He drew, and he was looking straight down the arrow at a white circle on a black background. Just look at the target. He held on it for three heartbeats, and then the arrow left him.

Dead silence, for the impossibly long time it took for the arrow to get there. Pilad's uncle Sen walked to the target with his armful of flags, picked one out and lifted it. Behind Teucer, someone let out a yell they must've heard back in the village.

Well, he thought, that's forty-five with nine; good score, enough to win most matches. And still one shot in hand. Let's see what we can do.

The draw. He had a lovely draw. This time, he made himself enjoy it. To draw a hundred-pound bow, you first use and then abuse nearly every muscle and every joint in your body. There's a turning point, a hinge, where the force of the arms alone is supplemented by the back and the legs. He felt the tip of his middle finger brush against his lip, travel the length of it, until it found the far corner. Just look at the target. It doesn't matter, he told himself. *It matters,* said the voice. *But that's all right. That helps.*

He'd never thought of it like that before. It matters. And that helps. Yes, he thought, it helps, and the arrow flew.

It lifted, the way an arrow does, swimming in the slight headwind he presumed he'd allowed for, though he had no memory of doing so. It lifted, reaching the apex of its flight, and he thought: however long I live, let a part of me always be in this moment, this split second when I could've shot a hundred-yard possible; this moment at which it's still on, it hasn't missed yet, the chance, the *possibility* is still alive, so that when I'm sixty-six and half blind and a nuisance to my family, I'll still have this, the one thing that could've made me great—

Uncle Sen walked to the target. He wasn't carrying his flags. He stood for a moment, the only thing that existed in the whole world. Then he raised both his arms and shouted.

Oh, Teucer thought; and then something hit him in the back and sent him flat on his face in the grass, and for a moment he couldn't breathe, and it *hurt*. He was thinking: who'd want to do that to me; they're supposed to be my friends. And then he was grabbed by his arms and yanked upright, and everybody was shouting in his face, and Pilad's grin was so close to his eyes he couldn't see it clearly; and he thought: I did it.

He didn't actually want to go and look, just in case there had been a mistake, but they gave him no choice; he was scooped up and planted on two bony shoulders, so that he had to claw at heads with his fingers to keep from falling off. At the butts they slid him off on to his knees, so that when he saw the target he was in an attitude of worship, like in Temple. Fair enough. Arrows nine and ten were both in, clean, not even touching the line. They looked like a bunch of daffodils, or seedlings badly in need of thinning. A possible. The only man living. And then he thought: they won't let me pull my arrows out, and they're my match set, and I can't afford to buy another one—

And Pilad, who'd been one of the bony shoulders, gave him another murderous slap on the back and said, "Nicely, Teuce, nicely," and with a deep feeling of shame and remorse he realised that Pilad meant it; no resentment, no envy, sheer joy in his friend's extraordinary achievement. (But if Pilad had been the shooter, how would he be feeling now? Don't answer that.) He felt as if he'd just betrayed his friend, stolen from him or told lies about him behind his back. He wanted to say he was sorry, but it would be too complicated to explain.

They let him go eventually. Pilad and Nical walked with him as far as the top of the lane. He explained that he wanted to check on the lambs, so he'd take a short cut across the top meadow. It's possible that they believed him. He walked the rest of the way following the line of the hedge, as though he didn't want to be seen.

It was nearly dark when he got home; there was a thin line of bright yellow light under the door and he could smell roast chicken. He grinned, and lifted the latch.

"Dad, Mum, you're not going to believe—" He stopped. They were sitting at the table, but it wasn't laid for dinner. In the middle of it lay a length of folded yellow cloth. It looked a bit like a scarf.

"This came for you," his father said.

He said it like someone had died. It was just some cloth. Oh, he thought. He took a step forward, picked it up and unfolded it. Not a scarf; a sash.

His mother had been crying. His father looked as though he'd woken up to find all the stock dead, and the wheat burned to the ground and the thatch blown off.

"I shot a possible," he said, but he knew it didn't matter.

His father frowned, as though he didn't understand the words. "That's good," he said, looking away; not at Teucer, not at the sash. "Well?" his father said suddenly. "Tell me about it."

"Later," Teucer said. He was looking at the sash. "When did this come?"

"Just after you went out. Two men, soldiers. Guess they're going round all the farms."

Well, of course. If they were raising the levy, they wouldn't make a special journey just for him. "Did they say when?"

"You got to be at the Long Ash cross, first light, day after tomorrow," his father said. "Kit and three days' rations. They're raising the whole hundred. That's all they'd say."

It went without saying they had records; the census, conducted by the Brothers every five years. They'd know his father was exactly one year overage for call-up, just as they'd known he had a son, nineteen, eligible. It would all be written down somewhere in a book; a sort of immortality, if you cared to look at it that way. Somewhere in the city, the provincial capital, strangers knew their names, knew that they existed, just as people a hundred years hence would know about Teucer from Merebarton, who'd once shot ten with ten at a hundred yards.

He wasn't the least bit hungry now. "What's for dinner?" he said.

He woke up out of a dream, and all that was left of it was someone saying, *he must've had eyes like a hawk,* and then he remembered: what day it was, what he had to do. He slid off the bed, found his clothes and wriggled into them by feel, because it was too dark to see.

The idea was to leave the house before anyone else was awake. Nice idea, but Teucer had always been clumsy. He sideswiped a chair with his thigh, and the chair fell over, and something that must've been on the chair clattered on to the flagstones, making a noise like chain-making at the forge, only a bit louder. He realised that it was his bow, quiver, knapsack and tin cup. He lowered himself to his knees and groped on the floor till he'd found them all. The noise he made would've woken the dead, but there was no sound from the other room. Mum and Dad would be wide awake, so presumably they'd guessed what he was doing. Well.

He'd put his boots in the porch the night before, the sash stuffed into the leg of the right boot. He wasn't sure whether he was supposed to wear it yet; in theory, he knew, you were a soldier from the moment it was handed to you (so when he shot the possible, was he already a soldier?) and so he guessed he was entitled to wear the damned thing. But old men in the village who'd been in the service told all sorts of blood-curdling stories about what happened to raw recruits who broke the secret laws of military protocol. There were, he knew, thirty-six different ways of wearing the sash: only five of them were correct, and two of those were reserved for twenty-year men. Unfortunately, either the old men hadn't specified, or he hadn't been paying attention. He fished it out, shoved it in his pocket and put his boots on.

The sky was cloudless, before-dawn deep blue, and it had rained in the night so everything smelt sweetly of wet leaves and slaked earth. He walked up the yard, stopped by the corner of the hay barn and looked back. He knew this moment. It was one of the best, getting up early and walking round the fields to see if he could shoot a couple of rabbits, maybe a fox, a deer if he was absolutely sure nobody was looking. On such days he'd always stop and look back at this point, just in case there was a rabbit sitting out on the edge of the cabbage bed. No such luck today. He grinned, turned easily and walked on, taking care to make no sound, out of force of habit.

Pilad and Musen were waiting for him by the oak stump on the top road, silhouettes against the blue sky. Musen was wearing a hat and a scarf, which seemed a bit excessive for the time of year. He nodded as Teucer came up, grunted, "All right, then?" Pilad was eating an apple.

"Where's Dimed?" Teucer asked.

Pilad shrugged. "Shacked up, probably. Last taste of home, that sort of thing."

"Do we wait?"

"No chance." Musen stood up. "Catch me getting in trouble because he can't be arsed to get up in time."

Teucer glanced at Pilad, who nodded, threw away the apple and rose to his feet. "He'll catch up," he said.

On the way to Tophead, Pilad told them the latest from the war; Pilad knew these things, though nobody knew how. By all accounts, it wasn't good. General Belot had crushed the enemy Third Army in the foothills of the mountains, which was all very well; but it turned out that the incursion was just a feint, designed to draw him away while the enemy unleashed their main offensive, which was headed straight at Choris Anthropou. Right now, there was no army in being between them and the capital, which was why they were scrambling all the levies and reserves in the north-east and rushing them south to block the way. Nobody expected them to turn back the invasion, no chance whatsoever of that; the idea was simply to buy time for Belot to get back across the sea and sort the buggers out for good. Whether even he would be able to do that was uncertain; it was a stupid time of year to be crossing the sea south to north; there wasn't time to hug the coast round, and sailing across the middle with the summer storms just starting, you could end up anywhere, very likely the bottom. This time, it looked like Belot had been taken in good and proper—

"Don't say that," Musen interrupted. "Belot's the best, there's no one like him. He'll get there, don't you worry."

"No one like him except his brother," Pilad replied. "That's the point."

"What if he doesn't get here in time?" Teucer asked.

Pilad shrugged. "They still got to take the city," he replied. "If they can't carry it by storm, there'll be a siege. That'll give old Senza plenty of time to get here and do the business, so I guess Forza's putting everything on being able to bash his way into Choris damn quick. Don't suppose he'd take that chance without he's got a damn good reason. They reckon he's got some kind of new weapon. But they always say that."

They'd reached the stile at Clayhanger, where they were joined by the Lower Town contingent. Interestingly, Dimed was with them, which tended to support Pilad's theory. Someone said that the Higher Town boys would meet them at the brook, and the West Reach crowd would be waiting for them at Fivehead. Lamin's mother had sent them a large basket of freshly baked honeycakes, with instructions to leave the basket at the Truth & Patience. "Does she want paying for them?" Musen asked with his mouth full, and nobody could be bothered to reply.

Sear Hill is the highest point south of the Lakes. Teucer had been that far out twice before, both times on droves, taking cattle to Southanger market. He recognised the blunt sugarloaf profile of the hill and knew where he was.

"Don't talk soft," Musen said. "That's not Sear; Sear's fifteen miles away, due east. That's Cordinger, and over there's the Wey valley."

"Right," Pilad said. "And in that case, we should be standing up to our ankles in the river." General laughter, and Musen pulled a sad face. "That's Sear, and just over the skyline's Southanger. We'll be there in time for dinner."

And they were. The muster was on Southanger Yards, the flat plain just outside the town where cattle were penned for loading on to river barges bound for Ennea and Choris Anthropou. Appropriate choice; when they got there, the whole plain was covered in sandy-white cotton tents, fifteen feet by ten, pitched in streets. The smoke from the campfires set Anser off coughing while they were still five hundred yards from the camp gates; they were burning coal and foundrymens' charcoal, and the air was thick and oily. They knew where to go because there was a queue, about a hundred men with bows and knapsacks, lining up to get through a small gap in a fence they could easily have climbed over. Welcome to the army, Teucer thought.

Pilad got talking to some of the men in front of them, East Riding men from over the other side of Sear. They were all wearing their sashes; the wrong way round, too. Teucer quietly suggested pointing this out, but Pilad only grinned. The queue moved painfully slowly when it moved at all. They were all hungry, but they were reluctant to break into the provisions they'd brought from home for fear of spoiling their dinner. The East Ridingers must've been there considerably longer. They were munching on bread and cold meat, and passing round big stone bottles of cider. Suddenly they were called forward; they passed through the gate and disappeared, as though they'd been eaten.

A very short man in a very big green coat was sitting on a stool in the gateway. "Next," he called out. Nobody moved. "I said next," the short man shouted. "You there, where's your sergeant?"

You there, who turned out to be Notker from Lower Town, shrugged and looked helpless. Pilad sighed and moved to the front. "That'll be me," he said. "We're from Merebarton. My name's Pilad."

The short man studied a sheet of paper. It had been folded many times, and the writing was very small. "Where?"

"Merebarton," Pilad said. "Just up from Coopers Ford on the South road."

"Got you." The short man looked surprised, as though the existence of Merebarton was too bizarre to credit. "Says here, twenty-six men."

"Are you sure?" Pilad said. "There's twenty-eight of us."

The short man stared at his paper, then looked at Pilad; then very slowly, like a man throwing dust on his father's coffin lid, he felt in his pocket, produced a little brass travelling inkwell, unscrewed the lid, put the lid carefully down on the ground, put the inkwell down beside it, felt in his other pocket, brought out a little bit of hazel twig with a nib served on to it with bootmaker's twine, leaned forward, dipped the pen in the ink, found his place in the paper, pressed it hard against his knee, scratched something out and wrote something in. "Twenty-eight," he said. "Is that right?"

"That's right, yes."

The short man nodded, then carefully reversed the procedure, with the tucking away of the inkwell as the final step. "You're late," he said.

Pilad didn't even blink. "Sorry about that," he said. "We got held up. Bridge down at Redstone."

The short man clicked his tongue. "Through there," he said, without the slightest indication of where there was. "See the master-at-arms, then the quartermaster."

They moved through the gateway. As soon as they were through, Teucer asked, "Where's Redstone?"

"No idea," Pilad said. "Right, over there, I guess."

Nobody seemed to mind that Pilad was now their sergeant, whatever that meant. Pilad had spotted the East Riding crowd who'd been in line ahead of them; they were now standing in another, even longer line that led to something Teucer couldn't see. The Easterners were, Teucer noticed, very quiet and subdued; also, they'd taken off their sashes.

The queue was to see a large, bald man with three teeth, sitting on a wooden box. He grinned at them. "Who're you, then?"

"Merebarton," Pilad said. "That's—"

"I know where it is," the bald man said. He didn't have any papers. "So where's the rest of you, then?"

"We're it," Pilad said. "Twenty-eight."

The bald man shook his head. "Merebarton," he said. "South Riding. Thirty-two men. Where's the other four?"

"Everyone's here," Pilad said. "There's nobody left in the village but old men. Really."

The bald man sighed. "No skin off my nose, boy," he said. "But your mates are going to catch it hot when the proctors come round. All right, over there, where you see the big tent. You get your kit, and someone'll point you to your tent."

"Thanks," Pilad said. "When do we get dinner? We've been walking all day."

"Suit yourselves," the bald man said with a shrug. "You brought your three days' rations, didn't you? Eat 'em soon as you like, for all I care. Right, move along."

"You know what," Teucer said, as they stood in line outside the quartermaster's tent. "This isn't how I thought the army would be like. It's, oh, I don't know—"

"All over the place," Pilad said. "Doesn't bode well, if you ask me."

"Quit moaning," said Notker from Lower Town. "I thought it'll be all bull and shouting and saluting, all that stuff. Can't say I was looking forward to it."

"Maybe that comes later," Musen said.

"No, I don't think so." Pilad was watching something; Teucer tried to figure out what it was, but he couldn't see anything. "I think this is how it's going to be."

"Hope you're right," Notker said.

"I hope I'm wrong," Pilad replied. "But I doubt it."

The quartermaster was tall and very thin, missing his left eye and his right ear. The hair on his head was sparse and fine, like grass growing back on fallow ground. "Unit," he said.

"Merebarton," Pilad replied. "Twenty-eight of us."

The quartermaster sat on an upturned barrel in the middle of a large tent, almost empty. There were about half a dozen tubs—old water barrels sawn in two. "Right, then," he said. "You get one pair of boots each free of charge—look after 'em because after that you got to pay for them yourselves. You get one sheaf each three dozen standard arrows, one bowstring, hemp, one sash—"

"We've already been given those."

"One sash," the quartermaster repeated, "one roll standard bandage, one inspirational medallion depicting the triumph of the true emperor, pewter, one cap, wool. When you're done, go out through the back; someone'll point you to your tent."

"Just a moment," Pilad said. "What about swords? Don't we get them?"

The quartermaster looked at him as though he'd just become visible. "Swords," he repeated. "What you want them for?"

"Well, to fight with."

The quartermaster shook his head. "You ain't here to fight, boy. You're here to shoot arrows. You get arrows. Swords cost money."

"But what if we're—?"

"Next," the quartermaster said.

"Is there an officer I can talk to?"

The quartermaster looked as if he'd been asked for a unicorn.

"There's one around somewhere," he said. "What you want an officer for?"

"Well," Pilad said, "I just want to—"

"Now you listen." The quartermaster took a deep breath, as though about to perform an act of charity for an unworthy recipient. "You boys aren't soldiers, right? You're levy. You need to be able to do three things, no, sorry, four. You need to shoot your bows. Can you do that?"

"Yes."

"You need to walk."

"Yes."

"You need to do what you're told. You boys all right with that?"

"Oh yes."

"And you need to be able to run," the quartermaster said. "Because when you've walked to where they tell you to go, and you shot off all your arrows, and them Western bastards are coming to get you, you want to be able to run like the fucking wind. You got that? Grand. All right, who's next?"

There was no one outside the tent to tell them where to go next. After they'd been standing around for a minute or so, Pilad said, "This way," and walked off.

Teucer trotted to catch up with him. "Where are we going?"

"Get a tent."

"But we're supposed to—"

Pilad smiled and shook his head. "Over there," he said.

They found a tent with nobody in it. There were no blankets or anything like that. They piled up their gear, and Pilad told Anser to go and look for the latrines. "Won't be hard," he said. "Just follow your nose."

The others were digging their provisions out of their packs. "I think I see what you mean," Teucer said.

Pilad nodded. He didn't seem to be hungry, so Teucer decided he wasn't either. "It's not good," Pilad said. "Still, we're country boys; we can fend for ourselves. Main thing is to stick together. If we do that, we'll be all right."

"We should go home," Musen said, sitting down on the ground next to them.

"We can't do that," Teucer said.

Pilad said nothing. "I don't see why not," Musen replied. "Nobody gives a shit about us. We might as well not be here."

"We'd get in trouble."

Musen laughed. "Nah," he said, "they'd just think we wandered off somewhere, got given the wrong orders, something like that. We should just turn round and go back home now, while we got the chance."

Teucer looked at Pilad, who was thinking. "Well?" he prompted.

"I don't know," Pilad said. "I don't think much to staying here. I mean, you heard the quartermaster. Doesn't look like they're going to make us into soldiers any time soon, and I reckon, if you're in a war, you need to be a soldier, or you won't last very long."

"That's right," Musen said. "So, let's get out of it while we still can."

"I don't know," Pilad repeated. "It's a mess all right, but they've got us down on a bit of paper somewhere, so if we just clear off, they'll know, and that won't be good either. I reckon the best thing is if we stick together, look out for each other, and think about what we're doing, instead of just doing what they say regardless. We're not stupid, we can look after ourselves, we should be all right. Just don't expect those buggers out there to do anything for us, because they won't."

Musen gave a loud sigh of annoyance, got up and walked away. Pilad didn't seem to mind. He lay back on the ground, his head propped up on his pack, and closed his eyes. Pilad slept where and when he could, like a dog, and always woke up instantly, fresh and ready for anything.

*

Six days' march. It's walking, Pilad told them; we can do that, we've been walking all our lives.

The first day was fine. The weather was good and so was the road. *March* had conjured up in Teucer's mind a vision of co-ordinated footfalls and relentless pace, but in fact it was more of a heavily armed stroll, since they weren't supposed to go faster than the ox carts. They stopped half a dozen times, always by water. Pilad got talking to men from some of the other contingents; he had family in the North and West Ridings, so the problem wasn't so much getting the strangers to talk as inducing them to stop without giving offence. In the evening, they set up a few caps on sticks and had an impromptu archery match between five villages; Merebarton came second, mostly because Musen flogged an easy one at fifty yards. There was still some cider left, though not for long.

The second day seemed to have rather more hours in it than the first, or else time passed more slowly west of the Blackwater. The road at this point was much used by carts, so they were walking in deep ruts, often flooded by the recent heavy rains; they got a sample of those around midday, and had to walk sodden until they dried out mid-afternoon. By the end of the third day Teucer's feet were beginning to hurt, and on the fourth day the ground started to rise as they tackled the foothills of the Hog's Back, a range he'd heard about but never seen before. At this point, the carts turned off and left them; apparently, they weren't their supply wagons after all, just a small convoy that had happened to be going in the same direction. On Pilad's advice, Teucer had kept some food back, but most of the others had long since finished theirs, and lack of food was the dominant subject of conversation on the fourth and fifth days. There must be a supply wagon somewhere, obviously; someone must've arranged for it to meet them at some point, but nobody seemed to know where or when. This raised the question of who exactly was in charge. Everyone Pilad spoke to seemed convinced that there was an officer with the column, but nobody had actually seen him; each village assumed he must be with one of the other contingents. On the fifth morning, before they started out, Pilad got up early and went round the camp. When he came back, he looked worried, which was never a good sign.

"No officer," he said.

"That can't be right," Musen objected. "If there's no officer, how do we know when to start and stop?"

Pilad sat down on the ground, took his boot off and examined the sole. "Good question," he said. "The sergeant of the Conegar lot reckons there was an officer to start with, but he sort of vanished after the first day. Nobody else figures to have seen him. I think whoever's in front starts walking when the sun gets up." He put his boot back on and smiled. "There's a fair chance we're on the wrong road, as well. I think when we crossed that river day before yesterday we should've taken the left fork, not the right."

Notker looked up sharply. "You what?"

"Sergeant of the Conegars was told we're headed for Spire Cross," Pilad said. "Spire Cross is on the Mere, and the Mere runs from the Hog's Back to the sea." He turned his head and nodded sort of north-east. "That's over there," he said. "Still, he could be wrong. He was only going by what he reckons this officer told him, and nobody else but him ever saw this bloody officer. For all I know, he might've been walking too long in the sun without his hat on."

There was a brief, quiet moment while everyone thought the same thing.

"So the supply cart—" Musen said.

Pilad shook his head. "Don't hold your breath for any supply cart," he said. "I reckon what we fetched from home was meant to last us as far as Spire Cross. So, if we get there tomorrow sometime, no real harm done."

"And if we're on the wrong road—"

"Well," Pilad said.

Anser from Middle Town said, "You don't actually know this is the wrong road."

Pilad grinned at him. "Course not," he said. "I don't actually know we're supposed to be going to Spire Cross, that's just what the sergeant of the Conegars told me, and he could be daft in the head for all I know."

Calo from Lopenhead said, "How can they send us off without an officer? That's crazy."

Pilad yawned. The sun was just starting to come up, and his face was blood-red. "Maybe there weren't enough to go round. I don't know, do I?"

"But if we're on the wrong road, we got to turn back, right now. We keep going, we could starve to death."

Teucer looked all around him, at the grey dry heather and the granite outcrops. "We're five days from the camp," he said. "All that time, we didn't pass anywhere where we could get anything to eat."

"Teucer's right," Pilad said. "God knows if this is the right road or not, but if we keep going we may well starve; if we turn back, we definitely will. Meanwhile, any of you see so much as a mouse, shoot the bugger."

No mice. The only living things apart from themselves in those hills seemed to be buzzards and crows, which stayed just out of range at all times, the way they do. By the end of the sixth day, it was clear that Pilad wasn't alone in his doubts. The pace of the column fluctuated wildly, from a slow trudge to a frantic quick-march whenever there was a horizon to cross beyond which there might be something to see, such as a town, or a line of carts, or even a plume of distant smoke. "Somebody's got to live here," Notker said, just after noon on the sixth day; apparently not. They realised they hadn't seen a living soul since before the Hog's Back.

"Figures," Pilad said. "This war's been going on a long time. When they call up a village, that's all the men gone. You think what happens when they don't come back, or just one or two. It means sooner or later everybody that's left packs up and heads for the city; that or stay put and starve to death. I reckon that's what we're looking at here."

Teucer thought of Merebarton, of who was left at home to do the work. His father, uncles, a few hired men; if something happened, how long could they carry on before it all got too much? They'd cope to begin with, but it wouldn't be like making shift while someone was away on a drove or off work with a broken arm. Gradually, the things left undone would begin to creep in: the fences not mended, the docks and thistles not grubbed out, the muck not spread so that the land lost heart, never quite enough hands to bring in all the harvest or the hay. Each year there'd be more left to spoil, less in the barn, another three or four pastures run to waste, another shed roofless or fallen down for want of time and stone to fix it; and all the time the men working harder, getting older, wearing out with use until in the end they were blunt and no good. It could happen so easily, while your back was turned.

On the seventh day, there was a horseman.

The column stopped dead and watched him, from a faint suggestion of moving dust into a man on a horse, in a grey cloak and a red felt pillbox hat, like the ones they'd been given. He galloped up the last rise towards them in fine style, his cloak floating in the slipstream; drew up, looked at them and yelled, "What the hell do you think you're playing at?"

They had, it turned out, taken the wrong road; they should've been in Spire Cross the day before yesterday, so the rider, a sergeant-at-arms from the Fifteenth cavalry, a *regular*, had been sent to find them. Being well versed in the stupidity of civilians, he'd glanced at a map, guessed what had happened and here he was. He looked at the desperate faces crowded round him and said, "Who's in charge of you lot, anyway?"

Dead silence; then Pilad said, "You are. What do we do?"

He'd brought his map with him. Teucer had never seen one before; he looked at it over Pilad's shoulder, but it made no sense. The cavalryman, however, seemed to understand it just fine. He had a little metal tool, like the carpenter's callipers but tiny and fine; he walked them across the map, measuring distances. "You cut across country here," he said, jabbing at the map with a long forefinger. "You'll be all right. Can any of you monkeys read a map?" Silence. "Can any of you *read*?" More silence. "Shit," the cavalryman said.

"You'll have to come with us," Pilad said.

"No chance," the cavalryman replied, "I got other things to do. Look," he went on—he was talking to Pilad as though he was the only person there—"all you got to do is, keep the sun on your left in the morning, keep looking at that slight rise—there, you see it? That's Stonecap, here, look." He prodded the map with the steel measuring tool. "Head straight for that till you come to this belt of trees, then head sharp north. That's an extra half a day, but that way you won't get lost. There's a village here, look: ask them nicely and they'll give you something to eat and point you to Spire Cross. You got that?"

Pilad frowned, then nodded. "If you're going back to the camp, can you get them to send a cart to meet us on the way? We haven't eaten since—"

"Sorry, no carts," the cavalryman said. "Nothing due in, so nothing to send out. You're country boys, you can look after yourselves."

"Not in this."

"Do the best you can," the cavalryman said. "You've only got to get as far as the village, and then you'll be just fine. Try and think about something else."

*

Easier said than done. Nobody said anything the whole of the second day after the cavalryman left them. From time to time, as they crossed small combes and valleys, inevitably they lost sight of the small bump on the skyline on which all their hopes depended; it was a terrifying feeling, and in spite of their sore feet and aching calves they quickened their pace until they were back where they could see it again and feel safe.

There was no belt of trees. They were a few degrees off complete panic when someone pointed out a line of nettles and briars. On investigation, these proved to mask tree stumps, and the ash of burned lumber, which had sweetened the ground and made the briars grow. "That's all right, then," Pilad said. "So now we head north, and there we are."

"I'm not sure I like being a soldier," Teucer said later, as they climbed the long hill towards where the village was supposed to be. "We've been in the army seven days, we'll be lucky if we survive another two, and we haven't come anywhere near the enemy yet."

"The enemy's not the problem, far as I can see," Pilad replied. "It's the daft buggers on our side we want to worry about."

They reached the village just before dark. They were in no hurry. They knew it was deserted from miles off; no smoke from the houses, no livestock in the fields. They kicked down a few doors, but all the houses were bare, stripped to the walls, the floorboards taken up, because nobody would abandon good sawn lumber. They found one barn with half a loft of damp, black hay. The Sticklepath boys shot and ate a stray dog. Nobody else had the energy to go looking.

Six miles or so outside Spire Cross, they were met by five cavalrymen in red cloaks, who arrested them for desertion.

Pilad dealt with all that, and got them tents, and made the quartermaster-sergeant keep the kitchen open an extra hour so everyone got enough food. Then he ate something himself, went back to the tent, lay down on the floor with his boots on and went to sleep.

Some bloody fool blowing a trumpet in the pitch dark woke them up. That, apparently, meant morning parade. Teucer was stunned. He'd never seen so many people in one place before in his life. He tried counting—so many rows, so many men in each row—but it was hard to see from where he was. Over two thousand, at any rate; and he thought, well, at least if it comes to actual fighting we should be all right, because two thousand of us, all shooting at once: what could possibly survive that?

They stood in their long lines, and a small group of men in red cloaks and red felt hats stood on the other side of the parade square and looked at them. That was all. Then someone yelled something Teucer didn't quite catch, and everybody started to walk away.

He looked round for Pilad and saw, to his horror, that he was headed straight at the men in the red cloaks. He hurried after him, and was in time to hear him clear his throat politely and say, "Excuse me."

Oh hell, Teucer thought. A redcloak turned round, looked at Pilad for a moment and said, "What?"

"Excuse me," Pilad repeated, "I'm Pilad, I'm the sergeant of the Merebartons."

"Good for you," another redcloak said.

"Could you please tell me," Pilad said. "Sir," he added. "What sort of training do we get?"

Brief silence, then one of the redcloaks laughed. Another one, an old bald man with white hair round his ears, like sheep on a hilltop, said; "Merebarton. That's South Riding, isn't it?" He had what Teucer had always thought of as a government voice, like the surveyors who came by every five years or so.

"West, sir."

"West Riding, thank you. Do you boys go to archery practice, like you're supposed to?"

"Yes, sir. It's very popular."

The man nodded. "I'm guessing you're all farm boys, shepherds, stockmen, foresters."

"That's right, sir."

"Fine." The man looked at Pilad's bow. "Made in the village, was it?"

"Yes, sir. Got our own bowyer."

"Listen," the man said. "You can shoot, you can get to places, you can look after yourselves, that's fine. You're levy, not regular soldiers, so we don't ask very much of you. Go where you're sent, stand where you're told, shoot three volleys, that's it. Run away if you like, we don't care. Rest of the day's your own. We simply don't have time or resources to train you, we definitely can't feed you or pay you while you're being trained, so we take a realistic view. Stand, shoot, run like hell. That's all. Savvy?"

"Sir," Pilad said, and walked away. The men looked at him for a moment, then resumed their conversation.

"Musen was right," Pilad said, as they stopped for the midday rest. They'd been walking for three days. The boots they'd been given didn't fit. "We should've gone home when we had the chance."

"Don't let him hear you say that," Teucer said.

"Don't worry, I won't. But we should've." Pilad opened his knapsack and took out two cloth parcels, tied up with tarred string. "Here," he said, "one for you. Don't know why I've been carrying it for you all this time."

Teucer took it. Heavy, but soft. "What is it?"

"Mail coif," Pilad said, keeping his voice soft and looking straight ahead. "We're not supposed to have them, but I traded with the quartermaster: bottle of brandy I fetched from home. It goes over your head like a hood. He wouldn't give us helmets.

Covers the throat and the top of your chest, too. No, don't open it now. Put it away before anyone sees."

"Thanks," Teucer said. "Why won't they give them to us, if they've got them?"

Pilad grinned. "Too many of us, is why. Those aren't ours, by the way, not for our side. That's Western stuff, off dead bodies. One careful owner. Quartermaster buys it off men coming back off the front, flogs it to the recruits. Says he'll take any mail we can get him, also helmets and leg plates if not too badly bashed up. So keep your eyes open, all right?"

Teucer nodded. "We could get in trouble."

"Bit late for that." Pilad yawned. "Want an apple? I got a couple left."

"Later," Teucer said. "You know, it doesn't seem right, taking things off dead people. It's like stealing."

Pilad gave him one of those looks. "Really," he said. "Where do you think those boots you're wearing came from? Anyway, it's not like we're stealing anyone's own stuff, it's what they were issued with, it all belongs to some government. It's not like pulling a ring off some poor bugger's finger."

"I guess," Teucer said. "Even so. I'm not sure I want to live off carrion."

"Crows manage." Pilad gave him a wide smile. "Clever birds. Did you know they can count? It's true. If two of you go and sit under a hedge and then one of you gets up and walks away, the crows won't come back in to feed till the other one's come out. Seen it myself, loads of times."

Teucer couldn't help grinning. "That's bullshit."

"True as I'm sat here. Would I lie to you?" He stood up, looked round. "Come on," he said, "we'd better be making a move."

Teucer hauled himself to his feet. It felt better now that there was an officer, though he hadn't seen him for three days. Still, he was out there somewhere, like the Skyfather, dimly aware of everything and presumably taking an intelligent interest. Someone or something to believe in; that wasn't too much to ask, surely.

A squadron of regular cavalry overtook them the next day, thundering past in a swirl of cloaks and dust. At the rear of their column, a dozen or so men were leading strings of riderless horses—remounts, or the horses of dead men; they went by so fast it was impossible to see very much. The day after that, they passed through farmland, the first inhabited and cultivated country they'd seen since they left home. Teucer could see sheep in a fold, smoke rising from half a dozen chimneys, a cart crawling along a distant road. By mid-afternoon they'd left it behind and were back up on the moors, where the only living things besides themselves were butterflies.

"I had the weirdest dream," Musen said suddenly, as they started to climb again after a long march across a high, flat ridge. "I dreamed the war was over and we arrived too late, and everybody got something to take home except us."

Notker said, "What sort of thing?"

"I don't know. Big, all wrapped up in sacking. I remember we were standing in a great long line, and when we got to the front, this man in armour said, 'Sorry, boys, it's all gone.'" He shrugged. "Maybe the war really is over," he said. "Maybe I'm a prophet, like in Totona."

Pilad shook his head. "Don't think so," he said. "For a start, the prophet in Totona's a girl."

Laughter. "So?" Musen protested. "I never heard it was only girls. My uncle, he reckons there was an old man in his village could tell what the weather was going to be, smack on every time. So it can be men, too."

"Let's hope you're right," Pilad said. "But I'm not holding my breath."

Just before nightfall, they met a cart; big, bigger than a haywain, and piled so heavy that its axles were bowed with long parcels, wrapped in sacking. They could smell the cart long before and after it passed them. Musen went quite pale. Notker was about to say something but Pilad scowled at him and shook his head.

"War's still on, then," Teucer said quietly.

Pilad shrugged. "Could be they died of camp fever," he muttered. "That's what kills most people, so they reckon."

"What's camp fever?"

"The shits," Pilad said. "But so bad it kills you. Mostly you get it from drinking bad water."

"Oh," Teucer said.

The next day they had to climb a very steep rise, which took them most of the morning. From the top, they could see for miles, though the view wasn't particularly interesting: moorland, with tall mountains a long way to the north; a river like a slash oozing green blood. "That'll be the Sannis," Pilad said. "I'm guessing we follow it east till we reach Longamen."

"Where's that?"

"Where the fighting is," Pilad replied, "or at least, that's where it was when we were at Spire Cross. Anyhow, following the river won't be so bad. We'll have water, that's for sure. And I'll bet you there's deer, or pigs. Bound to be rabbits, anyhow."

They lost sight of the river soon after they started to go downhill, but knowing it was there made Teucer feel almost absurdly hopeful; a river, a clear line drawn across the landscape to guide them, this way to the war. He wasn't so sure about that part of it, but at least there was finally something to see, aim for, follow. That had to be better than all the blank empty space.

Mid-afternoon, he heard Notker say, "Who do you reckon they are, then?" He looked round but he couldn't see anything. Pilad stopped and turned his head. He was that much taller, of course. "Not sure," he said. "Must be more cavalry, the speed they're going at."

"Headed this way?" someone else said.

"Can't say. They're moving away from us now, but the road loops and doubles back down in the valley. We'll know soon enough," he added, shifting his pack on his back. "Must be nice to ride everywhere, instead of having to damn well walk."

Teucer took a few steps left and tried to peer round Pilad's arm, but there was a rock outcrop in the way; he could see a slight smudge of dust in the air, but that was all. "I think they must've gone the other way," Notker said. "Can't see them any more."

"Screw them," Musen said.

Notker was trying to stuff a scrap of rag between his shoulder and the carrying strap of his bow case. "Give me my own two feet every time," he said. "I hate riding. It's such a long way down."

"There's nothing to it," Pilad said. "You just sit there."

They carried on for a while, climbing steadily. A lark burst out from the heather, making Pilad nearly jump out of his skin, and flew away shrieking. Musen muttered something about looking out for snakes, because you tended to get them wherever you found larks. That's just not true, Notker said, because—

"They're back," someone said.

Teucer leaned back and craned his neck, and this time he could see them; at least, he could make out dust, rising almost vertically from the valley floor, a long way below. "You sure that's the same lot?" he asked, but apparently it was too stupid a question to merit an answer. Whoever and whatever they were, there seemed to be a lot of them, moving quite fast. "First they're above us; now they're down there," Oseir from East Reach said. "Wonder what they're playing at?"

"Showing off," Musen said.

"Could be." Pilad uncorked his water flask and took two big gulps. "Bloody fools if they are."

"You sure they're on our side?" Notker asked.

Someone laughed. "With the cavalry, who knows?" said one of the Conegar men. "Don't suppose they do, half the time."

"Wonder if they've got any biscuits?" Oseir said. "We could trade them."

"What would we have that they'd want?" Pilad said.

They caught a few more glimpses of the horsemen through the afternoon and early evening, and when night fell and they lit their campfires it was in their minds that the riders might come across and join them; they'd have news, perhaps, or better food, or both. Come dawn, though, there was no trace of them to be seen, so it seemed likely they'd pulled out at some point in the night. "Maybe they're escorting us," Bajo from Stoneford said, "and they've gone on ahead to make sure the road's clear or something."

"You'd think they'd tell us, if they were doing that," Musen said.

"Not necessarily. And anyhow, just because we don't get told doesn't mean they haven't reported to the officer."

"Him," Musen said darkly. "Anybody seem him lately?"

"Could've done, for all I know," Bajo replied. "On account of, I don't know what he looks like."

Thoughtful silence for a moment. "Well," Notker said, "he'd be in uniform, wouldn't he?"

"Like we are, you mean," Pilad said.

"That's different. He's a regular." Musen threw another chunk of dead thorn branch on the fire. It burned quick and cold, a lot of light and not much else. "I think he's buggered off somewhere and we're on our own again. That's not right. We should have proper officers."

Pilad laughed. "Then we'd have to act like real soldiers," he said. "The hell with that." He looked up at the sky. "Time we were on the road," he said, and everybody got to their feet.

It took them the rest of the morning to get down the hill on to the plain; hard going, heather, bracken and shale, the gradient quite steep, the road broken and crumbling. By the time they reached the flat, the calves of Teucer's legs were sore enough to slow him down, and he knew they'd be worse the next day. The level ground, though, was as good as a holiday. Something grazed here. The grass was short and soft, thick with clover and creeping buttercup. Teucer was tempted to string his bow, just in case they saw deer, but they were making far too much noise, so he left it in its case. When they reached the river, the smell of water was almost overpowering after so many days on the dry moor. They stopped, waiting for the officer to bawl them out for wasting time, but nobody spoke. Then they unslung their bow cases, quivers and packs and flopped down on the grass. It was flag iris season, and the riverbank was blue with them, knee- or even waist-high. Oseir and Notker stood up after a while, scrabbled about in the shallow water for flat stones, and started skipping them across the deeps between the stepping-stone reefs. Teucer watched them for a while, then asked, "Can you do that?"

Pilad shook his head. "My dad tried to teach me, but when I do it they just go splash."

Suddenly, in spite of his sore legs, Teucer didn't feel tired any more. He stood up and walked to a place on the bank where something (sheep, most likely) had broken down an easy ramp into the water. There was a small apron of shale, and he bent down to look for good skipping stones. He found one, then something caught his eye (upside down, seen from between his legs): horsemen, trotting towards them beside the water.

He straightened up. "They're back," he called out.

There were a lot of them. Pilad sat up and spat out the blade of grass he'd been chewing. Some of the others further downstream were waving and calling out. No need; the horsemen were headed their way.

"Been sent to find us, I bet you," he heard Musen say to Oseir. "Probably we're going to get a bollocking for wandering off."

Odd-looking people. The first thing he noticed, once they were close enough to be more than horse and rider shapes, was the helmets they were wearing, because they flashed in the sun; tall and elegantly conical, like elongated steel onions, with a little tuft of white or black horsehair sticking out of the point on top. Whoever they were, they must have come from a very hot place, since they felt the need, in midsummer, to wear long wool cloaks with fur collars. Bowmen—something in common, except that their bows were absurdly short and round, like a pretty girl's top lip. It hadn't occurred to Teucer that they might be foreigners—but why not? It was a big empire, and if they were regulars, they could be serving hundreds of miles from home. If so, would he be able to talk to them and understand them? It'd be a pity if he couldn't. He'd never met a foreigner.

"They ride with their bows strung," someone he didn't know said. He looked; true, and strange. You don't keep your bow strung all the time, or it takes a set and loses its cast. Maybe it was different with the short cavalry bows, which were made out of horn and sinew rather than wood. It'd be nice if he got a chance to ask them, possibly even have a shot or two with a horn bow. He straightened up and lifted his arm to wave.

Something flew past him, level with the water. He guessed it was a dragonfly.

"Bloody lunatics," said one of the Conegar men. Teucer wondered what he meant, and then he saw one of the riders draw an arrow from his quiver.

It was interesting how he did it. In Rhus, the quiver is worn on the back, a long way up, so that the fletchings of the arrows stand quite high over the right shoulder. The horseman's quiver was on his belt, on the left side, so that the fletchings brushed the mushroom-shaped pommel of his saddle, around which his reins were knotted. To draw an arrow, he had only to reach down a few inches from his loose point. He did it without looking, fingering the arrow upwards from the quiver into his palm and nocking it in a single, fluid movement. When he drew, he didn't lodge the string against the pads of his fore and middle fingers; he caught it between his thumb and a big, oddly shaped thumb ring made of horn or tortoiseshell. You'd have thought it'd be impossible, or at the very least awkward and excruciatingly painful, but apparently not. As he drew, he swivelled his left arm out sideways, peering over the bow for a target. He drew to the chest, and let the string pull itself off his thumb—

He'd shot one of the East Reach lads, Corden or Corder, something like that. He'd ridden up level with him, as he'd straightened up from a crouch to shout or wave his arms, and shot him, from a distance of seven or eight feet, straight into the chest, dead centre, just below the bone. Teucer saw the feathers sitting on the man's chest, like a big horsefly.

And everything changed.

(There used to be an old man in Higher Town who had a trick he liked to play. He'd get a bit of charcoal and draw on a plank of wood: twelve black lines, forming a sort of sideways-on cube. You'd look at it, and to start with you thought you were looking down on it, but after you'd been staring for a second or two, it seemed to change, and in fact you were looking up at it from underneath. You actually felt a little jolt, as though you'd been nudged, and a very slight trace of dizziness.)

They're the enemy, Teucer thought. Not our lot; the enemy, and they're going to kill us, and there's absolutely nothing—

Something bit him; he winced and yelped. It felt so much like a bee-sting. He felt something wet trickle down his face, just like rain when you're caught out in a sharp shower. The horsemen were surging along the line, shooting as they passed. He saw Notker on the ground, and Pilad and Oseir. An arrow came so close to his face that he felt the breeze and heard it, *swish-swish*. Somewhere very deep inside his head, a voice he didn't recognise said, *fall down*.

He obeyed without thinking, only realising as he lay with his head under his left arm that he was doing this so as to make it look like he'd been hit and killed, so they wouldn't shoot at him. But the horses will trample me, he thought. They'll ride over me; trouble was, he didn't dare move, because he could hear, and feel, the hooves going past, appallingly close: they made the ground bounce. Anyway, he was too cold to move, like the winter when he'd lost his way in a snowstorm and dropped down in his tracks; it hadn't hurt and he hadn't been scared because he was too frozen to feel anything at all. But his mind was racing, or a part of it, imagining and predicting all sorts of ways he could come to harm if he moved so much as an inch—shot, trampled, speared, a hoof on the side of his head or his ribs, the crunch and the splitting noise. *Stay where you are*, said the voice, and for all he knew it was the Skyfather. The hooves were so loud they made his ears ring. I'm probably going to die, he thought, and it didn't seem unreasonable. He closed his eyes.

There was noise for a long time, and then it dwindled quickly, and then it was dead quiet. Teucer considered moving, but it wasn't as easy as that. He'd dropped in an awkward position, his left leg hinged at the knee under him; it had gone to sleep, and he couldn't move it, not without using his hand and actually lifting it. In his mind he made up pictures; the horsemen all gone, everyone else dead; or the horsemen sitting quiet watching to see if anyone stirred, arrows on their strings. Both pictures were entirely credible. He stayed where he was.

And then he felt something; a tug on his right foot, a sort of side-to-side levering movement. It took him a moment to figure out that someone was trying to pull off his boot. The enemy, robbing the dead. He froze and held his breath, but maybe he tried too hard, because something tickled his throat. He fought it desperately hard, but he couldn't stop it. He sneezed.

"Teucer?" said a voice.

He opened his eyes. "Musen."

There was Musen, looking down at him, gripping his right foot in both hands. "Teucer."

"What the hell do you think you're doing?"

Musen dropped his foot. Its impact on the ground jarred his whole body, and his numb left leg erupted in savage pins and needles. "I thought you were—"

Musen had one bare foot. Teucer lifted his head to look past him, to see who else—

"Just me," Musen said. "God, am I glad to see you."

"Musen." Indeed. On the one hand, he wanted to smash his face in for trying to steal his boot. Also, he'd known him all his life and never liked him very much. "What about the others?"

"There aren't any. Come on."

Made no sense. "What do you mean? What about—?"

"*There aren't any others.*" Musen froze for a moment, as though his own raised voice had startled him, then took a deep breath. "Are you all right? Are you hit?"

"I don't think so. But I've got pins and needles in my leg."

Musen stared at him. "Teucer, don't be such a fucking *girl.* They could be back any minute. We've got to go."

Out of the question, obviously. First, they'd have to go through the bodies, make sure there weren't any other survivors; then they'd have to bury the dead, and then carefully select as much in the way of supplies and useful equipment as they could realistically carry; best part of a day's work, even under ideal conditions. They couldn't just—

"*Now.* Or I'm going without you."

"They can't all be—"

"Now."

Musen turned away, and it was as though there was a rope round Teucer's neck; he felt himself being pulled to his feet, and staggered as his numb leg refused to take his weight. Musen was walking away. Teucer staggered again, nearly lost his balance, found it again, skipped a step or two to catch up. "Where are we going?" he called out.

"How the hell should I know?" Musen said. "Home. Anywhere. Away from here, before they come back."

Musen had always been a fast walker. Pilad reckoned it was because he was so much shorter than everyone else; he'd got used to going very quick, just to keep up.

Teucer stopped dead. Musen hadn't noticed. "Wait," he shouted.

"What?"

"The others." He meant Pilad. "We can't just—"

"Screw you, then," Musen said, and walked on.

Teucer gazed at his back as he got smaller and smaller, and he felt himself filling up with panic, like a bucket under the pump. Bastard, he thought; callous, unfeeling bastard. Then he broke into a run.

Musen, he realised, was marching up the slope. That wasn't a good idea, because once they reached the top they'd be against the skyline, visible for miles. He wanted to point this out, but he had no breath, from running uphill. He tried to go faster, but it simply couldn't be done; he couldn't run any more, and walking flat out he was just about keeping up. He opened his mouth to yell but sucked in air instead. He filled his lungs till they hurt. It wasn't anything like enough. The backs of his legs felt like they were about to burst.

When they were nearly at the top and he'd finally got close enough to be heard, he saw that Musen was heading for a fold in the hillside, just under the skyline. It was practically a sunken lane, and they'd be more or less invisible until they reached the end of the ridge. Smart. The sort of thing Pilad would've done. Also, they'd both come the same way, earlier, but he hadn't noticed the fold in the hill, and Musen had. It suddenly occurred to him that Musen wasn't stupid. He wasn't sure what he thought about that.

"Right." Musen stopped, bent forward, his hands on his knees. He was breathing hard. "What were you saying?"

"What?"

"Earlier. You were saying something."

Yes, but it was too late now. From there, they couldn't see the place, or the bodies. "Nothing," Teucer said. "Forget it."

Musen had no problem with that. "The way I see it," he said, "we've got no food, no water, we don't know if those bastards are going to jump up at us any minute. I *think*—" He paused and straightened up. "I think the way we came is that way there." He didn't point, barely nodded. Teucer had no idea where he was referring to. "But if the bastards knew to hit us back there, stands to reason they know the country, which means the roads. So, if we go back the way we came, there's a good chance we'll see them again."

Teucer shivered. He'd never have thought of that on his own.

"So," Musen went on, "we need to head back in the same direction, but not following the road. Which means picking our way across this shit. It just keeps getting better." He scowled, then turned to face Teucer. "What've you got?"

"What d'you mean?"

"Food," Musen explained. "Water. Got any?"

Teucer had to think. "No."

"Shit. Nor me." He pulled off his quiver and threw it away.

"What are you doing?" Teucer asked.

"We've got arrows but no bows," Musen said. "The hell with that. Also, the last thing we want to do is look like soldiers. Get rid of it."

Slowly, Teucer took off his quiver. Only three viable arrows: the rest had got split or cracked when he'd fallen down. His quiver. Not his match set, with which he'd shot the possible; his best business arrows. Somehow, he couldn't believe the possible had ever happened. He dropped the quiver on the ground. "Good boy," Musen said. "Well, nothing for it. We'd better start walking."

"Where are we going?"

"Home, of course. Don't know about you, but I'm through playing soldiers."

"But they'll—"

Musen gave him a scornful look. "Like hell," he said. "If they ever find out what happened to our lot, they'll assume we died, too." Suddenly he grinned. "Cheer up," he said. "We're dead. Which means we're let off. It's just you and me now, God help me."

He'd been vaguely aware for some years that Musen didn't like him very much. There was no reason. It was just that Musen said and did things that irritated him, and clearly it worked the other way around. It really didn't matter, hadn't mattered; they'd always been with the others, never alone together for more than a few minutes. There were plenty of people in Merebarton, after all. Had been.

"We can't just wander off like this," he said to Musen's back. "It's not right."

"You do what you like."

Musen was right, of course. It surprised Teucer how little that seemed to matter. But then, he thought, kingdoms and empires are like that, too. If there's a war, it stands to reason, one side must be in the right and the other side must be wrong, and the wrong side must realise that: people aren't stupid. But they go on being wrong, all through a war, to the last drop of blood, because—He had to think about that. Because the side you're on matters more than pure Truth; it has to, otherwise people couldn't live their lives; everyone's wrong sometimes, and you don't just weed them out and throw them away, like rotten fruit in the apple loft. You stick by your family, your village, your country. Now, here was Musen, clearly very smart, clearly quite right, and every instinct was urging him to argue, dispute, induce him to change his mind and do the wrong thing, just because they didn't like each other.

The horrible thought struck him that Musen was his side now, all of it. Pity about that.

He ran to catch up.

"So," he said, "you reckon it's this way."

"Yes."

"Fine. How far till we reach some water?"

"How the hell do I know?"

Uphill now, a long, steep climb. It was getting harder not to think about water, and food. Musen turned out to be considerably fitter than he was, or he had more stamina or willpower. The better man, in any event. Probably, Musen didn't need him at all, he'd be faster and better off alone. If this is a joke, he thought, I'm not laughing.

Two days in Musen's company, without food, with black ooze from bog pools to drink. It tasted strong rather than foul, but that evening he was convulsed with stomach cramps that made him whine out loud. Musen was fine.

On the third day, he saw a river. It wasn't even that far away. "Look, over there," he called out, but Musen was already scampering down the steep scree slope. Teucer, figuring that a twisted ankle wouldn't really help matters, followed on rather more carefully.

"This is good," Musen said, when he finally stopped drinking. "This must be the Swey, so we're past the Greytop. It should be all downhill to Spire Cross from here."

Teucer was on his knees beside the water. He couldn't wait to stick his face in it and drink till he burst. But first, there was something he needed to point out. "We've been here before," he said.

"Don't talk stupid." Musen was lying on his back, staring up at the sky.

"We've been here before," Teucer said. "This is where it

happened. Well, a bit further on. But look, that's the hill we climbed, and that's the fold of dead ground where we went so the horsemen wouldn't see us. You can just see the edges."

"Balls," Musen said, but he sat up, wriggled round and scowled at the hills behind them. "Nothing like it," he said.

Teucer cupped his hands and plunged them under the water. "We've come round in a circle," he said.

"We can't have."

The water was wonderful, clean and cold, and the more of it he drank the more he wanted. "All right, then," he said. "You take a walk down the riverbank, can't be more than half a mile. I can tell you exactly what you'll find."

"Fuck you," Musen said. He got up and walked away until he was out of sight. Not long after that, Teucer heard a familiar noise and looked up. A column of crows was twisting up into the sky, shrieking and yelling. Disturbed while feeding, Teucer guessed.

Sometime later, Musen came back. He had two bows, four quivers looped over his neck and two big knapsacks hanging off his elbow. He looked terrible.

"I got us some stuff," he said, dumping the packs and scrabbling at the quivers until he was free of them. "Looks like the bastards went through it all pretty good looking for food, but they missed a bit. There's a water bottle each, too."

Teucer stood up. "I thought you said no bows."

Musen shrugged. "Changed my mind. Well, there might be deer, or hares or something. Anyhow, I figure the bastards are long gone. We've been walking around here for three days and not seen them."

There was something Teucer wanted to ask, but he didn't. "Fine," he said. "So, now which way?"

Musen sat down, took a leather bottle out of one of the packs and plunged it in the river. "I figure where we went wrong was, we went up that fold instead of down it. We go down it, pretty soon we should be able to see the beacon on Greytop, and then we'll know exactly where we are."

Teucer thought for a moment. "There's a beacon."

"Of course. Part of the military relay. Everybody knows that."

"You knew there should be a beacon," Teucer said, "and you couldn't see it, and you still kept on going."

"Sure." Musen lifted the bottle out of the water and pressed the stopper in tight. "Your fault. I couldn't bear the thought of the smug look on your face if I'd said I thought we'd come the wrong way."

"Ah," Teucer said, and filled his bottle.

The village appeared out of nowhere. They climbed out of a steep, dry combe on to a skyline littered with granite outcrops, and suddenly there it was: two dozen buildings, with smoke rising from the chimneys. They hadn't seen it because the valley in which the village lay was so deep. There were springs running down the hill into a lake; the village was at the far end. The valley was absurdly green, as though it had been painted.

"Not on the map," Musen said, as they scrambled down the slope. "Maybe the government doesn't know about them. Well, it's possible. Some people don't like paying taxes and sending their sons off to fight. Crazy, but there it is."

"Oh, come on," Teucer said. "You can't hide a whole village."

"You say that." Musen stopped to tug his leg free from a briar, the first one they'd seen for a month. "You know Ranmoor, over between Merebarton and the old top road? Never been on the map, not ever. Surveyors came round, time before last, never heard of it. They only stumbled on the place because one of their mules broke loose and they had to go look for it. And the Ranmoor people weren't even trying to stay hidden."

"How do you know this place isn't on the map?" Teucer asked.

"Because I saw it," Musen replied. "The officer's map, at Spire Cross. Made a point of studying it, just in case."

"You can't read a map."

Musen laughed. "If you say so."

"You can't *read*."

But he could, apparently. A man of infinite resource and many hidden talents. It was a shame he was so objectionable. "Who taught you?"

Musen didn't answer. Bastard, Teucer thought. Not that it mattered; couldn't matter less, and it was just as well he had such a useful skill, as well as such a splendid memory. But who had taught him? And why had either of them bothered?

It took an agonisingly long time to get down to the valley. Each ridge they crossed proved to be hiding half a dozen more, and in places there were sheer drops or steep slopes of shale, guaranteed to break a leg, probably a neck as well. Going round meant going back up again. "You'll notice there's no road to this place," Musen said, as they headed uphill for the fifth time. "You ever been to a village with no road?"

"No road this side of the valley," Teucer pointed out; "could be one the other side," but he was rapidly coming to the conclusion that Musen was right. A green paradise with a lake in the middle; enough grazing for enough sheep, and, at the far end of the lake, where the biggest stream came down off the hills, there was a flood plain, fat with accumulated silt. You could grow anything. And fish, too. Who needs the world when you've got all that?

In which case, he thought, maybe they won't want strangers.

Maybe the same idea had struck them both at the same time. They slowed down, kept off the skyline as much as possible; they were dawdling, as though waiting for dusk. Eventually Musen said, "Chances are, they don't bother locking their doors."

Teucer had been thinking the same way. "You mean stealing."

"I think it's called foraging when you're a soldier."

"If they catch us—"

"Then they'll string us up, just exactly like they'd have done if we'd walked in and said hello, but with a good reason. Same difference."

No arguing with that. There was a stand of ash trees on the west side of the village. Maybe two hours to sunset. Musen was already heading that way.

From the edge of the trees they could see the village street. Windows glared yellow, like eyes. "We'll wait till everything's gone dark," Musen said. "That one there looks like an inn, so I'm guessing that outhouse back and left is a hay barn."

Teucer couldn't help grinning. In Merebarton, everyone strung up their sausages in the hay barn rafters under the thatch, where it was cool, dry and dark. And cheeses, in racks on the back wall, and shelves of store apples. And it wasn't really stealing, because—well, it wasn't, that was all.

"So," he said, after a while. "Where do you think we are?"

Musen thought for a long time before answering. "I *think*," he said, "that the other side of those hills in front of us is a long, high moor, and the far side of that's the Asper. If we can find that and follow it south-east, we go round the side of Spire Cross and from there on it's due south, downhill all the way. I think," he added.

Teucer realised that he trusted him. "How wide's this moor?"

"Two days," Musen replied. "Maybe three, I don't know. But I reckon, if we can load up enough stuff for seven days, that ought to do it. By missing out Spire Cross we cut off a bloody great big dog-leg. And there's that much less chance of running into anybody, and if we do we can see them a long way away. Don't know about you, but I don't want to meet *anyone* till we're safely back in the Ridings."

Seven days. How long since he'd left home? He realised he'd completely lost count. Also, he'd known Musen for eighteen years and completely misunderstood him. "When we get back—"

"If."

"When we get home," Teucer said, "we're going to have to tell—"

"Yes, all right." It was too dark for Teucer to see Musen's face, but he didn't have to. "Cross that bridge when we get to it. Right now, let's just think about getting some food."

Teucer straightened his leg. He'd been lying at a bad angle and he'd got cramp. "When did you learn to read?"

"None of your business."

Teucer and Musen had only been out together with the long net twice, because usually Teucer went with Pilad and his two cousins and their friends, and Musen netted with his father and uncles over Rawbarrow. On those two occasions, they'd been on opposite ends of the operation. Teucer had sat completely still in the pitch dark, seventy yards out in the field, clutching two stones, while Musen and Ecnas from Spin Pike crept forward to hang the net. That was the difficult bit; agonisingly slow, patient work, because you're between the wary, long-eared rabbits feeding out in the headlands and the safety of their home, stringing the thirty yards of net on to pre-planted stakes along the bank. One sound, one sneeze, one faint rustle of cloth as one trouser leg brushes the other, and the rabbits hear you and bolt for the warren, before the net's in place; ruined, wasted, and everybody's stayed up all night for nothing. Teucer had been a net man five times; one time he'd trodden on a snail, of all things, crunch, too soft for Pilad to have heard it at the far end of the net, but plenty loud enough for seventy-odd rabbits. When Pilad gave the signal and the beaters came out of the dark, yelling, whistling, clashing rocks, they ended up with four rabbits for a whole night's work. Pilad had shrugged, said he guessed he must've made a noise; nobody believed him. Just bad luck, they'd said, a fox must've come by earlier, something like that. But both times when Musen hung the net, they'd taken more than sixty.

Please, Teucer thought as they set off towards the hay barn, don't let there be any snails.

Nor there were. Instead, there was a man who'd stepped out of the inn for a piss. He'd finished, and was contemplating the stars or something of the sort, dead still and quiet, invisible. Musen walked straight into him.

"Watch it," the man said, staggering and clutching Musen's arm for balance. Musen punched him in the eye. But the drinker wasn't so easily disposed of. He still had Musen's other arm, and he was very big and strong, and now he was furiously angry. "What you do that for?" he roared. "Hey, I don't know you. Who are you?"

Musen tried again. The drinker caught his fist as he drew it back and crushed it until Musen squealed. Teucer froze. More than anything in the whole world, he wanted to run away, but somehow he didn't. Nor did he join in the action. Thinking about it later, he realised that he just wasn't a fighter. Some men are, some aren't, simple as that.

A blaze of yellow light as the door opened, and three men came out. Musen kicked one in the knee, making him roar. A moment later, he was on the ground with two men sitting on him; there had been a heart-breaking cracking noise, as his arrows broke under him. At least that made Teucer drop his bow, though he couldn't do much about the quiver. Then someone behind him put an elbow round his throat, levering up his chin like the lid of a jar. He wondered, quite objectively, if his neck was going to snap.

"Fucker hit me," the drinker was complaining. "Barged into me, then bashed my head in."

Someone had brought out a lantern. Someone else shoved it in Teucer's face, then said, "Bring them inside."

There must have been something happening that day, or else the people here were inveterate drunkards; the inn was packed, barely an empty place on the benches. Not an inn, of course, no travellers. Didn't these people know how to brew at home? "Who the hell are they?" someone said.

"They hit me," the drinker explained. "No reason. Just came out of nowhere and hit me."

The number of people aside, it could easily have been the Poverty back home: same rectangle of scarred, glowing oak tables around the same long fire, the same roil of smoke floating just above the crossbeams of the roof, searching for the tiny flue. The same people, essentially, except that they seemed to want to kill them both. "Excuse me," Musen said.

Everyone turned and stared at him, as though a dog had spoken rather than a human. "Excuse me," Musen said. "Look, I'm really sorry about what happened just now, it was really dumb of me. I didn't actually mean to hit anyone. I guess things just got out of hand."

Nobody spoke, but Musen seemed immune to the stares. He went on, "Actually, we came here because we need help. Axle on our cart's busted. We need a smith to fix it for us. You have got a smith here, haven't you?"

Long silence, then someone laughed. Someone else said, "Oh yes."

"Could you tell me where I can find him, please."

"You just met him."

Oh hell, Teucer thought. The drinker was the smith, the man Musen had punched. It was one of those moments.

"We can pay," Musen said.

They didn't seem interested. Quite likely they didn't use money here, if they kept themselves to themselves. "Bloody wonderful," the drinker said. "First he smashes my teeth in, then he wants me to fix his fucking cart."

It wasn't that funny, Teucer thought; but the villagers disagreed. They laughed till the walls shook, and then someone stood up, gave the drinker a slap on the back that made Teucer wince, and said, "You fix his damn cart for him, all right?" Whoever he was, he had the authority. The drinker, the only man among them who wasn't laughing, nodded sadly. What cart? Teucer thought. We don't have a cart.

They slept in the inn's root store, with their heads on piles of empty sacks. The room smelt of damp and onions. The only way in and out was a trapdoor, and when it had swung shut on them they'd heard the sound of something heavy, probably a full barrel, being dragged on to it.

Morning took the form of a piercing shaft of light through the trapdoor hatch, followed by the return of the ladder they'd come down the night before. Teucer was so stiff and cramped he could barely stand, but Musen was wide awake, springing, bouncy. He gave the smith a great big smile. The smith had a black eye.

"How are you feeling?" Musen asked him.

The smith didn't answer. "Where's this cart of yours?"

"A bit of a way out of town," Musen replied. "Probably best if you came with us and we can show you, and then you can decide what needs to be done."

During the night, in the pitch darkness of the cellar, Teucer had tried to find out what the non-existent cart was all about. Musen had pretended to be asleep.

"What about your horses?" someone else asked. Teucer didn't like the look of him—short man, bald, fat, broad shoulders, smallest nose he'd ever seen on a human being. Whoever he was, he gave the impression that he didn't believe anything about the two mysterious strangers, not even that they were real.

"They'll be fine," Musen said.

"I wouldn't leave my horses out standing in their traces all night."

Musen smiled at him. "You didn't give us much choice."

The suspicious man looked at the smith, who shrugged. "Might as well go and take a look," he said.

"Suit yourself." The suspicious man turned to Teucer. "The bow," he said. "What's that in aid of?"

"Bandits." The first thing that'd come into his head. He regretted it instantly.

"No bandits round here."

"Good," Teucer said. "In that case, with any luck, our cart might still be there."

The suspicious man was coming with them. Teucer wasn't happy about that, but Musen was horrified; he tried not to show it, but Teucer could see fear, just this side of terror. "Please," Musen said, "don't put yourself out on our account. We'll be fine."

The suspicious man gave him a nasty grin. "No trouble," he said.

They stopped by the forge, where the smith filled a big canvas bag with tools. "You," he said to Teucer, "make yourself useful." The bag was very heavy and didn't have a strap or a handle.

They walked for a long time, uphill, all the way up to the crest where they'd first seen the village. "Not far now," Musen called out. "Should be somewhere right here."

Teucer winced. The smith was scanning the bare, open moor. "Should be able to see it by now. Where is it?"

Oh well, Teucer thought. "It's gone."

The suspicious man was looking at him, he could feel it. "Is that right?"

"It was right here," Musen said. "Someone's stolen it."

The smith looked blank. Behind him, Teucer heard the suspicious man say, "You'd have thought there'd be tracks."

Don't say anything, Teucer thought. But Musen said, "Tracks?"

"You'd have thought so," the suspicious man said. "I mean, here's this cart with a busted axle. In order to get it away, they'd have had to come up here with another rig and chains, and dragged it away on three wheels. There'd be ruts, from the end of the busted axle digging in. You're sure this is the right place?"

"Here or hereabouts," Teucer said. "Sorry, we don't know this area as well as you do, obviously."

"There ought to be tracks," the suspicious man said. "If there was ever a cart."

The smith, meanwhile, had had enough. He grabbed his bag of tools out of Teucer's arms, turned round and stumped off back the way he'd just come. Musen started after him as though the two of them were linked by a rope. "You know what," he said, his voice a little bit higher than usual. "My uncle's a smith."

"Really."

"Yes, he is. A master blacksmith. But he keeps his hammers at our house. On the third floor."

The smith stopped and looked at him. "You what?"

"On the third floor," Musen said. "Where I live. That's where he keeps his hammers. And his anvil."

The smith frowned. "Oh," he said.

"There's five floors in our house," Musen said. "At Merebarton."

"If you say so." The smith walked away, rather faster than before. Musen didn't follow. He looked drained, as though he'd just used up the last of his strength, and the look on his face was very sad. Musen hasn't got an uncle who's a smith, Teucer thought. And they live in an ordinary house, one floor and an attic.

"I don't think there ever was a cart." Teucer had forgotten the suspicious man for a moment. "I think that was all bull, so you could get out of town." He looked at Teucer, then at the rapidly diminishing figure of the smith, charging downhill. If there was to be a fight, it'd be two against one, and all over before the smith could get back and join in. "Just piss off, the both of you. And don't come back."

"We won't," Teucer said eagerly. "I promise."

The suspicious man shook his head one last time, then ambled off down the hill without looking back. Musen was still rooted to the spot. "Musen."

"What?"

"Have you gone crazy or something?"

"Don't start."

"Why the hell did you tell them—?"

"Don't *start.*"

Teucer looked at him. On the one hand, Musen could easily have been the death of both of them; if the blacksmith hadn't been so eager to get home, they'd have been frogmarched back to the village, and things could quickly have turned very bad. On the other hand, without Musen he'd probably be dead already, back at the river or out somewhere on the moors. He hated to have to admit it, but Musen was his side, the entirety of the remainder of a tribe of precisely two, lost in the wilderness. "Look," he said, "just tell me what's going on. Please?"

"We're going home," Musen said. "That's it, that's all there is to it. And when we get there, I don't ever want to see you or talk to you again. Got that?"

Teucer breathed in deep and let it go again. "Sure," he said.

"Good. That's just grand." Musen was turning his head slowly, reading the landscape like a page. "This way."

"What?"

"Home. This way. You coming, or what?"

They had no food, no water, even their knives had been taken from them. In every direction, the world was ridiculously big. Assuming they could find a spring or a pool, they had nothing to carry water in. "All right," Teucer said. "Wait for me."

The next day they found a river. Whether it was the same river as the one they'd started from or a different one entirely they had no idea. According to Musen it wasn't on the map. By rights it shouldn't even be there. But it lay in a shallow-sided green combe, with head-high bracken and dense hedges of briars. There were dragonflies, and kingfishers. And fish.

"I know how to do this," Musen said. "Stay back and keep absolutely still."

Musen lay on his stomach in the shallow water, on the edge of a deep pool, his arms out in front of him just under the surface, palms turned upwards. Teucer couldn't see how anyone could keep that still without being dead. Just as he was about to drift off to sleep, Musen suddenly lifted his arms, arched his back and hopped to his knees. Something flashed in the air; "Catch it!" Musen yelled, and Teucer found himself diving at the glistening shape, closing his hands round something slippery, which squeezed out between his palms and landed thrashing and jack-knifing on the grass, a foot or so from the water. Musen hurled himself at it, his boot clouting the side of Teucer's head, and whooped for joy. He'd caught a trout.

Musen also knew how to light a fire with two sticks and a clump of dry moss. They spitted the trout on a dogwood shoot and turned it slowly over the fire until the skin was hard and black. It was mostly bones.

"How do you do that?" Teucer asked.

"Mostly it's just patience," Musen said. "You keep really still, and when the fish swims right over your hand, you flick it up in the air. Come on, I'll show you."

Teucer spent the rest of the day failing to learn, during which time Musen caught four more trout trying to teach him. "You're just stupid," he said eventually, and Teucer didn't have the heart to contradict him.

Teucer woke up out of a dream about picking apples and opened his eyes.

It was still pitch dark, but there was a light, three lights, moving. He poked around with his foot until he located Musen, who woke up with a snort. "What?"

"Lights," Teucer whispered. "Over there."

They were two days away from the river, and it was the first time they'd spoken since they left it. "So?"

"So they must have food, and water. And that noise is cart-wheels. Listen."

"So?"

"Fine," Teucer said. "You stay here. See you back home."

He started to get up, but Musen grabbed his ankle and pulled him down. "All right," he said. "But we'll wait till morning and catch them up. We can't go barging in on them in the middle of the night."

Fair point. "All right," Teucer said. "We'll follow them, and as soon as it's light we'll go and talk to them."

"Oh, for crying out loud." Musen got to his feet. "Just keep the noise down, will you? And if they've got dogs with them, it's your fault."

Dogs hadn't occurred to Teucer, but it was too late to back down. "They won't have dogs," he said. "Trust me."

They had dogs. Five of them, big dogs, *huge* dogs, long and thin and growling horribly in the first red light of dawn. Musen and Teucer stopped dead, realising they were now part of a very delicate mechanism. The slightest movement on their part would release the dogs, who'd tear their throats out before they could do anything at all. The carts, meanwhile, had stopped. Men jumped down. They were holding spears.

"Over here," someone called out. Then someone else whistled. That was all, and the dogs turned and trotted away, as if to say that it had all been in fun.

Maybe a dozen men, wrapped in dark cloaks with hoods, holding spears. "Who the hell are you?" one of them said.

"We're lost," Teucer replied, before Musen could open his mouth. "We haven't eaten for days. Please will you help us?"

Another man said, "Got any money?"

"Yes," Musen said. He stooped, pulled off his boot, shook it out over his outstretched left palm. Four silver coins fell out, like dandruff. Where did he get that from, Teucer wondered; then he recalled Musen trying to steal his boots by the river, and thought, Oh.

"All right," said a third man. "But you're not riding on the carts. You'll have to walk."

"That'll be fine," Teucer said quickly. Then he added, "Where are you going?"

"Spire Cross."

"That's good," Teucer said. "So are we."

The carts were full of weapons; also armour, helmets, clothes, boots, belts, pots and cooking utensils, a few mattocks and spades. There were eighteen of them in all: fourteen men, four women. The men walked.

"How do you know where to go?" Teucer asked.

"That's easy." The man was called Iser; he was short and thin, like the rest of them. "We just follow the cavalry."

Teucer nodded, then asked, "Which side?"

"Doesn't matter. We keep our distance, and watch out for crows."

Yes, Teucer knew about that. "Don't they mind?"

"The soldiers?" Iser shrugged. "We keep our distance. They don't like us much, but they don't go out of their way to bother us. And we save them a job, burying the dead. Soldiers don't like doing that. It's a sort of a deal. We bury them, we get to keep the stuff. And the quartermasters love us, of course. Shortages of everything, these days."

Teucer remembered the two mail coifs Pilad had bought. He'd thrown his away some time ago. "Must be hard work," he said.

"No kidding. We're just a small outfit. It's the big contractors who get the big battlefields, where the real money is. We just do little skirmishes."

Teucer nodded. "What breed are the dogs? I've never seen any like that before."

Iser laughed. "Oh, they're all sorts. But very good for finding places. You need a good dog in this line of work." A thought struck him; he went silent for a bit, then looked straight ahead and said, "You could do worse."

"What?"

"You and your mate. You could do worse than join us."

For a moment, Teucer didn't understand. "What, Musen and me?"

"Sure. If you don't mind digging. Got to be better than wandering about starving."

He could see Iser's point. Musen was a head taller than the tallest of the men, and Teucer was nearly a head taller than Musen; and the men weren't just short, they were skinny. Arms like sticks. "No," he said. "Thanks, but we're on our way home. We're farmers; we've got homes and families. We can't just go wandering off."

"Then how come you're out here?"

Iser wouldn't have asked the question if he hadn't already guessed the answer. Not exactly difficult. After all, he and his people had just buried a large number of practically identical bodies. "It's really good of you to offer," Teucer said. "But I've got to get home, as quick as I can. They're going to need me."

Iser looked at him, as though he'd just said something really stupid. "And what makes you think your home'll still be there when you get back?"

"He could be right, at that," Musen said. "I mean, the last thing we know is, their cavalry's roaring around the place killing everything that moves. God only knows where they are right now."

The light glinting on distant metal had to be Spire Cross. They stood and stared at it for quite some time.

"Well?" Teucer asked.

"I'm thinking."

They'd left Iser's caravan at dawn. The debate was, should

they bypass Spire Cross, as Musen had originally planned, and go straight home, relying on the provisions and directions Iser had given them and hoping the enemy weren't between them and Merebarton; or should they head for the relative safety of the camp and look for an opportunity of slipping quietly away once they were satisfied it was safe to proceed?

"Spire Cross," Musen said.

"But you said we should go straight home," Teucer pointed out. "You said—"

"Changed my mind."

Food, Teucer thought, and a blanket to sleep under. Not to mention the sheer unimaginable bliss of being with people who weren't Musen, "They'll send us off to the war," he said. "Do you really want that?"

"I'd rather take my chances than starve to death, thanks all the same."

Teucer wriggled his toes in the new left boot Iser had given him. It was slightly too big, but it had a sole. What a difference that made. "I don't know," he said. "I don't want to be a soldier any more."

Musen laughed. "Me neither. But I've had it with wandering about in the fucking wilderness. I'm tired, I'm hungry, and every friend I ever had is dead. I just want to get home quick as I can." He lowered his head, and spat. "They've got maps at Spire Cross. Just one look at a proper map, that's all."

"Who taught you to read?"

"So," Musen said, "if you don't fancy Spire Cross, that's fine. See you back home, maybe. Look after yourself."

"Fine," Teucer said quickly. "Spire bloody Cross. But if it all turns to shit—"

"Of course," Musen said. "My fault. Every damn thing can be my fault."

*

The heather was dry and springy, and under it the soil was flaking into dust. "You'd think it'd be worth someone's while to fetch a few sheep out here," Musen said, as they followed the zig-zag path downhill. "People are always moaning about the grazing being flogged out. It wouldn't kill them to drive out over this way."

"There's a war on," Teucer said.

"This close to the barracks, you'd be fine." Musen stopped for a drink of water. It was almost noon. "And you could make good money, selling to the military. In fact, if anyone in there had half a brain, they'd have a flock of their own. I mean, it wouldn't cost them hardly anything, they've got all those men sitting round all day with nothing to do, and I bet you half of them were farm boys before they joined up."

Thin lines of smoke rose from the camp, straight up in the air, no wind at all. At least they could be sure someone was home. "Well, there you go," Teucer said. "In five years, you could be rich."

All bullshit, of course. One thing that wouldn't be in short supply, once they got home, was land in need of working. Two of them, and the old men, to farm the whole of Merebarton. He didn't want to think about that. Instead, he asked, "What was all that about, back at that village?"

"You what?"

"All that about a cart," Teucer said.

"I told you, don't—"

Yes, but they were nearly at Spire Cross, and then Teucer wouldn't need Musen any more; so offending him no longer mattered. "It was bloody obvious we hadn't got a cart," he said. "If I hadn't had a brainwave and put the idea of it getting stolen in their heads—"

"Shut up about that."

"You could've got us both killed."

"They'd have killed us anyway," Musen snapped, "if they'd

wanted to. People don't just kill other people because they don't like them."

Musen was walking fast again, and it was costing Teucer breath to keep up. "They kill people who might be a nuisance," he said, panting slightly. "Like, if they've managed to stay hidden for years and years, and then two strangers show up, soldiers, who might go and tell the authorities."

"So," Musen said. "In that case, they'd have killed us anyway. But, oh look, we're still alive. So don't you give me a hard time, all right?"

"So you made up all that shit about a cart just to get us out of the village."

"Worked, didn't it?"

"Yes, but—"

"It worked," Musen said. "So shut your face."

The last hour was a long trudge across the flat. "So what are we going to tell them?" Musen suddenly asked. It was the first thing he'd said for a long time.

"How about the truth?"

"Fine. Two survivors of a massacre. You clown, you just don't get it. We don't want to be noticed. We don't want to get *involved*."

"All right," Teucer said. "We'll say we're deserters. After all, that's what they're bound to think anyway. And we can spend the rest of our lives rowing a galley in the middle of the fucking sea."

Maybe, just possibly, Musen hadn't considered that. "All right," he said. "We tell them about the river. They're going to shove us in with a bunch of strangers and send us straight off to the war."

Teucer stopped dead. "You arsehole," he said. "This was your idea."

"It was my idea not to starve to death on the moor," Musen said. "Teucer, for once in your life, use your head. Now, say after me, we are not soldiers."

"Oh, right. So what the hell are we doing out here?"

"We're drovers," Musen said. "We were driving sheep, all right? From Cleeve."

"To where from Cleeve?"

"Here, of course. To the army camp. Figuring they might want some nice fresh meat. But these enemy cavalry came out of nowhere. Friends all dead, sheep all gone. We can do that bit, easy."

Teucer thought about it. Practically impossible to prove otherwise. "Musen, why have you got to lie all the time? What's wrong with telling the truth?"

"It gets you in the shit," Musen replied. "So let's run it through one more time. We're drovers, from Cleeve. That's fine, we know where Cleeve is, they can't catch us out there."

"You ever been to Cleeve?"

"Once," Musen said. "There's a big old apple tree in the square, and they hang lanterns in the branches at midsummer. That's all anybody knows about Cleeve."

"I went there a couple of times with my cousins."

"Well, that's all right, then. So, we were out on the open moor, about two days from here. Actually, we were lost. Got lost in the fog. Happens all the time."

"What fog?"

"*The* fog."

"We've been on the moor for I don't know how long and there hasn't been any bloody fog."

"All right, we just got lost. Easy as anything, God knows. The sheep got spooked, and by the time we rounded them up again, we'd completely lost our bearings. So there we were, lost on the moor—"

"Why do we have to have been lost? Why make it complicated?"

"Lost on the moor," Musen said, "and suddenly these horsemen appear. We can do the horsemen, just tell it how it was. We had the wit to pretend to be dead. Horsemen bugger off, there we were, alone and screwed. See? Nothing at all about being soldiers."

Teucer nodded. "How about the army boots?"

"What?"

"We're wearing army boots. How do we explain that?"

Musen paused for a moment. "Took them off some dead men."

"What?"

"No. Listen, it's perfect. We took them off some dead soldiers we found by the river. And then they'll say, what dead soldiers, and they'll be much too interested in that to bother about us. And then they give us food and clothes and we go home to Cleeve. It's perfect," he repeated. "It's a lie with the truth sort of folded up in it, like cheese in a chunk of bread." He grinned. "Always tell as much truth as you can when you're lying," he said. "Nothing deceives like the truth."

The main gate of the camp was open. When they'd left it, Teucer could remember the gate closing behind them. "Musen," he said.

"What?"

"What's that? Lying in the gateway."

They stopped. The gate was maybe six hundred yards away. The shape on the ground could've been anything.

"Shit," Musen said.

"Could just be a log. Or a crate."

"Who'd leave a log lying about in a gateway?"

"There's smoke," Teucer pointed out. "That's cooking fires. It's all *right*. It must be just a log or something."

Not cooking fires. Much later, Teucer found out that the Jazyges don't bury their dead, they burn them, on great big bonfires, which can go on smoking for days, sometimes a whole week. Six bonfires; they'd smashed up rails and fences to get the firewood. They hadn't bothered with the dead soldiers, or else it was deliberate. Some people, savages, believe that until the body is buried or burned, the soul can't be released; so they leave their enemies to rot, on purpose—total war, in this world and the next.

"They can't have taken all the food," Musen said. "Not every last fucking scrap."

He was wrong about that. What they couldn't do was take all the water out of the well, so they'd thrown some dead men down it instead. Musen drew up a bucketful, looked at it and said, "I'm not drinking *that*."

There had been water barrels all round the parade ground, which the enemy had smashed, and a rainwater tank, which they'd allowed to drain, so that the earth all round it was still slightly damp. "How about if we boiled it?" Teucer said.

"In what?"

In, eventually, a helmet. They finally managed to punch four holes in the rim, using an arrowhead they found embedded in a door and a brick. They hung it from bowstrings over a barrel-stave fire, which took for ever to light. They also found a jar of pickled walnuts; the Jazyges had opened it, but clearly hadn't identified it as food. What they'd thought it was, Teucer hated to think.

"Right," Musen said. "Well, that's one problem solved."

It was getting dark. Fixing a drink of water had taken them all afternoon. They'd managed to recover two unsmashed chairs from some officer's quarters, and took them out into the parade yard, where the water was simmering. Solemnly, they each ate three walnuts.

"Musen."

"What?"

"What about Merebarton? Do you think—"

Musen shook his head. "There's a lot of other villages," he said. "And why would they bother? It's a war. It's soldiers they're after."

Teucer sipped some warm water from the edge of the ladle they'd found in the quartermaster's store. There was a definite taste, of something. "They were a bit bloody thorough, looking for food. I reckon they're hungry."

"There's a lot of other villages," Musen repeated. "Also, by now, our lot's going to be out there looking for them. We do have an army, you know."

Had an army. "Maybe the war's over already. Maybe we lost."

"The war's been going on for years," Musen said. "And we've got General Belot." Musen waved his hand vaguely. "This is just—"

"What?"

"Temporary," Musen said. "It happens. The tide comes in, it goes out. Any day now, Senza'll be along and he'll give them a bloody good smacking. Then it'll be our turn."

"What if—" Teucer stopped. What he wanted to say was: what if everybody else is dead, except us and Iser's people, who go around robbing the bodies? What if we're all that's left? "What was all that stuff you said to the blacksmith? There's no smiths in your family."

"Just making conversation."

"Who taught you to read?"

"None of your business."

Teucer yawned. "If we empty the jar and wrap the walnuts up in a bit of cloth, we can use the jar to carry water."

"Good idea," Musen said. "We'll do that."

"Should we take the helmet?"

Musen shook his head. "No army stuff," he said.

"If we took the helmet, we could boil the bog water. Heather burns. There's loads of those muddy boggy patches."

"No army stuff."

They hung around all the next morning, on the off chance that Iser and his people showed up, but by noon there was no sign of them. "They can't just have vanished," Teucer said. "They were headed this way."

"They should have got here before we did."

True; in which case they should have arrived to find bodies

being stripped and buried. But Iser and his men were nowhere to be seen, no indication that they'd ever been there. There were fifteen walnuts left. Why, Teucer asked himself, couldn't there have been an even number?

"Toss you," Musen said. "For the fifteenth walnut."

He'd accumulated a fistful of coins. The Jazyges had taken all the silver, but copper was apparently beneath their notice. "You have it," Teucer said. He noticed that Musen didn't argue. Bastard.

"No maps," Musen said sadly. "No paper of any kind. I'm guessing they used it all for kindling."

"Or they ate it."

"I hope it gave them the shits."

Part of Teucer didn't want to leave. After all, it was a shelter, a man-made structure in the middle of the empty moor, like a tiny point of light in the dark. Besides, sooner or later the army would send someone to find out what had happened. And the enemy had already been there, stripped it of everything they wanted and left it for dead; it stood to reason, therefore, that they'd be unlikely to come back. "We should bury the bodies," he said.

"You're being funny, aren't you? There's hundreds of them."

Dozens rather than hundreds, but the point was valid. "What do you think happened to Iser?"

Musen shrugged. "Don't know."

"I mean, this sort of thing, it's what they *do*. They wouldn't have just taken one look and run away in horror."

"I said, I don't know, all right? Why do you expect me to know every damn thing?"

Pilad had said that once, the exact same words. But Pilad always knew everything, or figured it out. "We'd better go," Teucer said, "while it's still light."

"I guess so," Musen said. "It's a bloody shame about the maps."

Quite. All those dead men, but the maps would've been useful. "Why won't you tell me who taught you to read?"

"Shut your face," Musen said.

"When we get home, you could teach me."

"Like hell."

They left the camp with four or five hours of daylight left—"This way," Musen said, but he was frowning—and walked slowly until it was too dark to see. Teucer had an odd feeling, of not being human any more; what he'd turned into he wasn't quite sure, but it was something allied to rather than inhabiting the weary, rather unsatisfactory body he was obliged to take with him. He felt about it the way he was sure Musen felt about him. At least it meant that he was able to take a rather more objective view of the countless aches, pains and niggles that had been building up since he joined the army: pulled muscles, blisters, the foundations of a trick ankle. He despised them, put up with them, but they weren't really his fault any more.

They found a shepherd's hut. The roof was turf, and it had sagged and slipped, crushing the lintel, squashing the doorposts, like a mouth trying to chew something a bit too big. There was just enough room for them to squeeze in sideways. Inside, the floor was covered with a thick growth of tall, thin-stemmed yellow toadstools. In the far corner, they found a complex of bones, but it was too dark to form an opinion as to whether they were human or animal. Rather more to the point, they found a coat and a pair of boots, hanging from a rafter and therefore relatively undamaged, except for mould. Musen decided he wasn't that desperate, so Teucer tried on the coat; the arms parted from the body as soon as he opened his shoulders. Without really thinking, he put his right hand in the pocket and found something: a leather purse, with coins. Five of them, blackened silver, completely unlike any either of them had seen before. There was also a bow leaning against the wall, but it was riddled with woodworm.

"You know what." Musen was trying to light a peat fire, using the broken-up bow as kindling. "I think this is as good as our luck is going to get."

"If this was a shieling," Teucer said, "there should be a village down in the valley. Maybe we should drop down and look for it."

"After the last time? Don't be stupid." Musen had achieved a tiny red spot on a patch of the dead coat, which quickly went out. "If there ever was a village, it's probably long gone. Nobody lives here now."

"The war?"

Musen shrugged. "This war, a different war, something else. Who knows? Who gives a damn? No bloody good to us, that's for sure."

Teucer thought of Merebarton; of its long and intricate history, of his own imperishable glory within it. "If there ever was a village," he said, "there's probably a river down in the valley."

"Not necessarily. If there is a river, we're completely lost. Shouldn't be any rivers till we reach the Brett, and that's way over there, to hell and gone." He sighed and rocked back on his heels. "I have no idea where we are," he said. "Sorry about that."

"Not your fault."

"No," Musen said, "it isn't. Still, I'm disappointed. I thought I'd be able to cope. I mean, walking across the moor, how difficult is that? Too hard for me, apparently."

"You didn't ask to come here."

"That's no lie."

They each ate two walnuts. Ridiculous; they couldn't help laughing. "We're not going to make it, are we?" Teucer said.

"It could go either way," Musen replied. "But no, probably not. Still, it'd have been a shit life anyway. There'd have been just us to do all the work. We'd have had to pack up, head for—" He paused, frowning. "God, I don't know. We'd all have starved inside a year anyhow."

"All the—"

"They're dead," Musen said. "Hell of a way to go, too. Fucking war. At least Anser and Nical and Pilad got it quick, never knew what hit 'em. It's like they took the short cut and we get to go the long way round. I'm going to go to sleep now," he added, rolling on to his side. "We want to set off early as possible in the morning, get as far as we can before it gets hot."

The next day, about three hours after dawn, they saw horsemen.

"Oh come *on*," Musen shouted. He was furious about something. "That's just not fair. All that fucking long way, and they still catch us."

"Maybe it's not them," Teucer said. "Maybe it's our lot."

"I don't think so," Musen said.

Hard to say how far away they were; half a mile, maybe less. They'd come out of nowhere, which presumably meant a folded-in combe or valley. "They won't have seen us," Teucer said, kneeling down as Musen had done.

They changed direction.

"They can't have," Teucer said, as they ran up the slope. "We weren't on the skyline, we weren't even moving. They can't have seen us at that range."

They came to a flat top, a table. The heather was about eight inches tall. No rocks, trees, anything like that. "They're not bloody eagles," Teucer said. "They can't have seen us."

Musen sat down in the heather. "The hell with running about," he said. "You haven't still got that stupid sash, have you?"

"What?" Teucer suddenly realised that he had.

"Get rid of it, quick."

Get rid of it where? Teucer dragged it out and crumpled it into a ball; they tried to scrabble a hole, but the heather roots were woven into a mass thicker than armour, and they only had their fingers. They tried tearing it into little strips, but the weave was too dense. "Eat it," Musen yelled, but Teucer knew better than to try. "All right, shove it up your arse. Just get rid of it."

Teucer seriously considered that for a moment, but decided it wouldn't fit. He jumped up and ran, a real sports-day sprint, a hundred yards in no time. He stooped, panting furiously, and tied the sash round a heather root. You couldn't help noticing it. He dragged off his boot, stuffed it down inside the leg, and threw the boot away.

"How's that going to help?" Musen said, when he'd limped back.

"I got rid of it."

Musen pointed. The boot was plainly visible, even at that distance. "They're coming up the slope," Musen said. "We're dead."

They could hear them now, thumping hooves they could feel through their feet, and a jangling noise, like someone throwing tools around. "Lie down," Teucer said.

"And have them ride over us? No, thanks."

They came over the crest of the hill at a slow working trot. Not the same horsemen. Teucer froze. He had no idea if they were the enemy or not. They were heavy cavalry; chainmail from the feet up, and a jacket of small steel plates, laced together into a complicated mechanism of moving parts. Their helmets had cheekpieces that covered nearly all their faces, and tall plumes of white horsehair that nodded wildly with every movement. They looked like gods; the thought that anyone could possibly harm or resist them was simply ludicrous. The small area of skin visible between the cheekpieces was dark brown, almost black.

"Not ours," Musen said.

Oh, Teucer thought, and the horsemen stopped.

"Keep still," Musen said. "It won't take long."

One of the horsemen dismounted; he slipped his feet from the stirrups, lifted his left leg over the pommel of his saddle and slid to the ground, wonderfully graceful. He was maybe five feet tall, if that.

"They're so *short*," Teucer said.

"Shut *up*."

Now he was unfastening the chinstrap buckle of his helmet. He lifted it off with an unconscious flourish. He had a white scarf twisted tight around his neck, and his hair was black and very short. He came towards them, stopped and smiled.

"Gentlemen." His voice was high and beautiful, like birdsong. He had an accent like the surveyors'. "Could you possibly tell us the way to Spire Cross?"

They're ours, Teucer thought. They're our side. He felt a smile bursting on to his face. But Musen was radiating terror in all directions.

"That way." Teucer realised he was pointing; not the right way, either. He adjusted his arm. "We just came from there. It's about two days' walk."

The black man smiled. "You just came from there."

"Yes, that's right."

Now he shook his head. "You can't have. We left no survivors."

Hell, Teucer thought. "We're not soldiers."

"Yes, you are." He was still smiling. "You're deserters. Where's your unit?"

"All dead." The words came out of Musen like vomit, in a rush, involuntary. "Your people killed them. Down by a river."

The black man nodded; that made sense to him. He knew what was going on. Well, he would. Gods do. "How many of you escaped?"

"Just us."

He considered the statement, and his divine insight recognised the truth. He nodded. "Kill them," he said.

"Just a minute," Musen screamed. "Wait. My uncle's a blacksmith."

The black man stopped; and his men, who'd been about to do something, stopped too. He turned slowly and looked at Musen. "Is that right?"

"Yes. He lives in Merebarton, in the second street. The fifth house, on the third floor. He keeps his hammers and his anvil at our house."

The black man frowned a little. "Go on."

Musen clearly didn't know what to say next. Panic. The black man's face was starting to cloud over. "He's a long way from home."

"Of course he is," the black man said. He sounded impatient, annoyed. "So?"

And then Musen must have remembered, because Teucer could feel him relax. "He shoes the horses that plough the lower meadows."

"Mphm." The black man was satisfied. "All right," he said, "you're with us. You're lucky we've got spare horses. Him too?"

Musen looked at Teucer. *I'm sorry but you're not worth it.* "No."

The black man nodded. "Shoot that one," he said.

He turned away. A horseman moved, somewhere behind Musen's head. "Musen," Teucer started to say, and then the arrow must have hit him.

He opened his eyes and couldn't move. Fine, he thought, I'm dead. That didn't seem such a big deal.

Then he realised he couldn't move because there was an arrow. It was right through him, between the collarbone and the round muscle of the shoulder, and it was pinning him to the ground. He peered sideways, and saw the feathers, sitting on his sopping-wet chest like a big, fat hornet. His shirt was glistening wet. He tried moving again, and a swarm of angry flies got up and buzzed in front of his eyes; that made him squirm, and it hurt really badly. Some fool, he thought. Some idiot, careless with a bow. Hadn't he realised, bows and arrows can be dangerous? It's the first thing they tell you.

"I said," came a voice, "are you Teucer?"

Not at home; not in Merebarton. He turned his head the other way, and saw two feet. Very strange feet. They were covered in chainmail, with thick leather soles sewn or served in between the rings. He looked up. It was the black man.

So he really is a god, Teucer thought. No wonder we lost, if we're fighting gods. "Yes," he said.

"Teucer from Mere Barton?" He made it into two words.

"Yes."

"You shot a perfect score at a hundred yards."

He couldn't help grinning. Definitely a god. Not just eternal glory but eternal life. "Am I going to heaven?"

"Did you shoot a perfect score at a hundred yards?"

"Yes," Teucer said, "that's right, that was me."

The god turned his head. "Patch him up," he said, and walked away.

They'd pulled out the arrow, and it hurt so much he went away again, a very long way indeed. He considered not coming back, gave it serious thought. On balance, though—

He opened his eyes, and saw blue sky. Then a face appeared, directly over him. A black man, a different one, older. "You'll live," he said.

He had to ask. "Are you gods?"

"What? Yes, sure we are. Compared to you, anyhow." The man did something to him, and it hurt. "Keep still," he said. He was poking about inside the arrow hole with a bit of stick. He took it out; there was a tuft of wool wrapped round it, messy with blood and some yellow stuff. "Try not to move," the black man said. "If it starts bleeding again, you'll probably die."

He couldn't see much, but he was sure it was a different place. There were hills on the skyline that hadn't been there before. "So you're the champion archer," the black man said.

"What? Oh, yes. Yes, that's right."

"You won't be drawing a bow for a while," the black man said.

His voice wasn't like the surveyors'; Teucer understood the words, but it was a totally different way of saying them. "Eventually, maybe, but not for a while. You were lucky."

Define luck. "Am I going to be all right?"

The black man shrugged. "Keep still and quiet," he said. He unstoppered a small glass bottle, dabbed liquid on another tuft of wool and poked it into the arrow hole. It hurt badly, then stopped hurting altogether. "We aren't going any further today."

"Where's Musen? My friend?"

The black man walked away. Teucer stared up at the sky, trying very hard not to move.

The black man came back a long time later, looked at him, nodded and went away again without saying anything. Later, when it was dark, Musen appeared over him. He leaned down, and his face blotted out the world.

"You let them shoot me," Teucer said.

That made Musen angry, for some reason. "What else could I do?" he snapped. "For crying out loud. I couldn't tell him you were one of us; you don't even know—" He stopped, made an effort. "Then I'd have been in the shit, for vouching for you. You do see that, don't you?"

"One of who?" Teucer said. "Who's us?"

"You wouldn't understand. Anyway, you're all right. They've *heard* of you."

He made it sound like Teucer had done it on purpose. "Who's us?"

"Anyway," Musen said, "it's not so bad. This lot are Blueskins, Western regular heavy cavalry. The other bastards, at the river, they were auxiliaries, they'd have killed us without even thinking about it." He stopped, breathing hard. "You do know, this is all your fault."

Teucer opened his eyes wide. "Really."

"Too bloody right. They didn't just happen to come along. They were looking for us. Looking for *you*."

Too much to take in. "So who told you this? Your new friends?"

"Listen," Musen hissed. "We're on bloody thin ice here, so don't try and be clever."

Something in the way he'd said it. "You mean, you are," Teucer said. "They came looking for me because I'm the champion archer. How the hell did they know about that? Nobody knows outside Merebarton."

That put Musen on his guard for some reason. "I don't know, do I? Somebody must've said something back at Spire Cross."

Teucer tried to shake his head, but every muscle and tendon in his upper body was horribly stiff and sore. "Don't think so," he said. "And I think these friends of yours were too busy killing everybody at Spire Cross to stop and ask, hey, do you know any really good archers round here? How did they know, Musen? Who told them?"

"Just shut your face and don't rile them," Musen said.

"If you're a prisoner of war, how come you've got the run of the place, walking about talking to people? Shouldn't you be tied up or something?"

"It's complicated," Musen said. "You wouldn't understand. I'm not a spy, if that's what—"

"Course you're not," Teucer said; "you don't know anything. Musen, who taught you to read?"

"Piss off," Musen said, and left him.

In the morning, the doctor came and examined him. "Not bad," he said, prodding the huge black scab with his fingernail. "No sudden movements, you'll be good. Amazing luck, the arrow didn't hit anything important on the way through. Now we've just got blood poisoning to watch out for."

After that, four cavalrymen in full armour came and put him on a horse. "I can manage," he said, but they weren't interested.

One of them knelt down so Teucer could use his shoulder as a mounting block. "Any chance of a pair of boots?" he asked. They didn't answer. They took the reins off his horse's bridle and tied a leading rein to it instead.

Much to his relief, they walked rather than galloped. By now he'd completely lost any inkling of direction he might once have had, and the landscape was completely unfamiliar; just the moor, endless and featureless, though he guessed Musen would have an idea where they were. He rode with a horseman on either side of him, in silence. All the horsemen were short, and the horses were no bigger than large ponies, by back-home standards. They had the same short, bent-back bows the men at the river had used, carried unstrung in smart wooden cases, painted red.

Around midday they stopped and dismounted; there was a man kneeling for him to step down on to, and then they made him lie on the ground. There was the most delicious smell, which made him feel savagely hungry. The doctor came and nodded at him, and then they brought him some food. They spooned it into his mouth with a shiny bronze ladle. It was the most delicious thing he'd ever tasted, and he had no idea what was in it.

Then back on the horse, another long ride. At nightfall, when they stopped, the first black man, presumably the officer, came to see him. A soldier fetched an ingenious folding chair for him to sit on, and a green cushion.

"You're Teucer the archer," he said.

Teucer nodded.

"We came all the way out here to find you." He smiled. "You should've stayed in Mere Barton."

Again, two words. The fact that this man knew the name of his village scared Teucer to death. "Not my idea," he said.

The officer laughed. "I'm Captain Guifres," he said. "You're a feather in my cap. Get well. Don't die." He peered at Teucer's shoulder. "Have you had anything to eat?"

"No."

Captain Guifres stood up and clapped his hands. A soldier appeared from nowhere, and Guifres said something Teucer couldn't hear. "They'll be along in a minute. Sorry about that."

"What are you going to do to me?"

Guifres laughed. "You'll be all right," he said. "You're valuable. Collector's item." He was still smiling. "Don't ask questions," he said. "Understood?"

Teucer nodded.

"Good man. Tell me something," he went on. "How big's the aiming mark in your country?"

"What?"

"The aiming mark. The target. What you shoot at."

"Archery?" Guifres nodded. "Two feet," Teucer said.

"And the gold?"

"Ten inches."

Guifres seemed impressed. "Imperial standard. And you hit ten inner golds in ten shots at a hundred yards."

"Yes."

"With a hundred-pound bow."

"Well, yes. That's what we use."

Guifres stood up. "And the others from where you come from. They can shoot well, too?"

"Pretty well."

"Just as well we killed them all, then. Take it easy, now."

He started to walk away. Don't ask questions, he'd said. "Captain."

Guifres stopped. "Yes?"

"Why didn't you kill my friend?"

Guifres turned a little and grinned at him. "Ask him that," he said, and walked away, and a soldier came and folded up the chair.

*

Riding was better than walking, even with a hole in his shoulder. He learned to forget about his body from the waist down—it was part of the saddle, nothing to do with him—and made an effort to keep his back straight. One of the cavalrymen even complimented him on his riding style; he had a good seat, whatever that meant. The Blueskins rode as though they'd been grafted on to their horses, like you do with apple trees, so he felt vaguely smug. They were polite and kind to him, on the rare occasions when they spoke to him. He didn't know which one of them had shot him, and decided not to ask.

Whenever they dismounted, the doctor would look at him, occasionally prod the scab—"Does that hurt?" "Yes" "Good, that's very good"—and Captain Guifres made a point of talking to him once a day, immediately after the evening meal. One time Teucer asked, "If you were looking for me, why did you shoot me and leave me for dead?" Guifres didn't mind the question. He opened the flat leather satchel that was always looped round his neck, and took out a little scrap of paper.

"Sorry," Teucer said, "I can't read."

Guifres grinned. "It says, *he has red hair.*"

"Oh."

"We'd been given a description of you," Guifres went on, "but it said, look for a very tall, big man with blue eyes, nineteen years old, and that applied to practically all your lot we came across, dead or alive. When I first saw you, no offence, I thought you were younger than nineteen, so it couldn't be you. A courier rode eighty miles in a day to bring me this bit of paper, and by the time we got it we were on our way back. Soon as I read it, I knew it had to be you we'd shot. Luckily for us both, you were still alive."

Teucer frowned. "Why am I so important?"

Guifres shrugged. "Don't ask me. Apparently, I don't need to know the reason. All I was told was, bring him in alive or don't bother coming back. Somebody wants you for something."

"Why did you spare my friend?"

"You keep asking me that."

The next day, he asked, "What sort of thing do you think someone would want me for?"

"Ah." Guifres smiled. "Actually, I've been giving that a certain amount of thought myself. I've more or less narrowed it down to three possibilities: a template, a specimen, or a gift for the man who has everything. I'm just guessing, though." He paused, and looked at Teucer with his head slightly on one side. "Would you like to learn how to read?"

Teucer felt as though he'd just walked into a low branch he hadn't known was there. "Yes," he said, "very much. Why?"

"I'll teach you, if you want."

"Thank you. Why?"

Guifres shrugged. "We've got a long way still to go. Anything to pass the time."

Which wasn't a credible answer. Still. "Can we start now?"

"Why not?" Guifres opened his satchel and took out a long, thin, flat rectangle of wood. It was coated on both sides with beeswax, and there was a hole drilled down into it to hold a nail. With the nail, Juifrez scratched a symbol in the wax. "Right, then," he said. "This is Amma."

It looked like a wall with two poles leaning against it. "Amma."

"Very good. This—" two triangles, one on top of another "—is Bose."

"Bose," Teucer repeated. "What are they for?"

Guifres' face had a look-at-me-being-patient look. "Each letter stands for a sound," he said. "Amma is the *a* sound. Bose is the *bu* sound. Writing and reading is where you take a word and break it into the sounds that make it up. So." He made more scratches. "Here's your name. Tamma, Eis, Umma, Ceir, Eis, Ro." More scratches. "Here's me. Jao, Umma, Ins, Ferth, Ro, Eis, Sim. Any word you like, all the words that exist in the world, you can break them down into twenty-seven little pictures. It's really easy once you understand how it works."

"I see," Teucer said. "It's pictures of sounds."

Guifres frowned. "If you like," he said. He turned the wooden rectangle over. "I'll write out the letters for you, and you can learn them. Now, watch closely. Ferth, Umma, Thest, Amma, Ro, Ceir—"

"Just a second," Teucer said. "How am I meant to remember which picture goes with which sound?"

"You just do."

Musen appeared to have made friends with the soldier who carried the trumpet, and four or five others who generally sat with him in the evenings. They'd found something to talk about, and Teucer heard them laughing together, several times. *I'm not a spy*, Musen had said. Teucer believed him. After all, what was there in Merebarton anybody in the outside world could possibly care enough about to recruit a spy? Except, he reflected, me. And that made no sense whatsoever.

On the day when Teucer first wrote his name on Guifres' wax tablet, they rode up to the top of a hill, and there was a strange-looking plain in the distance. It was dead flat and dark grey.

The horseman riding on his right said, "That's the sea."

Teucer looked at it again. "That is? That there?"

The horseman laughed. "A bit of it, anyway."

"I've heard about it," Teucer said. "But I thought it would be—"

"What?"

"I don't know," Teucer said. "Different."

"Quite right," Guifres told him that evening. "To be precise, that's Beloisa Bay, and what you're looking at is the North Mese." He smiled. "Moir, Eis, Sim, Eisma. On the other side of that is where I come from. If there's time, I'll show you a map."

If there's time. "I'd like that," Teucer said. He looked at Guifres, trying not to be obvious. "How far are we from where I come from?"

"You don't want to know," Guifres said. "And I'd try and forget about that, if I were you. No point dwelling on things that'll only upset you."

Ah. "Where are we going?" He'd never asked that before.

"Beloisa," Guifres said. "Which is fine," he added, "if you like that sort of thing."

He smelt the city before he saw it. "What's that?" he asked the horseman on his left.

"Fish," the horseman replied. "Fish, drying in the sun."

It wasn't a foul smell, exactly; just different, and very strong. "You get used to it," the horseman said.

The city itself was extraordinary, at least until you got up close, and saw that it was really just lots of small, badly looked-after houses, stacked together like logs in a pile. The plaster was cracking off the walls, and the windows were bowed and drooping, only held square by the shutters. Lots of houses, and no people.

There were sheds, rows and rows of them, identical, with huge doors you could drive a cart through. Still nobody to be seen. Small tufts of grass were starting to grow on the crests of the ruts cut by cartwheels. He guessed it wasn't supposed to be there. Tall, thin plants with grey stems and yellow flowers had taken root in the walls of the stone-built barns at the far end of the row of sheds. He knew all the plants round Merebarton, but he didn't recognise these. The roofs were mostly tiled, not thatched. He realised he was missing a sound he expected to hear, one that went with houses. It was some time before he figured what it might be. No chickens. He saw water bubbling up out of the ground and swirling away down a channel alongside the road. The flat stones on either side of where it came out had been cracked open. There was probably an explanation, if you knew about how houses were built. It looked all wrong.

"Whose city is this?" he asked the horseman.

"Ours," he replied. "Now."

He felt cold. He'd grown to like Guifres and some of the horsemen. They'd been kind to him, for no reason he could see except that it was in their nature to be kind unless there was a valid reason to do otherwise. Perhaps war constituted a valid reason. He wouldn't know about that. "Who's drying the fish?" he asked.

The horseman shrugged. "It takes a while to cure," he said. "We haven't been here that long."

The previous day, the same horseman had told him about his home. They lived in houses carved out of solid rock, he'd said, like caves, only on purpose; you could stay cool that way, and the sun was so very hot all the day, and at night it could be bitter cold. He had two sisters; his father had died in the war. There were only women and old men left in his village now.

They turned a corner, and there was the sea again, a sheet of rippled slate, unnaturally flat. Teucer could see things like rounded sheds, with trees growing straight up from them. So that's a ship, he told himself, but it was hard to work up any enthusiasm.

"They left before we got here," the horseman said.

"Where did they go?"

Another shrug. "A long way away, if they had any sense."

The city wasn't completely deserted; about a dozen soldiers appeared from somewhere, important-looking men, dressed like Captain Guifres, some but not all of them Blueskins. Guifres talked to them for most of a day, sitting outside in the sun with several jugs of wine, but they didn't seem to be enjoying themselves very much. The rest of Guifres' men kept themselves busy with domestic chores, polishing boots, darning holes, patching new links and plates into their armour. They worked steadily, with an air of mindless confidence, tackling jobs that would always need doing. They reminded Teucer of his mother.

That evening, Guifres came to see him as usual. He brought with him a small rosewood case with a brass handle, which he put down on the ground at Teucer's feet before sitting down. "Go on," he said. "Open it."

There were two brass catches, beautiful delicate work. The box was full of brass tubes.

Guifres leaned forward and picked one up. "Like this," he said, and stuck his finger in one end. From the other end emerged a tightly coiled roll of paper. "Go on," Guifres said.

Teucer took it and unrolled it an inch or two. All covered in writing; the letters were tiny, but so clearly formed that Teucer could make them out. "Well?" Guifres said.

Teucer concentrated. He was getting good at this. He took his time, not opening his mouth until he was quite sure he'd got it right. "The art of shipbuilding," he said.

Guifres grinned. "By Iosarius of Tianassa," he said, "in twelve volumes. And a little extra something as well, but I won't spoil the surprise. Hope you enjoy them. It was all I could get."

It took Teucer a moment. "They're for me?"

"Of course they are. Something to read on the journey."

"What journey?"

"And relevant, too. If anything breaks on the ship, you can tell them how to fix it."

Teucer looked at him. "What journey?"

Guifres took a deep breath. "You're going to Rasch Cuiber," he said, "you lucky sod. Wish I was."

"Where?"

"Oh for—Rasch Cuiber, the capital city of the Western empire. Centre of the known universe, best place on earth."

"Across the sea? On a ship?"

"Well, you wouldn't want to walk."

"No," Teucer said. "I can't."

Guifres was still grinning. "Sorry," he said. "Orders. We're soldiers, we do as we're told, right?"

"I'm not a—"

"You're a prisoner of war, and you're going to Rasch Cuiber." Guifres stood up. "Read the books," he said. "It'll be good practice and you might learn something." He hesitated. "Trust me," he said; "you'll be better off there. It's a civilised place: they don't just kill people out of hand in Rasch."

"What do they want me for?"

Guifres looked unhappy. "I don't know," he said. "But whatever it is, it's worth their while going to a hell of a lot of trouble to get you. You're valuable. People take care of valuable things." He smiled: an apology. "So long," he said. "Look after yourself."

"Thank you," Teucer said.

Guifres shrugged. "If they make you a duke, put in a good word for me." Then he walked away.

The ship was much smaller than it looked from a distance. Teucer had been in bigger barns. "Get used to it," one of the men said. He wasn't a Blueskin, but he wasn't like the Rhus people either; he was short and skinny, with long brown hair, like a girl's. "The crossing takes twenty days, if we're lucky."

"What if we're unlucky?"

"You don't want to know."

The planks were slightly warped; he could see down through the cracks between them. Barrels, mostly. "Where do I go?"

"Where you like," the man said, "so long as you don't get in the way." He paused, and looked at Teucer. "You been on a ship before?"

"No."

"They tell you anything about it?"

"No."

"Right. Nothing to it, really. Just remember, no matter how bad it gets, you won't actually die." He grinned. "Unless we sink, of course."

"Is that—?"

"Who knows?"

The ship kept moving slightly, but nobody else seemed to think anything of it. He found a space next to the tail, sat down and opened the box, which was his only possession. *The Art of Shipbuilding.* Well. He closed the box carefully, lay down and rested his head on it.

He must have fallen asleep. When he opened his eyes, the ship was in the middle of the sea.

6

The Thief

Captain Guifres watched the sail until it was hard to see. Then he turned to Musen.

"Well now," he said. "What are we going to do with you?"

Musen's mouth felt dry, as though he'd been working in the sun all day. "How about you let me go?"

Guifres shook his head. "Can't do that," he said.

"Oh. What can you do?"

Guifres pulled a face. "It's depressing how little discretion I've got, actually," he said. "Well, that's not strictly true. For instance, I could have you killed, right now, and nobody would say a word; it'd come under general expediency in the field. But if I let you go, they'd have me up in front of a board of enquiry and I'd be lucky to keep my commission. And if you can make any sense of that, please enlighten me." He scratched his chin. He'd lost his razor. Actually, Musen had taken it, the day before yesterday, while the captain was talking to Teucer; it had an ivory handle, and could at a push serve as a weapon. He'd hidden it in one of the troopers' saddlebags, wrapped in a spare scarf. "No, as I see it, I've got two options. I can turn you over as an ordinary prisoner of war, or I can find someone on the staff here to take you off my hands."

"A craftsman."

"Well, yes, obviously. But that wouldn't be a problem. Plenty of them."

Musen relaxed a little. They might be savages, but they took the craft seriously; far more than anyone had done back home. He wondered, not for the first time, what he'd have done in Guifres' shoes. *Kill them both*, probably, and spared himself all the inconvenience. After all, who'd ever have known?

"Do that, then," Musen said.

"It's not as simple as that." He was getting on Guifres' nerves. "For a start, what would anyone possibly want you *for*? Sorry." He smiled. "No offence. But really. You aren't a skilled man, you don't have a trade, and I can't see any of my brother officers wanting you as a servant."

"I can read."

"Yes. So can every soldier in the army. I'm sorry," he repeated, "but you can see, it's a problem. Even for a fellow craftsman, there are limits as to what can be done." He thought for a moment. "You could always escape."

"But I thought you said—"

A sort of give-me-strength look. "Yes, that's right. I can't let you go. But if you escape, I can quite legitimately take a command decision that I can't spare the manpower to chase after you and catch you. Once you're two miles from here, what the hell difference will it make if you've escaped or I let you go?"

"I wouldn't have a safe passage."

"Well, no," Guifres conceded. "There's that. But you're a smart fellow: you can look after yourself."

"I'll get caught again. By your lot."

"Not necessarily. You only got caught the first time because I was looking for your friend. But for him, you'd probably be home free and clear by now."

"I'd have starved to death on the moor."

"God, you're hard to do favours for. All right, you don't want to escape and I can't let you go. You suggest something."

Musen gave him a flat, stupid look. It was one of his best: versatile and effective. "We're craftsmen," he said. "You've got to look after me."

"Actually, that's not what it says in the rules—" Guifres stopped. "All right. I can leave you here in the custody of the garrison commander, who just happens to be a craftsman, too. Then you can be his problem. How about that?"

Musen thought for a moment. The sad fact was, he wasn't really sure what he wanted any more. Going home to Merebarton, alone, the only man under fifty in the village; be realistic, no future in that. At first, after the slaughter at the river, he'd had such visions—all the unclaimed land, the huge estate there for the taking; then the sober thought, as they'd crossed so much empty space, that land is useless without men to work it, and by the look of it there were *no more people*; because he knew for a fact, ten years ago the country they'd crossed, from Merebarton to Spire Cross and then on towards Carney, had been a settled, prosperous network of hill farms and small villages, all duly marked on the maps, and where the hell were they all now? So, no labour to be hired in from outside, no value, no point in all that land that should have been his for the taking. Waste; useless. In which case, why the hell go back? Nothing there but hard work and sorrow. But if he didn't, what was he supposed to do?

And the answer, coiled seductively round the base of his mind like a fat snake; these people obviously have far more things than they need, and plenty of money—

"Fine," he said. "After all, I wouldn't want to be a burden to anyone."

The city was a miserable place, hostile, empty and miserable, but eventually he found a buyer, a short man (they were all so short), in a coat even older than he was, sitting in a doorway. The man had called out, "Hey, want to buy? Good stuff, very cheap." He hadn't bothered looking up.

"Not buying," Musen said. "Selling."

"Uh." The man looked up at him. "You're not a soldier."

"No."

"What're you doing here, then? You're not from these parts."

"I ran away from home to seek my fortune."

That got him a grim look. "What you got?"

Musen dropped down beside him, looked round and fished in his pocket. "Here," he said, and unrolled the cloth bundle.

"Where'd you get that from?"

"Family heirlooms. Been handed down from father to son, twenty generations. Where do you think?"

Sixteen bone buttons, various. A small folding knife, bone handle, some pitting, the blade missing the tip. A man's ring, small, almost certainly gilded bronze, the blue stone slightly chipped. A man's razor, best quality, ivory handle. A silk handkerchief, some slight bloodstaining. "Well?"

The old man brushed aside the buttons. "Don't want them." He picked up the ring, put it down again; unfolded the knife and tried to wobble the blade, but it was sound in its bolsters; sniffed the handkerchief and dropped it; didn't even look at the razor, which meant he knew what a good piece it was. Thought so. "Ten rials."

"Oh, please."

"Nah." The old man covered the stuff with the cloth. "Ten rials. I'm not bothered."

He was so good at it that, for a moment, Musen almost believed him. He felt desperately provincial, but managed to keep his face straight. "No worries," he said. "Thank you so much for your time."

He'd got to his feet and was actually walking away when the old man said, "Fifteen," in such a sad, weary voice that Musen couldn't help feeling guilty for imposing on him so. He stopped, counted to three under his breath and said, "I don't think so."

"Twenty."

Musen had no idea what a rial was. It could be tiny, like a fish scale, or big as a cartwheel. He was guessing it was silver, but he didn't know. "Oh, go on, then."

Money changed hands. A five-rial turned out to be silver, about the size of his thumbnail but surprisingly thick. "That silk thing," the old man said. "Got any more?"

"I know where I can get some."

"Four rials each."

"Five."

"Four."

"I'll see what I can do." He closed his fist around the coins. "Army stuff any use to you? I can get stirrups, horseshoes, pliers, spare plates for breastplates, that sort of thing."

"Wouldn't touch it, son. You neither, if you got any sense."

Worth knowing. Clearly the Imperial army took a dim view of pilfering official stores. "Cheers," Musen said. "You here tomorrow?"

"I'm always here."

Depressing thought. He turned away and walked quickly till he was out of sight. Then he opened his fist. Four fat silver coins. He pulled off his boot, wedged the coins between his toes and pulled the boot back over them. Then he walked a couple of steps, stopped, removed the boot and the coins and put them in his pocket. Better poor than a cripple, his uncle used to say.

He walked back to the barn where Guifres' men had stabled their horses. A soldier he'd talked to once or twice was sweeping the yard. "How much is a loaf of bread?" he asked.

"Rial. Why?"

Oh well, he thought. But quite possibly bread was dear and luxury goods were cheap right now. It'd be different, surely, if he could get to a proper town, somewhere where there wasn't a war. The razor would've been useless in Merebarton. Nobody could have afforded it.

He thought about taking a quick scout round the hayloft where the men slept. There'd be nobody around; they were all out doing whatever soldiers do, and they were so trusting—Before he could make up his mind, a soldier he knew by sight came up to him and said, "Been looking for you."

"Me?"

Nod. "Captain wants you."

Surely not, Musen thought. And anyway, how could he prove anything? The razor was long gone by now. "Where is he?"

"I'll take you."

Didn't like the sound of that. Still, he couldn't let it show. "Thanks," he said.

The captain wasn't alone. There were two men with him, one Blueskin, one normal-sized man with red hair (for an instant, he'd seen Teucer; but it wasn't him) in ordinary clothes, not army. They both had little hammer brooches on their collars. "That's him," Guifres said.

The Blueskin frowned. The redhead stood up and smiled. He was about thirty-five, with long hair and a short beard, and clothes that had been cut to look much cheaper than they actually were. Boots to last a lifetime.

"I'm Oida," he said. "Pleased to meet you."

Musen had absolutely no idea what to say. Fortunately, the red-headed man was just leaving. He smiled warmly at the two soldiers, nodded to Musen and left. When he'd gone, Guifres said, "Do you have any idea who that was?"

"No."

Guifres and the other soldier looked at each other. "Fine," Guifres said. "You've just met one of the most important men in the empire, that's all."

"Really?"

"Yes. Still, no harm done, let's hope. This is Major Pieres, garrison commander. I've told him about you."

Pieres was what Guifres would look like in ten years' time, if he got plenty to eat. "He's a craftsman."

"Yes, believe it or not," Guifres said.

"What for?" Pieres gave Musen a long, sad look. "What did you join for? I don't suppose it was an unquenchable thirst for esoteric knowledge."

"My dad was a craftsman," Musen answered. "And my uncle."

"He can read and write," Guifres said, "after a fashion. I thought maybe you could use him in the stores."

"What stores? They're empty." Pieres shrugged. "Oh, go on, then." Musen managed not to smile at that. "What can he do?"

"Farm labourer," Guifres said. "But he's quite bright."

"Doctrine and works," Pieres sighed. The phrase was familiar. "Mind you, I reckon this ought to do me for works for the next five years."

Doctrine and works, anvil and hammer; of course. Musen was to be Pieres' good deed for the half-decade. Thank you so much. "Thank you," he said.

Pieres flexed his left hand, a cursory hammer and tongs. "Quite all right," he said. "Get over to the mess tent and have something to eat."

Musen had already done that, without asking, some time ago. "Thanks," he said, and got out of there quickly.

"Who's a man called Oida?" he asked.

The sergeant stared at him. "Seriously?"

"If I knew, I wouldn't be asking."

The sergeant was a craftsman. He put down the chunk of bread dipped in gravy he'd been about to eat. "You've never heard of Oida."

Musen found a grin from somewhere. "I'm the enemy, remember?"

"He's famous on both sides," the sergeant said. "Only musician in the world who's played for both emperors. Great man. *Great* man."

"A musician," Musen said.

"Don't say it like he's just some fiddle player." The sergeant was angry and amused at the same time. "Know what? Four years ago, something like that, he reckoned it was time to stop the war, right? They actually had peace talks. They actually sent ambassadors, both sides, just because he said so. *Not* just some fiddle player."

"But the peace talks—"

"It was because your lot kept asking for stupid stuff. Wasn't his fault. Kept asking for stuff they knew we couldn't give them. Deliberate, like sabotage."

"Oh," Musen said. "What kind of—?"

"I don't know, do I? Anyway, that's beside the point. You said, who's Oida. *That's* who Oida is. Right?"

"I see," Musen said. "Only, he was here."

"What?"

"Here," Musen repeated. "Just now. I saw him, in with the captain and Major Pieres."

For a second or two, the sergeant was so stunned he couldn't breathe. "You're pissing me."

"No, straight up. That's why I asked who he is."

"You saw Oida?"

Musen nodded. "He said he was pleased to meet me. Only because we're both craftsmen, of course."

"*I'm* a fucking craftsman," the sergeant protested. "Here, you sure it was him?"

"The captain seemed to think so. You've just met one of the most important men in the empire, he said. That's what made me curious."

The sergeant tried to speak, but his feelings were beyond words. He shook his head, stood up and walked away, then and for ever a man who had been so near and yet so very far. He was so preoccupied that he went all the way back to his tent before he realised he'd left his horn and silver drinking cup (for ten years' good service) behind in the mess tent. He hurried back but someone must've taken it away by mistake.

I don't suppose it was an unquenchable thirst for esoteric knowledge, the bastard major had said. Which showed how much he knew.

As always, raw materials were the problem. Back home he'd tried wood first of all: birch bark, carefully flattened over time under flat stones, but it split; then thinly sawn oak, fifty years old, cut from the heart of an ancient gatepost, but the ink just drained away into it, and there was nothing to see. Then he'd hit on the idea of thick rawhide, and that was just right, once he'd smoothed it right down with brick dust. The only way was to pour the dust into the palm of his hand and rub. Brick dust cuts skin. Fine, because rawhide is skin, but so were the palms of his hands. He had a devil of a job explaining why his hands were always raw and bleeding. But before very long, he had twenty-six identical rawhide rectangles, a palm long and an index finger wide. Ink was just oak apple gall and soot; everyone knew that, but nobody had actually ever made any, so he had to figure out the proportions by trial and error. It took an amazingly long time to get it right. For a brush, he used the pin feather from a woodcock's wing—tiny little thing, hardly bigger than a needle, and he had to keep rinsing it out in water to keep it from getting clogged.

The first attempt was all right, but he wasn't satisfied with it, so he made another one, and then two more, before he ended up with something he felt happy with. The problem was that you only got one shot at drawing the pictures. In theory, you could grind out your mistakes with brick dust, but he'd tried it and ended up with a horrible mess. He'd never drawn anything in his life before, went without saying. He tried practising beforehand, scratching on slates with a nail, but that was a totally different thing, it didn't prepare you worth a damn for brush and ink. The fifth try, though; not perfect, for sure, nothing like the real thing the Master had shown him, with colours; but good enough. The first time he'd used them had been the happiest moment of his life.

That pack was somewhere by the river, in his abandoned rucksack, unless one of the savages had taken a fancy to it. Now he had the whole job to do again.

Instead of rawhide he used parchment. Not a problem. The city was full of the stuff. He broke into a merchant's house and helped himself to a beautiful new roll, unused, milk-white. While he was there, he took two bottles of ink—black and *red*, for crying out loud—and three brushes, horsehair, and a stick with a fine steel blade shaped like a cut-off goose feather; a pen, he guessed. Wonderful thing.

Time wasn't a problem, either. The less he was visible, the happier everyone was. He appropriated a hayloft over a stable in the yard of an inn. If he half opened the door there was loads of good light, particularly in the morning. He sat on a barrel of nails, with the work on his knee. So this is happiness, he thought.

Part of him wanted the pack finished as quickly as possible; part of him wanted the drawing to last for ever. Instead of starting at the beginning, with one, the Crown Prince, he began with the easiest: nine, the Gate (which is just a closed gate in a wall; arch, the boards of the gate itself, four ornate hinges, the bricks of the wall; nearly all straight lines, which he ruled with the back of a knife which some fool had left lying around in the barracks dormitory). That gave him the confidence to move on to seventeen, the Table—mostly straight lines, the legs and flat of the table itself, but with the hills and the city in the background, and the dog and the fox on either side. He got the dog more or less right, but the fox came out looking a bit like a polecat.

He got a bit overambitious after that and went straight on to eight, the Castle of God. The castle ended up looking like it was falling backwards. He thought about that, and decided it probably wasn't a bad thing. He spent a whole day on the besieging army, now that he had a rather better idea of what soldiers actually looked like. The defenders were Rhus archers, of course, and the attackers were Blueskins, though he decided not to try shading them in, because that would just look strange. The figures were too big for the castle, but they'd been like that in the Master's pack, so that was probably all right.

Eventually, the day came when there was only one left to do, the one he'd been putting off. Five, the Drowned Woman. Well, yes; but it had to be done.

In the event it came out really well. He drew her floating on her back (not as he remembered), with a flower in her left hand, her eyes closed, her hair spread out round her on the surface of the water. Properly speaking, the sun-in-glory should've been overhead—for noon, the Great Noontide—but he put it well over to the right, for mid-afternoon, the only personal concession, but he felt it was the least he could do. As he drew the last strokes and inked in the number he was almost shaking. He told himself it was because he was scared of dropping a blot off the pen and ruining the whole thing at the last minute. When he pulled his head back to look at the finished article, he simply couldn't say if it looked like her or not. It was too long ago, after all, and he'd pictured it so often in his mind, he no longer had any idea what he was remembering.

Then he hung them up to dry from a string, each one fastened by a peg of green hazel, and went out to find a suitable box. Luckily, the major had one; he kept pens in it. The old man gave him three rials for the lot.

*

And then, after all that, he found out that the quartermaster-sergeant had a pack. They were coloured, just like the Master's, and drawn on the same light, not-wood stuff, and the box was rosewood with a brass clasp. But for some reason Musen preferred his own, and let him keep them.

"The Moon reversed," the quartermaster-sergeant said. "That means you're going on a long journey."

He was making it up as he went along. Fortunately the lieutenant of engineers wasn't a craftsman and knew no better. "Does that mean I'm going to get posted back home?"

"Let's see, shall we?" The quartermaster-sergeant turned up the next card. Number three, Shipwreck, natural. "Oh dear," the quartermaster-sergeant said. "Well. Speaks for itself, doesn't it?"

Musen made himself stay quiet. Shipwreck, natural is best interpreted as resourcefulness in the face of adversity, an opportunity disguised as a misfortune; that's if you believe the pack is for fortune-telling, which only fools do.

The lieutenant looked miserable. "So if I get offered a posting back home I should turn it down, is that it?"

The quartermaster-sergeant gave him a wise look, and turned up the last card. "Well, that's good," he said. "Number twenty. True Love."

The lieutenant cheered up at once, and Musen looked away. Number twenty, the Wedding, not True Love, coming after the Moon and the Dragon reversed, could only be bad; the forced marriage, unhappiness, disaster, coming at the very end of the sequence quite possibly death. Musen, who really didn't believe in fortune-telling, couldn't help shivering a little. Still, it served them both right, for abusing the Mystery. "That'll be three rials," the sergeant said, and Musen heard the sound of coins on wood. Then again, he thought, if someone's stupid enough to pay money for a load of old rubbish, why not? And he had his own pack now—

No, couldn't do that, it wouldn't be right. The lieutenant went to the bar and paid, his tab and the sergeant's. Musen got up to leave, but the sergeant was between him and the door.

"So," the sergeant said. "What's your game, then?"

"What?"

"I saw you," the sergeant said, "sitting there pulling faces the whole time, like you'd got the runs. I'm doing a bit of business here. What's your problem?"

It doesn't matter, Musen thought. And I'm here on sufferance, I need for these people to like me. Most of all, I need not to make life difficult for the major. And then he heard himself say, "You shouldn't be doing that."

"You what?"

"You're a craftsman. You're using the pack to take money off people. That's wrong."

"You *what*?"

I really need to stop now, Musen thought. "The pack's special," he said. "If you do that stuff, you shouldn't be in the craft."

The sergeant was a head shorter than Musen, and not much above half his weight. The first punch—solar plexus, inch-perfect—drained all the breath out of his body. The second one landed Musen on the floor. It was some time before he realised where the sergeant had hit him: the point of the chin, for the record. A boot in the pit of the stomach came after that, but by then he was too far out of it to care.

"Arsehole." The sergeant stepped over him and left.

Later, when the world came back and stopped moving, Musen took proper note of the fact that no one came to help him up or see how he was, though that seemed to be the usual etiquette after fights. Curiously, none of the twelve or so men in the place seemed to have noticed that he'd been knocked down, or that he was making a pretty poor job of walking to the door. You didn't need to be a Master to interpret those signs. Pity about that, Musen thought. He got out into the air, sat down with his back to the wall and concentrated on his breathing.

That's what an unquenchable thirst for esoteric knowledge gets you, said the voice in his head. He disagreed. It wasn't the unquenchable thirst, it was the being too stupid to keep his face shut. The question was whether the damage he'd done could be put right, or whether it was permanent, meaning it was now time to move on. Probably the latter—he wasn't sure how he knew, but he was pretty certain. In which case, where to?

Merebarton. Across the moor to the country of the walking dead. Merebarton wasn't an option any more. There was no guarantee it'd even be there. What if he were to make it back across the moor, only to find the houses empty, the roofs dragged off or burned, the people dead in the street? He wasn't sure he'd be able to overlook that, and it made sense not to do anything that would force him to hate the enemy; not if they were winning. The trouble was, thanks to the war, he couldn't rely on anywhere still being there—just empty land, from sea to shining sea.

When he felt well enough to stand, he got up and made his way back to the barracks, weaving and staggering like a drunk. As soon as he closed his eyes, he was fast asleep.

On the major's desk was a little bronze statue: a blacksmith, bent over his anvil, hammer hand raised, tong hand steadying the work on the anvil, forging a human heart. On the base, in small but elegant lettering: *Am I not a man and a brother?*

"You're starting to get on my nerves," Pieres said. "I had to spend half an hour this morning calming down Sergeant Egles. He's agreed to let the whole thing drop—"

"*He* hit *me*."

"You insulted him," Pieres replied angrily. "You cast aspersions on his worthiness to be a craftsman. That makes it an honour claim, recognised as such by military law. He was perfectly within his rights to challenge you, and you wouldn't have lasted two minutes. Fortunately, as I said, I managed to calm him down. Believe it or not, I do have other things to do with my time."

"He was fortune-telling," Musen said, "with the pack. He was making it up, and he took money off that lieutenant. That's wrong."

"Yes, well." Pieres scowled at him. "I did actually point out to the sergeant that obtaining money by deception from a superior officer is a court-martial offence, and if he survived the duel I'd have no option, et cetera. But you know what? I couldn't give a damn. Egles is a good soldier; he runs the stores damned efficiently, and you're a complete waste of space. I wish he'd called you out on the spot and killed you, and then we'd be rid of you and I wouldn't have had to do anything about it. So," he went on, "I'm giving you fair warning. Don't make trouble. You talk about abusing the craft. Seems to me that's all you've done since you got here."

Am I not a man and a brother? Only, apparently, up to a point. "I'm sorry," Musen said.

Pieres swallowed a mouthful of water. Rather a nice cup: silver, embossed with vine leaves. On a major's pay, Musen doubted he'd come by it honestly. He made a mental note of it. "First," Pieres said, "you apologise to Sergeant Egles. Next, for God's sake find yourself something to *do*. I can't have paroled enemy prisoners wandering around the post all day like rich men's sons, it's ridiculous. So make yourself useful, understood?"

No hard feelings, the sergeant said. By that point, the bottle was less than a quarter full. He'd traded the old man two mirrors, the sergeant's hairbrush and a solid silver buckle for it.

"No, I mean it," Musen said. "And to make it up to you, I'd like to do something to help out. Round the stores, maybe."

The sergeant squinted at him. "Like what?"

"Fetching, carrying, heavy lifting. Anything you tell me to."

The sergeant looked at the bottle, thought better of it. "What the hell," he said. "Great big bastard like you, why not? I spend half my life lugging stupid great boxes around. And fuck it, you're a craftsman." He paused, and a cunning look covered his face. "Pieres gave you a hard time, did he?"

"Just a little bit."

"Nah, he's all right. All fart and no turd. You don't want to take any notice. All right, then. Meet me up the stores after first change tomorrow."

Everything is a matter of perspective; from one point of view, the stores was an earthly paradise. A long, wide, low-roofed shed crammed with boxes, in the sort of chaotic mess that suggested it was under the authority of someone who didn't have quite enough time to do everything that was asked of him. Inside the boxes, all manner of useful and desirable objects. Two huge ledgers on the table by the window: Stores In and Stores Out. At each weekly audit, they balanced exactly, but only because Egles habitually under-recorded the incomings; if Supply delivered thirty-six gross boots, black, cavalry, medium, he recorded thirty gross in Stores In, which allowed a civilised margin of six gross for pilfering, private enterprise and genuine misplacement. Musen thought about the old man's misgivings about handling military goods, and dismissed it as an outsider's ignorance. Who the hell could ever possibly find out, except Egles, and he was in no position to get self-righteous about anything. As for finding an outlet for all this stuff, there was a campful of eager customers on the doorstep. Egles never issued anything for free if he could help it. So, sod the old man and his incessant bloody haggling. Why bother with civilians when you can do business with the military?

"You're really into this craft stuff, aren't you?" Egles said to him, one day after they'd unloaded a consignment from Supply.

Musen was tired and his back hurt. "I guess so, yes."

Slight hesitation; not something he'd usually associate with

Egles. "Do you think you could read the pack for me? Find out if I'm going to get posted home soon?"

I could explain, he thought. The pack is not for telling fortunes. "Sure," he said.

"Thanks. I'd like that. When can we do it?"

Furthermore, if you mess with the pack, the pack will mess with you. The Master hadn't put it quite like that, of course. "Tonight, after mess call."

"Thanks."

Later he broke the bad news to the old man, who didn't seem unduly bothered. As a parting gesture, he tried to sell him eight pairs of gloves, brown, non-commissioned officers'. "Nah," the old man said. "They're army. You can tell by the stitching."

"You could say they're off dead bodies. It's legal if they're battlefield."

"Don't be stupid, son. Anyone can tell they're unissued."

"Dirty them up a bit."

"You know what they do to you if you get caught receiving army stuff?"

"Have them," Musen sighed. "No charge. Present. Keep your hands warm."

That was different. "All right."

"My pleasure." For what we are about to receive, may He make us duly thankful. "If I get any civilian stuff—"

"What about the silks? You said you'd get some more."

He put the gloves down by the old man's feet. He left them there. "I'll see what I can do."

"I got a buyer. But you need to get a move on."

He never expected to see the old man again. But he did, a week later. He was with three other men, hanging from a big ash tree outside the Prefecture. He'd been there some time, but Musen knew him at once, if only by the smell of his feet.

*

"There was a woman in here looking for you."

That made no sense. Musen hadn't seen a woman, young or old, rich or poor, since the secret village on the moor. He'd sort of assumed they were extinct. "When?"

"Just now. You only missed her by a minute."

Damn, Musen thought; and then it occurred to him that not all surprises are pleasant. "Did she say what she wanted?"

Egles shook his head. "Left something for you."

On the bench where the soldiers sat while they were waiting. Just a sack, folded very small. "What is it?"

"How would I know?"

Egles was watching him out of the corner of his eye, a sort of oblique stare of great intensity. He picked up the sack and stuffed it in his coat pocket. "You want to do another reading tonight?"

"Yeah, why not?"

Musen managed not to sigh. It had come as a surprise to him how many, how very many ways there were of arranging the cards of the pack to spell out the same message: promotion, followed by a posting back home. The weird thing was, Egles never tired of it. Each time, his face lit up, his eyes sparkled and he bought drinks afterwards without being asked. "Well?"

"Well what?"

"Aren't you going to see what it is?"

"Liniment," Musen said. "For my back. Don't suppose it'll work, mind. Nothing works on my back."

"Could I try some?" Egles asked. "My back's been killing me lately. I think it's the hot weather."

"Sure. But I'll give it a go first, just in case it brings you up in boils or something."

He made a mental note: back wall, fifth shelf down, siege catapult winch ratchet lubricating grease, two-ounce pots; he'd have to scrape it out and put it in something else first. "You're too young to have a bad back," Egles was saying. "Me, I've had backs for years. It's the lifting."

"Maybe you should transfer," Musen said. "Go back on the line or something."

"What, with your load of bastards out there trying to kill me? Catch me doing that, son."

He had to wait the rest of the day before he was able to get some peace: in the latrine, while everyone was in the mess hall. He unfolded the sack. It seemed to be empty. Then he felt something right at the bottom, cloth, and pulled it out. A silk handkerchief, with faint traces of blood.

I got a buyer; practically the last words the old man had said to him. Now he came to think of it, the old man had mentioned it several times; the only line of goods he'd specifically asked for. But if the woman was the buyer, why had she sent this one back?

He tried to remember where he'd got it from. That was the trouble: so many things passed through his hands these days, some of them from the soldiers, some from locked-up houses, a few bits and pieces he'd genuinely found in the street. He racked his brains, tried to picture himself acquiring it. Then he remembered. Teucer: it had been sticking out of Teucer's pocket, the day after they left the hidden village. And he hadn't had it before—Musen had been quite familiar with all Teucer's possessions, at all times—so he must have got it there, somehow. A strange thing to find in a cut-off village in a fold of the moors, so remote that they didn't even know about the craft. Sure as hell hadn't been made there, so it had to have come from outside. He cursed Teucer for getting him in trouble, and then not being there when he was needed.

Then he examined the handkerchief, looking for anything distinctive. Nothing he could see; no embroidered monogram or anything like that. It was a sort of vague buttermilk colour, and the stains were very slight, a repeating pattern, in one corner, almost as though something had been wrapped up in it.

He thought of the old man hanging on the tree and shuddered. But that had been for receiving military stores, and this was nothing to do with the army. Only missed her by a minute, Egles had said. He wasn't sure if he was sad or happy about that. Also, it wasn't like Egles just to say "a woman." He was well aware of the sergeant's views on women, their uses and drawbacks, and "woman" was a surprisingly neutral term, coming from him. That suggested there had been something about her that had put Egles on his guard, at the very least. He fished out the sock he kept his money in, feeling the coins through the cloth, though he knew the total without needing to check—six gold angels and thirty silver rials, a worthwhile sum (and all through his own diligence and industry, in such a short space of time—and his aunts reckoned he'd never amount to anything) but not nearly enough to represent a stake or a fresh start somewhere, even if there was anywhere in this uncannily emptying world worth going to. Besides, making a run for it just because an unidentified woman had sent him a hanky was probably over-reacting. Probably.

He lay awake trying to make sense of it, eventually fell asleep, overslept and woke up late for work, with an eyeful of sun streaming in through the hayloft door. He pulled on his coat—quick check to make sure his money was still there, yes, good—and stumbled down the ladder.

"Sorry, I couldn't sleep, and then—" He broke off. Egles wasn't alone.

"That's him," he heard Egles say. She turned round and smiled at him.

It was probably, he later decided, because he'd grown up in a small village out in the country. Nobody left, no strangers ever arrived; you knew everybody from birth. So, with regard to women, you'd seen them grow up, from kids to girls, from girls to mature women; people you know change gradually, and you don't tend to notice, at least not consciously. Eventually the day comes when you discover you've known for some time that so-and-so isn't a skinny little nuisance with sticking-out teeth any more, she's now something quite other and extremely interesting, but nobody comes as a surprise.

"You're Musen," she said.

"That's right. Who—?"

She turned back to Egles. "Mind if I borrow him for a minute? I'll bring him back, I promise."

Egles was trying so hard not to grin. "You go ahead, miss. Stay here if you like. I'm just going out back."

Later, he realised she wasn't really beautiful. Her face was a long oval, her eyes were very big and dark, there was something odd about her nose, which was long, thin and flat. Her mouth was rather low down, and her cheekbones were exaggeratedly high. Tall as a Rhus woman, but thin, narrow-shouldered, almost bony. Between thirty and thirty-five? Merebarton women didn't look like that past twenty-four, but she was definitely older than that. Analysed objectively, though, not beautiful at all.

He was having trouble breathing. "Sorry," he heard himself say, in a nervous, squeaky voice. "I don't think I know you."

"Of course you don't." Same accent as the major's, but it suited her. A high voice, remarkably clear. "But I carry charcoal down to the fourth hearth."

"You're a—" He stopped, not sure what to say. "I didn't think—"

"Women in the craft? All right. Ask me something."

His mind, of course, went completely blank. The only question he could think of was about six minutes into the lesser office of the tongs, and he wasn't sure he could remember what the correct answer was. Still. "What came after the seventh fold?"

"Easy." She grinned. "He folded it seven times and laid it in the fire till it was white. Then he forged it five times with five hammers. Want me to tell you what they were?"

Perfectly right. As she said it, he remembered the Master, trying to teach him. "No, that's fine. I'm sorry. Only, where I come from—"

"Now, please be quiet," she said. "I haven't got all day. You know a man called Teucer."

"Yes."

"You stole the handkerchief from him."

"No, I—"

"Please," she said. "Now, was there anything inside it? Wrapped up."

He was going to say no, but instead he stopped and tried to remember. Teucer had been asleep. The corner of the handkerchief had been sticking out of his pocket, just the corner; it had snagged his eye, the way a bramble catches lightly on your sleeve and hooks in. He'd made sure Teucer was in deep—watched his eyes, listened to his breathing, the usual; then he'd pinched the visible corner between the thumbnail and forefinger-tip of his left hand and tugged, slowly and very gently, no more than half an inch at a time. It had taken a while. You learn to be patient, it's like tickling fish. Every two inches he stopped, let go and counted to twenty, his eyes fixed on Teucer's face—you never look at the thing itself, because if the sleeper wakes up, and there you are with your eyes glued to something half in and half out of his pocket, it's hard to be plausibly innocent. He remembered that there were a couple of times when he'd come up against an obstruction, when the fabric jammed and he had to use extra strength. You have to be so careful; pull evenly, building in a straight, rising line, just like drawing a bow, and as soon as you feel the resistance overcome, stop pulling and have a rest. And those obstructions could have been—

"I don't know," he said.

"You don't know."

"There could have been," he said. "Maybe there was something in there, and it came out in his pocket while I was—"

"Right." Something about how she said that suggested to him that he didn't have to explain, not the technical stuff. She knew about taking things from people's pockets, quite possibly rather more than he did. Another craft that women could belong to, apparently. "So it'd still be there, that's what you're saying."

"I don't know," he repeated, feeling ashamed. "Depends what it was."

She was considering him as a problem to be overcome and there were several different ways of tackling it. "The village was called Old Street," she said. "And there was a craftsman there, but it wasn't the blacksmith. I know, it usually is, but not there. They're a bit unfriendly in Old Street; they're scared of the war, they don't have anything to do with the outside world any more. So, nobody comes or goes. But the craftsman needed to send something out, it was quite urgent, and then you two turned up. So she wrapped it up in the handkerchief and stuffed it in your friend's pocket while he was asleep. The idea was, when he was caught by the cavalry—"

"Hold on," Musen said. "This—"

"Craftsman."

"She knew Guifres' troop was looking for us."

"For Teucer, yes. It was ideal. Teucer would be picked up but not harmed, and a fellow craftsman could get the handkerchief back from him and pass it on where it had to go. Only," she added, "you stole it. And nobody figured that out until now. Apparently it never occurred to them that friends would steal from each other in a situation like that."

"I—"

She ignored him. "As soon as Diudat showed me the handkerchief—" She stopped. "The old fence. Didn't you know that was his name?"

"I didn't, no."

"Soon as I saw it, I knew what had happened. Too late by then, of course. Teucer was on a ship. He's arrived safely, by the way, in case you're interested."

"What'll happen to him?"

"He's fine," she said. "But he hasn't got it, what we're looking for. You haven't, either." He wondered how she knew that. No, he knew how she knew that. When? Whoever it was that had searched him must've been very good. "I'm levelling with you," she went on, "because you're a craftsman, because you're serious about it or you wouldn't have made these." She took them out of her sleeve—impossible, there wasn't room for them in there—and fanned them in her hand with a casual skill he couldn't help admiring. "Believe me when I tell you, this is all about the craft, and what we're looking for is very important to us. If you love the craft, you'll help me and not lie any more. Well?"

"Yes," he said. His eyes were fixed on the pack in her hand.

"Fine." She nodded. "So, you really haven't got it?"

"I don't know. I don't know what it is."

"You'd know," she said. "It's not the sort of thing someone like you would find in his pocket and mistake for something else." She sighed and lowered her hand, still holding the cards. "It's beginning to look like it's got lost somewhere, genuinely lost. You didn't sell stuff to anyone else, did you? Apart from Diudat?"

"No."

"Fine. I know about everything he had from you. So, either Teucer lost it before you stole the handkerchief, or it was loose in his pocket and fell out. There wasn't a hole in the pocket; we checked that."

It occurred to him that this checking of pockets must've happened after Teucer arrived in the city across the sea, but she knew about it. How many days' journey was it? Someone had told him, but he couldn't remember. She was looking straight at him now. He wondered what she'd decided.

"Don't go anywhere," she said. "I'll keep your cards, for now;

sort of a hostage. I don't think you'll run away and leave them behind. If you're very good, you can have them back."

He considered taking them, but not for very long. "What have I got to do?"

"You? Nothing. Just stay put and keep out of trouble, and if you do happen to remember anything else, for God's sake tell me."

"How? How do I reach you?"

She sort of grinned. "When you read the cards for Sergeant Egles, rig the pack so he gets the Chariot, followed by Mercy, followed by the Drowned Woman. Then I'll find you, all right?" The cards had gone back in her sleeve; he'd been looking at them, but he'd missed how she did it. "Don't ask anyone about me, and stop thieving from the stores. You're not very good at it, and you'll get caught, and they'll hang you, and we might need you again. All right?"

He knew that whenever he came up to a group of soldiers and they suddenly went quiet, they were talking about the war. The rest of the time, they were fine, like he was one of them, and he quite liked that. But people were going quiet on him rather a lot lately, from which he gathered that something was happening.

"We're not supposed to tell you," Egles said.

"Fine. In that case, you can do your own readings."

Egles gave him a hurt look. "Don't be like that," he said. "It's an order, from the major."

"Who'd know?"

The war wasn't going well. General Belot had been recalled to deal with a new offensive in the South, which had turned out to be a feint specifically designed to get him out of the North. Now his brother, the enemy's general Belot, was somewhere out on the moor with a large army, heading straight for Beloisa Bay. It'd be suicide to be there when he arrived, but if they withdrew from Beloisa they'd lose everything they'd gained over the last eighteen months; the lines would go back to where they'd always been and it'd be as though the big push had never happened. The area commander, General Lauga, was an experienced officer with a sound record and three or four good victories to his name, but he'd never fought Belot. He wouldn't stand a chance. The question was, would the emperor make them stay and get slaughtered, or pull them out before Belot arrived? There was politics back home involved, apparently, so nobody had the faintest idea what was going to happen.

"That's stupid," Musen said. "It's no good to anyone if you lose a whole army."

"You don't understand politics, boy. If we lose an army on the Optimates' watch, it's bad for them and the KKA look good. There's war elections coming up in the city. So the KKA want us to stay here and get wiped out, the Optimates want us out of here soonest. Trouble is, the Optimates are the government."

"That's good, surely."

Egles smiled at such innocence. "They pull us out, the KKA'll say they're running from a fight, really bad for morale and how foreigners see us. Could lose them the election. They leave us here, we die, the KKA give them all sorts of shit for a major defeat that could've been avoided. Fucked both ways."

Musen frowned. "That's really how things work?"

"Politics, boy. Our only hope is if the emperor makes the decision, because he can do anything he damn well likes. Sometimes he does; sometimes he leaves it to the government. Usually he only gets involved in stuff if he thinks'll make him look good."

The war, again. He'd hoped it had gone away. The stupid thing was, he felt at home in Beloisa, as much or maybe even more so than he'd done in Merebarton. There were craftsmen here, his people. Being a craftsman, he had a place, guaranteed; and he was better than the ordinary soldiers, who didn't seem to be allowed into the craft under the rank of sergeant. Also, he liked them rather more than Rhus people, especially the Blueskins; they'd gone out of their way to be friendly, even though he was technically the enemy. And they had far more in the way of portable possessions, it went without saying, and if anything went missing they assumed they'd mislaid it. Nice people generally.

If they left, would they take him with them? He'd asked Captain Jaizo, Pieres' second in command, about signing up, joining the Western army; he'd said he wasn't sure, he'd have to look into it, and that was some time ago. Egles thought probably not; and if Musen did, he'd have to go to a training camp and go through basic, and probably a specialisation as well; he couldn't just stay in Beloisa and carry on working in the stores. His best bet, Egles reckoned, if they were going home, would be to stow away on one of the ships and stay hidden until they were well out to sea. Trouble was, he'd never be able to fade away into the crowd back in the South, he was just too damn tall.

Just possibly, there was another option. So—

"Next card, Mercy," he said, turning it over. "That's good."

"Is it?"

"Mercy's always good," Musen said. "And coming after the Chariot, that's very good indeed. Definitely looks like you'll be going home."

Egles beamed. "That's great," he said. "Well, we should all be going home, because of Senza fucking Belot. But you predicted it," he added. "Long before the news got out. You foresaw it in the cards."

"Well." Musen did the modest shrug. "What's next? Ah, that's good."

"What, the Drowned Woman? That's terrible, isn't it? Means the ship'll sink."

"Not really," Musen said. "Not following Mercy and the Chariot. You've got to remember, it's all about context. The woman's *floating*, remember. What it actually means is, once you get home, you're going to get that extra stripe. *Colour*-sergeant Egles is what that means, unless I'm very much mistaken."

Egles glowed slightly. "Well," he said, "you were right about going home, I'll give you that."

"Trust me," Musen replied. "We're craftsmen, aren't we?"

It worked. She didn't come to the stores this time. She materialised in his hayloft, like an angel; he opened his eyes, and didn't know if it was a dream.

"Well?" she said.

She'd brought a lamp, and the loft was filled with soft golden light. Number twenty-seven, he thought, Mercy. "You came."

"Yes, and I'm in a hurry. You've remembered something."

He looked at her. It was difficult. "You've got to get me out of here."

"What?"

"When the enemy get here and we pack up and go home. You've got to get me on a ship."

He'd said something that amused her. "Why should I?"

No suggestion that she couldn't do it. "I can't stay here," he said. "I tried to join up, but I think there must be difficulties."

"Why should I put myself out for you? You haven't remembered anything. You don't know where it is."

"You're wrong. But I'm not saying anything unless you get me on a ship."

"Sorry." She started to move away.

"I know where it is. I remembered."

She hesitated. She didn't believe him. "Well?"

"A place," he said. "On a ship."

"What is it? The thing we're looking for. If you've remembered, you must've figured out what it is."

"I didn't see it clearly, just a shape—" He was losing. "About as long as my finger."

"What?"

"It was about as long as my finger." He pinched his forefinger and thumb together. "About this thick."

She froze. "Go on."

"Not till you get me a place."

"You're guessing," she said. "You're thinking, what shape would something be if you could wrap it up in the handkerchief."

"It was something flat," he said. "Thin and flat, rolled up."

She looked at him for some time. "I'll see what I can do," she said. "You sure you want that, though? This is your home, surely. It's your lot who's winning."

"Get me on a ship," he said. "Please. Craftsman to craftsman."

"Suit yourself." She picked up the lamp. Just the usual red clay type, but it gave off far more light than they normally did. "Soon as you're on the ship, draw the pattern of six wedges on the rail."

"The what?"

She sighed. "Wooden thing to stop you falling in the water. You'll know what I'm talking about as soon as you see it. Got that?"

Bad news from the war. General Lauga had resolved that Beloisa must be defended at all costs. He'd asked for reinforcements from home; meanwhile, all units were being called in, and Beloisa was to be fortified and placed in a posture of defence. Meanwhile, Belot was reported to be at some place called Spire Cross, wherever that was; it didn't show up on any of the maps.

"I know where Spire Cross is," he told Captain Jaizo.

"Is that right?" Jaizo looked startled. "What about it?"

"That's where Belot is, right?"

"You're not supposed to know that." He picked up a big brass tube, poked in one end with his finger. "Show me on the map," he said.

Musen studied it. "This map's all wrong," he said.

"Excuse me?"

"It's all wrong. Nothing's where it's supposed to be. Are you sure this is the right one?"

Jaizo nudged him out of the way. "All right," he said, jabbing with his forefinger. "We're here, Beloisa."

"Yes, but the rest's all wrong. There's no mountains here, look, and they've missed out two rivers."

"Impossible. This is the Imperial Ordnance."

"There's mountains marked here, look," Musen said. "There's no mountains anything like that anywhere in Rhus. This is all rubbish."

"Yes, well." Jaizo pursed his lips. "Yes, there's problems with these maps, we know that. They've got proper maps back home, the old pre-war ones, but they won't copy them. Restricted. So we've got to make do with these."

"All right," Musen said. "Got some paper?"

Musen had never drawn a map. It was such a strange idea, like drawing a picture of a thought, or a piece of music. "We're here," he said, squiggling a line for the sea. "Now, those hills you can see out the window are here, in a sort of horseshoe, like this—"

When he'd finished, Jaizo looked at the result for a while, then said, "So we're here and Belot's here."

"Yes."

"That's bloody close."

Musen nodded. "Yes," he said. "But how come you didn't know? Captain Guifres knew where Spire Cross is."

"Guifres' lot were dragoons," Jaizo replied, as though that explained everything. "So, naturally, they got issued the good maps. That really is terribly close. I'd better tell the major. He's not going to like it."

Major Pieres had enough on his mind already. Orders had been issued to all the units in Rhus to fall back on Beloisa. That should have been enough to give them the advantage in numbers. So far, though, nobody had come. It wasn't hard to draw a conclusion from that, though nobody said it aloud.

"But if he's that close," Egles theorised, "and he hasn't come for us yet, and none of our lot's shown up yet—"

"There's other explanations," Musen said.

"Right? Such as?"

He came up with a few—Belot was having supply problems; the missing units had defied orders, or the orders had been superseded; they'd joined together and fought Belot out on the moors and beaten him; both Belot and the missing units were wandering about on the moor in the fog somewhere, hopelessly lost—and Egles was convinced enough to cheer up dramatically, but Musen wasn't fooling himself. And what was the point of arranging a place on a ship, at God knows what cost, if there weren't going to be any ships? And, if there were no ships, why hadn't she known that? Or maybe she had.

Finally the ships came.

Marvellous. Thank God. But they weren't troopships. They were freighters, loaded down with supplies and provisions for the siege. Thousands of barrels of flour, bacon, salt beef, salt fish, butter; hundreds of tons of oatmeal, in sacks; thousands of gallons of lamp oil, vinegar, birch syrup, honey; onions, dried peas, lentils, chickpeas; one ton of turmeric, for crying out loud, and a quarter of a ton of nutmeg. "There's enough here to last for years," Jaizo said, raising his voice over the thunderous rumble of rolling barrels.

"Yes," Pieres replied miserably. "Think about it."

Jaizo wasn't the sharpest knife in the drawer, but he got it. He immediately posted guards on the quayside and more guards on the ships, to catch stowaways. The roll was called four times a day. Musen was told to report to the guardhouse at the start of each watch. "Don't take it personally," Egles told him, but Musen was furious. They couldn't have it both ways, he argued. If they wanted to order him about and condemn him to death by making him stay and be killed, they should at least have the decency to let him join up. If they didn't want him, they should let him go. Simple as that.

"Fine," Egles said. "So desert. Go back to your lot. Bet you they'd be really pleased to see you, with what you could tell them."

"I can't do that," Musen snapped. "I can't betray craftsmen. You know that."

Egles stared at him. "Really. You don't mind screwing your own people, but not craftsmen."

"You don't understand anything," Musen said.

Egles just laughed. "Get the rest of the barrels shifted," he said.

And rumours, of course. Scouts had gone out and found the battlefields where Belot had slaughtered the Fifth, Sixteenth, Ninth Auxiliary, the entire Southern Army, recalled from the far distant frontier to relieve Beloisa and intercepted somewhere on the high moor. Furthermore, the relief fleet, carrying thirty thousand regular infantry and two field artillery divisions, had been caught in a storm, or sunk by the enemy fleet, or both. The good news was that plague had broken out in Belot's army and killed two men in three; his supply chain had been cut and he was starving; hundreds of his men were deserting every day; the Queen of Blemya had finally joined the war on the Eastern side, and was sending fifty thousand armoured cavalry on stone-barges—

"But none of it's true," Musen protested.

"Probably not," Egles conceded. "But it makes people feel good. Like Temple."

Don't go there, Musen told himself. "Who's the Queen of Blemya?" he said.

Scouts—real ones—reported a large body of men approaching the city from the east. They hadn't been able to identify them for sure—you had to get uncomfortably close to do that, since both Eastern and Western regulars used basically the same patterns of kit—so they couldn't definitely say whether the army was Belot or the missing friendly units. Pieres sent heralds, who didn't come back.

The supply freighters sailed home again. Musen hadn't bothered trying to stow away; he'd have been caught, and things were bad enough already. Everyone else in the camp was working flat out on the reinforced defences, hacking stone blocks out of temples and municipal buildings, hauling them on rollers, lifting them into position on rickety improvised cranes; when Musen volunteered to help he was turned away, with or without courteous thanks. It's because you're one of the enemy, Egles explained helpfully. That made him much angrier than he'd thought possible, but he did his very best not to show it. A few ships appeared in the harbour: small, fast diplomatic couriers, which anchored well out to sea and sent their passengers ashore on launches.

Pieres ordered the city's four gates to be walled up solid. ("You know why, don't you? It's not to keep Belot's men out, it's to keep us in.") To get blocks big enough, they dismantled the façade of the White temple, the oldest and biggest in Beloisa. Whoever was in charge of the operation did his best to shore the temple up with scaffolding, but there was only a limited supply of seasoned poles and beams, and the gangs working at the gates had priority. Without warning, the spire, bell tower and north portico of the temple suddenly collapsed, killing thirty men and completely blocking North Foregate, thereby cutting the city into two isolated halves. The granaries and water tanks were in the western half, which meant that three quarters of the garrison, working on the gates, had to go without water and food for the forty-eight hours it took to clear a way through the rubble.

The main water tank sprang a leak. Normally this wouldn't have mattered, since a tributary of the Los flowed in through a watergate in the east wall; but Peires' crews had dammed the river to form a moat and walled up the watergate. The breach in the tank flooded one of the three principal grain stores before it could be found and stopped up, by which time the tank was nearly half empty. The cause of the breach proved to be damage to the foundations of the tank, caused by the collapse of the White temple.

A fire broke out in the Tannery quarter. The district was deserted and there were no strategic stores there, but the intense heat cracked the west wall and made it subside; on investigation, it turned out that the fire had spread to an extensive network of cellars under a vintner's warehouse, where empty casks were stored. These had burned out, setting fire to the wooden props supporting the galleries, which caved in; the displacement of earth made the whole wall shift six inches. Pieres' men tried to shore it up with beams, but they didn't have any long enough so they built three buttresses out of rubble and half-fired bricks from one of the city kilns. They partly collapsed during the night, and had to be done all over again with finished stone from the hospital outbuildings.

The scouts confirmed that the approaching army was General Belot, with approximately fifteen thousand men. The garrison numbered precisely seven hundred and thirteen.

"These things always go the same way," Jaizo told him. "It's a set procedure, a sort of unwritten protocol. There were classes on it when I was at the Institute."

For some reason, Jaizo had started talking to him. He guessed it was because he was outside the chain of command. Since Jaizo always brought a bottle with him, and left what he hadn't drunk behind, Musen encouraged him.

"Go on."

Jaizo filled his cup. "Sure you won't join me?"

"I don't drink."

"Wise fellow. Bad habit." He swallowed half a cupful. "It goes this way. They launch an assault. If they get through, it's all over; most of us will probably get it during the fighting, they'll be so pissed off with the rest of us that they'll slaughter us like sheep. So, we fight back like mad and drive them off. That's stage one."

"I see," Musen said. "What's stage two?"

"Investment," Jaizo said. "They dig in round the walls, set up siege artillery if they've got any, start building it if they haven't. Their sappers set about undermining the perceived weak points of our defences. If we feel like it, we can launch a sortie or two, to steal or spoil their food supplies or set fire to their siege engines. We don't have to, but it sort of shows willing. Anyway, that usually lasts about ten days. Then we move on to stage three."

"What's stage three?"

Jaizo drank some more. "Terms," he said. "They offer terms, we reject them. They come back with a better offer. We put forward terms of our own. We haggle a bit, and then we surrender. Depending on the deal we've struck, we get to leave the city with or without our arms, armour and regimental insignia, provisions for the march, escort and safe passage, et cetera. We go home, our commanding offer is court-martialled and hanged for cowardice, we get reassigned without blame, life goes on. Ninety-nine times out of a hundred, that's what happens."

"I see. What if it doesn't?"

Jaizo shrugged. "There's stages four through six," he said. "Basically, they bombard us with rocks, dig under our walls and make them fall down, launch assaults with scaling ladders, rams and siege towers, that style of thing. Each time they have a go and we beat them off, there's an opportunity to go back to stage three. Stage *seven* is where they make it through the wall, burst into the city, kill everything that moves and burn the place to the ground. But that's pretty rare."

Musen was silent for a moment. "So Pieres—"

Jaizo shook his head. "He knows the score," he said. "It's a fact of life; you live with it if you accept a garrison command. After all, the only alternative is stage seven, so you're dead either way, only then you take hundreds of your mates with you. And, of course, the senior staff wouldn't stand for that. If we thought he was thinking along those lines, we'd cut his throat."

Musen thought a bit more. "So if everyone knows the city's going to surrender sooner or later," he said, "why bother with all this? Why not just—?"

"Give up straight away? Forget it." Jaizo wiped his mouth. "You never know, the government back home might send us reinforcements, or there could be an outbreak of plague in their camp, or heavy rains washing shit down into their water supply, or they could be recalled and sent somewhere else. That's what motivates the garrison commander to stay at his post, the one in a hundred chance of staying alive. Not very likely," he conceded, "but you never know. That's why we fight. Just in case."

"But usually—"

"Usually, yes." Jaizo poured a thimbleful into his cup. "The vast majority of these things end with surrender. Like, if the government back home really gave a damn they wouldn't have let it come down to a siege in the first place. Or they don't do anything because they can't, because they haven't got the men or the money." He shrugged. "Slightly different here, because we were fooled; we thought it was a trick and we were wrong. Our only hope of keeping the city is if our Belot wins a really big one on the other side of the sea, and they have to recall their Belot to deal with him before he's winkled us out of here. Not that it matters," he added with a shrug. "We don't actually *want* this godforsaken place, we only came here to open a second front and take the pressure off down south. It's all just strategy and tactics, isn't it?"

This godforsaken place. The trouble was, Musen realised, he thought of it in those terms, too. The moor, waste, empty, useless; their Belot and our Belot, but which was which? He really didn't want to be cooped up inside the city if there was a siege, neither soldier nor civilian, sideless. And another thing—

"Can I ask you something?"

This time, Jaizo was definitely drunk. Every day he went a little bit further; the previous evening, he'd brought two bottles, though he hadn't actually opened the second. Tonight, he was a quarter of the way into it. "Sure," Jaizo replied. "So long as it's not troop movements, because then I'd have to kill you."

"The war," Musen asked. "What's it *about*?"

Jaizo laughed. "Good question," he said, and fell asleep.

General Belot was building siege engines. Since Beloisa stood at the edge of the treeless moor, his only source of lumber was the joists, beams, floorboards and lintels of the handful of farmhouses scattered around the elevation where grass gave way to heather. The only way he could get nails was to burn them out of planks too rotten or warped to be useful; as for rope, he had a thousand men stripping and twisting nettles, of which the abandoned market gardens to the south-east furnished an ample supply.

At least water wasn't a problem, even though the garrison had deliberately cut itself off from the river; it rained non-stop for a week and all the tanks were full. Unfortunately, so were the gutters and the drains, and then the streets, and then the basements and cellars, including several that housed provisions and supplies. Forty-six miles of best flax rope were ruined in one night, engulfed in thirty tons of cement, earmarked for making good the damage soon to be inflicted by General Belot's artillery. As for Pieres' beautiful new moat, in places it was lapping up against the top of the battlements, and the engineers were frantically trying to figure out a way of draining it without flooding the whole city.

He wasn't in a good mood. They'd demolished his hay barn, where he slept—something about firebreaks in the heavily built-up zone next to the north wall, in case Belot bombarded them with incendiaries—and his blanket, pillow and spare clothes were now under three feet of compacted rubble. Also buried beyond recovery, though at different sites, was his stock in trade, but he couldn't see how he could register a formal complaint about that.

Having nowhere else to go, he decided to sleep in a temple. There weren't quite so many to choose from as there had been; the Old, the New, the White and the Refining Fire had all been pulled down or collapsed, the Perpetual Grace was flooded and the Eastgate had been turned into a hospital for men injured during the building works. That just left the Reformed and the Mercy, and the Reformed, next door to a major granary, was alive with rats. Musen went to the Mercy.

The door was locked, of course, but he didn't even need to force the vestry window; someone had done it for him, and very neatly, too. He wandered into the nave, and saw with a degree of surprise that the Flame was still burning, its glare reflected in the gilded walls and polished marble floor, so that the nave was flooded with light to roughly the same extent as the street outside was flooded with water. That made him feel oddly comfortable and also rather guilty. It meant that, in theory at least, the fire god was still here, at His post, on duty; a good soldier, though Musen suspected that He was no longer in practical control of the situation. Nevertheless, he made a perfunctory grace, bobbing his head and patting the left side of his chest, the way kids do. At the same time he was thinking: there must be a big reservoir of lamp oil under there somewhere, enough for several days. Lamp oil was at a premium right now. Query: if he doused the flame and stole the oil, would he drive the god out of His own temple? Could he actually do that, evict the god, as though He was behind on the rent? Define rent, he thought.

He went back into the vestry and found the chest where the priests stored their vestments. Good stuff, actual silk; you'd have thought they'd have spent out on a decent padlock. He gathered a heaped armful, went back into the nave and made himself a silk nest, like a caterpillar, in front of the fire, although the actual warmth it gave off was negligible. Our Father, he prayed, keep me safe, tonight and always.

Two chasubles made a fairly effective pillow, and he was just slipping into a dream when he heard someone cough. The voluntary sort. He sat up. "Hello?"

"That's so sweet," she said.

"You."

She was wearing deep red, an extraordinary choice in a city under siege, where people instinctively tried not to be noticed. Maybe she'd looted the dress from somewhere; maybe she'd been caught in the rain and got soaked to the skin, and the red number was all she could find. Red, of course, is the proper colour for the fire priestess. A terrible thought struck him. "Are you—?"

She grinned. "Actually, yes. At least, I'm ordained, but I'm not in offices. I sort of collect qualifications. They're useful." She changed the grin to a frown. "You're pretty hard to find."

Her shoes, he couldn't help noticing, were dry. "Am I?"

Over her shoulder, he could see the main door. It was slightly open. Did that mean she had the key? "Yes, you are. I've wasted a good hour looking for you. Mind you, I should've thought of a temple to start with. You really do believe, don't you?"

An odd time to discuss religious conviction. "Yes," he said, "of course."

She nodded, as though he'd given the right answer. "And when your friend Sergeant Egles insulted the pack, you hit him."

"Actually he hit me."

Shrug. "Same difference. You're a good craftsman, and a true believer. I suppose I shouldn't be surprised. Country people have stronger faith, I've noticed that." She'd produced his pack of cards, from somewhere. He tried very hard not to look at them. "It says in Scripture, you must not steal."

"I know."

"But you do."

"I'm not perfect."

"Do you try to be?"

He thought about that; it was a good question. "Yes," he said. "I fail, obviously."

"Lesson one," she said. "Nobody's perfect. To seek to attain perfection is to presume that you are capable of being equal in grace and substance with Him. That's very bad. Don't do it. Instead, you should confess your imperfections, to show that you regret them, and seek to make them good."

"You mean stop doing them."

Roll of the eyes. "No. *Make them good.* You don't understand, do you?"

For some reason, he wasn't scared, even though he knew he should be. But there was a sincerity in the way she spoke that had caught his attention, as though these questions mattered, urgently, here and now. "Sorry."

"Fine." She sat down, folded her hands, composed herself: the start of the lesson. The Master had done the same. "A smith makes a thing, let's say a hinge or a scythe blade. He makes it, but it comes out wrong. He can throw it in the scrap and start again, or he can try and make it good. With me so far?"

Musen nodded.

"The Great Smith makes us. Sometimes we come out right, sometimes we don't. Some of us are so badly flawed, we go in the scrap. Some of us are worth making good. Yes?"

"Yes."

"The Great Smith works on us through us; we are his hands and tools, his anvil and hammer. To make us good, He inspires us with awareness of our error, which leads us to recognition and repentance. Still with me?"

"Yes. Go on."

She smiled. "He then inspires us to make ourselves good. It's very important you understand what that means. It doesn't mean we throw ourselves away and start again. That'd be presumption. It's not for us to throw ourselves away, only He can do that. Well?"

"I understand."

"Good boy. When He made you, he gave you a shape, a form. He made you how and what you are. If you try and change that, be someone else entirely, you're throwing away the thing He made. Which is wrong. Isn't it?"

"I suppose so, yes."

"That's right. The shape and form He gave you is your character. That's actually what *character* means, it's a word in Old Imperial meaning a stamp or design."

"Oh. I didn't know that."

"Of course you didn't, but you do now. What you have to do is *make good.* You've got to work on that flaw, the flaw in your *character,* and make it good. Like, the smith draws out the hinge too thin on one place. So, he draws the rest of it down until it's all one even thickness. Or he burns the edge of the blade, welding it to the back; so he jumps up and draws down all round it and makes the burned bit good. He takes the flaw and makes it good. Do you see?"

"I think so."

"Excellent, we're nearly there. What you have to do is identify that flaw of yours—in your case, taking things that don't belong to you—and make it good. That's all. But it's really important. Because that's what He's doing, through you. If you fail Him, you're a bad tool. Bad tools go in the scrap."

She was silent for a while. He asked, "But I don't see what I'm meant to do. You're saying stealing is a flaw, but it's wrong just to stop doing it."

Another smile. "It depends on the flaw," she said. "Is it just a blemish on the surface that can be beaten out and filed smooth, or does it go all the way through the iron, like a cold shut or an inclusion? In your case, I'm guessing, it goes all the way through, right down deep inside you. You won't ever stop thieving, because you can't. He made you that way. But He made you. So, two choices. Throw you away or make you good. Which do you think He should do?"

Musen thought about it. "Throw me away."

"Wrong." She scowled at him, mock-ferocious. "You have faith; you're a sincere craftsman. He wouldn't have made you that way if He didn't have a use for you. So, you need to be fixed."

"I'm not sure I—"

"Also," she said, "you're a good thief." That made him blink, like a bright light shoved in his face. "Or you could be, if you're taught properly. I've been watching you very carefully, and in my professional opinion you show genuine promise." She pursed her lips. "You're a bit old for training, you're woefully ignorant of basic general knowledge and you've got the manners of a pig, but we can fix that. So, cheer up. I've decided. You're getting out of here."

A surge of uncontrollable joy, like the rainwater flooding the cellars. "You can—"

She nodded. "I've got a ship," she said. "Well, call it a ship, it's more a sort of overgrown dinghy, but it'll get us where we're going." She paused. "Now you ask, where's that?"

"Sorry. Where—?"

She beamed at him. "It's a really nice place," she said. "You'll like it there. Nice shady cloisters, so you won't boil to death, like most Rhus do in the South. Board and lodging completely free, and the food's actually quite good. Also, I think you'll enjoy learning. I should say you're quite an intellectual, for a farm boy."

He wasn't sure what that meant, but she seemed to think it was a good thing. "You've got a ship," he repeated.

"I said so, didn't I? It's all right, it'll still be there in the morning." She stood up, walked to the fire. "Sorry about this," she said, and threw his pack of cards into it. They burned up quite quickly, and the reflection of the brief flare on the gilded walls was like daybreak. "No valued possessions, it's the rule. Essential, actually, when you think about it. Five hundred thieves under one roof, the one thing you simply can't afford to let them have is *property*. Otherwise, there'd be chaos."

"Five hundred thieves," he repeated.

"There or thereabouts," she said. "At the Priory. People just like you."

His head was swimming. "The Priory. That's where we're going."

"That's it. Or you can stay here and die, of course, if that's what you'd prefer. This place has got absolutely no chance. That's official, direct from the General Staff."

He took a deep breath. "Sorry," he said. "Can I just get this straight? You're sending me to a sort of thief school, in the South."

"You could call it that."

"And this is to do with *religion*. It's a holy school."

She gave him a fond smile. "It's all right," she said, "they'll explain it all when you get there."

"And you can do this. Make the decision, I mean."

"Me? No, of course not." She paused for a moment. "Well, the actual decision, whether you're suitable or not, yes, that's me. But we've been watching you for a long time."

"You have."

"Since you were eight. Quite a remarkable thing, two of you in one poxy little village out in the middle of the bush. We thought it was just an inexperienced observer trying to make a name for himself. But no, you both measured up. And, of course, a linked pair's always a good thing to have up your sleeve. Anyhow, that's enough about that. Be here, first light. I'll send someone." She stood up and walked towards the open door. "Nice meeting you. You won't see me again for a bit."

"You're not coming on the ship."

She shook her head. "Too much to do here," she replied. "I

expect I'll see you at Beal Defoir, I don't know. Cheer up," she added. "Smile. You're going to get out. You're going to *paradise*."

He woke up and assumed it had all been a dream. Then he saw the toes of two pairs of boots.

"You coming, or what?"

His mouth tasted of mud. Sleeping with his mouth open. "The ship?"

He'd said something amusing. "Yeah, the ship. You coming?"

Musen scrambled to his feet, not so easy on a dead-smooth marble floor. "I'm right behind you," he said.

They were both short, broad men, very dark but not Blueskins; black curly hair and beards that made them look much older than they sounded. "I'm Loster and that's Coif," one of them said. They both wore long coats, bilberry-stain blue. He couldn't really tell them apart.

"Musen."

"Yes, we know."

They were going west, towards the docks, but he'd never been down these streets before. Didn't look like anyone had been that way for a very long time. They walked until Musen's feet began to hurt. "Is it much further?"

Another joke; he wished he could be that amusing on purpose. "Nearly there."

They stopped. By the looks of it, a carpenter's shop; the shutters had been stripped, the planks prised out, and the workbench was open to the air; tools lying everywhere, as though someone had gone through them in a hurry, looking for something in particular. "Wait here," Loster said. He went inside, and Musen heard his feet on stairs. Coif grinned at him, as though they were co-conspirators in some mildly antisocial venture. "Won't be long," he said.

"We are going to the ship, aren't we?"

"Oh yes."

Two pairs of feet coming down the stairs. He'd hoped it would be the woman. Instead, it was a man. He had a hood drawn round his face, but Musen recognised him immediately.

"Hello," he said. "It's Musen, isn't it?"

"That's right."

"The thief. You're on your way to the Priory at Beal Defoir."

He wondered if Loster and Coif knew who the red-headed man was. "That's right," he said.

"Splendid," Oida said. "We'll be shipmates as far as Tirres."

Wherever that was. "That's nice," Musen said. He felt such a fool.

13

Poverty

She watched the ship until it was out of sight, then clambered down the bell-tower ladder. The flowing skirts of the ridiculous red dress hampered and obstructed her, like bored, hungry children. Number-one priority, change into something else.

The panic was still there, it was always there these days, like a faithful but unfashionable dog, but she pretended she could ignore it. The side buttons were tight in the buttonholes and she ended up tearing two of them off: small, satin-covered buttons, unique, she couldn't be bothered to look for them in among the junk and rubbish on the vestry floor. She pulled on her smock and apron, her cloak of invisibility. That made her feel a little bit better.

Not to worry, she ordered herself. True, she'd given up her place on the last ship but one out of Beloisa to someone she personally regarded as almost certainly worthless, but there was still one ship to go; her chances of getting on board it, objectively assessed, about forty per cent. Not good odds, but not the worst either. She tried to squeeze her feet into the horrible wooden shoes. What am I *doing* here? she thought.

She left the twenty-angel silk dress draped over a broken chair. The door was wide open, but she didn't feel like going that way.

She climbed out through the vestry window, tearing her hem. In the street, the water was up over her ankles. It flooded her clogs and made her toes squirm. Thank you so much.

There were no clocks in this horrible city. Not that they'd have been any use today—the sky was low, black cloud, so no sun—but even so. A clock isn't the end of the world, technically speaking. It's a brass disc with numbers on and a thing sticking out the middle to cast a shadow. You'd have thought even these people could've got the hang of that. A city with no way of telling the time can by no stretch of the imagination be called civilised. It's just a mob with walls.

She hurried down Coppergate, splashing water up her legs. Oida had offered her his place on the ship, but he hadn't meant it, she could tell. Oida, of course, was about the only man in the world with nothing to fear in a city about to be taken by storm. Our Father, she prayed, whip up a gentle storm halfway across, just enough to make him chuck his guts up. She composed a mental picture of Oida bent double over the rail, making retching noises. It was a good picture. It made her grin.

There were two kettle hats on the main door of the Prefecture, but either they didn't know about the side door in Longacre or they didn't have the manpower. It wasn't locked; it couldn't have been, because she'd stolen the key. She clumped up the back stair, squelch squelch, let herself into Major Pieres' office, sat down in his chair and pulled her clogs off. A cupful of water drained out of them into the floorboards. I want to go home, she thought.

Pieres had locked his despatch case, bless him. That held her up for as long as it takes to boil a pint of water. Nothing new since this morning. She closed the case and locked it, breaking a fingernail in the process. One of those days.

"Hello," he said, when he finally showed up. "That's my chair."

She gave him a look and stood up. "You've got it all wet," he pointed out.

"I'm so very, very sorry."

He sighed, took off his cloak and draped it over the seat before sitting down. "Well?" he said. "Did you get them off safely?"

Pointless question. "Now, then," she said. "About me."

"I wanted to talk to you about that." Bare-faced lie. She could tell from his face, it was the last thing he wanted to talk about.

"You've given my place to someone else."

He had the grace to avoid her eye. "Not my decision," he said. "It's one of Division's damned politicals, turned up this morning at the South gate, we had to lower a basket on a rope and haul him up. Bloody fool was wandering about in the bush somewhere on a fact-finding mission—" (She loved the way he said that.) "Got separated from his escort, somehow managed to get back here, and now he's bouncing up and down pulling rank on me, so I'm really sorry, but there's nothing I can do." He paused. He always paused when he was about to tell a lie. "There'll probably be one more ship after this one, though obviously I can't guarantee it. But I promise you, the first available place—"

She gave him the sweetest smile she could manage. "That's perfectly all right," she said. "I quite understand."

"Don't be like that," he called out after her, but she didn't turn back. Instead, she ran down the main staircase, only realising when she was halfway down that she'd left the clogs behind and had nothing on her feet. Not to worry, she'd gone barefoot often enough. Just one shot at this, she told herself, so for crying out loud guess *right*. Now then, where would he be?

She went to the guardhouse of the Fifteenth, on Rook Street. Good guess. Poor little Captain Jaizo was there, surprisingly sober. "I need to see your political," she said. "Now."

"I'm not sure—"

"Now," she repeated. "I need to give him a top-priority message to take back to Central Command. The ship leaves in an hour."

Jaizo gave her an agonised look. "Give me the message, I'll make sure he—"

"You're not cleared," she snapped. "Fine. I'll go and drag Pieres away from his lunch, and he can order you. I'm sure he won't mind."

The political officer was a big man, tall, built like an athlete. He'd got on one of those marvellous vests of small steel scales that overlap like fish scales; light enough so you hardly notice you're wearing it, but proof against everything below light artillery. Not that it mattered, because she stabbed him in the ear.

"Bad news," she told Jaizo. "Your political won't be going."

He gave her a hazy stare. "What, after the fuss he made?"

"Dead," she said. "Someone got to him."

"Dead? You mean killed."

"Quite. Wonderful security you've got here, Captain. Might just possibly cost us the war, but there you go." Jaizo opened and closed his mouth, but no sound came. "You do realise, if that message doesn't reach Command—"

Jaizo was one step away from tears. Was I ever that young? she wondered. "What are we going to do? The ship sails in—"

She nodded at the sand clock on his wall. "Twenty minutes."

Despair; then sudden, wild hope. "Can't you go?"

"What?"

"You'll have to go. On the ship. Take the message yourself."

She needed just the right pitch of exasperated fury. "Don't be ridiculous; I can't go. I've got far too much to do here." She shook her head. "It's no good, I'll just have to write it out and give it to the captain, who'll probably lose it or wipe his arse with it. Not to mention it's a direct breach of standing orders."

"There isn't time," Jaizo wailed. "Not if it's got to be ciphered: you know how long that takes." He bit his nails, she noticed. Only weak people do that. "How the hell did they get someone in here? I've got guards on all the doors and windows."

She shrugged. "That doesn't really matter much now," she said. "Here, give me some paper."

"No." Jaizo had made up his mind, what was left of it. "You'll have to go. I mean it. I'm *ordering*—"

"You can't," she pointed out. Then a sigh. "But you're right, of course. *Hell*," she added, with feeling. "It's just one damn thing after another these days."

She made the ship with a couple of minutes to spare. She was wearing men's boots; she looked like a clown. The captain looked at her. "Where's the political officer?"

"He's not coming."

"I need to see a written—"

She had her warrant ready, folded in her sleeve. She pulled it out, unfolded it and held it two inches from his nose. Hooray for melodrama. "Well?"

"Fine," the captain said. "Do you really need all that stuff?"

"Yes."

The soldiers stowed it for her, wedged between the foredeck rail and a water barrel. It was only three sacks and a small steel trunk. On balance, she decided, she should've left a note for Pieres, to get Jaizo off the hook. It would've been the decent thing to do. But too late now.

No disrespect to the fire god, naturally; blame it instead on His administration, presumably made up of officers of roughly the same level of ability as their terrestrial counterparts. That would explain why the mild storm she'd ordered for Oida hit her instead.

Just as well she hadn't eaten for two days. Even so, it was hell. The sailors, nervous enough already about having a woman on board, wisely gave her a wide berth, six feet of rail all to herself. It was inconceivable that any human being could retch so much and still have all their insides. By the time Cape Pinao appeared on the skyline, she was sure she weighed a stone lighter. She lifted her head and scowled at the scenery. In five hours' time, she'd have to be in the General Office in Numa, looking *beautiful*. No chance.

Amazing, however, the difference dry land can make. Also, she had a spoonful or two of the stuff left (you swallow it and it makes your skin positively glow, and your eyes shine, and you look like the moon goddess, and six hours later you're as sick as a dog) and mostly it's just mental attitude, anyway. In the end she coped just fine, and the evening was pretty bad but could've been worse. Anyway, she was home, which was rather more than she'd dared hope the same time yesterday.

In the morning she felt fine, apart from a painfully dry throat that didn't seem to respond to water, so she went to Temple, which made her feel a lot better. She caught the noon stage to Rasch Cuiber; three days in a coach, with two provincial moneylenders and an actuary.

"Excuse me," she said brightly, as the coach bounced painfully over the Saddleback hills. "What's that game you're playing?"

The moneylenders looked at her. "It's called Bust," one of them said.

"It looks like fun. Can I play?"

The moneylenders looked at each other. "Don't think so," one of them said. "Man's game, Bust. Also, you play for money."

From her sleeve she took her last two gold angels. "Oh, I've got money," she said.

The actuary turned away, as if he couldn't bear to look. The moneylenders laughed. "Well, in that case," one of them said.

So that was all right. By the time they reached the inn, she had plenty of money: for a room, food; she could've bought the inn itself if she'd wanted. The moneylenders didn't want to play cards the next day, but she'd got a book out of her luggage so it didn't matter. She had a nasty turn in mid-afternoon—the stuff did that sometimes, came back at you for a second go—but she managed to keep it down until the driver stopped to water the horses. After that, she felt better than she had for weeks. The moneylenders left the coach that night and an elderly man and his granddaughter took their places. The man was a professor from the Imperial Academy at Fort Nain, specialising in moral philosophy; he was reading Eustatius on Transubstantiation, while his granddaughter looked at herself in the back of a small silver hairbrush. Once she'd broken the ice, she had a really quite invigorating discussion with him about the Six Degrees heresy, on which subject he was surprisingly well informed, for a provincial.

"I'm so sorry," he said, after a while. "I don't think I caught your name."

"Telamon."

"Ah." He clearly liked the name. "And which temple did you say you were—?"

Well, she hadn't actually told him she was a priestess, but she hadn't denied it either. "The Poverty and Patience," she said, "in Oudei Mavia. You won't have heard of us," she added, quite truthfully, since she'd just made it up. "This will be my first time in Rasch. I'm terribly excited."

No indication that the professor was a craftsman, which was more disappointing than surprising. It was becoming fashionable in academic circles not to belong; perverse, but no more so than most fashions. She tried not to hold it against him. "Do you know Rasch well?" she asked.

"Reasonably well," he said. "Where will you be staying?"

"The Blue Spire," she lied. "Can you tell me where that is?"

The directions he gave her were almost but not quite accurate; if she'd followed them, she'd have ended up in Sixty Yards, a place which, if he ever went there, would freeze his blood. "Thank you," she said gravely. "I must admit, I'm a bit apprehensive. Cities—"

The professor raised a hand. "You have to be careful," he said. "But the capital has so much to recommend it. The Old Library. The Opera."

She smiled. "You like music."

He had plenty to say after that. Seleucus, of course, and Scadia, and some of the Moderns; Avares, Procopius himself—

"What do you think of Oida?"

He paused; she could see him being scrupulously fair. "His sacred music is certainly charming," he said, "and of course *Caladon and the Wolf*. But I find much of his recent orchestral stuff is sadly derivative, and of course he wastes so much time and energy writing for the popular stage. I believe there's rather less to him than meets the eye."

"I do so agree," she said, with feeling. "Terribly overrated. Very much a minor talent, if you ask me."

"Oh, I wouldn't go that far."

Civilised conversation; before she knew it, they were rolling through the vineyards, with the Foregate dead ahead on the skyline. She felt a surge of joy which was hard to conceal. The professor was talking earnestly about Carrana's *Winter Requiem*. The girl must have noticed something; she looked at her and grinned, then went back to combing her hair. Through the Foregate and into New Town. Almost there.

The professor was kind enough to point out objects of interest; that's the Mausoleum, that spire is the Golden Hook, and if you look carefully you can just see the dome of the Offertory, and on our left is the Infirmary (No it's not, you old fool, that's the Guards barracks; *that's* the Infirmary.) and we're just approaching the Milk Cross now.

The coach stopped. "We're getting off here," the professor said. "So very nice to have met you. I do hope you enjoy your time in Rasch."

She smiled and stood up to let them get past to the door. As she did so, her short knife dropped from her sleeve and clattered on the floor. She picked it up immediately, but too late. "Thank you," she said, "I'm sure I shall." She tucked it away under her bracelet. "Thank you so much for showing me the sights."

They stared at her and got out. An old woman in a blue silk dress got in, with a small white dog in a basket.

"You killed a political officer," the abbot said. "Just like that."

"He was in the way."

"You can't do things like that."

The look on his face told her that actually she could, and that bothered him, quite a lot. She could sympathise. "It was him or me," she said. "There was one place, on the last ship out. The garrison CO didn't have the authority."

"He's going to report you," the abbot said gloomily. "And then we'll have all sorts of aggravation. You know what people are saying about how we're abusing benefit of clergy."

She shook her head. "No, he won't," she said. "If he's not already dead, he soon will be. And don't say he'll have sent a letter, because he couldn't have. Last ship out, remember."

He gave her a despairing look, which she stared down. "Fine," he said. "I wish you hadn't told me."

"I tell you everything," she said. "Oh, come on," she added. "A political's no great loss."

"Was he a craftsman?"

Sore point. Score one to the abbot. "No idea," she said briskly. "He didn't say and I didn't ask. It's all as broad as it's long," she went on, before he could say anything. "When Senza Belot storms Beloisa and slaughters the entire garrison, what difference will one more body make? They're all dead anyway. That's what happens in war, which is," she added gravely, "an institution of which I do not approve. Can we talk about something else now, please?"

The abbot gave her a long look, then asked her questions about other things which she was both able and willing to answer. Her answers put him in a good mood, and the subject of the dead political didn't come up again. "Thank you," he said, when the debriefing was over, "you've done marvellously well, as usual.

I honestly don't know how this faculty would manage without you."

She gave him a don't-be-silly smile. "Where next?" she asked.

"Not quite sure," the abbot replied. "There's a number of situations developing which would benefit from your touch, I don't yet know which one's most important. So, have a few days off."

She beamed at him. "Thank you," she said. "I could do with a break. Do you realise, I've been on the road continuously for six weeks now?"

"Good Lord." Of course he knew perfectly well. "Then you definitely deserve a break. How are you for money?"

"Oh, fine," she said quickly, and he knew better than to ask further. "In fact, the first thing I'm going to do is go out and get measured for some new shoes. I'm sick to death of sore feet."

There were several hundred workshops in Rasch that professed to make footwear, but only one that anyone with even the faintest idea of style would consider buying from. The Gargon brothers were on the far side of town, but she didn't mind that; she was going that way in any case.

Her first stop was Drolo's, in the Old Market. The old man recognised her, a sort of oh-it's-you look. He didn't hold with selling weapons to women.

"Too long," she said, handing the knife back.

The old man was trying not to scowl; it was really rather sweet. "That's all I've got right now."

"Could you cut it back an inch?"

She'd wounded him. "I could," he said, as though she'd asked him to blind his firstborn child. "The balance won't be right, though."

Perfectly true. The Drolo family didn't make pretty things; plain, with a dull oil-black finish. But piking a Drolo knife back an inch would be an atrocity. "Fine," she said. "How long to make me one, like this, but five inches?"

He shrugged. "Ten days."

"I'll pay you now, if you like."

"No, when it's ready will be fine." He waited till she was almost through the door, then asked, "What happened to the last one?"

She smiled at him. "I'm so careless," she said.

Next, to the Carrhasius twins, on Moorbank. A much better welcome there. "We've got something special put by for you," they said. No kidding. Four out of six volumes of Bartagen's *Reflections*, the pre-war edition, with the full marginalia. "How much?" she asked.

Wicked grin. "Does it matter?"

"Yes," she lied. "How much?"

The figure quoted made her head swim. "Ten days?"

She'd said something amusing. "As a special favour, we can hold them for three days. But only because we love you."

"Yes, please." Worry about the money later. "The other two volumes. You wouldn't happen to—?"

"Alas."

Liars, she thought, as she walked up Temple Hill. Liars and thieves; they knew perfectly well where the other two volumes were, just as they knew that once she'd got the four there was no price on earth she wouldn't pay to complete the set. Never mind. The *Reflections*: just the thought of it made her glow inside, as though she'd drunk good brandy. And then all she'd need would be time to read them.

Corsander, on White Cross; five angels for three silk petticoats and a scarf. Daylight robbery.

A quick stop at Peldun's for ink, sealing wax and nibs—tempted by a delightful silver and ivory travelling set, early Revival, though the sand shaker was a modern replacement; but she had three like it already, so no—then up the steep, narrow lane to Ash Yard, where the Gargon brothers had raised their temple to footwear. These days the Gargons didn't see customers; they had a woman, reputedly a field marshal's widow, to attend to all that. She was perfectly civil, while giving the impression that she wasn't really there. That didn't last. The look on her face—

Smile. "Is something wrong?"

The woman took a moment. "No, of course not. Do forgive me."

Naturally, the field marshal's widow had never have seen feet like it before; not unless she was given to acts of charity among the homeless and destitute. "I know," she said, "my feet are a bit on the wide side. It's so hard to get shoes that don't rub."

Then she went back to the abbey and slept for twenty hours, and then woke up. Nothing to do. At a loose end. Her skin started to itch. She wanted to scream.

Just the reaction (she told herself, as she walked to the library) to a month of constant frenetic activity, plus having to kill five people, plus the very real prospect of death. It'll wear off, she told herself. It'll wear off, just as soon as I find something to *do*.

She went, as always, straight to the Ethics section. The assistant librarian gave her a shy smile. He was twenty-one, and spotty.

"*Dahasius on Moral Expediency*," she said. "Is it—?"

He gave her a sad look. "Sorry."

"Damn."

"Just went out this morning. If you'd been here an hour earlier—"

"That's fine. Thank you. Why the *hell* don't you people get another copy made?"

He winced, and mumbled something about copyists' time being limited, and having no discretion, and the war—

"What's the war got to do with anything?"

He looked like he was afraid of getting hit. "Well, you know how it is."

Deep breath. "I understand; that's perfectly all right. I wonder, could you be awfully sweet and let me know the moment it comes back in? Only I've been looking forward to reading it so much, and it's always bloody out." Another deep breath. "Thanks again," she said, and wandered back to the open shelves.

Coryton's *Celestial Anvil* was where it always was; nobody read it these days, which was silly. She lifted it down and opened it at random, and a few minutes later she realised she was reading standing up in the middle of the central aisle. Dear, wonderful Coryton. She looked round for a seat, found one, in the corner by the pillar. She knew whole chapters of Coryton by heart, but it didn't seem to make a difference. Reading it was like a hot bath, with soap and honey.

"Hello," someone said. She looked up and saw Oida looming over her. Damn, she thought, and smiled.

"May I?" He sat down beside her without waiting for an answer, which at least stopped him looming. "You got out all right, then."

Did he know about the political? "No trouble," she said. "What are you doing here? I thought you'd be in Mase, for the chiefs of staff."

He shook his head. "Postponed," he said. "No reason given. Which means something's going on, but I don't know about it. How about you? Heard anything?"

What every other female in the two empires saw in him, she really couldn't guess. "No. Actually, I've been asleep ever since I got back. What sort of thing?"

He shrugged. "If I knew, I wouldn't need to ask. You sure you haven't come across anything?"

She frowned. "Well," she said, "I've just been given the week off. Now that was a surprise. I was assuming I'd get just enough time to comb my hair and shave my legs, and I'd be off on the road again." Her frown deepened. "You know, that should've put me on notice. Too tired to think straight, probably."

Clearly he thought so too; down a couple of degrees in his estimation, not that she gave a damn. "Sounds like a rest will do you good," he said. "What's that?" He leaned over her book. There was so *much* of him; rather more, she felt, than was strictly necessary. "Oh, Coryton."

"Yes. I find him relaxing."

"Mphm. I've got a spare copy; you can have it if you like." Just like that; her own copy of the *Anvil*. As it says in Scripture, to the gods all things are possible. If he remembered, of course, and if it didn't come at a price.

"Thank you," she said. "I'd like that. Drop it in at the lodge next time you're passing."

He grinned at her. Bloody mind reader. "Sure," he said. "And if you do hear anything, you will let me know."

"Of course."

He stood up and moved away, stopped, turned, gave her another grin, disappeared among the freestanding shelves. Even so, she thought; her own copy of Coryton. That'd be something.

She realised she was now too wound up to read, so she put the book back and went out into the small East quadrangle, up the back stair into the New Building, short cut through the lecture hall and up the private stair to the Neus tower. Out on to the roof; she was pleased to note that she'd climbed all those stairs without getting out of breath. She brushed dust from the handrail off her sleeves. You could see the whole City from there, on a clear day, when the foundries weren't working, and, this high up, the air was clean and sweet. She took a dozen long, deep breaths. Better.

Oida thought something was going on. He was almost certainly right. He was also worried, which was rather terrifying: he'd have to be, if he was reduced to asking someone like her if she knew anything. Omniscience was a fundamental part of the Oida persona, along with the charm and the red, red hair. I suppose I ought to try and find out, she told herself, but just the thought of it made her feel tired. Why have I got to be on duty all the damn time? she thought. Because you'd hate it if you weren't, she conceded.

On the way back down, she met Diracca, one of the lodge

masters and a friend from way back. He smiled at her. "I didn't know you were in town."

Her instincts were all flight and evasion—only passing through, terribly busy, can't stop, sorry. She repressed them firmly. "Just got back," she said. "Actually, I've got a few clear days, which is wonderful."

"Good," Diracca said. "In that case, would you like me to get you a seat for the concert?"

"Concert?"

His eyebrows shot up. He was married, of course, which was probably just as well. "The concert," he said. "The New Academy choir. Premiere of Procopius' magnum opus. You know, the one that's going to knock us all sideways. It's the day after tomorrow."

"I've been away," she said. "Actually, I'd love to hear that. I remember people talking about it, what, a year ago."

"Oh, it's been on the stocks a hell of a lot longer than that." Diracca knew about music. "Rumour has it, it's going to be really rather special, and old Scar-face himself will be conducting. Everybody's going to be there, naturally. You really should go, if you possibly can."

"I'd like that," she said firmly, before she could think herself out of it. "Hell," she added, "I'll need a dress."

He looked at her. "Definitely."

"Yes, thank you. Where?"

"In the concert hall at the Port Royal, obviously. I'll get you on the list today. Oida will be there," he added as an afterthought. "Who knows, you might get a chance to meet him."

"That'd be nice," she said vaguely. "What's he like?"

"Surprisingly genuine," Diracca said. "Good craftsman. And, of course, that voice."

Well, quite.

*

Her mother, that poor, long-suffering creature, had always maintained that she had an eye for clothes, and on balance she'd had a point. She could tell straight away if a particular style would suit someone, and she was never wrong about colours. Other women came to her for advice and went away delighted with the result. Dressing herself, however, was another matter. Her theory was that she had a picture of herself in her mind that didn't actually correlate with the real thing; she believed she was shorter and wider than she really was, and not nearly so dark, and as a result she ended up in things she'd never have allowed someone else to go out in public in. Maybe, she further speculated, it was because deep down she didn't want to look nice, because if you do, people notice you.

So, this time, she went to the Corsander woman, handed her twenty angels in cash, told her what the occasion was and abdicated any further responsibility in the matter. The Corsander female gave her a rough verbal outline of what she had in mind, which sounded awful. "Thank you," she said. "When do you need me for a fitting?"

She got back to the abbey and found two letters waiting for her. One from her sister; she stuffed it up her sleeve for later, when she had a minute. The other one was from the Director of Resources: my office, right now. So much for her week off. She was ashamed of herself for feeling so relieved.

"I'm very sorry," he said. "I know you were looking forward to a break, but this is urgent. You hadn't got anything planned, had you?"

The concert. Twenty angels on a dress. "No," she said.

"It's not a very nice job, I'm afraid."

Oh dear. That usually meant either sex or killing somebody. On balance, she'd rather it was killing. Both were grossly intimate, but a killing is over far more quickly. Also, she was better at it. "Go on."

Neither, thank God. Just an interrogation, and she didn't mind that at all. But she had to ask, "Why me?"

"Specialist knowledge," he replied. "That's all I know. Apparently, none of the regular interrogators can understand what they're being told, so they don't know if they're getting the truth or not, or if it's important or just waffle."

She tried not to smile, but she could see how embarrassing that might be. *All right, I'll tell you everything, damn you,* and then you had to keep stopping them every two minutes so they could explain to you what such-and-such meant. Hopeless.

"Where?" she said.

He nodded downwards; so here, in the building, probably the holding cells that nobody was supposed to know about but anyone could direct you to, if you asked nicely. In which case, maybe she'd be able to make the concert after all.

He was an Easterner, a High Imperial, so at least there'd be no language barrier, even if their awful flat whining accent made her head hurt after a while. He was lighter than most Eastern Imperials, almost a sort of rust colour. They'd beaten hell out of him, approximately three days ago.

"A woman," he said, as the cell door closed behind her. "That's unusual."

"Not in the West," she said. She looked round for something moderately clean to sit on. Should've brought one of those little folding stools.

"Right," he said. "Manpower shortages. We have killed rather a lot of your pay grade recently."

The cuts on his face needed seeing to, or they'd go septic. "Women make better listeners," she said. "I can get them to send a man instead, if you'd rather. He could hit you some more."

He grinned. "You'll do."

"Thank you. Now, then. You're Colonel Pausa, Eastern military intelligence, assigned to the land survey."

"That's in the file, surely. Haven't you read it?"

"I enjoy the sound of my own voice. You're a specialist, second grade, surveyor specialising in rock formations and mineral deposits. Well?"

He was looking at her. "You'd be all right," he said, "but you're a bit flat-chested. You want at least a full handful, or there's nothing to hold on to."

"I'll take that as a yes," she said. "You were captured by our landing party at Beloisa, just over a year ago."

"That's right. I gather your lot's getting a bloody nose down that way. Senza giving you a hard time, is he?"

That'd be the guards, discussing current affairs in the corridors. Too stupid to realise that sound carries, even through steel doors. "It was touch and go for a while," she said. "But it's all under control now, thanks for asking. What was so interesting about the rock formations in Beloisa Bay?"

He shrugged. "Nothing much. Just lots of rocks. We were going to cut a road along the bottom edge of the cliff."

"To link the harbour with the south quay," she said. "Good idea. Save carting stuff all the way up the hill and down again."

She'd impressed him. "You know Beloisa?"

"I was there, a few days ago. I particularly liked the Arch of Sarpedon. So much late Mannerist stuff's been ruined by insensitive restoration."

"They're going to knock it down," he said, smiling. "For the new road. It's in the way."

"Too bad." She glanced down at the papers she'd brought in, though she didn't need to. "Why would your people send a geologist of your grade to see to a simple road-building job?"

"Unstable cliffs," he said, straight away. "Can't trust the local clowns; they'd bring the whole lot down on their heads. I have a bit of experience. Also, we were short-handed, I was available and had nothing else to do. I like to be useful. So I said I'd go."

She'd have believed him, except that someone had had to inflict unspeakable pain on him to get him to say more than name, rank, number. She rather liked him, probably because he had a nice voice, in spite of the accent. "Would you like me to see if I can get you a doctor?" she said. "A couple of those look like they could do with stitches."

"Thanks." She'd amused him. "But I'd rather wait till you've finished beating me up, and then do the whole lot at once, if it's all the same. Bit of a waste of time otherwise."

She smiled. "You're probably right," she said. "And torn stitches can be a pest. You're not a craftsman, are you?"

"Wish I was," he said ruefully. "Maybe you wouldn't have smashed my face in, I don't know. But, no, I'm not. For what it's worth, I'm not a believer."

That shocked her, just a little. "More fool you," she said briskly. "Did you find anything interesting while you were doing your survey?"

"Depends what interests you. There's a big fat seam of blue lias, which is unusual for the north coast but not unheard of. Apart from that, nothing really."

As quickly as she could, she leaned forward, grabbed the little finger of his left hand and bent it back until he yelled. She applied just the right amount of pressure, then a little more. Then she sat down again.

"Let's try that again," she said. "Did you find anything interesting?"

He was breathing deeply, and there was sweat on his face. It makes some men do that. "I just told you, no."

"Did you find anything interesting?"

He'd folded his hand into a ball. "Piss off and die, you whore."

"I'm guessing," she went on pleasantly, "that you found silver there. Or lead, which is more or less the same thing. I know those cliffs; there's no blue lias, they're sandstone. But there's a disused lead mine five miles inland, worked out in Flavian times. I think you may have found silver."

"Think what you like."

She felt sorry for him. Really bad luck, to have been there when the invasion barges suddenly appeared. Probably he'd stayed to help organise the defence, because the local militia officers would've been in a dreadful panic. A lesser man would've ducked out on the last boat. "Sorry," she said, and repeated the operation on his right hand. This time, she used too much force and felt something give. Of course, he wasn't to know she hadn't meant to do so much damage.

"Now then," she said. "Where is this silver?"

For an intelligent man, he wasn't very smart. The fire god only saw fit to give us ten fingers, and she was afraid she'd run out and have to think of something else. "The silver," she said, for the twelfth time.

"All right, there's silver." He was croaking now, like a frog. "Since you know already, what's the point of all this?"

"I've had a look at the map," she said, "and I'm guessing the vein starts somewhere in the Creen hills and runs down to Hillsend, where you've got that big fault line running north–south. I can show you the map if it'd help."

He gazed at her. At some point during the interview, it had dawned on him that he wouldn't be getting out of this alive. "I don't know," he said. He was close to tears.

"Obviously, now that we're back in control in that region, we can send our own surveyors and they can figure it all out for themselves. But it'd save a great deal of time and bother if you'd just tell us what you found. No point in duplicating your work, is there?"

"Forget it." He'd come to some sort of decision. "Before you can do that, Senza'll be right up you and he'll drive you into the sea. You don't stand a chance."

She did a light frown. "Oh, didn't anyone tell you? Senza Belot is dead. Gangrene. Just a little scratch. You've got to be so careful."

If she hadn't done all the careful spadework, breaking him down inside and hurting him just right, he'd never have believed her. It's such a delicate thing. "You're lying."

"Afraid not, sorry." She'd damaged him far more with four words than with anything physical she'd done. "You look tired," she said. "I'll let you get some rest, and we can carry on where we left off later. I'm surprised nobody told you about General Belot. We're all very excited, as you can imagine."

So simple after that. The only problem was getting him to shut up.

There was a vein of silver; not where she'd said (well, it was just an educated guess). The first indications had come to light only quite recently, but he'd had a chance to explore it pretty thoroughly, and in his opinion it was a truly substantial find, as big as Rhomespa, quite possibly bigger; not too far down, easy enough to extract from the lead using standard techniques. It could've turned the tide of the war, he said sadly, if only—

Once she was sure she'd got everything out of him that there was to get, it crossed her mind to tell him that Senza wasn't dead after all. She decided against it; the pain of knowing he'd been fooled into parting with such crucial information would probably be greater than what he'd gone through already, believing Senza was dead. Leave it at that, she thought; don't meddle.

If only, she thought, as she made her way to the Director's office. If only General Belot was dead—their General Belot or ours, makes no odds—and the war was really about to end. She smiled at herself for believing something like that was possible.

*

"Excellent work, as usual." The Director was preoccupied, as well he might be. The news that the enemy was about to come into a huge sum of money was enough to flood anyone's thoughts. "I'll definitely be putting you in for a distinction."

She thanked him nicely. Pointless, of course, since she was a woman and therefore not eligible for any form of recognised promotion. Shouldn't be in the service at all, properly speaking. "One thing," she said.

"Sorry, miles away. Yes?"

"Colonel Pausa."

"What? Oh, the man you've been—"

"That's him. I was thinking. It might be a good idea to let him live."

The frown. "I'm sorry," he said. "You know departmental policy."

"Yes, of course. But he is actually a really good geologist." She paused, then added: "Sort of a collector's item, if you follow me. It'd be a dreadful waste. There's not many of his calibre, certainly not on our side."

The special words hadn't been lost on him. "As good as that?"

"I think so, yes. At any rate, worth passing along, let them decide. Of course, it's up to you," she added, "but I thought I'd mention it."

"No, I mean yes, quite right." He was thinking about it. In two seconds, it'd have been his idea. "I'll send up a note," he said. "Thank you."

"My pleasure."

Well, she thought; maybe the good colonel would turn out to be a top-notch geologist after all, and then everybody would be happy. She hoped so. It had been a silly thing to do, to stick her neck out like that for someone of no obvious value to her, but so what; she reckoned she'd earned the right to indulge herself, after all the aggravation she'd been through lately. *Calibre,* she thought;

did I really say that? I'm starting to sound like departmental communiqués.

The dress was beautiful. She loved it, even though it showed a lot of arm (she didn't like her arms), and she thought the warrior-princess look was silly. Seeing herself in the dress in the Corsanders' full-length mirror—an extraordinary thing, one of only four in the whole of the West—she revised her opinion. The warrior-princess look was silly when worn by other people. On her, it looked just fine.

Maybe it was just the dress, or the combination of the dress and the successful interrogation: on the evening of the concert she was in a better mood than she could remember in a long time. Walking under the great arch of the Port Royal put a slight crimp in her feeling of wellbeing—the last time she'd been here, she'd been a leading prosecution witness against an old and dear friend, convicted and subsequently executed for treason—but the size and splendour of the crowd in the covered garden counteracted that to a certain extent. The men were either in formal academics or parade armour, and the women were simply glorious, so that she could enjoy her dress and still be inconspicuous, just another bird of paradise in a huge flock. There were just enough people she knew to make her feel comfortable, and she had tremendous luck avoiding the people she didn't want to talk to. They'd laid on eunuchs with their skins gilded, dressed as fire angels, bringing round trays of hors d'oeuvres, and the four alabaster fountains were running water—snow melt, piped in from the Black hills and deliciously cool—so she didn't have to drink wine.

As she refilled her cup from the Winter Fountain she met Colonel Vaudo, an old friend from her first lodge, now attached to the Ordnance. He'd put on weight since he'd come off the front line, and there was a long wedge of scarlet tunic showing up one side, where his gilded dress breastplate and backplate no longer quite met. "I know," he said, observing and interpreting her grin. "It's hell when I sit down. I had them punch extra holes in the straps, but the bloody thing's still tight."

"Get a new one," she said.

"Can't be bothered. Only the second time I've worn it since I've been back. You're looking good."

She nodded. "Girl clothes," she said. "I treated myself."

He leaned awkwardly against a pillar. There was an audible creak. "I gather you were at Beloisa."

"That's right. Any news?"

He frowned. "Not particularly good," he said. "Of course, what we're getting is what they're telling their own people, but it looks like Senza carried the town at the first assault. All over in an hour or so."

"You surprise me," she said. "Colonel Pieres had got it done up pretty tight. There was a bloody great big moat, for one thing."

"They reckon Senza used pontoons under cover of heavy pavises," Vaudo said. "Anyway, no doubt we'll get the details in due course. The point is, we've lost our last foothold on their ground and we're right back where we were eighteen months ago. The usual bloody stalemate."

She did her cheerful voice. "Yes," she said, "and Senza's back up north on his side of the line, instead of down here on ours. Meanwhile, it's Forza's move. Our turn to beat up on them, for a change."

"I guess so." He smiled. She noticed he had a few grey hairs in his beard now. Actually, they suited him. "Anyway, screw the war. Have you seen Oriden recently? Last I heard, she'd got engaged to some Imperial in Internal Communications."

She twitched her nose. "He's called Iuppito, and he's Director of Waterways for the whole of the north-west. Very good-looking but five feet nothing in his army boots. I got a letter from my sister, and apparently they're talking about getting married in the spring."

Vaudo raised an eyebrow. "Well," he said. "How is Philemon, anyway? Still at the same place?"

"And doing very well, apparently. She reckons it's between her and some Northern female for Prioress when the old battleaxe retires, which should be any day now." She grinned. "Nice to think that one member of our family's making something of herself in the world."

"Well, quite." Vaudo stopped a gilded angel and helped himself to white wine. "Are you still dashing around all over the place?"

"Pretty much. No idea what's next. Here, hopefully, but I just don't know. I'm sick of sleeping in barns."

He gave her a sympathetic look. "You should put in for a priory," he said. "You've got seniority, God knows. Hang up your boots, nothing to do all day but shout at a bunch of nuns."

She shook her head. "Women's work," she said. "I'd go berserk inside of a month."

He sighed. "What you should be doing is running a big City lodge," he said. "It's ridiculous, someone with your background and ability still nominally a lay sister." He frowned and lowered his voice. "I've heard it said they're ordaining women in the East. So why the hell not here?"

"Fine," she said, "I'll defect. I'll leave a note saying you suggested it."

A fanfare of trumpets, and everyone started to move. "See you later," Vaudo said. "I'm with a party from Supply. Enjoy the show."

"You too," she called after him, and then the stream of moving people separated them. She followed it into the main auditorium. They'd draped garlands of blue and red flowers round all the pillars, like at Spring Festival, and the roof was open. She found a seat about halfway down on the end of a row at the right. She liked being on the end, in case there was a fire.

After what struck her as an unnecessarily long time, the choir appeared through the double doors at the back and processed up the main aisle, followed by the orchestra. They took their places on the raised semi-circular platform, and the instrumentalists started making the usual raucous tuning-up noises. Then they stopped, and there was a moment of rather uneasy silence; then the single door at the side of the platform opened and all around her people were standing and cheering. Being on the end, she was able to peer round; she caught sight of a big man in a long black academic gown, but she was too far away to make out anything more precise than that. Certainly, no chance of seeing the scar. He moved towards the centre of the half-moon of choristers, and she lost sight of him for a while until he emerged on to the choirmaster's podium. He stood there for a while and nothing happened. Then he turned towards the orchestra and raised his hands.

It began with a sudden thrill on the strings that seemed to cut her to the bone. Then the horns launched into a harsh, wild theme that soared, gathered, repeated, gaining pace and mass before hovering as the rest of the orchestra rushed in behind it, like flood-water through a breach in a sea wall. A countermelody cut across it, like a parry, like enfilading fire; there was a duel between the two, scrambling up into a crescendo, into a sudden savage thrust of the strings, and a dead stop. Five beats of silence; then the horns led the woodwind in a gentle, solemn melody so lovely that it caught in her throat until she could barely breathe. The melody developed over two building repetitions, and then the first theme reappeared, muted to begin with but growing to frantic intensity; it was like watching weeds and brambles growing up through a bed of flowers, but speeded up so that they moved as fast as snakes. Just when she could bear it no longer, a frantic ascent on the strings scattered both themes and drove them aside, and a new theme, major, glorious, triumphant, rose from the orchestra like the sun. As the melody burst like a flower opening, the choir took it up and launched it across the hall like a missile.

*

"Hello, you," someone said, and she looked round to see Oida, advancing on her with a grin outstretched like a spear. She found a smile from somewhere.

"Well," Oida said. People got out of his way, with is-it-him looks on their faces. "What did you think?"

"Incredible," she said.

He was holding a plate with a slice of honeycake. "You reckon."

"Yes."

He pulled a wry face. "Yes, it was rather, wasn't it? You've got to hand it to the old devil. Just when you think he's losing it and dwindling away into a pillar of the establishment, he comes up with something like that. Makes me wonder why I bother, really."

Indeed, she thought. "You make it sound like a fight to the death," she said. "I've never thought of you and Procopius as, well, *rivals*. You do such different work."

"Quite," Oida said. He handed his plate to a fire angel. "He writes music. Still, there you go. That's me put firmly in my place for a while. I guess I'll have to go back to playing the three-string outside tea houses." He smiled. "There's a bunch of us going on to dinner at the Vetumnis house, if you fancy coming along."

"I'd better not, thanks," she said vaguely. "Early start in the morning."

He didn't seem exactly heartbroken. "Next time, then. Meanwhile, if you've got five minutes, there's someone I think you should meet."

Hell, she thought; but there's just so much refusing you can get away with in one evening. "Love to," she said, and followed his slipstream through the crowd towards the left-hand side door.

Through the door into a corridor, then some stairs. At least it was quiet. She really needed some silence, after the music; silence, and somewhere dark and safe where she could come down. The last thing she wanted was to make conversation to some lodge grandee or politician.

At the top of the stairs there was a door. He breezed through it, she followed, and found herself in a small panelled room; there was a table, covered with piles of sheet music, and a dozen or so men and women down the far end of the room, drinking and talking quietly, and at the other end, eating cold beef wrapped in flatbread, a huge man in a black gown.

She stared at him. She couldn't help it.

The scar, an inch wide, ran from his left eye to the right corner of his mouth, drawing a white line across the deep mahogany brown of his skin. She could see at once that it had been appallingly badly stitched at the time; the upper side of the scar overlapped the lower, forming a mound, like dried glue left around a joint by a slapdash carpenter. It occurred to her that it was the sort of job you'd do if you didn't expect your patient to survive, so why bother?

"Telamon, I'd like you to meet Director Procopius. She loved the show, by the way."

He must have seen her staring. She imagined a knife cutting her throat; it made her feel a tiny bit better. She opened her mouth, but froze, having no idea how to address him. There was a silence that lasted till the end of the world.

"I gather you're not long back from Beloisa," he said. He had the most amazing voice. She felt like she heard it through her skin. "That must've been pretty rough."

He gathered. He'd heard of her? "Towards the end, yes," she heard herself squeak. He had thick black hair in braids down his back, with just a few filaments of grey. He was tall and broad enough to be a Rhus. "I'm afraid I ducked out. I gather things ended badly."

"I've read about Beloisa before the war," he said. "It was supposed to be one of the most beautiful cities in the empire, in its day. There was a mosaic ceiling by Garheil in the apse of the White temple."

"Gone now, I'm afraid," she said. "We pulled it down."

A slight frown. "That's a great shame," he said. "It's terrible when beautiful things are lost, no matter what the reason. Still, I expect the commander was only doing what he felt he had to do. I'm not sure I could ever take a decision like that, so it's just as well I'm not a soldier."

She had no idea what to say. "I loved the music" sort of slipped out before she could stop it, like a bad dog after a cat.

Procopius frowned a little, as though she'd said something in slightly bad taste. "Thank you," he said. "How about you?" he went on, turning a few degrees to the left. "A bit staid and academic for you, I imagine."

"I loved it," Oida said. "If you don't get the Crown this year, there's no justice."

"I can guarantee I won't get the Crown. I'm on the panel of judges."

Oida clicked his tongue. "You shouldn't let them take advantage of you like that," he said. "Every year you put yourself out of the running, and some kid gets it who hasn't got a tenth of your ability. Result: people stop hearing your name, and next thing you know they stop playing your stuff. Next year, you really ought to tell them, enough's enough."

Procopius nodded slowly. "You haven't entered for the Crown for five years. Not since you won it."

Oida shrugged. "I guess I'm not competitive by nature. As someone very wise said to me recently, it's not a fight to the death. But there's such a thing as proper recognition."

"Oh, people recognise me," Procopius answered quickly. "That's not a problem."

A very short but intense pause, then Oida laughed loudly. "I guess not," he said. "But you know what I mean. It's different for someone like me, churning out junk for the masses. For you—"

"Not nearly as many people like my music," Procopius said. "Quite." He turned back to her and smiled. The scar stretched.

"I've always taken the view that the best music is what people like the most. What do you think?"

She opened her mouth. Her mind was a complete blank. They were waiting for her. "You're asking me which is best, lamb or honey. I love both."

Procopius sighed. "Born diplomat," he said. "Let's go and have dinner."

The dinner at the Vetumnis house, to which she'd refused an invitation. Oida said, "Are you sure you won't join us?"

But then, you wouldn't want to have dinner with the fire god; you'd be all burned up before they'd finished clearing away the soup. "I'd love to but I really do have to get an early night. Otherwise I'll be useless in the morning."

"Another time, then," Procopius said. "So nice to have met you."

By her standards, she slept late. There were broad red stains in the eastern sky when she closed the side door of the Old Cloister behind her, put the key (she'd cut it herself, from an impression taken in a pat of butter) safely away in her sleeve and started to climb the long hill up to Cyanus Square. A tune was going round and round in her head, the way tunes do; nothing from the Procopius last night, but, rather, a theme from one of his earlier pieces in the same vein, the second movement of the Sixth Symphony. It fluttered around inside her head like a trapped bird, until she could barely think.

"Oh," said the duty priest at the Golden Light. "It's you."

She nodded. "Is he in?"

"In body. His soul will be along in an hour or so, after he's had his breakfast."

Clearly the priest knew him well. She went up the narrow spiral staircase to the top of the tower, knocked on the door and went in.

Dawn was a good time to visit. During the Bonfire of the Images, three hundred years ago, nearly all the pre-Republican stained glass in Rasch had been smashed by the mob. According to the story, Precentor Argantho and his monks, canons and deacons had crowded into the staircase she'd just come up, literally filling it with human bodies, to keep the rioters from getting up into the tower. Three quarters of the way up—four turns of the spiral—the rioters had grown sick of killing monks and heaving them out of the way; they'd given up and gone and burned down the Gynaeceum instead. Ever since, art historians had argued whether Argantho's sacrifice had done good or harm, the Macien glass in the Prefecture tower versus the neo-Mannerist frescoes of the Gynaeceum. Contemporary sources, which she'd bothered to dig out and read, tended to suggest that Argantho wasn't actually there that day, and a couple of dozen monks had tried to barricade themselves in the tower and failed. That was probably why she'd always preferred theology to history.

Father Icadias sat on a low stool in the exact centre of the Rotunda, as he always did at this time, marinading in the reds and blues streaming in through the windows. The tower builders had placed it so that the first light of dawn seemed to come in from all round, three-sixty degrees. Provided the sky wasn't overcast, a man sitting dead centre in the Rotunda would appear to be bathing in flames that illuminated but did not consume; a graphic if somewhat literal illustration of the fundamental miracle of the faith. Among other miraculous properties ascribed to it, the dawn light in the Rotunda was supposed to cure all bodily ailments, provided the soul was ready. Icadias made a point of telling people this when they came there for confession for the first time. He'd been the incumbent for thirty years, and he had chronic rheumatism.

"Hello, Telamon," he said. He had his back to the door. She'd taken pains to tread as lightly as possible, so he wouldn't hear her, let alone be able to identify her by her footsteps. She had no idea how he always knew it was her, no matter how hard she tried, though she suspected there was a perfectly good mundane explanation.

"Father," she said.

"Close the door, for heaven's sake. You're letting the draught in."

She did as she was told and sat down on the floor. He turned round slowly and faced her. "How was the Procopius?" he asked. "I had a seat, but something came up."

"Glorious," she said. "One of the best thing's he's ever done."

"Ah." Icadias nodded, so that the reds and blues seemed to flow up his face like tears. "I miss all the good ones, but when Zembra premiered his Sacred Cantata I was there in the front row. About halfway through I remember praying for death, but no such luck. What can I do for you?"

"Hear me, Father, for I have sinned."

"Oh, right." He pulled his hood down over his eyes. The gold overstitching on the hem blazed like beacons. "In the name of the Five and the One I absolve you. What've you been up to this time?"

"I killed someone."

He sighed. "Yes, you did, didn't you? Still, he was a political, so I imagine the All-Seeing will turn a blind eye. Anything else?"

She paused for a moment. "I have lied, stolen, betrayed a trust. I have inflicted pain, not through necessity. I have neglected appeals for help from fellow craftsmen."

"Well," Icadias said. "Five solemn indemnities, and don't do it again. That's it?"

"Yes."

"No luxuries, adulteries, immodesties or unnatural fleshly practices."

"No."

"You should get out more. No, really," Icadias went on, "I'm a bit worried about you. I mean, you're still a beautiful young woman, but time's getting on. You ought to find a nice steady young man and settle down."

"Yes, Father. Is that it? Five indemnities?"

He grinned at her. "Telamon, I've known you since you were six; you're a craftsman to the bone. I think you can take it from me that your immortal soul is the least of your worries. I heard you saved the life of that enemy surveyor. There's not many in your position that would've done that."

"It seemed such a waste. He was a clever man."

"Not a craftsman."

"One day the war will be over. They'll need people who can build roads."

"Or find vast new deposits of silver. Quite. About that," he added. "Do you think it'll change things?"

"It's got to," she said.

He nodded. "Would it surprise you to learn that we have also found silver? A very large amount of it, on the flood plain just below Hyperpyra?"

That was news. "Really?"

"Really and truly. Oh, you didn't hear it from me, of course. No, by all accounts it's a truly significant strike. They were rather hoping it'd be enough to buy victory, but now the other side have got one that neatly cancels it out, and we're back where we were." He hesitated for a moment. "Very neat," he said. "A sort of divine symmetry that suggests to me that our heavenly Father has a wicked sense of humour, at the very least. At the worst, He wants us to carry on slaughtering each other till there's nobody left. Blessed be the name of our god," he added serenely. "And you can see His point. But it makes you think."

She thought of the moors above Beloisa: empty land, abandoned farms. "They've kept it very quiet," she said.

"Believe it or not, they can keep a secret, when they really want to. So," he went on, "it was a good concert. Many people there?"

"Everybody," she said. "And you'll never guess. I actually met him."

"Excuse me?"

"Director Procopius," she said. "Oida introduced me, of all people. He was so amazingly—" She tailed off. Icadias smiled.

"I knew his father," he said. "Charming fellow, fine draughts player. I suppose I should say it came as a terrible shock, but it didn't. Like so many charming people, he had a vicious streak. Were you surprised? At being introduced, I mean?"

"God, yes. Sorry," she added, and he grinned. "Yes, of course. And the strangest thing was, he'd heard of me."

"Strange indeed," said Icadias, who didn't seem the least bit surprised. "Your explanation?"

"I haven't got one." She thought for a moment. "I mean, I sort of suspect that Oida's after me. Who knows why, considering the sort of women who'd be only too glad—"

"I think he wants the complete set," Icadias said solemnly. "Like the coin and medal collectors; the one you want most is the one you haven't got, regardless," he added kindly, "of condition. That wouldn't account for Procopius knowing who you are."

"No," she said. She waited. Then: "Any ideas?"

He stretched his legs out with a faint groan. "Doctrine states," he said, "that the clergy, duly anointed through the chain of apostolic succession reaching back in an unbroken line to Medra himself, are the mortal conduit for the divine flame. When I speak, provided I'm wearing the right bits and pieces and I haven't got them on back to front, the voice that issues from my lips is the voice of the fire god, my thoughts are His thoughts and my wisdom is His wisdom." He paused, took the heavily embroidered scarf off from around his neck and laid it reverently across his knees. "Sorry," he said. "Not a clue."

"Oh." She frowned. "But you know everything."

He laughed; genuine pleasure. "By no means," he said. "I only know everything that *matters*. Therefore, by implication, the reason why Scar-face has heard of you can't be terribly important. I hope that's some comfort to you."

She looked at him. "You didn't seem terribly surprised, that's all."

"I'm eighty-one years old, and I've been a priest sixty-two years. Surprise is just one of the faculties that atrophies with age. Actually, it's the one I miss most, I'm ashamed to say. What exactly did he know about you?"

"That I'd been at Beloïsa."

"Ah." He nodded. "He'll have read your report. The name at the bottom will have stuck in his memory, since not many women file war despatches. Next miracle, please."

"I suppose so," she said. But then: "Why would he be reading third-level classified despatches? He's an academic."

"I would imagine he's something high up in the craft. Not the main line, perhaps, one of the side orders. If he's sixteenth or seventeenth degree, he'd get to see everything, if he wanted to. And before you ask why would he want to, there's all sorts of possible explanations. Maybe he has family in those parts. A surprising number of people keep up their connections across the boundary, particularly in the older families. And the Procopii are old Imperial, right back to Carnassus and the First Ships. That's a guess," he added, pointing to his unadorned neck. "You can probably come up with half a dozen more, equally plausible. Or you could ask him."

"Me?" She felt a sudden wave of panic. "Don't be—"

"Why not? You've been formally introduced. People tell me he's very approachable. Write him a letter."

"I couldn't."

Icadias was mightily amused by that. "So you do know the meaning of fear after all. What's this, hero-worship?"

"And then some."

"I don't blame you. There's only half a dozen men in the two empires I genuinely respect, and Director Procopius is one of them." He smiled. "Did you know, my lodge archdeacon was on the panel that assessed him when he applied for the priesthood, what, twenty-five years ago. Turned him down. Said it'd be a crime against gods and men to have a fellow with his talent wasting his time in the ministry when he should be writing music. I remember being deeply shocked, but the old devil was perfectly right, of course."

"Procopius wanted to be a priest."

"Yes."

"And your archdeacon stopped him. That's dreadful."

"Oh, come on. Think of the effect it'd have had on his work. No secular music whatsoever."

"If he wanted to be a priest, you should've let him."

Icadias looked at her, head slightly on one side. "Spoken with true feeling."

"You know it's all I've ever wanted. And it's impossible."

He was silent for a while. Then he lowered his voice. "You do know," he said, "they're ordaining women in the East."

She looked at him in surprise. "You know," she said, "you're the second person in two days to tell me that. Why is everybody so dead keen on me defecting? Is it something I said?"

He shrugged. "It's what you always wanted. And, no, it's not impossible. I'm just stating a fact, that's all."

She sat up straight. "Hear me, Father, for I have sinned. For a split second, I was tempted to betray my country, my lodge and my craft. Fortunately, I was able to overcome the temptation quickly and easily." She looked at him. "What do I get for that?"

"One lesser indemnity and light a candle in the chancel." He shrugged. "I thought I owed it to you to mention it. Same god, after all. I'm not sure it matters to Him all that much which side you happen to be on in this stupid war. If He cared, He'd have done something about it by now."

"You'd have thought." She stood up. He looked disappointed.

"Are you leaving so soon?" he said. "I thought we might have a hand or two."

That made her laugh. "Oh, why not? It's ages since I played."

He got up—it was distressing to see how much effort it cost him—and crossed to the wall. With practised ease, he teased a single loose stone out of the wall, felt behind it, retrieved a small rosewood box, replaced the stone. He handed her the box; she opened it and took out the pack. "With or without trumps?" she asked.

"Without, I think. After all, we're on consecrated ground."

She nodded and went through the pack, taking out the picture cards. They reminded her of the Rhus thief, Musen, and his home-made versions. Then she gave him the pack to shuffle. As always, his dexterity amazed her. "Do you cheat?" she asked.

"What a thing to suggest."

"Well?"

"Not against you."

He handed her the cards and she dealt: sixteen each, the remainder placed on the floor between them. Talk about a rotten hand; four of each suit, all high cards, including the dreaded Twelve of Spears. "Are you sure about that?" she said.

"I don't need to cheat against you. You're a terrible card player."

Not true. She opened with five, which he immediately doubled. She felt in her sleeve and fished out some coins. "Excuse me," he said. "Enemy money."

"What? Oh, sorry." She scooped the coins up and put them back. "Souvenirs from Beloisa. Here we go, the good stuff. Come on, then, let's see yours."

He smiled. "I seem to be a trifle short today. Instead, I wager two blessings and a conditional indulgence."

"Seems fair," she said. "Thirteen with none."

"Call," he said. "Confident, aren't we?" he added, as more of her money hit the floor. "I'll cover that with an act of grace. All right?"

"Sure. I don't think I've ever had one of those."

"Don't hold your breath." He smiled, and laid the Three of Arrows.

"You *do* cheat." She had the Four. He smirked as she gathered up the cards. One to her. The Four had been her lowest card, and the lead was now with her. Somehow she had to contrive to lose four tricks, with this load of rubbish. "Do you say penance afterwards, when nobody's looking?"

He played the Eight of Spears to her Ten. "Not to rejoice in a victory sent by the Almighty would be a sin," he said. "To pretend to regret such a victory would be blasphemy indeed. Your lead."

She won all sixteen tricks; five over the line, in other words, which meant he could throw away five cards and draw from the pack. She dealt. No chance he'd draw an ace, because she had all four. Might as well concede now and pay the fine, while she was still nominally solvent.

"It's a shame," he said. "You'd have been a good priest."

She looked at him. "What makes you say that?"

"A special blend of piety, humanity and ruthlessness. I have two, but I'm rather lacking in the third."

"Which one?"

"Your declaration."

She went six. Doubled. She called. No use. When the game was finally over and he was counting his winnings, she asked, "What do you do with the money?"

"Charitable works," he replied, not looking up.

"Such as?"

"With this lot, I might just endow an order of monks. Or I could rebuild the Grand Temple, only with solid ivory pillars." He looked at her. "Do you need it back?"

She shook her head. "Plenty more where that came from."

"I shall pretend I didn't hear that."

"If you win money off people by cheating and then spend it on good works, is that an act of grace?"

"Qualified grace," he said. "But I don't cheat."

"And if it's stolen money?"

"Rectified by outcome. Not the fact, remember, the intention."

"Of course. Sorry."

He peered at her. "Was it stolen money?"

"No."

"That's all right, then. Had breakfast?"

She looked at him warily. "It's not fermented cabbage, is it?"

"That's tomorrow. Today is pancakes."

"In that case I haven't."

He proved to be almost entirely right. It was indeed pancakes; but, since it was the second recess day after Ascension, the archdeacon had authorised pancakes filled with fermented cabbage, as a special treat.

They came in the middle of the night. She was just dropping off to sleep again—the Sixth Office bell over in the New Building had woken her up, and then she was wide awake for an hour—when the door opened. She heard boots on the floor, managed to remember where she was before instincts took over and led her to do something drastic and unfortunate. "You Telamon?" said a man's voice. Low-class, southern, about thirty, thirty-five.

"Yes." No point making a fuss. Someone who bursts into your room at midnight and asks to confirm your name can only be the government. "Don't light the lamp."

She could hear a tinderbox whir as she said it. "Why not?"

"I haven't got any clothes on."

Dim glow, then enough light to see by. Too smart to fall for that one; she might have a knife under her pillow—she did, actually, though obviously she wasn't going to use it this time. She grabbed at the sheet and pulled it up. "Do you mind?" she said.

Six kettlehats—*six*. She was flattered. Full armour, too. He was looking at her, but not in that way; she was just dangerous freight. "All right if I get dressed?" she asked.

He nodded, just the minimum of movement. A sergeant, by

his collar, but he and his men all had new armour, all the plates matching, no obvious make-do-and-mend repairs. Not many like that these days. Not just any grab squad, then. Just as well she wasn't going to try anything.

She waited for him to turn his head, which he didn't. "Fine," she said, trying to sound outraged. She slid her legs off the bed, stood up and grabbed yesterday's dress, which was lying on the floor. It was a rather splendid object, red with white and yellow slashed sleeves, seed pearls on the collar, one of her old outfits she'd got out of store. Not really suitable for being arrested in; a shade too frivolous. For being arrested, you want something smart but sombre in dark blue or slate-grey worsted. She had a bit of trouble with the buttons at the neck, for some reason.

"Right," she said. "Where to?"

Of course they didn't tell her. It wasn't close arrest, they didn't tie her hands or grab hold of her; just that dreadfully embarrassing boxed-in walking, where you have to try really hard not to step on anyone's heel.

She didn't know him. A large bald man, craftsman, in dark brown ecclesiasticals (but he was government, not Temple: that was only too obvious); a broad face, quite good-looking, forty or thereabouts. The fact that she didn't know him was quite eloquent in itself.

"Please sit down," he said. The chair was old black oak, very nicely carved, Restoration or maybe a shade earlier, worth money. The table was even older, though quite plain. She sat down, and he nodded to the kettlehats, who left and closed the door. "Apologies for the melodrama," he said. Quiet voice; he'd been to the Seminary, but where he came from originally she wasn't quite sure. "It's all right, you're not in trouble."

"That's nice," she said. "Who are you?"

Like shooting arrows at a wall. "Just a few questions to start with," he said. "When you were in Beloisa, did you meet a couple of

Rhus prisoners, brought in by a Captain—" a glance at the papers in front of him. "Captain Guifres."

"One," she said. "Not a couple."

"Mphm. Did you catch his name?"

"Musen."

Slight frown. "One prisoner, called Musen."

"That's right."

"Describe him."

She took a moment to get it right. "About six four," she said, "two-twenty pounds, big man, broad shoulders. Brown hair about the colour of your robe down to the shoulders, nineteen or twenty years old, brown eyes." She paused, then went on: "Clean-shaven, no scars or distinguishing marks, narrow face, long nose, small mouth, good teeth."

"Yes?"

"That's about it. He was a Rhus. They all look pretty much the same."

A faint not-good-enough look. "You didn't see a red-headed man, same height and build, blue eyes."

"I don't think so, no."

"Does the name Teucer mean anything to you?"

"No."

"This Musen didn't mention anyone called Teucer."

"Not to me."

He was perfectly still for a moment; then he wrote something on a wax tablet with a very thin ivory stylus. Too small for her to read. "You sent Musen to Thief School."

"Yes. I thought he showed promise."

He nodded. "They're pleased with him," he said. "They say he shows a remarkable degree of innate spirituality, possibly even worth considering for ordination at some point. Did you sleep with him?"

"What?"

"Did you have sexual intercourse with him?"

"No, certainly not."

"No matter." What was that supposed to mean? "How well did you know Captain Guifres?"

"I didn't do him, either."

"How well did you know Captain Guifres?"

She made herself calm down. Business, she thought, just work. "I knew him by sight, I didn't talk to him. He wasn't anything to do with me, just some soldier." She paused. "You know why I was there."

No acknowledgement. Information went into him, not out; like a sort of valve. "In your opinion, was Captain Guifres a loyal officer?"

She shrugged. "He *looked* loyal," she said. "At least, from about ten yards away. That's as close as I ever got. I don't know, what do traitors look like?"

He did something odd. He reached down on to the floor, picked something up, put it on the table between them. It was a little silver inkwell, highly polished. Oh, she thought. "Did Colonel Pieres ever mention a second Rhus prisoner? One that came in at the same time as Musen?"

"Not to me."

"Captain Jaizo?"

"No."

He nodded. Another glance down at the paperwork. "Now then," he said. "You murdered a political officer, Captain Seunas."

"No."

"I said," he said, "you're not in trouble. We can't prove it; you've already admitted it. You killed this Seunas."

"Yes. He was going to take my place on the ship."

"Did you know him? Talk to him?"

"No. First time I met him was when—"

"Do you know what he was doing upcountry? What his mission was?"

"No, I just told you. I went to his room, drew a knife and stabbed him. Just here," she said, pointing. "He may have said hello, who are you, I don't remember."

"You didn't look through any papers he may have had."

"No."

"Ah." Mild regret. "And neither Pieres nor Jaizo said anything about the work he'd been doing."

She tried hard to think. "Pieres said he was on a fact-finding mission. He was late coming in because he got separated from his escort. I saw that name you said on a document while I was flicking through Pieres' despatch case, but I didn't read it; I was in a hurry and it wasn't anything to do with me. I didn't know his name was Seunas till you told me just now."

A flicker of interest. "What sort of document? The one with his name on."

"I don't know. I can't remember."

"Try." Pause. "Orders? Despatches? Memorandum? Personal letter? Was it parchment or paper, sealed or unsealed? What sort of writing, court hand or freehand? Pro forma or narrative? Come on, I'm asking you a question."

"Freehand," she said. "Half a page of writing, standard military paper, not parchment. Not sealed, not orders or any sort of a form. Not a personal letter." She paused, trying to see it clearly in her mind. "It was a name in the middle of a paragraph. I think it only occurred once. I was scanning the letter for names, capital letters; you know, like you do."

"Go on."

"I'm sorry, but that's all. I didn't read it."

"Were there any other names you remember from the same document?"

She shook her head. "I'm sorry."

He looked at her. He was deciding whether to kill her or let her go. "Thank you," he said. He made his decision. "You've been most helpful. Did you enjoy the concert?"

"What?"

"The Procopius. Did you like it?"

"Yes, very much."

Another nod. "I missed it," he said, "but everyone says it was excellent. Would you like a score?"

"A what?"

"A score. A copy of the music. Would you like one?"

"Yes. Yes, very much."

Just a trace of a smile. "I'll have one sent to you." He balled his fist and brought it crashing down on the table. The door opened, and the kettlehat sergeant came in. "Please show the lady out," he said.

The sergeant led her down about a mile of corridors, completely unfamiliar, not the ones she'd come in by. Eventually he opened a door and she could see New Market Square, a dazzling blaze of gold in the early morning sunlight. "Thanks," she said, stepping carefully round him. "I know my way from here."

It took her about ten minutes to get home. When she got there, she found a parcel on her bed, wrapped in fine linen cloth and tied up with official green tape. It was the score of the Procopius. She hurried to the balcony and threw up into the South Cloister garden below.

"Another nasty job, I'm afraid," he said. He didn't look particularly remorseful. It occurred to her that maybe he thought she liked doing that sort of thing. Revolting thought.

"Ah well," she said. "Home or away?"

"Away," he replied. "Somewhere you know quite well, actually. That's why it's nasty."

Her heart sank. "Go on."

He was in no hurry. "Drink?"

"Water?"

The idea of drinking water was clearly disturbing to him. "Wine or brandy."

"No, thank you. Where are you sending me?"

He leaned back in his chair, making it creak. She wanted to tell him, for crying out loud, don't do that, it's Age of Elegance and very fragile and valuable. But the lodge house was crammed with stuff like that, and nobody bothered about it. One dark night, she'd have a cart waiting out back of the stables and a dozen strong men to do the lifting, and then she could retire—

"You spent a year in Blemya, is that right?"

"You should know. You sent me there."

Smile. "Not me, my illustrious predecessor."

"You're quite right, so it was." She frowned. "You're sending me to Blemya."

"Yes."

"Well, that's not so bad. What've I got to do?"

He leaned forward again, and her heart bled for the delicate joints of the chair. "When you were there last, you met the queen."

"Well, she wasn't the queen then. The prince was still alive, so she wasn't anybody special. Just so much stock-in-trade, waiting to be found a husband." She paused. "Nice girl, I liked her. She'd be, what, twenty-four now?"

"Twenty-two," he said. "A girl of twenty-two is the most strategically important asset in the world. Sometimes I can't help wondering, no disrespect to the Almighty—"

"Indeed," she said briskly. "So, what do you want me to do to the poor kid?"

He beamed at her. "I want you," he said, "to present her with a copy of the score of Procopius' new choral symphony. You know, the one that premiered the other day. Were you there, by the way?"

She nodded. "Were you?"

"Front row," he said smugly. "I liked it, though I thought it dragged a bit in the middle. Anyway, in light of the special relationship between ourselves and the Blemyans, and knowing that Her Majesty is very fond of music, Director Procopius has kindly allowed a copy of the score to be made, and I'd like you to go there and give it to her."

She frowned. "Just me, or me and some other people?"

"We were thinking of a party of twenty. Keep it quite low-key."

"I see. And that's a nasty job, is it?"

"That's not quite all we want you to do."

A nasty job all right; but she'd done worse, and at least she'd be out of the country. Probably not a bad idea to be a long way away, in a neutral foreign country, until whatever that other business about Beloisa was had blown over. It was, of course, quite unspeakably hot in Blemya. The thought made her feel sad. And she had absolutely nothing to wear—

I. The sovereign Kingdom of Blemya (see map)—

There was no map, but that didn't matter. She knew where Blemya was. She stretched out her legs and drew the lamp a little closer.

> I. The sovereign Kingdom of Blemya (see map) lies between the Eastern and Western empires on the southern shore of the Middle Sea. Originally a province of the united Empire Blemya rebelled shortly before the outbreak of the Civil War, and has remained independent ever since. The rebel commander, General Tolois, proclaimed himself king and ruled for seventeen years until his death. He was succeeded by his eldest son, Dalois I. Given the strategic location of Blemya and its considerable resources of manpower, agricultural produce, timber

and minerals (including iron ore and gold, see Appendix), it was inevitable that after the partition of the Empire at the end of the Civil War, both sides should have made assiduous attempts to enlist the Blemyans as allies. Equally inevitably, first Tolois and then his son and grandson have maintained a policy of strict neutrality while playing off both Empires against each other. Blemya trades extensively with the West, supplying timber and finished lumber, wheat and wine, and the East, predominantly metals, barley and palm oil. Blemyan citizens are forbidden to enlist with the armies of either side, on pain of death and confiscation of family assets. The Blemyan army, well-organised, superbly equipped and professionally led, is believed to number in excess of one hundred thousand, the majority drawn from the Settler smallholder class (see below) . . .

She yawned. Who wrote these things, anyway?

II. Blemya's population is seventy-five per cent indigenous desert tribesmen, twenty-five per cent Settlers, the descendants of the Northern Imperials who first conquered and occupied the territory in the reign of Clea IV. The Settler aristocracy own large estates in the north and west of the country, largely worked by indigenous labour; relations between the two ethnic groups are generally held to be distant but friendly, with no recent instances of sectarian disorder. The south and east are mostly tribal homelands, but there are substantial areas of small and medium Settler farmsteads, concentrated alongside the two forks of the Blee river, the arable heartland of the country. These Settler communities provide the bulk of the Blemyan infantry, although the officer class is predominantly northern and western aristocratic. The Blemyan cavalry is recruited from the tribes and is regarded as highly effective;

their officers are drawn from the upper echelons of the tribes, and are treated as equals by the upper-class Settlers. All the regions of Blemya are generally prosperous, and considerable wealth is concentrated in the coastal cities and the three tribal capitals in the far south. Indeed, the national average standard of living throughout Blemya is significantly higher than that prevailing in all but the most favoured regions of either Empire.

Overstating it a bit, she thought; but not that much.

III. . . . Following the death of Dalois II, the throne passed briefly to his uncle, Sinois, acting as regent for Irdis, the crown prince. However, both Sinois and Irdis were drowned en route to a religious festival, whereupon the crown passed to Dalois II's only surviving child, a daughter, enthroned as Queen Cardespan at the age of nineteen. Remarkably, Queen Cardespan has contrived to maintain the unity, independence and prosperity of her kingdom, thanks no doubt to the support and excellent advice of her council, about whom regrettably little is known—

Fibber, she thought. But maybe just as well not to put too much down on paper.

. . . is of paramount importance to the security of the Empire, and it has therefore been decided in Council that limited acts of destabilisation are necessary at this time. Equally important, however, is public opinion within Blemya, which currently tends to favour the East. This is largely due to the influence of the mine owners and the palm oil consortium, who derive substantial revenues from the Eastern trade, rather than to any political or ideological sympathy; the average

Settler is typically open-minded on the issue of sides, tending to regard both Empires with distaste, as being the direct descendants of the united Empire from which Blemya felt it necessary to secede in what the Settlers refer to as the War of Independence.

She nodded. Fair enough.

. . . possible at the same time to destabilise the Queen's regime and to attribute such acts to Eastern infiltrators and/or insurgents, such operations could well have a significant effect on popular attitudes in Blemya and might even result in the overthrow of the Queen and Blemya's entry into the war on our side. With the human and financial resources of the Kingdom at our disposal . . .

Well, quite. A hundred thousand men; more to the point, the Blemyan state arsenal, possibly the most advanced arms factory in the world, about which the report had been curiously reticent. But she'd been there and seen it, which the writer of the report presumably hadn't. And the money, of course. All that money. And victory was quite definitely something you could buy.

Acts of destabilisation. Interesting to see what they had in mind. She read on.

"Oh," she said. The wind caught her hair and tugged at it, like a child in a tantrum. "I didn't know you were—"

Oida smiled at her. "Surprise," he said.

Oh God, she thought. A porter lifted her bag, winced slightly at the unanticipated weight. What the hell've you got in here? he didn't say. The bag clinked slightly, and Oida raised an eyebrow. "I'll repack it so it doesn't do that," she said, and he laughed.

Oida's luggage consisted of three trunks, four large bags, two knee-high barrels and a long, flat packing case. "Just as well it's a big ship," she said.

"That's a portable euphonium, would you believe," he said proudly. "Designed it myself, and the lads at the Dula Arsenal ran it up for me. Folds away flat in five minutes, no specialist tools required. Got a nice sound, too."

The Dula Arsenal was in the East. "A *portable*—"

He shrugged. "You get used to a particular sound," he said. "Actually, if she likes it, I'll give it to her, I can always get another one made. You, by contrast, travel light."

"Spare frock and some weapons." She shrugged. "Who else is coming on this bun fight?"

"Nobody important," Oida said. "Diplomats, mostly, a couple of lodge bigwigs with a taste for foreign cuisine." He lowered his voice; still too loud, but the crack of the sails and the squeals of the gulls covered him quite effectively. "The only other one who's read the briefing is him there—you see, in the green? That's Cruxpelit." She looked at him: small, utterly nondescript middle-aged man with a bald spot and a very short beard; his coat was so long, she couldn't see what he had on under it, military, court dress or ecclesiasticals. "He's craft, but God only knows what he actually does. Rather a creepy individual, if you ask me."

She gazed at him in mock astonishment. "You mean to say there's something you don't know?"

"Quite." Not funny. "And I'm not exactly thrilled about sharing a ship with an unknown quantity, let alone an important secret mission. Bastard's as tight as a miser's arse. Oh, he'll talk to you all day long, but he never actually *says* anything."

There was genuine unhappiness in Oida's voice, and for the very first time she thought there might just possibly be aspects of this job that she might enjoy. "I think we can go on the ship now," she said.

"The proper term is *embark*. After you."

It was going to be a slow, lazy voyage. The sea was mercifully flat, with just enough wind to keep them moving at slightly more than fast walking pace. She found a barrel next to the forecastle stairs to sit on. She'd brought three books. She could think of ever so many worse ways to spend five days.

Oida, bless him, was bored silly. Just before daybreak each morning he did his voice exercises, a combination of roaring noises, scales, arpeggios and snatches of heartbreakingly lovely melodies suddenly cut off in the middle. At noon precisely he did scales on the flute and chords on the mandolin. The rest of the time, when he wasn't being seasick, he prowled round the deck getting in the way of the crew, or came and stopped her from reading.

"I have no idea," he said suddenly, "where we are."

She closed the book around her forefinger, to mark the place. "Of course you do. Just there"—she pointed to the place on the deck where he was standing—"is the exact centre of the universe. Nothing else really matters very much. Better now?"

He grinned. "Seriously," he said. "I tried figuring it out from the position of the stars last night, but I must've got it wrong, or we'd be in the middle of the desert somewhere. I hate not knowing where I am. I mean, if the ship sinks, which direction do we swim in?"

"This far out? Makes no odds. You'd drown anyway."

"Thank you so much." He sat down cross-legged at her feet, which annoyed her intensely. "I don't like the way this ship is run. It's all so bloody haphazard. All over the place, like the mad woman's shit."

"You know a lot about seamanship."

"No," he said. "But it's obvious. Half the crew spend half the time just lolling about."

"That's because the wind is gentle and constant. What do you want them to do, get out and push?"

He scowled at her, which she took as a slight victory. "We need to get our heads together and decide what we're going to do."

"We know what we're going to do. It's in the briefing."

"Yes, but we need to *plan*." He looked round. "Have you seen that creep Cruxpelit? I haven't set eyes on him for days."

"You sat next to him at dinner last night."

"Well, hours, then. But he disappears. How can anyone disappear on a poxy little ship?" He picked something up off the deck, a nail; looked at it and threw it over the side. "Someone could've trod on that," he said. "And he's never seasick."

"Nor am I."

"Yes, well, you're the proverbial woman of steel. But he's a little fat man. He ought to be chucking his guts up all day long."

"Like you."

"I'm much better now, thank you for asking. We need to plan," he repeated. "Work out a detailed plan of action, with alternatives and fall-back positions. This really isn't the sort of thing we should be making up as we go along."

It occurred to her that maybe he hadn't done much of this sort of thing before. "I wouldn't bother," she said. "Detailed plans and fall-back positions generally don't help, in my experience. Usually they just get in the way."

He looked at her. "Is it true you murdered a political, just to get his place on a boat?"

She closed her eyes, then opened them again. "Yes."

"I see."

For some reason she couldn't explain, she felt a need to justify herself. "It was him or me," she said. "There was one last ship out of Beloisa. Everyone left behind was going to die. What would you have done?"

He didn't answer that. "Talked to the diplomats much?"

Sore point. "They don't want to talk to me," she said. "If I didn't know better, I'd say they were scared of me."

"Probably they are."

"Don't be stupid. But it's true. I can barely get a civil word out of them."

He yawned, not covering his mouth, an uncharacteristically vulgar moment. "They're a poor lot," he said judiciously. "At least, the men are. Place-fillers. The Imperial woman's got brains but no charm, and the other one—"

She nodded. "Charm but no brains. Like the fairy tale about the three sisters with one eye between them."

"Indeed." He looked impressed by the analogy. "Mind you, they're just camouflage. I think—" He lowered his voice. *Still* too loud. "I think the main reason they were picked was because they're expendable."

"Excuse me?"

"Expendable. Nobody will miss them terribly much if they never come back. As in, if we make a bog of it and get caught and strung up, no great loss."

She considered that. "Same goes for me, I suppose."

That startled him. "I don't think so. They chose you because you're good."

"And expendable."

"No, not especially. After all, they chose *me*, too. And I'm definitely not expendable."

She couldn't help laughing. "Well then," she said, "that puts paid to that theory. If they're prepared to risk a national treasure like yourself—"

He gave her a serious look. "They wouldn't hang *me*," he said. "That'd risk pissing off the West *and* the East. No chance of that."

She nodded. "Hence," she said, "the portable euphonium made in the Eastern state munitions factory."

He grinned. "Clever old you. Well, it does no harm to drop the odd hint."

"Of course. Just out of interest—"

"Yes?"

"Whose side *are* you on?"

Big smile. "Silly girl. Ours, of course."

You must—all the old travellers' accounts insist, you *must*—approach Ezza for the first time from the sea. True enough, the approach from the landward side is very impressive, particularly if you're coming up the old Mail Road, and the first glimpse you catch of the city is the breathtaking view through the gap in the Axore mountains; and then you slowly descend through the lush river valley with its orchards and olive groves, until eventually you enter the city through the amazing Bronze Gate. But for the full effect—the authorities are united on this point—nothing compares with the long, almost painfully slow progress between the seamarks of the lagoon in the early morning, before the mist has lifted, culminating in the first heart-stopping vision of the white marble Sea Gate, with its four impossibly tall, slender columns and the massive statue of the Forgotten Goddess, vast and hideously, wonderfully, eroded into an abstract monstrosity by two thousand years of salt winds. Next, you begin to make out the gold and copper domes of the twelve fire temples crowded together along the Foreigners' Quay; to begin with, they're just vaguely disturbing coloured lights; then, as the sun breaks through, they become burning beacons, convincing you that you've arrived right in the middle of an invasion or a civil war; and then they resolve themselves into symmetrical, artificial shapes, a row of enormous chess pieces facing you across a board, daring you to make your first move. If you've come to Ezza, they seem to be saying, you'd better have brought your best game, or we'll have you.

This was, of course, her second time. The first time, she'd come to Ezza by night and been hoisted up over the wall in a herring basket. She'd felt horribly sick and her hair smelt of fish for two days.

*

Three days of diplomatic receptions. How she endured it all she wasn't entirely sure. Mostly she stayed close to Oida, like those little sucker fish that hitch rides on sharks. Everybody wanted to talk to Oida, and Oida just wanted to talk. She heard all about his early influences, his views on the development of the symphony, where he got his ideas from; she found him loathsome in this vein, but slowly it dawned on her that it was all just armour, interlocking plates of arrogance and charm, designed to attract and repel at the same time. That she could understand, even admire. But the other epiphany was simply baffling. Oida wasn't really interested in music.

("Well, no, actually," he confessed, when she taxed him with it, during a brief ceasefire in the middle of the deputy chief minister's reception. "I used to, but not any more, not for a long time. But I'm so good at it—")

So she stopped fighting from behind his shield and took the battle to the enemy; in particular, the Blemyan ministers' wives. They found her fascinating. With one huge, obvious glaring exception, women didn't participate in Blemyan politics. There were priestesses, of course, quite senior figures in Temple, but they confined their activities to reciting Scripture and enacting ritual, very occasionally being consulted on fine points of doctrine (but only in their capacity as conduits of the divine). There were no female craftsmen above the second degree; she got the impression that their principal function in lodge was baking honeycakes and arranging flowers. As for a woman doing a regular job of work in return for money—God, she thought, what a country.

The ministers' wives asked her three questions: is it too terrible having to work for a living; what's Oida *really* like; what are they wearing in Rasch? She had to struggle to get anything much in return. It wasn't that the wives were discreet or cagey. They simply didn't know anything, about politics or trade or the economy or sectarian divisions. That just left malicious gossip, and, although that wasn't too hard to obtain, she didn't really know enough about the people and the issues, though she was learning fast. All in all, not the three best days of her career so far.

"And the food," she protested to Oida, when they were finally clear of the finance minister's reception. "How can they eat that muck? If I see another sun-dried bloody tomato—"

He gave her a seraphic smile. "You know the two barrels I brought with me?"

"Yes, I—" Wasn't able to see a way of getting them open without being obvious. "Was wondering about them."

"One of them's a side of boned salt beef, Dirian-style."

"Oh *God*," she moaned.

"And the other's spring greens preserved in honey." He looked at her. "It's such a shame you don't like me. Otherwise, I'd be delighted to share."

"I never said I don't like you."

"Some things don't need saying." He shrugged. "Salt beef Dirian-style with six different kinds of pepper," he said. "There's a little man in Cousa who makes them for me, to an old North Imperial recipe. So tender you can carve it with a blade of grass. But I imagine you'd rather preserve your integrity and eat couscous."

"I've always liked you, Oida. You know that."

He laughed. "You *don't*," he said. "That's why I find you so intriguing and irresistible. Don't spoil it, please."

"Fine," she said. "You're arrogant and vain, you wear scent and you stand too close to people when you talk to them. Also, I don't like your vocal music. The instrumental stuff is fine, but you can't write songs for olive pits."

They were walking under the soaring pink granite arch of the Friary, where they were staying. "I'll pretend I didn't hear the last bit," he said. "The rest is freely admitted. I am who I have to be."

She found that statement rather unsettling. "And your attitude to women—"

"Ah." He shrugged. "The moths revile the flame, and why not? Let me tell you something. If I'd wanted to get you into bed, I've had done it long since."

She was aware that she was glowing red, like coke under the bellows. She hoped it was anger.

"But," he went on, "I don't sleep with colleagues, it's a rule. Just so happens, you're the only woman I count as a colleague. But it's a rule."

"You're so completely full of—"

"Yes," he said gently. "It's how I make myself useful. Let me put it another way. I don't sleep with women I care about."

She looked at him. "That's just silly," she said.

He shrugged. "Thankfully it's a very small category. And most of them are over seventy. Do you want some salt beef and greens or not?"

She gave him a solemn look. "I should very much like some salt beef and greens."

"All right, then. Because once it's opened, it'll only keep a couple of days."

And then they were presented to the queen.

Afterwards, long afterwards, she tried to picture her, but all she could bring to mind was the image of a huge golden throne—its arms were lions, its legs were elephants, and two gold and ivory double-headed eagles perched on the headrest—flanked by the biggest human beings she'd ever seen, head to toe in gilded scale armour; and it was as though someone had left a heap of bizarrely exotic ceremonial regalia piled up on the seat of the chair, intending to come back for it later. Somewhere under all that stuff—the *lorus*, the *divitision*, the greater and lesser *chlamys*, the purple dalmatic, the Cope of State with jewelled *pendilia*, the *labarum* and orb flammiger—she sensed the presence of someone small, frightened and angry, but she couldn't lay her hand on her heart and swear she'd seen her.

The diplomats did the actual handing over of the gift: a silver box containing the score, dedicated to Her Majesty by Procopius in his own handwriting. Nothing else with it—an eloquent gesture, that, because anything else would be mere junk in comparison, so why bother? A chamberlain took it from them and put it on a large circular silver tray carried by four enormous guardsmen, who lugged it away somewhere behind the throne. The chamberlain thanked them and made a sort speech, stressing the friendly relations between the kingdom and the empire. The chief diplomat then made a short speech stressing the friendly relations between the empire and the kingdom. Everybody bowed to everyone else, then everyone bowed to the Throne, and then it was time to go.

For sharpening knives she used three stones: first the red sandstone, then the coarse grey millstone, finally the black water stone, a tiny chip out of a mountain somewhere in the Casypes, a semimythical range in the far north of the Eastern empire, the only place in the world where the stuff had ever been found. Black water stone, weight for weight, was slightly more expensive than emerald, much harder to get hold of, and illegal to own in the West. She wore hers in a brooch, with a highly ornate silver setting.

Carrying the knife about would be easy. The Director of Protocol back home had sent the Blemyan Chamberlain's Office a twenty-page summary of Imperial court dress; on page seven, under Priestesses, was a list of sacred and ceremonial items which a priestess was required to have with her at all times: a mirror, a small silver phial of holy water, a tinderbox, a knife, a pair of white linen gloves for handling the sacramental chalice. The Blemyans had objected that no weapon of any kind was allowed inside the palace precincts unless expressly authorised by the Count of the Stables. The Director replied that the empire would of course respect Blemyan law, and it was a shame that the visit would have to be cancelled over so small a detail; however, no embassy could set out without a priestess, and no priestess could discharge her duties without a mirror, a small silver phial of holy water, a tinderbox, a knife and a pair of white linen gloves for handling the sacramental chalice. The Blemyans quickly responded by issuing the mission's officially designed priestess with written authority to carry a small ceremonial knife, signed and sealed by the Count of the Stables. Simple as that.

She gave the blade five more strokes each side on the water stone, for luck; then she wiped the slurry off her brooch with a small pad of cotton waste, which she threw on the fire, and slipped the knife into the pretty velvet sheath they'd run up for her in the lodge workshops. It was dark red (so practical as well as fashionable) and decorated with three rows of tiny freshwater pearls. She longed to hang on to it after the mission was over, but she was pretty sure they'd make her give it back. Lodge property, after all.

She took off her shoes.

Now, then. Time to go out and kill a perfect stranger.

Three essentials of the perfect political assassination: a sharp knife, a plausible excuse for being in an inappropriate place, if challenged, and a really accurate map.

She could see maps. One good long look, and she could see it in her mind, up to three days later. So, out of her door and turn right, down a long marble-floored corridor, past a statuary group representing Blemya Marrying the Sea, at the end of the corridor turn left; fifteen yards, second mezzanine, up six flights of stairs, left, then right, then thirty-two yards (she had a pair of excellent dividers, which doubled as a cloak pin), the door on the right. As anticipated, the room was empty and dark. She crossed it slowly and carefully, guided by the slight change in temperature, until she reached the unshuttered window. Out on to the ledge—she hated that—and shuffle along twelve feet in a state of blind, weak-kneed terror, until her groping right hand felt the wood of a shutter.

Next, the horrible part; the shutters opened outwards, of course. She inched along, letting her fingertips trace the shutter panels, until she found the line in the middle where they met. She crept on, two feet precisely, and inserted her fingertips into the join. If the shutters were latched, that would be that—mission aborted, try again later. But they weren't; she felt the right-hand shutter lift away from the wall. If it creaked and woke him up, she'd have no alternative but to jump. Eight floors up. No chance.

Getting off the ledge, in through the window, feet on to the floor, proved to be very nearly impossible. For some unaccountable reason, the bottom sill of this window was a good eighteen inches higher than the counterpart in her room, on which she'd practised so assiduously, and her legs simply weren't long enough. In the end, she had to hop, not knowing what she'd be landing on. Mercifully, it was a sheepskin rug.

Pitch dark, of course. She straightened up and stood perfectly still until she found where the bed was by the sound of his breathing. He'll be alone, the briefing had assured her; he's a married man, but his wife is a home body and doesn't like coming up to town. Therefore there'll be no need to identify which occupant of the bed is the target. That was, in fact, the principal reason why he had been chosen to die, rather than the equally eligible Director of Interior Supply.

She waited as long as she dared, giving her night vision as much time as possible to acclimatise to the very faint light coming in under the door from the lantern sconces in the corridor outside. Unfortunately, there was some bloody great big thing—a wardrobe or a linen press—directly in the way; she could see its outline, just about, but the space between her and the bed was dark grey fog. Way beyond the point now where any explanation would be credible. She closed the shutter, just in case the slight chill of the night air disturbed his sleep. You have to be really considerate, like a newlywed.

Two distinct patterns of breathing. Oh hell.

She'd have to kill them both, the minister and his unknown, inconvenient bedfellow. Nothing for it, had to be done. Could it be done? She rearranged the cutting list in her mind and decided that, yes, it could. You found the vital spot in the dark by touch, by tracing with the exquisitely sensitive tip of your left little finger until you found a landmark: an ear, the corner of the mouth, something definite to navigate by. Almost always, the subject started to wake up while you were doing it, and then you had less than a second, which is actually plenty of time. You could do two people in one second if you absolutely had to. What you couldn't do was flounder about distinguishing man from woman, and most certainly you couldn't leave a live, awake witness. Sorry, she thought. I really am sorry. It's such horribly rotten luck.

The hell with it, she thought. She made herself slow right down, a parody of movement. She knew from long practice exactly what the edge of a bed felt like against her shin. Killing people in the dark is so sensual, someone had told her once, before her first time; your whole body comes alive, every tiny patch of your skin becomes unbelievably sensitive. At the time she thought he was just being weird, but it was true. Hearing, too. She understood how blind men could find their way around by sound alone. It wasn't as though either the minister or his companion snored, or anything like that, but their breathing was loud and clear enough to find them by. She reached out, and the first thing her fingertip touched was hair.

She tried to remember. The minister, she'd seen him at three receptions: a medium man, medium height, build, medium-length hair. Several of the Blemyan council were bald as eggs, why couldn't they have set her on one of them? She followed the line of the hair, trying to gauge its length. It was soft, but some men had hair like that. A faint scent of peaches and apples, but the men here were incredibly vain. She thought of Oida. She touched an earlobe, instinctively drew her hand back. Too small to be a man's.

I have to kill them both, she thought. I can't, she thought.

Well, that was all there was to it. A wave of annoyance swept over her; damn the stupid bloody woman, some people are so *thoughtless.* She couldn't do it the usual way, she'd have to go by sound and intuition. Some people could do that, she'd never tried. She'd have to kill the man without waking the woman. Trade test. Thank you so bloody much.

She listened, trying to unravel the combined sound of breathing; like trying to listen to just the bassoons in an orchestral piece. Actually, she could do that. He was the quieter of the two, oddly enough, and he took longer breaths, slightly more widely spaced. Just as well she had ears like a bat. She listened some more, until she was as sure as she'd ever be where the man's nose was. What she didn't know was, was he lying on his back or on his side?

Very cautiously, she felt, and located a cheek; on his side, fine. That ruled out her preferred point of entry, the triangular hollow at the base of the throat, where the collarbones met. She was fairly sure he was lying on his right cheek, in which case the jugular vein would be just *there*; but she couldn't be sure—also, spurting blood might wake the stupid woman. In through the ear, then. Difficult when you can't see, because of the risk of hitting bone. She'd have to risk using force. It just got better and better.

She slid the knife out, reversed it, passed it into her left hand, positioned it, like a mason poising a chisel. This is all going to go horribly wrong, she thought; she could hear the lodge master's voice in her head, *how could you be so irresponsible,* though of course she'd never hear him say it, she'd be dead herself. So; so some tart's life is worth more than yours, but you killed a political officer. Bloody stupid, she thought, I'm just so bloody stupid. Then she cupped her right palm and used it as a hammer on the pommel of the knife.

There was a sound; a crisp, crunching, punching noise. It was so loud they must've heard it in Rasch. Only one breathing sound now, but still regular and even. She tightened her left hand on the knife and pulled. Stupid thing was stuck.

Leave it, yelled the voice in her head, *leave it and get out of there.* No. She tried again, felt the dead man's head lift off the pillow, stopped immediately, gently relaxed until she was sure it was resting again. She splayed the fingers of her right hand and put them on the dead head—insensible now, so no risk; she felt damp warmth, must remember to wipe her hands as soon as possible. She felt the steel of the blade against the web between middle finger and ring finger. She pressed down gently but firmly on the head, and drew on the knife with her left hand. It reminded her of the fairy story, the boy who pulled the sword from the rock to prove he was the true king. She pulled. Knife still stuck, a slight jolt, knife free and clear. She stopped for a moment, then gently withdrew her right hand, taking great care not to let it brush against *anything*. She wiped the knife on the pillow four strops per side, then did her best to wipe her hand; then the knife back in the sheath. One final listen; breathing still regular. One of those people who can sleep through anything. She envied her.

Why do I have to make things difficult for myself? she thought. Own worst enemy; always been the case. She steered warily round the wardrobe, chest, whatever the damn thing was, until she was basking in the light from under the door. She knew where the door was. Fingertips of her left hand, the clean one, to find the key, mercifully in the lock. Usually, all of this stage wouldn't be a problem, because you're alone in the room; you can fumble about, make a certain amount of noise, maybe even risk a light. But no, she had to be merciful, playing God. Her reward was that the key was in the lock. She turned it, agonisingly slowly, until she felt the wards relax. Plenty of follow through, even then, to avoid a sudden last-moment click.

Her information was, there was no guard on the door. The corridor would be empty. She could just leave, rest of the day's your own. She opened the door.

And nearly brained a soldier, in full-dress armour, standing about ten inches in front of it. He stepped sideways, swung round, looked at her. Just a very faint fleeting grin, and he stepped aside.

Among her gifts was the ability to get in character instantly. The woman in the bed, on being leered at by a guard, would give him a look like *this.* The guard immediately put on a stuffed-fish expression and directed his eyes to a space on the wall six inches above her head. She walked past him two paces, then slipped out the knife, shot out her arm and stabbed him at the base of the throat. His mouth opened; she left the knife in there until the light in his eyes went out, then took his full weight on her left arm and gently eased him down on to the floor. Sorry, she thought; but he was a soldier, they don't really count, and, anyway, he'd laughed at her for what he thought she was. No justification, really.

It just gets better and better and better.

But there was nobody else in the corridor, she'd been exceptionally quick and quiet, and she was going to get away with it, this time. She wiped the knife on his hair, taking a second to make sure it was really clean, then examined her right hand. One little smear of blood she'd missed. She spat on it, worked it out with her left forefinger, wiped it. Attention to detail. Then she set off down the corridor towards the middle stair, which took her down two flights, then left and right across the back gallery, rejoin the stairs she'd come up by, retrace steps, back to her own door, inside, turn the key, shoot the bolt. She walked quite calmly to the bed and sat down on it, and stayed completely still for quite some time.

Then she found her tinderbox, lit the lamp, took off her knife sheath, drew the knife. She washed the blade carefully, paying particular attention to the slight crevice where the blade went up into the hilt. She examined the sheath for even the tiniest speck of wet or drying blood, found two, scraped at them with her fingernail, teased the pile of the velvet until there was nothing to see. She'd have to be wearing this knife and sheath tomorrow, and the next day, or it'd be too blindingly obvious. Then she checked them both again, knife and sheath, and again, and again, and again, and again. Her head was splitting. She lay down on the bed, feeling dizzy and sick.

I'm so sorry, the City prefect said for the fifth time, I'm really sorry to have to ask you all these questions, but you do understand, it's a matter of the utmost gravity. Naturally, completely above suspicion, but we do have to ask. You do understand, don't you?

Oida understood perfectly. He was charming, sympathetic and completely cooperative. Yes, as it happened, he could account for his whereabouts all last night, and, as it happened, he did have a witness. He spent all night with his colleague, the priestess Telamon, and she could vouch for the fact that he was in his room all night, because neither of them had got very much sleep.

Conflicting emotions plainly visible on the City prefect's face; about to die of embarrassment, but oh so relieved that he could cross this overwhelmingly, lethally important man off his list of suspects and not have to bother him any more. The lady Telamon can verify what I've just told you, if you want to ask her. Oh no (very emphatic). No need, no need for that at *all*.

"Simple misdirection."

She wished he'd go away. It was gloriously warm on deck, there were pools of golden light like honey, and they were going home. He was spoiling the mood, and she didn't want to have to hold that against him. "Yes," she said. "I know."

Probably he wasn't listening to her. He sounded like he was giving a lecture. But he admitted that he did that sometimes—gave lectures to imaginary audiences, as a way of clarifying his mind. You understand something so much better when you're trying to explain it, he'd said.

"They suspect me," he went on. "I produce an alibi. It's entirely plausible. It never occurs to them it's the other way round."

"Quite," she said. "I'd rather like to close my eyes for five minutes, if that's all right."

"Sure, go ahead." He stayed where he was. "They said to me, that'll never work, but they didn't understand. It's not what you present, it's how you—"

Just a moment. She opened her eyes and sat up. "It was your idea."

"What?"

"The alibi thing. You thought of it."

"Of course," Oida said. He sounded too surprised by the question to be lying. "This whole show was my idea. We kill a minister known to be favourably inclined to us—"

"*Your* idea?"

"That's right. We kill a minister known to be favourably inclined to us, during a state visit by us. What are they supposed to make of that? We couldn't have done it; the dead man was our friend. Therefore the opposition must be behind it, therefore they must be trying to frame us. Meanwhile the balance of power on the council shifts dramatically—"

It had been, she had to concede, basically a good idea. Simple, therefore good. Create the instability, don't try and be greedy or clever. A remarkable plan for someone so arrogantly convoluted.

"Result," he went on: "the council collapses, the government falls, she loses her key advisers, meanwhile popular opinion's against the East because they're perceived to have murdered a very popular minister, adored by the poor Settlers for his economic and social reforms, so her new cabinet's heavily weighted in our favour. It picks up a momentum of its own with no further interference needed from us. Next thing you know—"

"It won't work," she said.

That stopped him dead in mid-flow. "Why not?"

She gave him a sad smile. Luckily, the sea was so smooth that even Oida's notoriously frail stomach had nothing to fear. The faint cry of gulls. Out of the corner of her eye, she saw the silver flash of a school of flying fish. "Think about it," she said. "Daxiles dies a martyr's death. His fellow Radicals on the council use the sudden upsurge in popular support to ram through the rest of his agrarian reforms. Nobody dares oppose them, it'd be seen as pissing on the martyr's grave. Result—" she tried to mimic the way he said the word, but couldn't quite catch the inflexion. "You get your instability, the government does indeed fall, but the new cabinet's going to be chosen for their economic policy, not which empire they favour. What you'll actually get is a council packed with Radicals, who either favour the East or couldn't give a damn either way. You should know by now, it's the price of bread that gets people excited, not foreign affairs."

The look on his face was a wonderful sight. Really and truly, he hadn't thought of it that way, and realisation had just dropped on him like a huge rock. She'd seen it, of course, the night she read the mission briefing. And, naturally, she'd assumed that there had to be more to it than that, and that whoever had thought up the plan was playing a much longer, deeper game than she could begin to understand. But in fact it was all the clown Oida, who'd failed to think it through—

"I don't agree," he said. "I think the fundamentalist faction on the right of the KKA—"

"Anyway," she said crisply, "we'll know soon enough how it's going to pan out. And we're free and clear and on our way home, so what the hell."

He was angry—with her, which was just ridiculous, but at least it made him go away. She opened her book and tried to read, but she'd lost the thread of the argument and couldn't be bothered to go back and pick it up. Something was wrong, but she couldn't figure out what it could possibly be.

She closed her eyes for a moment, and heard Oida's voice, right back down the deck. He was not quite shouting at someone, but definitely giving him the full force of his personality. She could only make out a few words here and there, but the general idea seemed to be, *can't you make this thing go any faster?* The captain, or whoever it was, was being too deferential to be audible. He wasn't doing much of a job of soothing Oida's tantrum; quite the reverse. She guessed this would be one aspect of the journey in the great man's company that the captain wouldn't be telling his grandchildren about.

Later it got very hot indeed, even when the sun went down, and since it was still calm she decided she'd sleep up on deck, where there was at least a trace of a breeze. Apparently the diplomats had chosen to do the same thing; she could hear them talking somewhere in the darkness, quiet and fast, not heated but anxious. She wondered if something had gone wrong; well, she'd find that out in due course. Maybe their tone of voice made her nervous. She took the knife and sheath off her belt, stood up and dropped them over the side into the sea. Pity about that; the sheath was lodge property but the knife had been her own.

She drifted off to sleep and was woken by what at first she took to be screaming; it proved to be nothing more than a very big gull, perched on the rail and complaining loudly about something. She sat up, and it spread its wings and flopped away.

Oida walked past. He had a plate of scrambled eggs resting on the upturned palm of his left hand, and a short wooden spoon in his right. He stopped and glowered at her. "You're completely wrong about the KKA," he said. "They'll go into coalition with the Optimates, you just wait and see."

She yawned. "Any eggs left?"

"No."

"You could've woken me."

He scowled at her and walked away, eating. She grinned.

Not long after that there was a storm, the sort that comes out of nowhere, threatens to tear the sky in half and then dies away into sweet serenity, as if to say "Who, me?" She was used to them; she'd already found herself a tight corner of the hold, with things to hang on to and no risk of being buried under falling cargo. She went there only to find it occupied: Oida, curled up in a ball and muttering the catechism, over and over again, very fast.

"Mind if I join you?" she yelled. He couldn't hear her over the roaring and creaking, and he filled all the available space. She swore at him and went back on deck, where she got under the feet of the crew and was scowled at.

It was early the next day, and the Silver Spire was just visible on the skyline, when she finally realised what it was that had been bothering her. She sat down on a coil of rope, because her legs were suddenly too weak to carry her weight. Oida. Oida planning operations, formulating policy; since when? Sure, he was really high up in the lodge, twenty-third or twenty-fourth degree, something ridiculous like that. But he was *neutral*; that was the whole point about him, he came and went between the two empires (each one naturally assuming that he was on their side really), playing his music, making (she assumed) absurdly large sums of money, courted and feted wherever he went, and everyone upon whom his radiance happened to shine was continually asked, what's he *really* like? And, yes, presumably both governments knew he was a double agent, a complete whore who'd turn a trick for anyone, impersonal, just business, no feeling; such an entity would be not just useful but vital, since even treachery is a form of communication, and otherwise the two sides couldn't communicate at all. Yes to all that; but Oida spearheading a serious attempt to bring Blemya into the war wasn't the same thing as a few names, pillow-talk secrets, troop movements. Was it possible that Oida had actually made up his mind at last and taken a side? If the East found out what he'd been up to, they'd be livid—

Yes, but it was *stupid* plan. It wasn't going to *work*. A good man dead, all that risk, and nothing to show for it whatsoever. Maybe that was the idea. Maybe his true masters, in the East, had told him: we want you to go to the West and sell them on this incredibly stupid plan, and it'll go wrong and the Blemyans will be furious and come in on our side—only that wasn't going to be the result. There would be the most appalling trouble in Blemya for a while, and then things would carry on *exactly the same*. So where the hell was the point?

It had been a stupid plan. Which raised two colossal issues. One: was Oida really that stupid? Part of her yearned to say yes, of course, he's an arrogant clown, shallow as silver plating, so full of it that he simply didn't see how bad the plan was; a clown and a coward, curled up in a ball, whimpering to the fire god because of a silly little storm. She wanted that to be true, so she was fairly sure it wasn't. And two: the great men of the lodge and the great men of the Western empire had given their blessing to this stupid plan, blinded by Oida's fiery glow or just too thick to see it wouldn't work. Now *that*—

"Hello, you." She looked up. She hadn't seen him since the storm. He'd brought her a plate of scrambled eggs. She realised she was quite hungry.

"Can't face anything myself," he said, sitting cross-legged on the deck beside her. "God, I hate the sea."

She laughed. "I don't think it likes you terribly much." He handed her a little wooden spoon. The man who thinks of everything. "Can I ask you something?"

"Of course."

She prodded at the eggs with the spoon. "When were you last in the East?"

"Let me think." He thought. "I came straight on from Belroch to Beloisa."

She looked at him. "You just strolled through the front line like nothing was happening?"

"Good God, no. I had a safe passage. Not that I needed it, because the country all round there was pretty much deserted."

"But you had a bit of paper, if you'd needed it."

"Well, yes. Not a problem. Why do you ask?"

She smiled. "What's it like in the East?"

He took a moment to reply. "Different," he said, "but more or less the same. They have women priests there, for one thing. And grace comes at the end of the meal, not the beginning. And they celebrate Ascension on the three-quarter moon, not the full, and the jam is poured over your pancakes, not served separately in a little dish. And if two people are shown to have conspired to kill someone but you can't prove which of them actually struck the fatal blow, they're both acquitted of murder but convicted of attempt, but they're both hanged just the same anyway; and they can try you up to three times for same crime, which I can't say I approve of. On the other hand, a son can't be forced to testify against his mother, and vice versa, which is quite civilised. Oh, and the country people use tanned bulls' scrotums for putting their money in, and in town they carry their small change in their mouths, which is pretty startling the first time you buy something from a street trader. You lift your head up for yes, and nod down for no, it's quite important to remember that. Summer solstice used to be a big festival where all the servants and apprentices went home to their families in the country and they used to burn a straw lion at sunrise and give each other presents, but that's terribly old-fashioned now. And only prostitutes carry handkerchiefs stuffed up their sleeves. That's the same in Blemya, by the way, which is why you kept getting all those funny looks." He shrugged. "That sort of thing, anyway. Otherwise, they're more or less like the West. About what you'd expect; five hundred years as all one big happy family, then ninety years apart hating each other to death. Why the sudden interest? Thinking of going there?"

"Just interested," she said. "As in, if they're really not all that different from us, what are we slaughtering each other for?"

He sighed. "Honour," he said. "Moral imperatives, to defend our country and our way of life. Money, of course, and eternal glory, and to defend our trading interests. Because we're right and they're wrong. Because evil must be resisted, and sooner or later there comes a time when men of principle have to make a stand. Because war is good for business and it's better to die on our feet than live on our knees. Because the fire god is on our side, and it's our duty to Him. Because they started it. But at this stage in the proceedings," he added, with a slightly lopsided grin, "mostly from force of habit."

4

Virtue

From behind the gilded screen he watched the throne come down, then gathered up his papers and put them in order. She joined him a moment later.

"I *hate* that thing," she said. "It's worse than camels."

"People will hear you," he said with a grin.

"Oh, people." She scowled at him. "Let's go and make pancakes, I'm starving. Oh *please*," she added, in that voice.

"No," he said. "You've got appeals to hear."

She sighed, and slouched after him down the corridor like a sad dog. "You didn't use the throne when the Westerners were here," he said.

"I couldn't face it. All those diplomats *and* the throne. Have mercy."

The Great Throne of Blemya and the Golden Birds had been a gift to the founder of the dynasty from some outlandish place far away where they were probably rather too clever for their own good. Unlike the Birds, the throne still worked. As the suppliant entered the Great Hall through the North door, he was astounded to see the throne, three tons of marble, porphyry, ivory and gold, rise slowly and steadily into the air, so that by the time he reached the braided red velvet rope that marked the limit of how far he could go, the throne and its occupant was ten feet off the ground. Up there—some clever trick of the acoustics—the Royal voice took on a booming quality and reverberated off the walls, giving the visitor the impression that he was being spoken to from all sides at once. He, of course, had to raise his voice so as to be audible at a distance without committing the unforgivable faux pas of shouting.

The works were down in the cellars, where a huge cistern of water powered a thing called a hydraulic ram. Water was laboriously pumped up into the cistern from the big rainwater tank; when the chamberlain's people gave the signal, someone opened a tap and water flowed down a horrendously complicated system of pipes; in one of the pipes was a thing called a piston, which was linked by camshafts and crankshafts and God knew what else to a girder riveted on to the back of the throne; the weight of the water coming down made the piston ride up in its pipe, taking the throne with it. When the audience was over and the duly astounded visitor had been led away, someone turned another tap, the water drained back into the tank and the throne gradually descended; except when it got stuck, in which case the only means of escape for the Royal personage was down a ladder. But, of course, nobody ever saw that.

The Old Man, King Tolois, had been delighted with it and thought it was great fun; his son, Dalois I, believed it had great symbolic value and devised a number of rituals based on it, which he included in his life's work, the twelve-volume *Ceremonials of the Blemyan Court*. His sons had put up with it, cursing the inconvenience while tacitly acknowledging the value of the impression it made on foreigners and the lower classes. One of the first things the queen had said, on her accession to the throne, was, "Anyway, I'm not going up in that thing, and that's final." Since then, of course, wise men had explained, and she understood. Didn't mean she liked it.

"Have I got to hear appeals?" She sounded like a little girl.

"Yes."

"Damn." The hem of the *divitision*, massive with gold braid and gold thread, pearls and lapis lazuli studs, made a sort of rasping noise as it trailed along the flagstones. Tolois had been a tall man. "How long till?"

He grinned at her. "You might get some lunch," he said, "or you might not."

She groaned, and gave the *divitision* a mighty hitch, making it skip like a breaking wave. "And I hate this stupid thing, too. Why can't I just wear a *frock*?"

They walked through the South cloister, the best short cut from the Great Hall to the Council Chamber. Access to it was forbidden to everybody except the queen, the Lord Privy Seal, the Count of the Stables, the Grand Logothete and a little bald man who swept it once a month; no courtiers, servants, equerries, no guards, even. The Count and Privy Seal were only allowed in by express invitation. It was his favourite place in the world.

She said, "After I've done the appeals, can we play chess?"

He shook his head. "Afternoon council, then state dinner, and then you've got a mountain of things to read and sign. Sorry."

She sighed. They'd reached the end of the cloister. A thin shaft of light from a high slit window pooled at their feet. "See you tomorrow, then."

"Mind you read the brief from the Navy treasury committee," he said. "You've got to make a decision on that tomorrow."

She pulled a sad face. "Can't you do it?"

"I've done you a two-page summary," he said, "but you *must* read the full brief. Got that?"

"Bully."

"You've got to make these decisions yourself," he said gravely. "We talked about it, remember?"

"All right." She was drooping, the wilted-flower pose. Then

she did that shrug of the shoulders, settling the *lorus*, dalmatic and lesser *chlamys* back into position, like a carthorse applying its strength to the collar; everything was back in place, her back was straight and her head was high. "But there'd better be almond biscuits when I get back, or someone's going to be in real trouble. Got that?"

"Your Majesty."

He opened the door for her and she gave him a regal nod, then stuck her tongue out at the last moment, before the last three inches of the *divitision* flicked over the threshold and she was gone. He closed the door almost reverently, then hurried back down the cloister to the Great Hall, which was empty apart from a few domestic staff, dusting and polishing. Two of them, allies from the old days, smiled at him as he passed and he grinned back.

Too much to do, far too little time to do it in: job description of the Grand Logothete of the Kingdom of Blemya. Actually, neither of them knew what a logothete was; she'd seen the word in a book, years ago, and it had stuck in her mind, and when (the afternoon of the king's funeral) she'd turned to him in the one quiet moment they'd had together and whispered, "You will help me, won't you? I can't do this on my own," he'd tried to say no and it had come out as "Yes, of course." "We've got to think of something to call you," she said later, after the ferocious council meeting, when she'd refused to back down. "What?" he'd asked. She'd looked at him. Chief Secretary and Grand Vizier were the only suggestions he'd been able to come up with; she'd just looked at him, and he'd nodded and said, quite. Then, out of the blue, she'd remembered Grand Logothete; and suddenly there was one, and it was him, and here he was doing it.

He glanced down at his crib sheet and his heart sank. Ordnance Committee; that was fortifications and siege engines and things, about which he knew nothing, and the committee was a bunch of fire-breathing old steelnecks who thought nobody under the age of forty-five should be allowed to speak. They scared the hell out of Daxin Paracoemenus, but the Grand Logothete was afraid of nothing. Well, then.

He waited in the little anteroom until the water clock told him he was five minutes late, then breezed in, slammed his papers down on the table, dropped into the only empty chair and said, "Gentlemen," in the loud braying voice his uncle Faras used for shouting at his bailiff. The steelnecks glowered at him, rose resentfully to their feet and bowed. "Sorry to have kept you, let's see, what have we got today?" He made a show of consulting the agenda, though he'd memorised it while he was waiting. When he was nervous in a meeting, his eyes got blurry and he couldn't read. "Procurement." He lifted his head, found the right steelneck and fixed his eyes on a spot on the wall two inches to the right of him. "General Auxin," he said. "I think you've got some explaining to do."

Which he had, of course; the old fool was behind schedule and well over budget on the refurbishment of the Bronze Gate, and even Daxin knew that the Gate was the only weak spot in the Land Walls, and its present deplorable state directly jeopardised the security of the City. The steelnecks sat down, and Auxin began turning the pages of some brief or other. "No," Daxin said, "don't read me your notes; you should know this. When are you going to start work on the second phase, and how much is it going to cost?"

It was a painful meeting. By the end of it, Daxin was more or less convinced that Auxin was fiddling (after all, his brother-in-law had the masonry contract, and Auxin's eldest son had lost a lot of money at the track lately) and that the rest of the committee knew about it and were helping him cover it up. Stupid. All the stupid fiddling and cheating that went on, everywhere you looked; ridiculously rich men who still managed to find ways of desperately needing money, or who were simply greedy, or regarded wealth as the only way of keeping score in the endless social and political warfare of court life. When he'd told her about it, she'd looked at him and said, "What shall we do?" and he'd had to explain: there is no *we*, there's just you, *you've* got to decide, and she'd accused him of being deliberately unhelpful and given him that yearning look: please deal with it and make it go away, I don't want to. She understood, of course, perfectly well. But just occasionally, he knew, the desperate urge to be twenty-two and not responsible for the fate of a million people was almost too strong for her, and because she daren't tempt herself, she tempted him.

So he'd thought about it, and decided that since the rules were no help, and she couldn't break the rules, it was up to him, on his own. And then, while he was trying to figure out a plan of action, he'd met that unbelievably helpful and sympathetic man Oida, the musician—

After the Ordnance, he had the Bank governors, followed by a delegation from the mine owners, followed by an unspeakably annoying man from the lodge gabbling away about the preferments list; and now, just to round it all off, the High Priest and some professor from the Royal Academy of Music were demanding to see him about an urgent matter of national security. One of those days. By now, of course, he was running late, so any hope of sneaking off to the Sun Tower and making himself a stack of pancakes had evaporated like water off a hot stove.

Actually, incredibly, he liked the High Priest. The old devil reminded him of his father; the same solemn, baleful stare and total deadpan delivery, so that there was a delay of five or so seconds before the joke exploded inside your head and made you laugh painfully through your nose; and the same reproachful glare to rebuke you for your unseemly outburst. The man was a total menace, and could cheer up an otherwise desperate day like no one else. The professor, on the other hand, was a completely unknown quantity—boring or difficult or both, and how in God's name could a music professor be an urgent matter of national security?

*

He sent her a note about it.

The notes were her idea. Officially, he could only send her formal documents—minutes of meetings, memoranda of audiences, petitions, factual summaries, all of them documents of public record which would end up in the Great Cartulary, for ever and ever, along with the foreign treaties and the pipe rolls. But formal documents were sent in a despatch case, the original case that Tolois had used at the Battle of Luxansia; and the case was pigskin lined with velvet, and there was a tear in the lining, which it would be sacrilege to mend, and you could wedge a little scrap of parchment in the tear and nobody would know.

This time the note said, *Before matins, south cloister, will bring honeycakes.* When the case came back, with countersigned orders in council and a refused petition from the Board of Works, there was a scrap cut off his scrap that read, *All right but why so early*? He grinned at that, and sent down to the kitchens.

She was in plain clothes. The cloak and hood he recognised as the property of her maid, which bothered him. By now, at least fifty interested parties around the court would know that the queen had borrowed her maid's cloak, and would be drawing conclusions like lunatics. He mentioned it.

"Do I look stupid?" she said. She was annoyed because it was so early. "I stole it from her when she wasn't looking and hid it at the bottom of the linen press. She's been searching high and low for it ever since, the silly cow."

She didn't like her maid, but was too soft-hearted to get rid of her just for that reason. He apologised. "It's just, you can't be too careful, all right?"

"I know. Anyway." She took a cake and stuck it in her mouth. "What's so important?" she mumbled through the crumbs.

He paused for a moment. "I don't know if it *is* important," he said, "or if it's just weird. I mean, it's definitely weird, but I can't see anything more to it than meets the eye, which is weirder still. I mean, it's such a lot of trouble to go to, if really it's nothing but an extravagant gesture."

"Daxin," she said, "you're talking drivel."

"Sorry."

"Well?"

He sighed. "All right," he said. "It's good for a laugh, if nothing else. This professor from the music school came to see me."

"What professor?"

"A professor. Juxia Epigennatus, if you must know. Never heard of him before."

"Nor me." She took the other cake. "So?"

"So," he said, and hesitated again. It was just so weird. "Apparently, he got hold of that musical score the Easterners brought. You know, the new Procopius."

She nodded. "I flicked through it," she said. "Not my sort of thing, really."

"Well," Daxin said, "this Juxia's done a damn sight more than flick through it. He's been working on it day and night for a week, and he—"

"Why?"

Daxin shrugged. "It's a masterpiece by one of the greatest living composers. That's what professors do. Anyway, he made a remarkable discovery. Well, a really strange one, anyhow."

She did the impatient frown. It was one of the few times she ever looked genuinely pretty. "And? Oh, come on, Dax, it's freezing out here and I've only got this stupid cape thing."

"Well," Daxin said. "Apparently one of the things you do with a piece of music if you're a professor is, you calculate the numerical values of the intervals of the main chromatic themes. Don't ask me to explain that," he added quickly, "and I could well have got the technical terms completely wrong. What it means in real life is that in every piece of formal music there's got to be certain elements, or it's cheating or it's not proper music or something like that. One of the ways you analyse these things, if you're a professor, is, you turn the music into numbers, using a universally accepted standard equivalence. All right?"

"It all sounds incredibly silly to me," she said. "But, yes, I think I see. Go on."

"The professor was doing his sums," Daxin went on, "and there was something about the patterns of the numbers that rang a bell in his head, and he couldn't think for the life of him what it was. He racked his brains for a day or so, and then, just for a laugh, he turned the numbers into letters, using the universally accepted—"

"He turned the letters into—?"

Daxin nodded. "W is one, D is two, so on and so forth. It's a craft thing. Hundreds of years old. Anyway, he did that, and guess what? The letters made words, and the words made sense."

She blinked at him. "That's weird."

"Told you so," Daxin said. "Apparently he's been through the whole thing five times, checking and rechecking, and it comes out the same thing every time. Turned into words and then into numbers, the Procopius thing is a poem."

"What?"

"A poem," Daxin said. "A fairly well-known one, by Corrhadi. One of the love sonnets. Do you know them?"

She frowned, and her nose wrinkled. "I think so," she said. "My mother made me read them. All soppy and over the top, I thought."

Daxin nodded. "That's the ones," he said. "This is the one that starts off, *If love were all, what would be left to say*. Book two, sonnet sixteen."

She was silent for about five seconds. "That's weird," she said.

Daxin grinned. "I guess so," he said. "I mean, on one level, it's the most amazing tour de force of utterly pointless cleverness. It's this really amazing piece of music that also happens to be a Corrhadi sonnet in *code*."

She shrugged. "Showing off."

"Indeed. Except, why the hell bother? Why make life so incredibly difficult for yourself? And why a Corrhadi sonnet, of all things? I mean, they're one notch above the *Mirror of True Love,* but that's about all you can say for them."

"Weird," she said. "All right, but how exactly is this a threat to national security?"

Daxin looked round. Unnecessary, since they were in the South cloister, but even so. "I have absolutely no idea," he said. "As far as I can see, it's just very, very strange. But I can't help thinking. After all, Procopius is sort of in their government, or at least he's what you'd call an establishment figure. What if this isn't just some smartarse showing off? What if it's, I don't know, a coded message or something?"

"A coded love sonnet."

"Well, yes. But if the Eastern government's behind it somehow—" He made a vague despairing gesture. "They come here," he said. "They hand over this bizarre thing. The same night a member of the cabinet is murdered by an unknown assassin. It's got to mean *something*. Well, hasn't it?"

She looked at him. "Oh, come *on,*" she said.

He pulled a sad face. "I've sent Professor Juxia away," he said, "and told him to make the same analysis of all Procopius' major orchestral works, see if they're all like it."

"Dax! You didn't."

"Serves him right," Daxin replied. "Also, I got the impression he'd have done it anyway. No, listen. If Procopius makes a habit of encoding third-rate romantic slush in all his compositions, then there's no special significance and nothing to bother about. If not—" No good. He knew that look.

"It's all right," she said. "I hereby pardon you for dragging me out of bed at this ridiculous hour of the morning. The thought of that poor man doing all those idiotic *sums*—"

He lowered his voice. That always made her listen. "You need to take it seriously," he said. "Right now, we've got to take everything seriously. Come on, you know what a horrible bloody mess we're in."

She gave him a cold look. "I had sort of gathered, yes."

"I'm sorry. Of course you know. It's just—" He ran out of words. He was twenty-three years old, chief executive of a big, rich country hours away from civil war, and he simply hadn't a clue. "I'm sorry," he said. "But Iaxas is taking it seriously, so I thought—"

She nodded. "It's just so weird," she said. "We'll see what your professor finds out, and then we'll know."

He felt the tension drain out of him. "You'd better get back before you're missed," he said.

"You make it sound like—" She stopped and frowned. "Yes, right," she said. "Now I've got to go and put on all that horrible junk. It's not fair. I look like a woodlouse. Why can't I wear nice clothes, just once in a while?"

One of the steelnecks, General Rixotal, had put it best. In an unguarded moment, among friends, he was reported as having said, "You know what's wrong with this country? It's being run by bloody *children*."

Daxin couldn't agree more. It struck him as ludicrous; almost as ridiculous as taking the second son of a minor nobleman, who'd picked up his education the same way a dog picks up scraps at table, and making him Grand Logothete of Blemya, simply because he'd played Rattlesnakes with the queen when they were kids. The truly awful thing was that he was a good Logothete, a brilliant one, born to it, a natural. He could guess why. Years of being careful, keeping his eyes and ears open, learning quickly, having to keep the peace between Father and his brother, doing and getting things for himself because nobody else was going to; it had been the perfect training. Mostly, he could understand people. If you could do that, the rest of it was just keeping calm and paying attention to detail.

"As far as we can tell," the colonel said, "he must've climbed the wall, come in here, through the window, done it, stuck the guard and made off down the corridor. That's what all the evidence tells us. It just doesn't make sense, that's all."

Daxin peered down at the brown-stained sheets. No sense at all. An assassin, skilful enough to climb the outer wall of the north elevation, cool enough to kill a man and not wake the woman sleeping next to him, instead of simply turning round and going back the way he'd come, took the huge and unnecessary risk of killing a guard and wandering off down a corridor, with half the palace to walk through before he could get out again. But the killer had definitely come in through the window; there had been the clear prints of toes and heels in the grime on the ledge outside, and traces of that grime on the sheepskin rug, which surely ruled out the possibility that he'd come from inside the palace. An inside killer would've had a much easier job, given that he was committed to killing the guard anyway. Clearly a man who knew what he was doing. The colonel was still baffled by the fact that he'd managed to open the door and come out into the corridor without the guard yelling and raising the alarm. You'd have to be so quick and so quiet. The only men the colonel knew of who were that good were the Eastern emperor's Pasgite bodyguards—tiny wild men from the far north, trained to kill from childhood, so strange-looking and alien it was a moot point whether they were genuinely human. That (the colonel said) tied in rather neatly with the size of the footprints; also, the Pasgites always went barefoot.

He took one last look round, then thanked the colonel and went to meet the Emergencies Commission. No further leads, he reported. All we can say for certain is that the clues we've found have yielded no definite information whatsoever about who the killer was, what country or party or organisation. It was possible that the assassin was a Pasgite, or a child, but even if that was true, all it implied was that the killer was a hired assassin, which was more or less certain anyway.

"We've got the City more or less locked down," the prefect said. "Two battalions of Life Guards on the streets, a big presence on all the gates, random stop and search, keeping the pressure up generally. General Ixion's brought down four regiments of marines and all the south-eastern cavalry and stationed them in a ring round the suburbs. It's working for now, there haven't been any more riots or anything like that. And he's pretty confident about the men themselves. They'll do what he tells them."

Daxin nodded. Ixion was a good man, for a steelneck, and the soldiers liked him. The trouble was, he was seventy-three years old and desperate to retire. "Outside the City," he said.

The Chief Commissioner pulled a sad face. "Not so good," he said. "Because Ixion's pulled so many troops out to secure the City, we've got trouble in the South and the West. Mostly quite peaceful, people out on the streets shouting and waving banners, but no real trouble so far. I guess it's because it's all so vague and mysterious, and nobody actually knows anything at all. It's hard to work up a really good head of righteous indignation when you've got a sneaking suspicion in the back of your mind that it might just have been your side that did it."

Daxin thought for a moment. "I think we can probably slacken off gently in the City," he said. "Nice and gradually, so people get the impression that things are easing up, but we can still come down like a ton of bricks if we have to. If we keep it too tight for too long, it's more or less inevitable that something'll strike sparks, and then we'll be in real trouble. I'm not too worried about out of town. Country people have got too much to do at this time of year, and I gather the miners have stayed pretty quiet."

"So far," said the Deputy Chief. "They never liked him anyway."

"Small blessings," Daxin said. "What about the lodges? They've been remarkably relaxed about the whole thing."

"I'm guessing they've come to the conclusion there's nothing in it for them," the Chief Commissioner said. "Either that or they're playing a very long game. I confess, I don't like it when they're quiet."

News from the war. The Belot brothers had fought a battle, a big one. It had come as a shock to the governments of both sides, who hadn't really known what they were up to; both brothers were experts at moving quietly and very fast. They'd fought to a standstill for the best part of a day just outside the oasis city of Rumadon, on the border, only thirty miles or so south of the Blemyan frontier. Early reports said casualties were in the tens of thousands on each side, and that afterwards both armies had pulled back and gone away, and nobody was entirely sure where they were now.

"The priestess," the Count of the Stables said, as they walked together into the Lesser Hall for dinner. "Did you notice her?"

"Hard not to," Daxin said. "Bright red dress."

"I thought they didn't ordain women in the West."

"They don't." Taxin stopped to let a server go past with a big tray of fresh bread. "Priestesses are different. They stand up in Temple and chant things, but they don't actually *do* anything. Like, they can't hear confessions or confirm you or anything like that."

The Count sighed. "It's confusing," he said.

"We used to have them here," broke in the Urban Tribune, who was behind them in the procession. "But they sort of died out about fifty years ago, when we introduced women deacons. They don't have women deacons in the West," he added. "All a bit primitive, if you ask me."

Later, when they were sitting down, the Count said, "I looked it up."

"Looked up what?" Daxin said, with his mouth full.

"Priestesses," the Count said. "In relation to foreign embassies. I read through all the relevant stuff in Porphyrion's *Offices*. Nothing at all in Imperial protocol says you've got to have a priestess on an embassy. They made that up."

Daxin frowned. "But that's pre-war, surely," he said. "How it was under the united empire, in the old days. Presumably the West's got its own protocols now. They like to invent new stuff to show they're grander than the East."

The Count shrugged. "That's probably it, then. I just thought it was funny, that's all. Considering how anti-women they are in most things."

Look who's talking, Daxin thought. "It's like conjurors do," he said. "Fetch on a girl in a red dress; at the crucial moment everyone's gawping at her, so they don't see you pull the Six of Thrones out of your sleeve."

"That's an interesting remark," the Count said, frowning. "So you think the Westerners did it?"

"The murder?" Daxin shook his head. "I don't think anything of the sort."

"Come on," said the Count. "You say they had the priestess along as a distraction, but on the surface, so to speak, they didn't actually *do* anything. Just handed over the music book and left. No distraction needed," he added, "on the surface. So, if there was a distraction, it must've been to keep us from noticing something we didn't actually see. Like the murder."

Daxin sighed. "You're putting words in my mouth," he said. "All I did was, I suggested that may be the reason why, as a matter of standard operating procedure, they routinely take women in red dresses along on embassies. On this specific occasion—"

"Pass the mustard, would you?"

Daxin reached across and grabbed the little silver pot. "Anyway," he said, "we know exactly what function the priestess was serving: she was there to keep the Illustrious Oida from browsing the local wildlife. Given his reputation, I should say it was a very sensible precaution, though if you ask me it's like inviting someone to lunch and he brings his own food. If you've finished with that—"

The Count nodded. He took back the mustard and spooned a little dab on to the side of his plate. The Count said, "What did you make of him?"

"Oida? As it happens, I know him from way back. He's one of those people who's actually a lot less objectionable than he likes to make out."

"Not sure I follow you," the Count said, "but never mind. You do know he's a distant cousin of Herself."

Daxin didn't know that. "Really?"

"Oh yes." The Count was mopping up gravy with a corner of bread. "Once removed or is it twice? Not sure. On his mother's side. Strictly speaking, he counts as a Royal. The chamberlain's office had a fit when they found out, because by then, of course, it was too late, the wretched man was already here, and there's all these protocols that should've been observed but weren't. Fortunately, nobody knew, so—"

"Oida's a member of the Royal family."

"That's right," the Count said, "and as you know, there's not a hell of a lot of them left, what with them slaughtering each other like sheep for the last hundred and fifty years. I seem to remember some clerk telling me that, theoretically, he's something like tenth in line to the throne."

Daxin frowned. "You said he was a second cousin or something."

"Yes, but that's beside the point. Strictly speaking—"

"So if ten people die, Oida becomes king."

The Count laughed. "Can you really see that happening?" He ate a last chickpea and pushed away his plate. "Besides, you know the man, you said. He seems all right. We could do worse."

At least he's a man, he meant. "The country wouldn't stand for it," Daxin said.

"Of course not," the Count agreed. "What's for afters?"

The senior librarian from the College of Heralds was typically efficient. Come back in two hours, he'd said, and he was as good as his word. When Daxin returned, he was presented with a proper formal family tree, complete with sources and brief biographical notes, where relevant. It was a huge document; there wasn't a table big enough, so they had to spread it out on the floor.

"No, it's all right, I can manage just fine," Daxin said quickly, as the old man began the slow and arduous process of kneeling down beside him. "I know how to read these things."

A bit of an overstatement, but he was able to get the general idea. Sure enough, Oida (Gennaeus Fraxiles Eurymedon Oida Mazentinus, in full Imperial nomenclature) was there up away in the middle of the right-hand margin. He was in blue, meaning he was still alive. Nearly all the names on the parchment were red, for dead. To his surprise, he also saw himself—Gennaeus Deas Eurymedon Daxin Epignatho—far out on the left-hand outskirts, in black, meaning correlative, or too remote to be family within the meaning of the relevant statutes.

He stood up. "Could you do me a favour," he said, "and write in who's what in line to the throne? I'm not quite clear just from looking at it—"

The librarian gave him a look. "We're not supposed to do that," he said. "Technically, in fact, it's treason."

"Is it? Good heavens. Oh well, don't, then; sorry I asked. Is it treason if you just tell me?"

"That would be something of a grey area."

"Tell me very quietly."

He didn't have a chance to talk to her for three days, which was infuriating. When finally they were alone in the South cloister and he'd blurted out his discovery, she looked at him and said, "Yes, I know."

It took him a second to recover. "You didn't tell me."

"I assumed you—Oh, well, it doesn't matter particularly, does it? I've got twelve cousins, as it happens. I don't *know* any of them. I mean, we don't send each other cakes at Ascension or anything. I bet you've got hundreds of cousins, and you couldn't name half of them."

Perfectly true. "Yes, but Oida," he said, and paused.

"What about him?"

"I met him," Daxin said, "about three years ago, just after the coronation. He was here with the Easterners. I can't remember how we got talking, but—well, it seemed perfectly natural at the time, he was interested and sympathetic and very well informed, and you know what we were like back then, didn't know what day of the week it was. I thought he was just being nice, and, anyway, he's supposed to be neutral and above it all, isn't he?"

She was frowning. "What did you tell him?"

"Oh, nothing he didn't know already, or at least he seemed like he knew it all, I really can't be sure. It's more what he told me."

"Sorry?"

"Everything, basically," Daxin said. "Sort of, a complete beginner's guide to politics. Really opened my eyes. Scared the life out of me. Suddenly I realised just how dangerous our position is, how many people are out to get us, all that sort of thing. We sat up all night in the New Gallery, and he more or less explained to me how things stood, what we had to look out for, the sort of problems we'd have to face, what we ought to do about them. Incredibly helpful. I don't think we'd still be alive today if it hadn't been for him. To be honest, everything I've done this last three years has been based on what he told me."

She was gazing at him. "You never said."

"No," he said, "I didn't. At the time I thought he was just this really clever, helpful man who felt sorry for us and wished us well. And he had nothing to gain that I could see. He was just—"

"Being helpful. Well," she said, "maybe he was." She paused for a moment. "He didn't say he and I are related?"

"No, didn't mention it."

"Maybe he thought you knew."

Well, he thought, with a sense of anticlimax, that would explain it. He felt stupid for not having thought of that. "Bit of an assumption, surely."

"Not really. Maybe he wanted to help us—help me—because we're family. And anyway," she went on, "I don't see what difference it makes to anything. I mean, it's not like there's anything *sinister.* The worst you could read into it is, he wanted to make his number with us in case he ever needs anything from us—money, a safe place to go, something like that." She grinned at him. "It's not like he's deviously and maliciously *become* my cousin, as part of some vast dark conspiracy."

Bad news. It came as a complete surprise. Daxin, whose entire strategy for coping was built around having plenty of notice of everything, realised he had no idea what to do. He felt as though it was all his fault, which was ridiculous.

The Mavida were a loose confederation of nomadic tribes, living in the vast desert to the south of Blemya. Part of their territory was nominally Imperial land, both East and West; in practice, they roamed at will over an inconceivably large area of sand, mountain and scrub that nobody else had any possible use for whatsoever. They had sheep, or goats, or something of the sort, and traded fleeces at the outpost cities for a range of commodities, mostly flour and weapons. It was vaguely known that, from time to time, they were prone to intense bouts of religious fervour, usually coinciding with the appearance of a self-proclaimed messiah. They were pagans, worshipping the sun as a god. Nobody knew exactly how many of them there were. They were no bother to anyone.

The reports were incomplete and unhelpful, drawn from refugees and the very few survivors, and it took a while to piece them together into a coherent narrative. What seemed to have happened was that the latest messiah, who went by the name of Goiauz, had taken it into his head to be mortally offended by the fact that the Belot brothers had chosen to fight their appalling waste-of-time battle on the edge of Mavida land; specifically, after the battle one side or other (unknown which) had disposed of some of the dead bodies by dropping them down a well, which by unlucky chance had tremendous spiritual significance to the Mavida sect to which Goiauz belonged. Prompted by Goiauz, who was said to have been speechless with rage for an entire day, the Mavida elders had cried out for vengeance; unfortunately, since both Imperial armies were long gone and the few Imperial outposts had been either stormed or evacuated during the Belots' campaign, there was nobody left to be revenged on. By now, however, Goiauz had built up such a head of steam among the tribes that something had to be done, if only to keep them from turning on each other. He therefore launched a surprise attack on the nearest walled city, the southern Blemyan regional capital, Seusa.

The Seusans knew the Mavida as peaceful traders, and were aware that the Imperials had been fighting recently in their territory. When they saw a large nomad caravan approaching the city, therefore, they assumed it was refugees, hastily got together all the food, tents and blankets they could spare and opened the gates to them. A few hundred Seusans survived by hiding in water cisterns and crawling out along an aqueduct; the rest were massacred in the space of a few hours.

By chance, just possibly something to do with the antics of the Imperials, General Raxilo and the Fifth Army were conducting manoeuvres fifty miles north of Seusa. The army, eight thousand regular infantry and two thousand tribal cavalry, marched day and night and caught up with the retreating raiders just before they crossed through the Split Hoof Pass. Slipping past them under cover of darkness, they took up a strong position in the pass itself. The intelligence they'd received suggested that the Mavida might number something in the region of three thousand combatants. The intelligence was wrong, by at least a factor of ten. The ensuing battle was very short. Afterwards, Goiauz sent four prisoners, with General Raxilo's head preserved in a jar of wild honey, to inform the queen that a state of war now existed between the Mavida and the Kingdom of Blemya. He added that the forces deployed at Seusa represented only a tiny fraction of the manpower at his disposal, all of whom would be honoured to fight to the death to avenge the defiling of the holy well. Tell your queen we are coming, he said. Tell her the sky is about to fall.

You couldn't really call it a letter. Letters are written on paper or parchment, in ink. They aren't generally inscribed in the wax seal of a jar of ginger preserved in syrup. Of course, a subject, even a Grand Logothete, never writes personal letters to a queen.

> *It's bitter cold,* he wrote, *which is stupid, because it's also unbearably hot. I mean unbearable. Hours at a time, you sit there thinking, I just can't deal with this any more, I want it to stop now, please. Yes, I'm whining. And, yes, I've got it really, really easy, because I'm lolling about in a covered chaise fanning myself with a great big fan, I think it actually did come from a tart's boudoir, it's all pink feathers and tastefully drawn erotica, which is an enormous joke for the men. They're the ones who are really suffering, because we're*

marching in full armour, day and night. They have to sleep in full kit because we have no idea when the bastards are going to attack. They haven't yet, but we can't take the risk. And then, at night, it's absolutely freezing, and no wood or anything for a fire, just a few blankets. We have about a hundred thousand gallons of water in oak barrels on pack horses, but the ration for the men is two pints a day; I really want to stick to the same as they're getting, but sometimes I just give in and beg for more water, which of course they give me; and you know what, they brought ice. Yes, really, ice, just for me, in a huge insulated packing case. I was so angry when I found out, I made them smash it all up and distribute it to the men—well, there wasn't nearly enough, there's forty thousand of them, but everyone in C company, first battalion Life Guards got a tiny little splinter. Now I really, really wish I hadn't done that. Ice, for crying out loud. I'd sell my soul for a fistful of ice, round about noon. Now, of course, I'd sell my soul for an extra blanket. I'm pathetic, aren't I?

Still, I'm glad I came. Let me qualify that. I really, really hate myself for being so stupid, I shouldn't have come, I have no place here, I'm an intolerable nuisance they really could do without and I'm suffering more than I thought humanly possible. But I promise you, if you aren't here, if you aren't going through all this hell, there's no way in a million years you'd ever begin to understand. Not that me understanding matters a damn, of course. But—amazing, and I can't understand it at all—I'm doing good being here. Honestly, these people are amazing—amazingly brave, amazingly strong and enduring and uncomplaining, amazingly cheerful. And they really do appreciate me being here—the Grand bloody Logothete, out in the desert with them, leading them. I'm doing no such thing, of course, I'm being carried in a covered chair. I'm—well—luggage. It's the idea of it that matters. It's always the idea—like you on the stupid throne, ten feet up in the air, like all those bloody stupid ceremonies and rituals, they make the idea, and the idea matters, it genuinely matters and makes a difference. These men are here, suffering all this, because of the idea—of Blemya, of a gold and ivory queen on a gold and ivory throne ten feet up, glorious, wonderful, divine. They love you so much. Honestly, they do. It's such an easy thing to say, the men love you so much they're willing to die for you, for you and Blemya. But, so help me, it's actually really true. Because of the idea. Because the idea is so much more real to them than the heat and the sweat and the thirst and the pain, and don't get me started on scorpions. Those things are just temporary, commonplace. Blink, and you miss them. One man in an army this size is so small you can't see him. But the idea is vast, eternal, hugely eternally true. I understand that now, like I never could back home. You and I, doing it every day, mistake it for a lie and a sham. You have to see it from a distance, like the frescoes on the ceiling of the White temple. Seen from a long way away, from here, you suddenly realise it's all true.

No space left. Look after yourself. Back as soon as I can. Dax.

He put the nail away carefully in the hole in the little folding table, so that only the head was visible. Then he replaced the cloth cover on the jar and bound it as tightly as he could with the original hemp string. It wasn't perfect. The string was too short to get a firm grip on, and tying the knot was incredibly fiddly. He did the best he could.

He opened the tent flap and called for a messenger. There was always one on duty, day or night, ready to saddle up and ride. He handed him six brass rolls of official despatches, a silver roll for the Council, two gilded rolls for the lodge. Then, as the messenger was about to leave, he called him back. "Do me a favour," he said. "This jar. It's just ginger in syrup, but I happen to know it's the queen's favourite. Mind you give it to her senior lady-in-waiting, tell her it's got to be tasted before it goes through to Her Majesty. You got that? Splendid, thank you."

He sprawled on the camp bed and tried to sleep, but he was freezing cold and his clothes were still wringing wet with the day's sweat. He lay on his back and tried to think of something useful, but no luck.

He was therefore wide awake an hour before first light, when some gorgeous creature in a gilded breastplate and helmet twitched back the tent flap and said that, if it wouldn't be too much trouble, the general would be grateful for a moment of his time. Oh God, Daxin thought; he stuffed his feet in his sopping wet shoes and stumbled awkwardly out of the tent into the pale blue darkness.

It was the only time of day when it was neither freezing nor roasting; the only time when anybody's brain worked worth a damn. The general was sitting outside his tent, in an old tunic with a faded regulation cloak over his shoulders. There were a dozen gilded men standing round him. There was also the usual folding table, covered in maps weighted down with stones and small glass bottles.

The general waited until the man who'd summoned Daxin had gone. Then he waved his hand, and one of the gilded men unfolded a chair. Daxin sat on it.

"Nobody here but us grown-ups," said General Ixion. Daxin liked him. He didn't look like a general, although he had a reputation as a diehard steelneck. But he was long and thin, bald, with a huge forehead; long, thin fingers, weedy clerk's forearms. You'd have said he was a book-keeper or at best an academic. He was notoriously short-sighted, and deaf in one ear. "I thought we could talk about a few things."

Daxin nodded. "Whatever you like," he said.

"Don't mind them," Ixion said, nodding at the gilded men. "My personal staff. You can pretend they aren't there. Obviously they're totally discreet, or we wouldn't be having this conversation. Would you like some breakfast, while you're here?"

Breakfast ration was a fist-sized chunk of munitions bread and a small cup of water. "Bit early for me."

"You sure? We're having pancakes and peach tea."

"That'd be lovely, thank you."

Ixion nodded, and one of the gilded men sort of melted away into the night. "Now then," he said. "Excuse me speaking frankly, but we've only got half an hour before it gets hot and my brains boil. Why are you here?"

Speaking frankly. Oh well. "I thought I ought to be here."

"Really? Why?"

"To see what war's really like," Daxin said, "and because the queen can't lead her men into battle, but I believe it's good for morale to have some sort of figurehead—"

"Yes," the general interrupted, "it is. The boys like it. They like it that you're mucking in, more or less. They know I don't do that stuff, but that's all right because they know and trust me. They say, Ixion likes his partridge soup and roast quail with onions, he needs to keep his strength up for all the thinking he does." He grinned. "If I mucked in and ate bread and water, they'd reckon I was no good. Do you understand that?"

"I think so."

"Good. You're smart. Now then, we're here." He placed a delicate fingertip on the map, in the middle of what looked like blank space. "The main Imperial road is here, of course." A pale red line. "Needless to say, we can't use it, because that's where they expect us to come from. So we're cutting down across the flat here, with a view to getting between them and the water at—" the fingertip moved to a tiny blue spot "—here, quite a major oasis. No name on the map but the locals call it Long Side. We don't actually know where the enemy is, out here somewhere, but as far as we can tell they've gambled on getting to the water before we do. That's what it's all about out here, getting to water. You have a certain amount of time to reach a certain place, or you're dead. Interesting rules to play by, I must say."

He paused for breath. Daxin thought about the huge oak barrels on the heavy carts. Lots of water, but not nearly enough. "How about us?" he said. "Are we gambling?"

"Of course," Ixion said. "But we have an advantage. They don't think very highly of us. They think we move more slowly than we actually do, and they think we don't know the desert. Which we don't, but, thank God, we can read books, and we can bully prisoners. They therefore believe that by the time we reach Long Side, trundling slowly down the road, they'll be there waiting for us, and we'll have to attack their prepared positions or else die of thirst. So, my idea is, we get there first, we prepare positions, they have to attack us or die of thirst. It's horribly simple, but it was all I could think of. Well?" he said. "What do you think?"

Daxin was mildly stunned. "You want my opinion?"

Ixion nodded. "You're a clever man," he said. "I've been watching you, the way you run things, the way you manage people. The fact you're here shows you're smart but also fairly—" He smiled. "I was going to say green or inexperienced, but I think the word I'm looking for is *young*. Anyway, if I'm to call the whole thing off and march back to Carna, I want to be able to say I was only obeying orders."

Daxin thought for a moment. "This is the point of no return, I take it," he said. "If we go any further, we won't have enough water to get back."

Ixion beamed at him. "I have to say," he said, "it's the safe thing to do. It's what I want to do. But I'm not going to do it unless someone orders me to, because *if* we can get to Long Side before they do and *if* we can kick the shit out of them there, we might just win this war and save Blemya. If we don't, I don't see how we're going to beat them."

"But I thought," Daxin said, "we don't know very much about them. So how do we know they're going to beat us?"

Ixion looked at one of his gilded men, who nodded. "We know enough for that," he said, "simply from what we got out of the survivors." He swallowed a long drink from his tea bowl. "Essentially, they fight like our own cavalry do—in quick, shoot fast and often, out again like lightning. Our boys who made it out of the battle say that their arrows went through sixteen-gauge steel like it wasn't there. You've never seen our cavalry in action so you wouldn't know, but, trust me, the thought of being on the wrong side of them's enough to scare me rigid. By the sound of it, these people are like them, but better. You know how Tolois beat the Imperials, back in the War of Independence? Cavalry. Cavalry just like these people, and the Imperial regulars couldn't do a damn thing about them; they just got shot up and died where they stood. Since then we haven't evolved a strategy against swarm tactics by mounted archers, why should we, we thought we had the monopoly. Turns out that's not the case. The same thing that's made us invincible makes them invincible too. Also," he added, lowering his voice, "you've got to ask yourself. Our tribal cavalry are marvellous soldiers, fight like lions, don't know the meaning of fear, and their officers are good men; I've served with them for thirty years, it never occurs to me to think of them as *different* any more. But the plain fact is, they've got a hell of a lot more in common with these savages than they have with us. If we start losing battles, if they take another city or two—well, you don't need me to draw you a picture. No, we need to beat them now, before it all goes any further. And not just beat them, wipe them out. Make sure only a tiny few ever get home to tell the tale. See, once they get the idea that the Kingdom's not unbeatable—" He shrugged. "It's all smoke and mirrors, isn't it? The whole business."

Daxin made himself take his time before answering. "I think we should turn back," he said.

Ixion's face didn't change. "I see. Why's that?"

Daxin said: "I think we'll get to the oasis and find they're already there. If it's that important, and they're anything like our tribes, they'll be there. I'm not a soldier, I don't know anything about tactics or the art of war or anything like that, and I can count how many tribesmen I've met in my life on the fingers of one hand. But I've met a few, and I've talked to them, and I've read a bit of history, and you say these invaders are like them only more so. If that's the case, they'll be at the oasis right now." He shrugged. "That's my opinion. You're the soldier. It's entirely up to you."

Ixion leaned back in his chair. "That's not a direct order, then."

"No," Daxin said.

"Pity." Ixion swilled the dregs round in his cup. "For what it's worth, I think you're wrong. I've got scouts out deep, they've got right up close to the oasis, and there's no sign of them, no dust clouds, no tracks, nothing. A caravan that size is going to throw up a dust cloud you can see for miles."

"Not at night," Daxin said quietly.

"Can't find your way in the desert at night," Ixion said crisply. "Can't be done. If it could be done, we'd be doing it."

Daxin nodded slowly. "If I wanted to win a really important battle," he said, "I think I'd try and find a way of doing something that couldn't be done. It'd give me an advantage."

"Some things really are impossible," Ixion said. "Like navigating the desert at night." He waved his hand, and someone took away the breakfast tray.

"That's all right, then," Daxin said. He stood up. "Nothing to worry about."

"You could give me a direct order."

"There's this thing called the separation of powers," Daxin said.

"Not out here."

Daxin tapped the side of his head. "In here." He took a step back from the table. "If you really thought we were walking into a trap, you'd turn back. But you don't think that. You're just worried. I can understand that. I was born worried. Thank you for the pancakes."

They went on until just before noon. Then they turned back.

Daxin asked to see the general. The general was sorry but he was rather busy. He would be delighted to speak to the Grand Logothete just as soon as he had a moment.

Ixion devised a drill, in the event of an attack. The column was to stop and fall back, forming a massive square, twenty shields deep, round the water barrels. They practised it three times, and the men's performance was deemed satisfactory. After the third rehearsal, Daxin asked one of the gilded staff officers if the general had a moment yet. Unfortunately no.

"Only," Daxin said—the gilded man was anxious to get away, but Daxin made it clear he wasn't finished with him yet. "Only, it seems to me that all these manoeuvres to form a square are going to be pretty hard to do if we're being shot at all the time. The men have got to fall back in order, so most of them at any given time are going to be just standing there, begging to be shot at. I don't know if the general's considered that—"

The gilded man gave him a scornful look. Not a problem. There would be plenty of time, because the enemy's dust cloud would be visible for at least an hour before they arrived, and the drill only took thirty minutes. However, if the Grand Logothete wished to raise a formal query with the commander-in-chief—Daxin assured him that he had no intention of doing that, and the gilded man went away, smirking.

He was sitting up reading Anthemius on sound money when he heard the first shouts. There were just a few of them, a long way away, then silence. He wondered about them, because usually the camp was dead quiet at night. But the enemy wouldn't attack in the dark, because they were archers, and you need to be able to see in order to aim. He took a sip of water and went on reading.

More shouting, and horses neighing, and a loud thump, like something very heavy falling over. The only things that heavy in the camp were the water barrels. He jumped out of bed, crammed his feet into his shoes and drew back the tent flap.

It was pitch dark, he couldn't see a thing. But he heard a scream, like someone in pain. As he stared into it, the darkness thinned a little. He could make out movement, a lot of movement. There were men running about.

The water. It was a logical thing to spring into his mind, because the water was the most important thing. Something was happening to the water; he had no idea what it could be, and it was a guaranteed, stone-cold certainty that he couldn't do anything, except get in the way. He ran out of the tent, and someone crashed into him and knocked him down.

He wasn't frightened or angry or annoyed. He picked himself up, his head feeling a bit light and dizzy. No light; no fires, because no fuel; no lamps or torches, because of giving away their position to the enemy. He scowled at the darkness as if it was doing it on purpose. Shouting all round him now, but he couldn't make out any words. He stood still, trying to listen. It sounded like orders being given, except that orders are delivered in a certain tone of voice—loud, maybe, sometimes angry, but not *scared*. That was what was wrong. It was the sound of orders being given, but not obeyed.

A soldier ran past him, didn't stop when he called out. He could see much better now; he could see shapes as shadows, black outlines. He decided to go back to his tent and get his lamp. Someone cannoned into his back and sent him sprawling.

The man who'd hit him was down, too. He was scrambling to his feet. Daxin grabbed, and caught hold of a leg. The man tried to pull free, but he clung on. "I'm the Grand Logothete," he shouted. "What's going on?" The man punched him in the face, and he let go.

Something's badly wrong, he thought.

His head was swimming and his nose hurt very much; he cushioned it in his cupped palm and could feel warm wet, which he decided was probably blood. The way he felt reminded him of the reasons he didn't drink. His instincts were telling him to run, hide, get away, but he fought them. Run where? Hide from what? He had no idea what the problem was, so there was nothing he could do.

A man was running straight at him; silhouette moving very fast, head down, legs pumping. "Hey," he shouted, "stop. What's going on? Stop." The man stopped. Or, rather, he fell, and the way he fell was vaguely familiar. Out hunting one time with his father, and Father had shot a running hare, and it tumbled three times, cartwheels. The man didn't do that, but the resemblance was there.

He tried to find him in the dark, floundered about, tripped over something. His fingers met flat steel plates, regulation lamellar breastplate. "Are you all right?" he yelled. He was shouting at a dead man. Only the second dead body he'd ever been that close to. His fingers drew back, as if the body was infectious. His knee brushed against something, and his instincts told him it was a withy or a sapling. No saplings in the desert. He groped for it with his hand, found a thin, straight rod. Feathers at the top. Feathers.

We're being attacked, he realised. But we can't be.

Suddenly he felt very, very aware of everything. It was the feeling he'd had once or twice when he'd cut himself badly, and immediately he'd been vividly, intensely, conscious of all the things in the world that could knock against the incredibly tender wound. He could see a little bit better—moonlight, he realised, it's a full moon. Some of the moving shadows were horsemen. We're being attacked. We're *losing*.

A strand of his mind became clear. Find General Ixion's tent and go there, it's bound to be the safest place. He tried to remember where it would be, picture the layout of the camp, but his mind was a blank. He didn't even know which way he was facing, or where his own tent was.

Lie on the ground and play dead. Inside his head, it was a clear, distinct voice, as though someone a few feet away was talking to him. Not a bad idea, but he decided against it, though he wasn't quite sure why. A horse thundered past him and he jumped back out of the way. He walked backwards and collided with something. It proved to be one of the willow frames for the water barrels. Immediately, a perfectly reasoned argument appeared in his mind; the barrels are heavy-duty seasoned oak and full of water, so even if they set fire to everything, someone hiding among the barrels will be safe. Before he knew it he was on his knees and crawling.

He crawled until he felt the cold iron of a barrel hoop against his wrist. Then he curled up into a ball.

The shouting and screaming went on for a very long time. Then dead silence; then faint shouting, desperate voices, some anger. He stayed where he was. He actually fell asleep.

When he woke up, the sun was shining. He was sitting inside one of the willow frames, surrounded by barrels. He wondered what he was doing there. Then he remembered.

He craned his neck, trying to see. He saw three dead bodies, an overturned flour barrel, a pair of empty boots, a crate marked *Rivets*. No movement. The only sound he could hear was his own heart beating. He thought, they're all dead except me.

He forced himself to think. It was very hard. Possibilities: they'd survived the attack, they were all dead and he was alone, they were all dead and the enemy were trudging round the camp (dog-tired, no sleep) looking for items of value. I can't stay here for ever, he thought. But I can stay here a bit longer.

He had the most appalling cramp in his left leg; he tried to straighten it, and it was the worst pain he'd ever felt.

He lay perfectly still for a while, then gradually, bit by bit, he got the leg straight and working again, though the pain had left him weak. You clown, he thought.

Really, he decided, there were only two possibilities. If they were all dead, it didn't matter if the enemy were still out there, he was going to die anyway, from thirst or starvation or something else. Hiding in the luggage was pointless. He crawled out, tried to stand up, couldn't; used his hands to grab the frame and drag himself upright. That was as far as his resolution was going to take him. He looked round, and saw a man.

"It's a miracle," the captain babbled. "We looked everywhere. We were sure you were dead only we couldn't find a body. I can call the search off now. This is wonderful."

A very strange word to use. The camp seemed to be mostly a place where dead bodies grew, untidily, like mushrooms. The captain had just stepped over one without looking down.

"Can we slow down a bit?" Daxin said. "I'm still a little dizzy."

Which was true, although it had nothing to do with the blow on the head he'd invented to account for his absence. "Sorry, of course," the captain said, shortening his enormous stride just a little. "Only there's so much to do. Thank God you turned up when you did."

There was a dying horse just a few yards away. It lifted its head. A pile of helmets, about waist high. Two soldiers making porridge over a charcoal stove.

"We're guessing they were waiting for us in those dunes over there." The captain waved a hand at an apparently blank, level horizon. "Needless to say, we have no idea how many there were, or where they've gone. We killed three," he added, as they stepped over another dead man, "caught one, but he died before we could get anything out of him. We believe it was quite a small raiding party."

"The water." He'd asked before. It had been the first thing he asked about, when he was found. But he needed to be sure. "Did they get the water?"

"No, thank God. All the casks are undamaged, and the frames are fine; about a dozen horses ran off, but that's not a problem, we've got plenty of spares. I guess they couldn't make them out in the dark, even with this incredible night vision they seem to have."

Two soldiers lifting a dead man on to a stack of dead men. The top of the stack was rather high off the ground. They swung the body by the arms and legs, once, twice; then one soldier's hand slipped, and they dropped it.

He had to ask. "How many did they—?"

"We haven't called the roll yet," the captain said, "but at the moment our best guess is about six hundred, so it could've been a hell of a lot worse. They couldn't bring fire, you see, because of the element of surprise. And the general was always so firm about it, no fires in camp after dark—" The captain stopped suddenly, and when he started talking again his voice was a little hoarse and high. "So that turned out all right," he said. "It's fire that's always the big problem in situations like this."

That waver in the captain's voice. "Is the general all right? Nothing's happened to him, has it?"

The captain stopped as if he'd walked into a wall. "Didn't they tell you? The general's dead."

They showed him the bodies, though he couldn't see the point. General Ixion and all his gilded men, laid out neatly in the sun to dry; and at their feet, about two dozen others, too old and well dressed to be ordinary soldiers.

"It was the most appalling bad luck." A different officer, an Imperial; maybe twenty-eight years old. His left arm was in a sling, and it was too short. The hand was missing. "The general was holding a council of war just as they broke in, and of course they came up the main street here, and practically the first thing they ran into was General Ixion and the staff."

For the first time, Daxin realised why his tent was always tucked away in a side street, awkward to get to, hard to find. But the general had to be at the centre of things. It seemed rather likely that the enemy had known that.

"As a result," the officer went on, "we have no field officers over the rank of major. To be precise, we've got two supply majors, an engineer and, well, me."

Daxin looked at him. "Sorry," he said. "Who are you?"

The Imperial did the little military nod; pure reflex. Daxin guessed he couldn't say his name without doing it. "Major Prexil, Fifth Infantry. I was duty officer," he explained, "so I wasn't at the council."

"So you're in charge."

A terrified look passed over Prexil's face. "Strictly speaking," he said, "the engineer's got seniority. He's over at the ablutions, I'll send for him."

"No," Daxin said, "don't do that. You're a line officer. Surely that means you're in charge."

"Well, I suppose so, yes." Prexil waited for a second or two, then said, "What do you want me to do?"

Ridiculous question. Then Daxin had a truly horrible thought. "I'm a civilian," he said.

"With respect." Prexil sounded quite desperate. "As Grand Logothete, you're acting deputy for the queen in all matters of prerogative, surely."

Daxin had never been entirely sure what that meant, even though he'd written it himself, or, rather, copied it out of a book himself. "Prerogative," he said.

"Absolutely." Prexil sounded relieved. "And command of the

armed forces is a royal prerogative, and you're the queen's deputy. Therefore you have military standing. That's right, isn't it?"

Daxin's mouth was dry. "Theoretically."

"Thank you. I was afraid I'd got it all mixed up." Prexil paused, then repeated, "What do you want me to do?"

They were moving again, at last. Daxin was riding Ixion's horse, because the commander-in-chief can't loll about in a sedan chair; but he'd drawn the line at armour. All he could think about was the heat.

"What happened to your hand?" he said.

He hadn't been so wet since the time he rode up from the country to town in a torrential downpour, wearing nothing but a hunting tunic and a light travelling cloak. And wet from the inside out is far worse.

"Carelessness," Prexil said. "It's just instinct, isn't it? Someone lashes out at you, you raise your hand to protect your head. Of course, the first thing they teach you is, don't do that, use your feet to get out of distance. And the first time in combat, what happens? Instinct takes over. Really, I've got nobody to blame but myself."

Sweat dripped off his forehead into his eye. He pawed it away with the back of his wrist. "First time in combat."

Prexil grinned. "I'm afraid so, yes. Strictly a parade-ground soldier, I'm ashamed to say. Like my father. Forty years in the service, never saw an arrow shot in anger." He shook his head. "To be absolutely honest, I'll be glad to be out of it. I always suspected I didn't have what it takes."

Daxin stared at him. Prexil had done everything: pulled the army together, figured out what had to be done, mostly from first principles, badgered and charmed and bullied forty thousand bewildered, terrified men and got them back on the march in good order, all in the space of a few hours. "Don't be stupid," he said. "You can't quit the service. First thing when we get back, I'm making you a general."

"With respect—"

"No, I mean it. You've done an incredible job. You've single-handedly—" He stopped, horribly aware of what he'd just said. Maybe Prexil hadn't noticed. "All on your own, you've saved the army. You're obviously a natural leader."

"With respect," Prexil repeated firmly. "Let's just wait and see how many of us are alive tomorrow before we start dishing out promotions. If that's all right with you."

Not just one dust cloud. Three.

Three clouds, sort of sandy grey: one dead ahead, one behind them, one over to the right. Impossible to say how far away, so Prexil sent out scouts. He didn't know what to do. If they stepped up the pace, they'd be heading directly at the cloud in front of them. If they slowed down, the one behind would catch up. It was just possible that at least one of the clouds was a sandstorm, not an army. They'd know when the scouts got back. The scouts didn't get back. They were slow, then late, then obviously not coming. Prexil sent out more.

"Really," he said, for the fourth or fifth time, "we've got nothing to be afraid of. We're forty thousand men, for pity's sake. They're the ones who should be scared."

Every time he said it, Daxin found it harder to be comforted. There was still enough water, and the men were making good progress, twenty-five miles a day, excellent going in these conditions. Prexil had worked out impressive new protocols for sentries and what to do in the event of another night attack. They'd run drills, and the responses had been first class. In theory, the army was in optimum fighting condition. It was also so brittle with fear that one reverse, one minor calamity, would wreck everything.

That afternoon, Captain Mesajer of the auxiliary cavalry

joined them at the head of the column and rode with them for an hour. Daxin had an idea that Prexil had sent for him, though neither of them said as much. Mesajer was a short, slight man with thinning hair, somewhere in his early thirties. He wore the usual tribesman's quilted coat, long-sleeved and ankle-length. If he was sweating, it didn't show. The only thing about him that might suggest he was a soldier was the beautiful red lacquer bow case, hanging from his saddle by an elaborately knotted silk rope, with tassels. Mostly they talked about desert geography, although Mesajer came from the grassy plains, two hundred miles to the north. He came across as a quiet man, extremely intelligent, exceptionally observant; softly spoken, precise, very polite.

"Excuse me," Daxin said—they'd been talking about mirages. "I can't help noticing, you don't wear a hat."

Mesajer looked mildly amused. "Sorry," he said. "I can wear one if you like."

"But the heat—"

"Oh yes." Mesajer nodded gravely. "It's very important to keep your head covered in the hot weather."

Daxin was too overcome to contribute much to the conversation after that; Prexil asked a few questions about how the cavalry were bearing up, to which Mesajer gave positive but uninformative replies. Then he said something about duty rosters and rode back down the column.

"I don't know," Prexil said, after a long silence. "I simply don't know."

Daxin looked at him. "What?"

"Whether they'll stick with us or go over to the enemy," Prexil replied. "You never know where you are with those people. One minute you're talking about the weather or some play you both saw in town, next minute they're coming at you with butcher knives. It's so difficult to tell what they're really thinking."

Daxin found that rather disturbing, on several levels. "What makes you think they'll go over to the enemy?"

"They've got so much more in common with them than with us," Prexil replied. "And they've never really liked us much, let's face it. After all, we conquered their country."

"Hundreds of years ago."

"I don't think that matters. I think they'd turn on us in an instant if the mood took them."

"I don't," Daxin said firmly. "I'm really glad we've got them with us. As far as I can see, they're our best bet for beating off an attack."

Prexil gave him a startled look. "Ixion didn't think so," he said. "His idea was to keep them well out on the wings and away from the action. He figured that if they weren't called on to choose between us and their desert cousins, there'd be less chance of them actually defecting. They'd just sort of watch and see who won."

"Ixion said that?"

"Oh yes. And he was a great admirer of the cavalry. I mean, look at the late charge at Farnaxa."

Daxin decided not to show his ignorance. "Well," he said, "there you are. The cavalry's always fought well for the Kingdom."

"Against other enemies," Prexil said. "I mean, it's perfectly understandable. How would you feel if someone ordered you to kill your own blood relations?"

"You never knew my aunt Loxor."

That got a wan smile, which was probably all it deserved. "Seriously," Prexil said. "We do need to be very careful with these people. Trouble is, what do you do? Can't send them away or they almost certainly will defect; can't keep them close in case they stab us in the back."

"That doesn't leave many options," Daxin said. "Unless you cut their throats here and now."

"The thought had occurred to me."

Daxin looked away so that Prexil wouldn't see the shock on his face. He'd meant it. "I don't think we need go that far," he said.

"It's the practicalities more than anything," Prexil replied. "How exactly do you go about slaughtering two thousand horsemen in cold blood in the middle of the desert?"

All three dust clouds were still there as the sun set, and no scouts had returned. Prexil hadn't said anything; nor had he sent out more scouts. The soldiers moved to their night attack positions without waiting for orders. There was a general air of bewilderment, as if nobody could quite understand how it had come to this. Shortly before midnight, Prexil had a blazing row with the engineer—something technical, about fascines and enfilading fire. Daxin wanted to get between them and stop it, but they were so angry he was afraid they'd hit him for interrupting. Prexil ordered the engineer confined to his tent. The engineer refused to go. Prexil yelled for the guard, who stood and did nothing, whereupon Prexil stormed off into the darkness, leaving the engineer swearing at him at the top of his voice. Then he went back to what he'd been doing, and nobody spoke.

A watch before dawn there was a sudden commotion on the far western edge of the camp. A thousand men of the mobile reserve ran across in full armour. When they got there, there was nothing to see, and the sentries swore blind they hadn't seen anything.

Dawn came, and after that, the heat. Nobody had got any sleep. It took considerably longer than usual to pack away the tents and break camp, and the sun was high before they eventually got moving. Prexil wanted to up the pace, to make up time. The junior officers tried to argue with him, and he started shouting about insubordination and courts martial. The orders were given. The pace slowed down a little, if anything. The dust clouds were still there.

"They're too scared of us to attack," Prexil said. "They know there's absolutely nothing they can do, so they're just tagging along, keeping station. Pretty soon they'll give up and go away."

Daxin had been looking at a map. He'd found it in Ixion's tent, and nobody had seemed to want it for anything. He'd been over it many times, not sure if he was interpreting the symbols correctly; a light blue dot was water, wasn't it, and if he'd calculated the scale correctly and if he was holding the damn thing the right way up, the three enemy units hadn't been anywhere near water for a long time. He wondered what that meant. But it was safe to assume that Prexil had all the relevant information and knew the answer, and as things stood he didn't feel like raising the issue with him.

A scout came back; just one, on a horse without saddle or bridle or shoes. He was from the second group, and they'd got up as close as they dared to the dust cloud directly behind the column. From six hundred yards away, it looked like an ordinary trading caravan. They closed in to three hundred yards: about ninety pack horses, fifteen camels, thirty-odd men walking, five women on horseback, a small flock of sheep. The scouts withdrew, taking care not to be seen, and started to ride back to the column. After an hour or so, one of them said something like, that's a pretty small caravan to kick up that much dust. The others said no, not really, and we ought to be getting on; we haven't got much water left. So they rode on a bit further, and the scout who'd made the fuss started up again; look, he said, the cloud's bigger than it was, a lot bigger. Don't be stupid, the others said, you're imagining it. I'll go back and take a look, said the difficult scout. Please yourself, the others said, we aren't going to wait for you.

He rode away, and the others cursed him and decided they'd better wait; they dismounted and sat in the shadows of their horses, and someone got out a pack of cards. They'd played four hands, and then one of the scouts fell forward, like he'd gone to sleep, but he'd been shot in the back. They all jumped up; all but one tried to get on their horses and were shot. One, the survivor, just ran. Arrows passed him—he said it was like one time when he'd put his foot in a hornets' nest, and the hornets had chased him half a mile—but he kept running until he was out of range, and didn't look back. He guessed they didn't bother chasing him, since without a horse or water he'd be dead in a few hours. He never saw the men who'd shot at them. He ran until he fell over, and then he was too exhausted to move, and he just lay there until it got dark, and in the night he very nearly froze to death—it was like there was an open door, he said, and all I had to do was take a few steps more and go through; I wasn't all that bothered, but I thought, no, not yet. At sunrise he got up and started to walk, slowly, no idea which direction, until it got hot. Then he must've collapsed and passed out, because he could remember waking up and there was this horse standing over him, shading him from the sun. Good caravan horses learn to do that, the scout said. He had no idea where the horse had come from. It held perfectly still while he scrambled up on its back; then he looked round for the dust clouds and headed for the biggest. He was pretty certain he'd die of thirst anyway. He got light-headed and stopped trying to guide the horse; just as well, because he dozed off and woke up, and there in front of him was a pan of filthy water about twenty yards across, with some rocky outcrops and a few scrubby thorn bushes round it, and a huge broad mess of footprints to show that a lot of people had been that way quite recently. Either the horse had smelt the water or it was used to coming that way. There was nobody to be seen anywhere. He drank too much and was violently ill, which wasted a lot of time. Then he aimed the horse at the biggest dust cloud, and that was about it, really.

Prexil didn't believe him, and put him under close arrest. "He's a tribesman," he said, which was true enough; regular cavalry, ten years' service. "And you don't just find horses in the middle of the desert. Obviously, he's a spy. I'll see to it he's tried and hanged when we get back."

Daxen didn't argue, because there was no point; but he couldn't see it himself. A lot of trouble to go to, he felt, to disseminate misinformation that couldn't possibly benefit the enemy. He decided the scout was telling the truth, in which case the enemy were clever, paid close attention to detail and knew about water that wasn't on the map. But he'd more or less figured that out already. He was getting more and more worried about Prexil, who was having to shout and scream to get anything done, even straightforward, routine things. He thought about relieving him of command, but there wasn't anyone else; the engineer was more or less in hiding, and the junior officers didn't inspire confidence. That said, the column was making tolerable progress; Prexil had cut the water ration by a fifth, which was just about tolerable and meant they should have enough to get home comfortably. The dust clouds were neither closer nor further away. Nothing is actually happening, Daxen thought, which is really very strange.

"That shouldn't be there," a junior officer said. He was looking at the flat-topped blob of rock that had suddenly appeared on the skyline dead ahead of them. It hadn't been there yesterday, and it wasn't on the map. It was as though someone had neatly cut down a mountain and left the stump.

Another officer explained. Although the gradient was so gentle it was easy not to notice it, they'd been going uphill for two days now. They'd just reached the top of the rise, which had hidden the mountain, or whatever you wanted to call it. Hardly surprising it wasn't on the map, because the surveyors had stuck to the military road, which was over there (vague gesture) and considerably higher up. You wouldn't see the mountain unless you left the road and came quite some way over; and even if you did, from a distance it'd just look like a big sand dune or something. Anyway, it didn't matter. It was just a lump of rock.

Prexil didn't like it at all. He didn't like the way it had reared up out of nowhere, like a predator lying in ambush. You could hide a huge army behind a thing like that, and nobody would be any the wiser until it was far too late. Daxen wanted to point out that in order to hide an army you'd have to get it there first; they'd have seen the dust cloud, and the three clouds were still exactly where they'd always been—unless you'd sent it on ahead weeks ago, in which case the army would have died of thirst long since; unless there was a well on the rock somewhere—did you get wells on flat-topped mountains? He had no idea—and in any case, that would presuppose that the enemy had known for quite some time that they'd be coming this way, which was impossible. He made himself stop thinking about it. He had an uncomfortable feeling he was starting to think, and sound, like Prexil.

They gave the mountain a very wide berth, heading east, back towards the military road. The change of course had a significant effect on Prexil, as though he'd just won something, or figured out a deeply laid plot against him. He started smiling again, and didn't shout nearly as much, and the junior officers did what they were told without the awkward silences. "In fact," Prexil said, "we might as well go the whole hog and get back on the road for the last leg of the journey. We could water at a way station, which would be wonderful. Clearly they're not going to attack us now. They've had their chance, God knows."

It was hard to argue with the logic of that, and Daxen made a point of agreeing with him; the road would solve a lot of problems, and they could hardly be at greater risk there than out here in the middle of the desert. He suggested sending scouts ahead, but Prexil only smiled. "They're not going to attack," he said. "Where's the point?"

Three days later, they found the road. It was a wonderful thing; something human and artificial in the middle of the desert. He made a point of appreciating it for the achievement it was. Dead straight; a five-foot-high embankment, twenty yards wide; the bed of the road was compacted rubble, levelled and paved with flat slabs of stone precisely two feet square. It had been built by the empire, long before the civil war. It was the sort of thing a god might make, if the gods ever did anything useful.

Prexil showed him the way stations on the map. "We're somewhere here," he said, stabbing at an area an inch wide. "So, at the very worst, we're no more than a couple of days from the nearest station, which is this one here. It's not manned, of course, but there'll be a water tank, and shade for a day while we have a breather and pull ourselves together. There may even be fodder for the horses, which would be just as well; we're getting low. Or the savages may have stolen it; you just don't know."

The enemy had become *the savages*; a recent development, ever since the decision to head for the road. It wasn't the word Daxen would have chosen. The enemy were clearly intelligent, sophisticated, patient, realistic, organised, all sorts of things that savages aren't. They'd seen Prexil's scouts and sent out the fake caravan to distract them, even had the wit to halt their advance until the scouts had been dealt with so there'd only be one dust cloud. On balance, he figured they'd been wise not to attack the column, even though their night raid had been so successful; wise also not to repeat it, correctly assuming that if they came again they'd find themselves up against men who were drilled and ready. Instead, they'd left the army to worry and lose sleep. It was mere chance that the sawn-off mountain had prompted Prexil to make for the road, but Daxen had his own ideas about that. A large body of men moving along the road would raise no dust; they'd be invisible until they actually appeared, and one thing they could reasonably assume about the enemy was that they had a healthy respect for the element of surprise. If they marched up the road by night, then got off the road and laid up still and quiet during the day—cavalry, of course, who could make up ground so much faster than men on foot. It's what I'd do, Daxen reflected, not that that meant a great deal. Still, he was inclined to wonder if it had been simple bad luck that Ixion and his staff had been killed in the night raid. Ixion had been determined to avoid the road, and yet here they were, walking cheerfully down it as though they were off to town to buy olives.

The way station was a perfect white cube that shone like silver. It grew bigger and bigger as they got nearer; when they were close enough for Daxen to get a sense of perspective, he realised it was larger than the Blue temple back home. It was built of what they called army stone—you mixed sand and water and some sort of powdered rock from a special mountain in Thyrnessus, and you could pour it in huge moulds like molten brass and it set hard like fired clay. It wasn't used any more, since Thyrnessus was in the East, but the refineries where it was ground into powder were just over the border in the West; presumably the method was written down somewhere, but nobody seemed to know it. Close up, it wasn't actually white but a sort of light grey.

Deserted, of course; but the enormous tank was three-quarters full of clean water under its heavy wooden shutters, and five long sheds built into the eastern wall were packed tight with hay, old but still good. The only thing that appeared to be missing were the station's four doors—according to specification, five inches of six-ply oak, cross-grained to resist battering, fitted with four hinges each weighing a quarter of a ton. No sign of any doors, which made the building useless as a defensive position. Prexil decided that they'd been stolen by the savages and broken up for firewood and scrap; he advanced no explanation for the fact that the hay was still there. There was no sign that anyone had been there recently, but the charcoal cellars had been filled to capacity, which wasn't scheduled for another three months.

"We might as well stop over for a day," Prexil said, "maybe

even two, get ourselves back into shape, that sort of thing. It's going to be bad enough when we get home telling everyone that we've achieved absolutely nothing. I don't want us marching into Erithry in this state."

True enough, the army didn't shine and gleam like it did when it set out, and the military put so much stock in things being shiny. Now they were on the road again, it would be no more than five days to Erithry, and Prexil would have to march his army through the Lion Gates, with crowds watching. A parade-ground soldier, he'd called himself. No wonder he'd been so irritable lately.

There was an empty cellar next to the charcoal stores. It was wonderfully, gorgeously cool, and if you left the trapdoor open there was plenty of light to read by. Daxen announced that he had despatches to write, and left them to it.

That night, for the first time he could remember, Daxen was actually warm. He had two charcoal fires, one on either side of him. He was a little nervous at first—the Emperor Glycerian, returning in triumph from the Second Jazygite War, had died in his tent, asphyxiated by the fumes from a charcoal stove—but after an hour or so he found he was still alive, so it was probably all right. Someone had found an amazing treasure in a remote storage room: a palm's width thick with dust, nine barrels of fermented cabbage, a little bit cottony on top but perfectly good otherwise, and four barrels of salted herrings. That, and all the water you could drink. Someone had tentatively suggested that really they ought to share it with the men, but someone else had pointed out that the ration would be one thin strand of cabbage and a pinhead of herring each, which would just be a waste. Rank, they decided, had its privileges. General Ixion always said that, and the men respected him for it. Besides, only the officers and two quartermaster-sergeants knew about it, so that was fine.

*

A day spent polishing things had a marvellous effect. When they set out the next morning, thirty-nine thousand men marching smartly in step, they made the ground shake, and the sun blazed on their sand-burnished spearheads like the epiphany of the fire god. It did occur to Daxen that the flash would be visible for miles around, cancelling out the absence of dust cloud that came with using the road, but he couldn't see that it mattered any more. On the road, five days from Erithry, at the head of a mighty army with polished boots and shiny buckles—an undefeated army, let's not forget, since you couldn't call the sneak attack a defeat; he thought about that, in his capacity of formulator of policy for the Kingdom of Blemya. Now that he'd seen the desert for himself, he could judge these issues sensibly. There was absolutely no point, he knew now, in a punitive expedition. The fall of Seusa had been a tragedy, but the simple, heartbreaking fact was that a city out in the middle of the desert was unsustainable. Seeing the road, the way station, had made him understand, the way no written report ever could. In order to rule the desert, you had to be able to build things like the road and the stations, works that even the gods would hesitate to undertake, and the stations had to be garrisoned. The old empire had been able to do that sort of thing, for a while, a short while, until the sheer weight of its obligations tore it in half. It had done it by bleeding the people white, confiscating their sons and sending them off to be soldiers, rounding old men and women up like sheep and forcing them to build roads at slave wages. Seusa—he'd never been there, but by all accounts it had been a fine city, in its day—simply wasn't worth all that. When the nomads calmed down and wanted to start trading again, they could come to Erithry, and have only themselves to blame for the extra journey. Meanwhile, if they wanted the desert, they could have it, with watercress garnish on a bed of wild rice.

An hour out from the way station, and someone pointed out that the dust clouds were still there.

"Bastards," Prexil said. "Why don't they just give up and go home? Still, I guess it's their way of seeing us off the premises. Next time—" That was Prexil's new phrase, *next time*. Daxen decided not to disillusion him. He felt sorry for him, in a way. But, all things considered, he'd done a pretty fair job. A minor honour, he thought, and a good pension, and let's not dwell on the petulance and the shouting.

"We ought to send out the cavalry," said a junior captain, Heuxo, or Geuxa, something like that. "We owe those devils a surprise visit, after all."

Daxen winced. To his relief, Prexil laughed off the idea, though there was an edge to the way he spoke. Later, he said, "You know, I've been thinking. Maybe I shouldn't resign my commission after all. I mean, it seems a bit *weak*, don't you think?"

"Yes, but your injury—"

"Oh, that." Prexil laughed. "Amazing how quickly I've got used to it, though I still catch myself reaching for things and wondering why I can't get hold of them. No, that shouldn't be a problem. I mean, look at Nausaiga."

Daxen had no idea who he was talking about. "That's a good attitude," he said. "If you like, I'll put a word in for you with central command."

"Oh, I wouldn't want a desk job," Prexil said firmly. "One thing this experience has taught me, I have a genuine vocation, leading men on the front line. It was a bit shaky to start with, admittedly, but I believe I've learned an awful lot. I'm sure that's what I ought to be doing, particularly now that I've got this special insight into the savages." He paused for breath, then went on, his eyes positively shining, "When we come back and give the bastards the kicking they deserve, I want to be in on it. You will make that possible, won't you?"

"Leave it with me," Daxen replied, making a mental vow to get Prexil transferred to Supply at the earliest opportunity.

They stopped at another station—a small one, just a well and a shed, for the messenger service—to sit out the noon heat; they'd made such good progress on the road that they could afford small indulgences. Daxen was sitting in the shade writing official despatches when he overheard two soldiers talking. There's another one, said a voice—he couldn't see them from where he was sitting. What do you reckon that's in aid of? A different voice said he didn't know. How long's it been there? Don't know, I wasn't looking. Bastards, said the first voice, without any special degree of rancour, and it suddenly occurred to Daxen that they might be talking about the enemy, any comment concerning whom was always rounded off with an epithet, like grace at dinner. He'd been assuming they were talking about kites or buzzards. Another one, he thought. He got to his feet and came outside. For a moment, as usual, he was blinded by the glare. Then he looked at the skyline. Three dust clouds, same as always. He felt a certain degree of relief; then he realised that from where he was standing he wouldn't be able to see the dust cloud to the south, because the building was in the way. He walked a dozen yards further and looked back past the corner of the shed. A fourth dust cloud.

"Oh yes." Prexil didn't seem too concerned when he pointed it out, five minutes of anxious searching later. "So there is. I wonder what the buggers are up to now."

Don't you think we should—Daxen stopped himself saying it. Do what? "Where did they come from?" he said.

Prexil shrugged. "Up the road, maybe, and then launched off cross-country. That'd explain why we didn't see them before. Not that it makes any odds. It's just a last bit of aggressive display, like peacocks. You know, my uncle had one of those green ornamental pheasants once, cock bird, mad as a hatter. Every time he walked down the lime avenue in the park, this stupid bird would come charging up at him, pecking his legs, fluttering up and scratching at him with its spurs. He'd boot the bloody thing like a football and back it'd come, madder than ever; and when he got to the end of the avenue, which was like the border of this bird's territory, he'd look back and there it'd be, perched on a fence rail, head held high, positively glowing with triumph at having seen him off. Fox got it in the end, of course. Anyway, that's what they're doing, they're seeing us off. Savages set great store by that sort of thing, you know."

Daxen couldn't help grinning. "Why didn't he just pull its neck?"

"What? Oh, my uncle. No, he got quite fond of the stupid creature, said it was a true hero. Boamund he called it, after the fellow in that poem. He got a scratch off it that went bad and he was quite ill for a bit, but even after that he always took a pocketful of grain with him. You've got to admire courage, haven't you? It's the supreme virtue."

No, Daxen thought. "I think we ought to start doing the night-watch drills again," he said, "just to be on the safe side. Don't you think?"

Prexil looked dubious. "We can if you like," he said. "But really, we're practically home now, I honestly don't think there's going to be any trouble."

Daxen made an excuse and left him, and went in search of the quartermaster. "I want a sword," he said.

The quartermaster looked at him as though he was mad. "Sir?"

"A sword. I haven't got one. I haven't got a weapon of any kind."

"Sir." The quartermaster walked slowly across to a mule, quietly browsing its nosebag under a towering pile of bags, sacks and boxes. He levered the top off a crate with a small jemmy and took out something wrapped in oily yellow cloth. "This do you, sir? It's just a Type Fourteen, ordinary issue. Get one of the men to clean it up for you if you want."

The cloth stank of rancid fat. "Yes, please."

"Sir. Bring it to your tent tonight, if that's all right."

By the time it arrived, bright and shiny, with a few grains of the sand it had been scraped clean with still lodged under the cross-guard, the sky was already dark. Daxen gave the sword a quick glance and stuffed it under the bed. What on earth do you think you're going to do with that? he asked himself, and no sensible reply came. The greasy leather of the scabbard had left marks on his hands. He wiped them off on his sleeve.

Only three dust clouds the next day: behind, and on either side. The one in front had vanished. Prexil grinned and said it proved his point. Daxen contemplated pointing out that the disappearance could only mean one of two things. Either the enemy unit was sitting still out there in the desert, which was suicide unless they were crowded round another unrecorded oasis (this close to Erithry? Unlikely) or else they weren't kicking up dust because they were heading down the road, straight at the army. He decided not to say anything. The road, after all, was straight and flat from here to the city. If an enemy force was approaching, they'd see it in good time. Also, despite his own irreproachable logic, he didn't think a hostile army was coming at them. They were, after all, only two days from the city, close enough for a fast rider to call out the city garrison and get back with a flying column of cavalry in time to play a useful part. If the enemy wanted to fight, why had they left it so late? In spite of himself, he was more and more inclined towards Prexil's crazy pheasant theory—an odd way to conduct a military campaign, but it did have the significant merit of having succeeded.

Instead, he suggested sending messengers ahead to the city, and Prexil agreed. They'd need a day or so to prepare, after all; forty thousand unexpected guests would be something of an imposition, even for a city as large and prosperous as Erithry. The messengers set off at a merry gallop, and Daxen watched them till they were out of sight. He felt as though there was now an invisible rope, by which they could pull themselves to safety out of the desert. The last time he'd been in Erithry was—what, fifteen years ago? In a different life. His uncle had a house there. He remembered it as a huge, empty white building, so cool inside it was practically cold, with an open cloister with a carp pool; he'd stolen bread from the dinner table to feed the fish, but he hadn't actually liked them much. The quick, almost savage way they snapped up the bread pellets was mildly disturbing, and afterwards he'd had nightmares about a sea monster. That, of course, was the year his brother was killed, so events from that time tended to stand out in his memory. The best thing about Erithry, of course, was that there'd be despatches and letters waiting for him there; and in a lining, or written very small on the back or in the margin of something, there'd be a few words from her. Maybe that was what he'd had in mind when he visualised the invisible rope.

He found a pretext for talking to Mesajer, the cavalry commander. Either he was very forgiving or thick-skinned as an elephant; he seemed not to have noticed the appallingly rude way Prexil had treated him—all that had changed once they reached the road, but even so. Maybe he was so used to it he hadn't noticed. Daxen considered apologising, but decided that would only make matters worse. Instead, he'd asked around and discovered that Mesajer was a theatre buff, mad keen on the Drula, the Sunifex brothers and musical comedy generally. Couldn't be better. Nothing breaks the ice like a shared passion, especially if it's one of which other people don't necessarily approve.

"People don't believe me when I say I'm a Drula fan," Mesajer said. "I guess they think it's odd, a tribesman with a penchant for mildly satirical social comedy. They reckon I should be into epic poetry and falconry. Or maybe they think I'm aping the tastes of my betters."

Daxen winced slightly. "The hell with people," he said. It was a quotation, and made Mesajer grin.

"Quite," he said. "I wonder, did you see Coloxa as Vissanio in *The Girl with Only One Shoe*?"

"Wish I had," Daxen replied fervently, "but that was before my time. The bit with the lobster—"

"*Desert* lobster," Mesajer corrected him, and he laughed. "You had to be there," Mesajer went on. "I was thirteen. My mother and my aunt took me for my birthday. I laughed so much, I can remember how much it hurt. I couldn't breathe, like drowning."

So that was all right. A man who liked Drula and had seen Coloxa do the desert lobster scene could no more betray the Kingdom than fly in the air, even if he did have a faded blue tattoo on his neck, just peeping out over the pauldron of his cuirass. Daxen wished he knew what it meant; interpreting them was a complex matter, so he understood, which was why the craze for tribal tattoos among young aristocrats with intellectual pretensions tended to cause so much quiet amusement in the cavalry officers' mess. But you couldn't just point and ask for a translation, unless you wanted to cause mortal offence—

Eventually, reluctantly, he steered the conversation round to other topics. True, the indigenous tribes of Blemya were related to the desert people—in the same way, Mesajer said, that wolfhounds are related to wolves; common ancestry, radically different viewpoint. Yes, it was hard not be offended sometimes, and, yes, there was always the sense of being different, even when the Settler talking to you was one of your closest friends. The dog analogy was, in fact, quite apt. A lot of men love their dogs, admire them, are proud of them; love them more than their wives and sons, are really only happy when in their company, weep inconsolably when they die. But dogs are dogs, and people are people. That said—Mesajer grinned—if it wasn't for people, dogs would still be wolves. Dogs, he felt sure, were well aware of that, as they curled up in the rushes in front of the hearth.

Daxen was mildly shocked by that, which Mesajer found amusing.

*

Two hours into the next morning's march, they came over a slight rise and saw Erithry. They saw it as a white blur surrounded by a green penumbra, the vineyards and market gardens that flourished along the irrigation canals dug by Ceuphro IV two hundred years ago. The white was the glare of marble, the local material, cheaper than sandstone; every stable, warehouse and outside privy was built of it. By noon, they could make out the faint pink of the better-class districts, where the masons had used the celebrated Erithrean Rose from the quarries in the northern suburbs. The messengers hadn't come back yet. There was no sign of any large body of men on the road ahead of them, or any dust rising from either side of it; the three clouds were, however, still keeping perfect station, behind them and on either side. Prexil found that offensive, so close to the city. As soon as they were back, he said, he'd send out cavalry patrols to shoo them away. Daxen made no comment, and his silence wasn't noticed.

Nobody really started to worry until they reached the fourteenth milestone, where there was a way station. It was deserted—it should've been manned—and the haylofts were empty and the tank was dry. There was no sign that anyone had been there recently, though a sandstorm would have covered any tracks completely, and there was three inches of sand on the road at that point. Prexil sent out scouts. A few sharp-eyed men at the front of the column said they might have seen movement, as of large bodies of men, in the fields to the north-east of the city. Nobody else could make out anything of the kind, however, and the illusion was put down to overexcitement.

There was a brief debate as to whether they should stop for the night at the tenth milestone, or press on to the city, even though it would mean marching the last hour or so in the dark. Prexil agonised about it for a while, then decided to press on. The road was easy enough to follow, after all, and as soon as the sun set they'd have the lights of the farms and suburbs to guide them.

But they didn't. The darkness slowly filled out, but there were no lights. The scouts hadn't returned, either. Prexil called a halt, and put the army on lesser alert. He was thinking, he explained, about the dust cloud, the one that had preceded them and then vanished. "It did occur to me," he said, "that the reason the cloud stopped was that they'd moved on to the road and were coming up it at us, though I wasn't all that bothered if they were. What I didn't think was that they'd joined the road and gone the other way, towards the city. I mean, what if we get there and find there's a siege? It's the only reason I can think of why the suburbs are dark."

"We'd see the enemy campfires, though, surely," suggested one of the captains. Prexil shrugged.

"You'd have thought so," he said, "but maybe they're staying dark, for some reason. Like we did, in the desert. Don't want to give their positions away. As I recall, there's some pretty high-class artillery on the walls, and I can't imagine they've got any engines of their own to keep our boys' heads down with."

That made an uncomfortable amount of sense, and everyone was quiet for a while. Then Prexil said, "Well, if that's what's happening, all I can say is, the bastards have got a nasty surprise coming. If we can get in close before they see us—"

"What about our scouts?" someone said.

Indeed; the scouts who'd so signally failed to return. "Well," Prexil said, "if they know we're coming, so what? I imagine they'll bugger off out of it before we get there, but if they don't, I'll take great pleasure in kicking their arses up through their ears. I don't know about you fellows, but I've taken a bit of a dislike to these people. It's about time we gave them a bit of a smacking."

Daxen sat through the meeting in silence, then went and sat alone in the dark for a while. They hadn't pitched the tents; by the time they stopped it was already too dark. It was bitter cold, of course, and naturally Prexil had forbidden the lighting of fires. The fall of Seusa was one thing; if the savages (he was doing it now) had dared lay siege to Erithry, however, something would have to be done about it. Something, yes; define something. Carrying the war out into the desert, he was now unshakably convinced, wasn't an option. Somehow, the savages managed to live out here, but civilised people, Blemyans, couldn't survive in this unnatural place, let alone conduct military operations. In which case, all he could think of was some sort of diplomatic retaliation—discreet infiltration, setting one tribal faction against another, that sort of thing. Which would take time, and the results, though potentially satisfactory, wouldn't be visible. What was needed was a grand gesture, to reassure the world, and he couldn't think of one. That made him feel depressed. He couldn't sleep, he couldn't read and he was freezing cold. He snuggled four blankets into a sort of nest and lay awake, looking at the stars.

There was no siege. That was apparent as soon as they reached the outlying vineyards. From the high ground, eminently suitable for growing fine-quality grapes, they had a good view of the city, and the Foregate was empty; no tents, earthworks, besieging army. No anybody. The vineyards were deserted, likewise the wide, flat, hedgeless fields of cabbages, turnips, leeks and beans, geometrically perfect and immaculately tended; a few chickens, and that was all. No signs either of assault and destruction. Someone murmured something about a sudden deadly attack of plague, and got no response.

They matched up the road in total silence, apart from the rather inhuman thump of forty thousand men marching in step. For some reason, they were parade-ground perfect—a slight lag between the very front and the very end of the column, making a weird sort of ripple-echo effect, but as near exactly in time as it's possible for such a large number of humans to be. It's because they're concentrating on what they're doing, Daxen guessed. Concentrate on keeping in step and you don't think about other things.

Between the market gardens and the wall, the suburbs; a concentric outer circle, like the blue on an archery target. In other places, you had shanty towns outside the walls, where the very poor built houses out of barrels, crates and boxes. Not at Erithry; here, the suburbs were mostly villas, sprawling single-storey blocks with an ostentatiously extravagant footprint, usually with a portico and cloister, formal gardens and an acre of kitchen garden enclosed by a wall. Normally you'd see small armies of gardeners, smoke rising from bonfires, carts everywhere taking the surplus produce into town; it could take half an hour to travel the last two hundred yards to the city gate because of the bottleneck and the queues. All empty, and the road shimmered in front of them like some absurdity out of a bad dream.

"They wouldn't have evacuated, would they?" said a nervous young lieutenant who didn't know when to shut up. "I mean, it'd be a huge operation—what's the population of Erithry, a hundred thousand?"

"Double that," someone said. "Easily."

The young lieutenant was quiet after that. Yesterday, he'd been telling anyone who'd listen that he had cousins in Erithry: they were in the silk business, they had a beautiful garden and a very fine cook. Now you could practically see him not-thinking, closing the gates of his mind against the unimaginable. He wasn't the only one with relatives in Erithry, not by a long way.

They could see the gate clearly. It was open. "There's got to be some perfectly simple explanation," someone said.

(Yes, Daxen told himself, I can think of one. But it can't be that, because there aren't any bodies. There's no *smell.* Two hundred thousand bodies, at least a week in the hot sun, there'd be a smell all right. But the only smell was jasmine, from the fields to the east where they grew it for the perfume trade. So it couldn't be that. The end of the world would never smell like jasmine.)

*

When Daxen was a boy and they lived most of the time at the country house, the housekeeper would send him to the farm for milk and eggs. He hated that, because he'd walk down to the farmyard and there'd be no one there. He'd wander in and out of the barns and sheds, looking for someone. There'd be chickens scuttling about, maybe calves penned up, pigs in the sties, lambs in the long barn, but no sign of the farmer, his wife or sons, nobody to issue him with milk and eggs so he could go home. He wasn't allowed to take the stuff without asking, so he was doomed to roam endlessly through the muddy, mucky yard until eventually someone turned up, back from the fields to fetch something. Someone always did turn up, eventually; but he often thought, what if they don't? What if there really is nobody at all, and I have to stay here for ever and ever?

They marched through the gate into Sheepfair. A dozen startled crows flew upwards, shrieking with rage, to reveal a split sack of grain. This was where the bakers had their market; three quarters of an acre of canopied stalls, but not today. The white marble pavement shone brilliantly, empty as the desert.

The coppersmiths' quarter; they went from shop to shop, and the doors were open, and the tools were neat in the racks and the hearths were cold. The lumber yards; long sheds with long saw benches, the great circular saws frozen, the mill trains disconnected, the waterwheels rock still beside their briskly flowing races. Nobody in the weavers' quarter, the looms all quiet. Nobody feeding the fish in the carp tanks (but the fish cruised up and down under the surface, swift, anxious; hadn't been fed in days. What was going on?). Nobody in the tanneries or the slaughterhouses or the empty stockyards, nobody in the potters' quarter or the fulleries, and the urine tanks were empty. So they tried looking in houses, and the beds were made and the cups and dishes were in the racks, coats hanging behind doors, cots and cribs empty. No horses in the mews, stables and livery yards, no carts in the trap-houses. No *dogs*, for crying out loud. How could there possibly not be any dogs in Erithry?

"They eat them," Mesajer said. It was the first time he'd spoken for an hour.

"What?" Prexil snapped. "Who eats what?"

"The desert people. They eat dogs."

Nobody in the goldsmiths' quarter. Plenty of gold, both finished goods and carefully stacked ingots, but no people. "That's just crazy," said the engineer. "Who captures a city and leaves the gold?"

No sign of looting or plundering of any sort, not anywhere. The only missing commodities were food—every kind of food, from bulk grain to salt pork to raisins to baby cucumbers in dill pickle. There was nothing to eat in the whole of Erithry.

"Cabbages," Prexil said.

The quartermaster nodded. "And a bit of curly kale. There's a few fields of early beetroot, turnips about the size of walnuts, hard as rock but just about eatable if you boil them for an hour. No beans yet. Nothing's ready for another month."

Prexil sighed. "How much flour is left?"

The quartermaster shrugged. "Depends on how you ration it. Maybe six days, if we really spin it out."

Prexil issued orders for the Sixth, Ninth and Third Auxiliary to go and cut cabbages. "This time of year they're just finishing up the store crops," the quartermaster explained. "Only all the clamps are empty; we looked. Just about the worst time of year for this to have happened, really."

Daxen had thought that, too. Twenty miles up the road and you came to the wheat belt, huge fields as far as the eye could see; but close to the city was all greens and other ephemera, things that don't keep. At any other time, half a dozen different crops would've been in season. The disappearance, the great absence, had taken place at the one point in the food cycle when there was hardly any fresh produce in the fields.

"We can't survive indefinitely on bloody cabbages," Prexil was saying. "Quite apart from the men, I've got fifty thousand horses and mules to feed, have you got any idea how much those bloody things eat? We're out of oats and barley—we had to give all we had left to the men for porridge—so right now I've got all the horses out grazing turnip tops, but we can't take three hundred acres of garden land with us when we leave. And why the hell aren't there any *carts*?"

"We'll have to build some," someone suggested.

"Oh yes, let's do that," Prexil snapped. "A thousand carts, just like that. We'd be here for *weeks*. We can't afford to be stuck here, doing nothing, when—" He stopped. It wasn't a sentence he wanted to finish. "We'll have to make big cloth bags," he said. "There's plenty of cloth, at any rate. How long do cabbages keep for once they're cut, anyway?"

They tried the less obvious places where people might hide—cellars, towers, cisterns, even the sewers. But the sewers smelt sweet. They looked for freshly turned earth, evidence of intensive burning. They tried the City hall; papers neatly stacked and no ink in the inkwells. "Whatever it was," said a lieutenant who claimed to know about these things, "it happened early in the morning, before they mixed the ink. That's how it's done," he added defensively, as people looked at him. "Every day, the junior clerks take turns to mix the ink and take it round the offices in a big jug. Then, in the evening, they go round and empty all the inkwells."

Actually, that made sense; not just the clerks' offices, but all the shops and workshops looked as though they'd been packed away for the night and not opened the next day. It wasn't much, but it was something to go on, the first tiny step towards a hypothesis. "A dawn attack," Prexil said. "No, it'd have to be before dawn. Maybe fourth watch. There's never anybody about then."

"There's sentries," someone objected. "And first thing they'd do would be ring the bells. And besides, we examined the gates. No sign of forced entry."

Daxen said, "Did anyone look for the keys?"

Everyone went thoughtful. "No sign of any keys," someone said.

"Did you look?"

"No," the speaker admitted. "But we'd have seen them if they were there."

"Go and look," Daxen said.

No sign of the keys, which was just bizarre, because the keys to a city are incredibly significant things, hedged around with procedures and ceremonies, duty officer rosters and guard changeover schedules. Judging from the size of the locks, they were also *huge*. "They've got to be somewhere," Prexil said. "For crying out loud. We can't secure the city unless we find them."

They looked. A whole brigade of the Sixteenth searched the gatehouse, watch house and guard rooms. No keys. "Someone must've taken them," a junior captain said.

"Oh come *on*," Prexil exploded. "They leave six million angels in gold coins in the Treasury, and they steal a bunch of keys. None of it makes any sense."

Without food, they couldn't leave. Without keys, they couldn't secure the gates. The engineer sent his smiths away to make bars, hasps and keepers; twelve hours' work, not including fitting. In the meanwhile, they jammed the gates shut with scaffolding poles. "Nobody is going to make me believe that a Blemyan army garrison surrendered the third biggest city in the Kingdom without a fight," Prexil declared. It was a statement of faith (defined as an irrational belief for which one can furnish no objective proof) and he clearly wasn't in the mood to be contradicted. "Someone betrayed them, opened the gates in the middle of the night, it's the only possible explanation."

And not a bad one, at that, Daxen was forced to concede. He sent men to examine the bakers' ovens; no bread, no flour, needless to say—but there were burnt-out ashes in the hearths, which told him that the fires had been lit. When do bakers start work? Early, he knew that. He buttonholed a captain.

"Somewhere in your unit there's got to be a man who used to be a baker before he joined up," he said urgently. "I need to talk to him *now*. Do you understand?"

The captain stared at him and nodded. "Sir."

"This is important. Life and death."

"Sir."

An hour later, the captain came back with two sergeants flanking a terrified-looking man, who confessed to having been born a baker's son. Daxen gave him a huge smile and offered him a chair. "What time of day did your father light the oven?"

"Third watch, sir."

"On the bell, or later?"

The man thought for a moment. "More like halfway between third and fourth, sir. He'd start laying the fire on the third bell, but it takes time, like; it's got to be done just right. So he wouldn't actually get it lit much before fourth bell."

"Thank you," Daxen said. He reached in his pocket, then remembered he didn't have any money. "Captain, give this man two angels. Thank you, dismissed."

Well, it was a start. Some time after the middle of the third watch, then; a time when any city is at its quietest, when even the drunks are asleep, but before the early risers start work. The perfect time of day, and at the perfect time of year; someone intelligent and well informed thought up this plan, he told himself, someone who knew about cities and how they operate. It didn't feel like a spur-of-the-moment reaction, the sort of thing you'd expect from a wild-eyed desert prophet outraged over the defiling of a sacred well. Perhaps. The time-of-year aspect might simply be chance and coincidence. The capture of the city, on the other hand, was work of the very highest quality. And why had nothing except food been taken? Nothing at all.

He climbed a long spiral stair that left him shamefully breathless and arrived at the top of the gatehouse tower. One dust cloud. He looked up and down the wall. There was nobody on watch. Furiously angry, he ran down again and stormed into Prexil's tent; but he wasn't there. Eventually, after a great deal of fruitless rushing about, he found him eating a bowl of porridge in one of the guardhouses.

"Why aren't there any sentries on the wall?" he yelled.

Prexil gave him a sad look. "Aren't there? Damn. Right, I'll see to it."

"You do that. And there's now one dust cloud, and it's coming straight at us."

Prexil jumped up, knocking the table and the porridge flying. "Oh hell," he said crisply. "Right, here we go." He grabbed for his sword, which was lying in its scabbard on the table; he fumbled with the buckles, gave up and left it. "It's about time, I guess. Did you see if they've done the bars on the gate yet?"

They were peening over the rivets when Prexil and Daxen got there. "Close the gates," Prexil yelled. "All units to stations." A count of three, and men started pouring out of doorways, ramming helmets on their heads, scrabbling at the loops and catches of their armour. "Mobile reserves to the bastions," Prexil shouted; he didn't seem to be talking to anyone in particular, but he had a loud voice, and things were certainly happening. He didn't draw breath for five minutes, by which time the walls were lined with archers, and a solid phalanx of spearmen was drawn up at attention in Foregate Yard. It was only then that Daxen remembered something he'd heard recently. He craned his neck to look, just to make sure.

"Aren't there supposed to be siege engines mounted on these walls?" he said.

"Yes, of course. Twelve tactical batteries, four long-range—"

"They're gone."

Prexil froze, staring at him. "Oh God," he said. "Are you sure?"

"Look for yourself."

Prexil's head shot up. "Oh *God,*" he repeated. "Well, there's absolutely nothing we can do. *Scouts!*" He ran off towards the gatehouse tower steps. Daxen didn't follow. He was suddenly very, very tired, and he didn't want to get in the way. He managed to cross the Yard without getting knocked off his feet, and found himself on the steps of the Sunrise Temple. He looked up at the glowing copper dome. Why not? he thought, and went in.

The temple was empty. He walked up the long aisle towards the nave, where light streamed in through the precisely angled rose windows and reflected off the gilded walls and floor, to create the sacred illusion of the Well of Fire. Walk into the Well, they promised you, and your sins will be burned away. Daxen grinned. It was worth a try, he supposed. Conscious of his boot heels on the marble, he marched up to the altar and knelt down. He said the words, but his mind was on other things.

This time, the scouts came back. They brought five men with them.

"Who the hell," Prexil demanded, "are you?"

One of the five unwrapped the scarf that covered his face. He took his time over it. The scarf fell away. "Now just—" Prexil said, and then stopped dead. All Daxen could do was stare. The man was an Imperial.

"But I thought—" Prexil said.

"My name," the man said, "is Genseric. Are you in charge of this circus?"

An Imperial; from the grey in his beard, somewhere between forty and forty-five. He spoke with an upper-crust Western accent; in fact, he sounded remarkably like Oida, only perhaps a little deeper. "Yes," Prexil said. "I'm Major Prexil. This is—"

Genseric nodded. "I know who he is." He lifted off his helmet and put it on the table. It was an old-fashioned Imperial pattern—four plates riveted into a frame—and covered in off-white canvas glued to the steel. His head was shaved smooth. "Where's Ixion?"

"He's dead," Daxen said.

Genseric kept his eyes on Prexil. "And you're the ranking officer."

"Yes. Answer my question. Who are you?"

Genseric sighed, relaxed a little into the back of his chair. "I'm a constable of the Faculty of Arms." He shifted slightly. Prexil was looking at his face, so he didn't see the little gold hammer and anvil that was now visible on the inside of his tunic lapel. "Oh come on," he said impatiently. "You don't know—"

"I do," Daxen said.

Prexil gave him a bewildered look. Daxen nodded, it's all right. Prexil shrugged, leaned back, folded his arms. Slowly, Genseric turned to Daxen and looked at him for a moment. Distaste, Daxen read with surprise, and no attempt to disguise it.

"You're lodge soldiers," Daxen said.

Genseric liked him even less for that. "Put crudely, yes," he said. "We're here to observe, and safeguard craftsmen and lodge property, as far as circumstances allow. Obviously, in this case—"

"Just a minute," Prexil said. "Lodge soldiers? What the hell does that mean?"

The look on Genseric's face would have poisoned a city. "The Faculty of Arms," Daxen said quickly. "It's like an order of chivalry, inside the craft. They have—well, resources of their own."

"Like a private army," Prexil said. He was clearly disgusted.

"No, not as such," Daxen said quickly. He realised he knew

next to nothing about the Faculty of Arms, except that it existed, and younger sons of impoverished nobles went off to join it. "It's attached to the University, isn't it? Like a sort of military academy."

"You could say that," Genseric said. "The Academicians study every aspect of human knowledge and endeavour, including military science. And, in every field we cover, we don't confine ourselves to the merely theoretical." He turned slowly to face Daxen; Prexil clearly no longer existed. "We came here to observe the battle between the two Imperial factions," he said. "Clearly, there was very little we could do. I have three thousand cavalry under my command, and medical and supply units. We were able to assist a small number of craftsmen left wounded on the battlefield; we recovered them and sent them under escort to our colleagues from the Faculty of Medicine. While we were doing this, we heard disturbing rumours about developments among the desert people; we decided to stay here and observe. We witnessed the events at Seusa, but were unable to do anything. Unlike you—" he paused for a moment "—we deduced that the next target would be Erithry. We also deduced that the tribesmen would lure your army into the desert, safely out of the way, while they attacked the city. We got to Erithry as quickly as we could, but since we didn't dare use the road we made poor time. When we arrived, the city had already been taken, and the evacuation of prisoners—" Daxen started to speak, but Genseric shut him up with a slight gesture of his hand "—was well under way. We met with the tribal leaders and received assurances that the craftsmen among the captives would be treated properly, pending formal ransom negotiations. I sent a note of the agreement to my superiors, who will in due course arrange payment. Then we turned back to see you. We felt you would wish to know what had happened."

"For God's sake," Prexil shouted. "You knew we'd been decoyed away, but you didn't send and tell us. That's appalling."

Genseric didn't look round at him. "This isn't our jurisdiction," he said icily. "We don't interfere. We observe, and we offer assistance to fellow craftsmen, where feasible. I have just arranged for the safety and eventual release of six thousand craftsmen and their families. If it had been left to you, I imagine they would have died, in the desert or as slaves. We came here as a courtesy, to let you know what happened. If you don't want to hear, we'll go."

Prexil was going to say something; Daxen managed to catch his eye in time. "Six thousand," he said. "That's going to cost a lot of money."

"Two million." Genseric dismissed the figure with a tiny shake of his head. "We can afford it."

"They left three times that in the Treasury here."

Genseric sighed. "You don't understand," he said. "That would be stealing. They don't steal. Ransoms are different: they're honourable. If you don't study your enemy, how can you ever hope to deal with him?"

"You've done that," Daxen said. "Studied them, I mean."

"Of course."

"And they talk to you."

Genseric smiled. "We have full diplomatic relations," he said. "Our scholars and theirs have been in communication for centuries. That's how respect is earned. They know we have no quarrel with them."

Prexil made an exasperated noise. "You're on their side."

"Prexil, be quiet." He hadn't meant it to come out quite like that, but never mind. "I'm sorry," he said to Genseric. "Major Prexil's been under considerable strain lately, as you can imagine. It's been difficult for all of us. The fact is, we don't know a lot about these people. Not nearly as much as we thought we did, anyway."

"You're out of your depth." Genseric said it casually, a statement of fact that it would be pointless to deny. At that moment, Daxen would've paid good money to be allowed to hit him. "That's unfortunate. These are difficult people you're dealing with, complex, sensitive. We've known them a long time, but they're continually surprising us."

Daxen looked straight at him. "You *are* on their side."

Quite unexpectedly, Genseric laughed. "Well, if I had to choose," he said. "Fortunately for all concerned, I don't. In fact, I'm expressly forbidden to. As I keep telling you, I'm here to observe and help craftsmen. Beyond that I couldn't go, even if I wanted to."

Daxen took a deep breath. He couldn't remember disliking anyone more than he disliked Genseric at that moment. "Naturally," he said, "the Blemyan treasury will reimburse you for the ransoms you've already paid. I'm officially asking you to use your good offices to negotiate the ransom of the remaining citizens presently in their hands. That wouldn't be taking sides," he said firmly. "That'd be helping both parties to get what they want."

Genseric sighed, shook his head. "You really don't understand, do you?" He picked up his helmet. "First, we can't take any money from you, I'd have thought you'd have worked that out by now. And if you think the tribes kidnapped your people with a view to extorting money, you couldn't be more wrong. They released our craftsmen as a special favour. They accepted the ransom because it would be a sin against their god to part with His property without getting something for Him in return. They don't want money. They don't use it, their laws forbid it. If I were to offer them money on your behalf for your people, it'd be an unforgivable insult tantamount to a declaration of war. The ransom payment will be dedicated to the god in a solemn ceremony and then buried somewhere remote in the desert." He stood up. "As far as they're concerned your citizens are now divine property, all of them, every man, woman and child in Blemya. That's good news, because once they've captured them they'll give them food and water and look after them, like they do with their sheep. But the only way you'd ever get them back is by force, and I strongly recommend you don't try." He paused for breath; Daxen could see he was struggling to keep his temper. "We're going to leave now," he said. "As a gesture of goodwill, I'll give you some badly needed advice. If you want to try and save your kingdom, get your army on the road and head for the capital. If you're lucky, you'll catch them up before they get there. If you honestly believe you can beat them, fight them as soon as possible, though I would suggest you send away all the craftsmen in your army beforehand, tell them to go home to their families. They've got a chance. Frankly, you haven't."

Daxen knew what he had to do, but it took him the rest of the day to nerve himself to do it. He summoned a full military council, and formally relieved Prexil of command. In the circumstances, he said, it was his clear duty as the queen's proxy to lead the army himself. This action was no reflection on anyone present, and he would of course continue to rely on their advice and assistance. The army would march at dawn for the capital. Desperate though their situation was, as far as food and other supplies were concerned, he could see no other reasonable course of action. He was taking command because he wanted it to be unequivocally clear that the responsibility for everything that happened from that point on was his and his alone.

Prexil waited till he'd finished speaking, then got up and walked away without a word. The rest of them stayed where they were, dead quiet.

Daxen's throat was so dry he could barely speak. "Any questions?"

Long silence; then someone whose name he didn't know said, "You believe it, then. About the savages."

He thought for a moment. "I don't think we can afford not to," he said. "If they had the power to do what they did here, we've got to assume Genseric was telling the truth. If we stay here and the kingdom falls—" He found he couldn't complete the sentence. No need, fortunately. He'd made his point.

There were a few questions about details, practical and sensible. He didn't know the answers and said so. "I'll have to leave it to you," he said. "We all know I'm no soldier. But you'll all do the best you can."

Nobody argued. There were no more questions. He dismissed the council, and they trooped out in silence. Daxen sat down in his folding chair and watched the oil lamp on the table burn itself out. After that, he sat in the dark until the sun rose.

The next five days were the strangest of Daxen's life so far, and the loneliest. He rode a white horse at the head of the army, agonisingly arrayed in the late General Ixion's golden breastplate and helmet. The helmet was too big and the breastplate was too small; the inside edge of the pauldrons chafed his neck raw, so he had to wear a scarf, which he had to change every hour because it became sodden with sweat and chafed even worse; the helmet was padded with four pairs of wool socks to stop it falling over his face, and the sweat pouring down his face made him look as though he was crying his eyes out; fortuitously, this went down very well indeed with the men, who thought he was grieving for Erithry; copious tears together with his bolt-upright seat in the saddle (essential because if he slouched even a little bit the pain in his thighs was unbearable) made him a heroic figure, strong and compassionate in equal measure. The junior officers congratulated him on the fact that the men had awarded him the supreme accolade of a nickname, which meant they really liked him; however, they were curiously reluctant to tell him what it was.

The supply problem didn't bother anyone particularly since, as they all assured him, once they reached the wheat belt everything would be fine. And so it was, up to a point. They marched through an endless ocean of wheat, just right for cutting or maybe the tiniest bit gone over. At one point he stopped, dismounted, picked an ear and bit into a few kernels: hard like a nut, no softness or milkiness. And there it was, still standing, uncut; and no human beings to be seen anywhere except for the soldiers. At this time of year the fields should be swarming with men, women and children, frantically busy with the three hardest weeks' work of the year. Instead, the only movement was explosions of rooks and crows, bursting up out of the laid patches where the weight of the grain had dragged the stalks down and the birds could pitch to feed. They erupted suddenly and unexpectedly, shrieking abuse, thick black clouds of furious movement that dissipated into twisting columns, thick curling smoke in the wind. Each evening the soldiers went out to reap with their swords, trampling trenches in the crop, spoiling five times what they stole; they threshed with their belts over spread-out cloaks, and every boot and garment in the camp was full of sharp, gritty chaff. There was no smoke from burning roofs, no bodies swollen on the road, no riderless horses; no sign that anyone had ever been there at all.

"It's all pretty desperate," young Captain Euxis assured him. "This lot's not just supposed to feed Erithry, this is the breadbasket for Cumnis and most of the South. If it isn't cut and carted damn quick, it's not going to be pretty, that's for sure."

Daxen had figured that much for himself. He'd seriously considered halting the march and sending the men out to harvest the wheat. In his mind he could see the pages of two books; one read, *by this sensible act, Daxen wisely secured the vital food supply and saved the kingdom from famine*; the other said, *meanwhile, as Daxen's army wasted precious time over their commander's futile gesture, the enemy column swept remorselessly on through the south, slaughtering and enslaving at will.* In the end, he figured that since he had no grain sacks and no carts to carry them on, there was no decision to make. He was painfully aware that this line of reasoning was deeply flawed, but he did his best not to think about it.

*

The market town of Tollens was famous for its brassware, its delicate blue and white glazed pottery, the Pauxen opera house, the annual flower festival, its traditional lattice-top meat pies and its distinctively nutty-tasting wheat beer. The gates were open. It was deserted.

"What I can't make out," Prexil said, "is how they reckon on feeding that many prisoners. Yes, granted, they've taken every damn item of food in the town, right down to walnuts and ground pepper. But that's not going to last very long, is it? Not with a whole town on the march."

A sound enough man within his limitations, Prexil, but no imagination. More to the point, in Daxen's view, was which direction the prisoners had been sent off in. Tollens stood at the junction of three roads: the Great South, which they'd just come up; the West High, which stalked off into the mountains and eventually petered out into cart tracks; and the East Military, which veered away south-east dead straight for two hundred miles before forking into the Great East and the South-East High. It stood to reason that the enemy would have sent their prisoners away under escort, so as not to impede their own progress, while their fighting men pressed on up the Great South towards the capital. Logic dictated that they should have taken the East Military, which would bring them back to the desert in a relatively short loop. Logic also dictated that they'd be mad to go the way their enemy expected them to go, so undoubtedly they'd taken the West High; struck out west for fifty miles or so, then cut across country, rejoined the Great South at some point between Tollens and Erithry, then merrily on their way to the tribal heartlands. The more he thought about it, the more loops and tangles formed in his mind, until he despaired of the whole issue. With forty thousand men—some of the time, forty thousand was an intolerable burden, a vast multitude to feed and water and move about, like trying to carry an anvil on your shoulder; other times, it wasn't nearly enough—detach five thousand to garrison Erithry, five thousand to cut the corn, send a thousand cavalry down the West High: if he started down that road, pretty soon there'd be no one left. When he closed his eyes he was surrounded by piles of books, all *The Rise and Fall of the Kingdom of Blemya,* all open at this precise moment, all different, some of them with alarmingly few pages left to go. No chance, Genseric had said; he'd sounded confident, as though he'd read to the end. No chance; don't bother, nothing you do will really make any difference. He'd said it with such feeling—

A sparrowhawk, hovering next to the road, on the left. You were supposed to be able to read the future by observing and interpreting the flight of birds; also the movement of stars and planets, the entrails of slaughtered animals, the fall of dice, playing cards. Was that the sort of esoteric wisdom the wise men of the craft devoted their lives to? Maybe Genseric had thrown the dice or made a detailed study of a fieldfare, and that was why he was so sure. *Our scholars and theirs have been in communication for centuries.* Not just their scholars, either. It seemed absurd that an Imperial could talk to these people rationally, conduct civilised negotiations with them; with these creatures of sand and darkness, who ate up whole populations and then vanished into the desert glare. Genseric had used the word respect. Bizarre. The tribesmen lived in the baking hot desert and thought the sun was God. For crying out loud. So was sweat running down your legs supposed to be some kind of sacrament?

On the sixth day they came across an army. Which army it had been, led by whom, was anybody's guess, because every single body had been stripped naked, and the heat had swollen them into unrecognisable lumps. You could just about tell the Imperials, because they were plum-brown rather than purple.

"We ought to bury them, surely," Euxis said. The crows were screaming again, and Daxen could see their point. First they chase us off the laid wheat, now the carrion. What harm did we ever do them? Nobody was inclined to walk up and down among the bodies and carry out a systematic count, so they made do with a rough guess; fifteen thousand, call it twelve regiments plus auxiliaries. Nearly all arrow wounds (but the enemy hadn't left a single arrow. Waste not, want not). From a distance, they looked like a spectacular crop of mushrooms, overgrown and just about to spoil.

Later, Daxen overheard some of the junior officers talking; they were riding behind him, he didn't recognise their voices and he couldn't see their faces. One was saying: fifteen thousand dead, doesn't that make it the greatest defeat in Blemyan history? No, another one said, that's Second Antecyra, sixteen thousand four hundred. Then there's Choris Axeou, sixteen thousand two-fifty. Yes, said the first one, but Second Antecyra, wasn't that where the bridge collapsed, you can't count that, it was a separate thing. Yes, said the second, but the bridge collapsing was during the battle, so properly speaking it counts. Choris, said a third voice, wasn't that where we lost about eight hundred to friendly fire from the garrison batteries? No, said the second voice, you're thinking of Gavetta; Choris was where five hundred men got marched off a cliff in the dark, during the night outflanking manoeuvre. Fine, said the first voice, knock off five hundred, you're down to fifteen seven-fifty, and bear in mind we didn't do an accurate count, it could've been more than fifteen seven-fifty. At any rate (said the first voice, resolutely defiant), it's got to be the second-worst defeat in Blemyan history. Well, hasn't it? And the third voice said, Hang on, though, aren't you forgetting about the Hyaxan Forks?

The next day, five hours before they reckoned on arriving at Laxen's Ferry, they met a cart.

The outriders raced back with the news: *there's a cart on the road.* About a mile ahead, just one cart, two people in it, possibly a man and a woman. For a moment or so, Daxen and his senior staff were too bewildered to speak. Then someone said, fetch them here, right now. Someone else said, hang on, what if it's a trap? One cart, someone else said, out in the open, it should be all right. The second voice explained that he'd meant it as a joke.

"Bring them in," Daxen said (and a part of his mind realised: trap, pony and trap, oh I *see*). "Quick as you can."

They were Oxelas and Ruxen, and they had a small coopers' yard in Laxen's Ferry, and they were on their way to a vineyard at a little place called Brown Reach, and if the soldiers didn't believe them, they could look for themselves. See? Two dozen half-hogsheads, as ordered. Yes, they'd left Laxen's that morning, end of fourth watch, soon as the gates opened. Invasion? What invasion?

When Daxen told them, they went deadly pale. We've got to get home, the woman said to the man, what about the children? The man gestured her quiet, and asked if the invasion had got as far as Brown Reach. Little place, he repeated, about four miles off the road, there's a track off to the left. Daxen said he didn't know, which seemed to surprise the man very much. Sorry, he said. You're the army, I thought you'd know something like that.

Daxen thanked them and sent twenty cavalry with them as an escort. Then he called a staff meeting. They sat on folding stools beside the road, while the army leaned on their shields and waited for orders.

"They can't just have vanished into thin air," Prexil said. "If they turned back, we'd have run straight into them. They can't have gone off cross-country, or we'd have seen signs. You can't march a huge army through cornfields without leaving a trail."

Daxen pointed out that they'd passed a major crossroads early that morning. He clicked his fingers for the map and found a thin blue line. Castle Street, he read out; runs parallel to the river, then forks, and one branch swings back down to join the East Military. He looked up. "Maybe they've gone home," he said.

There was a bewildered silence. "Why would they do that?" Euxis said. "I thought they were headed for the capital."

The engineer shrugged. "We don't know that," he said. "That lodge bastard sort of implied it, but we don't *know*."

"More likely," Prexil said, "they've changed course, trying to throw us off. Where's that map?"

Daxen kept hold of it. "I don't think so," he said. "If they turned off down this Castle Street thing, there's nowhere to cross the river for fifty miles, not till you get to Holden. And from Holden back to town is a hell of a hike, up through the forest and all sorts." He stopped and looked round. "Has anyone sent scouts to Laxen's Ford?" he asked.

No, they hadn't. The omission was swiftly rectified. "If they wanted to give us the slip," said the engineer, who'd got hold of the map while Daxen was occupied with other things, "surely they'd have carried on just past Laxen's and taken the Old Express. That way, they could've led us a merry dance through the Mesoge and still not have had to go very far out of their way. That's assuming they know the geography, but I think we can take that for granted."

Daxen stood up and tugged the map gently from his hands. "Why would they turn back?" he said.

Silence; then a young lieutenant whose name Daxen should've known by now said, "Maybe they've got what they came for, or done whatever it was they wanted to do. You just don't know, with people like that."

People like that—"Actually," Daxen said, "he could be right. Since we don't know what they want, we're in no position to guess if they've got it yet."

"I thought the lodge man said they wanted to wipe us off the face of the earth," Euxis said.

"Maybe they do," Daxen said. "It'd be so much simpler if we could just ask them."

*

The scouts came back from Laxen's Ford. Everything seemed normal. They'd asked a couple of farmers if they'd seen anything of the invaders, and been met with blank stares. No invasion here, friend, sorry.

Daxen gave orders to pitch camp. Someone pointed out to him that there was no water. They marched on another two miles until they came to an irrigation channel, and stopped there instead. Daxen announced that there would be a general kit inspection (which would give the men plenty to do) and retreated to his tent with all the maps. No interruptions, under any circumstances.

With the flaps drawn, he lay on his bed, closed his eyes and tried to clarify his mind. So far, they'd marched into the desert and back again, visited a deserted town and city, passed by the dead bodies of an entire army, chased an invisible enemy who'd dissolved into mist for no apparent reason. In order to carry out this mission, he'd taken direct personal command of the armed forces. He had absolutely no idea what he was doing, or what was going on.

So far, so good. He still had the army, nearly full strength, adequately supplied, undefeated in battle; the mighty Blemyan army, holder of the balance of power between empires, widely acknowledged as the finest fighting force in the civilised world. That should be enough, he thought, but somehow it wasn't. He had the wretched feeling of having been found out, as though he'd forged a document or impersonated someone. All along, he'd reassured himself by saying that whatever happened, she'd understand; but now he wasn't so sure. In his mind he could hear her: *How could you,* she was saying: *how could you have been so stupid?*

Suddenly he grinned. She was funny when she got all pompous, and she couldn't keep it up for very long. Then she'd break up laughing at herself, amused and angry and ashamed, and everything would be fine after that. He realised, for the first time, just how much stronger she was than him.

Then the bright moment faded, because there was nothing at

all she'd be able to do, if she was here, except quite possibly lose her throne; she couldn't take charge, lead the army. If she tried to, the soldiers would just stare at her, red with embarrassment. Oh God, he thought, why does it have to be us? Why can't we just offload it all on to someone else, a professional, a grown-up? Then he thought about the steelnecks and the politicians, and was forced to the unhappy conclusion that he was on his own.

Still, once he'd accepted that, at least he knew what to do. He got up, pulled back the tent flap and yelled for Captain Euxis.

"First thing tomorrow," he said, "we're going to the capital. I want to leave at dawn. Got that?"

Euxis was about to say, *Yes, but*. At the last moment, he drew back from the precipice and said, "Yes, sir."

"I want you to send the cavalry on ahead," he went on. "We won't need them, and I want some sort of military presence near the City as soon as possible. And there'll be despatches to the Joint Chiefs of Staff, so I'll need the fastest rider we've got. All right?"

After that, he went back and lay on the bed for a long time.

They crossed the river at Laxen's Ford and pressed on up the road. Mesajer had insisted on leaving him two squadrons of heavy cavalry—you can't have an army of just foot soldiers, he'd said, it's unnatural—and Daxen sent them on ahead to announce their arrival and gather any news at all of the invaders. At Coxin they found fresh fruit and vegetables waiting for them; at Piloessin they were joined by a convoy of a hundred and seventy carts, commandeered from the mines by a quick-thinking cavalry lieutenant. The military governor of the province rode out to meet them outside Argyra; what was the emergency, and what could he do to help? Daxen thanked him and told him to stand by, whatever that meant. Was it true that Erithry had been burned to the ground? Not quite. Just stand by, there'll be an official communiqué in due course.

An exhausted horseman appeared at the camp gate and was carried in to see him. Apparently, he'd been riding for four days, as fast as he could without killing the horse. He wasn't even a soldier, it turned out, or not a proper one anyway. He was a mulberry grower, the second in command of a militia unit from a place called Outemida, a miners' transit depot on the East Military Road. Early one morning he and his CO had been dragged out of bed by hysterical townspeople, who reckoned they'd seen a vast body of people and horses on the road, just as the sun was rising. When you say vast, he'd said; tens of thousands, they'd told him, maybe even hundreds of thousands, the line was three miles long, it took them nearly an hour to go past where we were hiding. There was no trace of booze on their breath, so he'd guessed they were telling the truth; his CO had sent him to tell the military governor, but when he got to Argyra he was told the governor was headed for Laxen's Ford. He'd cut across country, but the governor hadn't been there; so he'd followed the road looking for the army he'd been told about, and here he was—

Daxen thanked him, made notes and dismissed what he'd heard from his mind. If the enemy had passed through Outemida four days ago, he had no chance of catching up with them this side of the desert, and there was no way he was going back there again. Now at least he knew *something*; the enemy were headed back where they'd come from, and they weren't alone—people and horses, the mulberry grower had said, there were men and women on foot as well as the hostile cavalry. That could be interpreted as meaning that at least some of the prisoners from Erithry were still alive, at the very least. They take care of their prisoners, Genseric had said, like they take care of their other livestock. He shivered. Something else, about belonging to the god. Fine. If you're that pious, enough to go to war over a perceived insult to a well, you'd take pretty good care of God's property, now wouldn't you?

*

The ancient and beautiful city of Cortroche. Daxen had cousins in Cortroche, an elderly lady and her two jolly, stolid sons. He'd stayed with them once, seven or eight years ago; they had the most amazing pear orchard. Like a fool, he'd forgotten that this was the time of the celebrated Cortroche Goose Fair, to which people (and geese) flocked from miles around. Consequently the road was jammed with carts, people and several million geese, waddling in step like (the comparison wasn't lost on him) a large but badly led army. They came so far that the geese had to be shod, with little wood-and-leather pattens that strapped under the foot. The army spent a morning causing chaos trying to force their way down the road, covered a whole mile and a half, scattered seventy thousand geese over a huge area; then Daxen made the decision to go round the city, across country. The outskirts of Cortroche are ringed by orchards, some of the finest in Blemya. Marching forty thousand men through orchards was easier than marching them through geese, but only just. The people they encountered didn't seem pleased to see them; why don't you go and play soldiers somewhere else?

Back on the road, eventually. They were nine miles out of Cortroche and Daxen was thinking about where to camp for the night when someone told him there were riders up ahead. Not a big deal any more. He put them out of his mind until Euxis came and told him the riders were official, from the capital; from the queen.

Daxen's heart stopped for a moment. "Why the hell didn't you say so earlier?" he snapped, quite unfairly, and scrambled through soldiers pitching tents and driving in palings until he found them: six smartly dressed kettlehats watering their horses at a stream.

"Have you brought a letter?" he asked breathlessly. One of the kettlehats turned and looked at him for a moment, and asked if he was Grand Logothete Daxen.

"Yes, that's me. I'm expecting a letter from the queen. Have you—?"

The kettlehat looked round, as if assessing some tactical issue. Then he made an obvious effort and took a step forward. The other five closed in behind him. "I have a warrant for your arrest," he said.

It wasn't a cell, as such. As far as he could make out, it was an ante-room to the vestry of what had once been the private chapel used by the emperors of the united empire, before the civil war. Here, presumably, the supreme pontiffs of the one true faith had retired to meditate before performing the high sacraments in front of the emperor, the imperial family and the inner court; that would account for the exceptional quality of the mosaics that covered every square inch of the walls and ceiling. On all four sides of him was the Translation—the epiphany, the transmission of the holy flame, the miracle of the five red birds, the apotheosis of the Prophet and the transubstantiation of the flesh—while above him Our Lady of the Penitent Spirit stood in a posture of eternal supplication, her left hand raised, the single tear glistening on her mahogany cheek. If Daxen had been just a little bit more spiritual, he'd have said it was worth it just to be there, for hours on end, with nothing to do but sit and admire the artwork.

After a very long time the door opened; it was a footman with a silver tray. Cold beetroot and artichoke soup (very fashionable but he couldn't be doing with it), duck terrine with cherries, something with noodles and bits of chicken in a creamy mushroom sauce, and nothing to eat it with; no knife, no spoon, even. He looked at it.

"Can I get something to drink with that?" he asked. The footman looked over the top of his head and withdrew, and he heard a bolt grind in a hasp outside. Apparently not.

He wasn't hungry anyway. He put the tray down on the floor and sat down again. The chair was three hundred years old and hard as nails, but he was damned if he was going to sit on the ground. He tried to think, but he couldn't: beyond anger, beyond fear. He just wanted something to happen.

He must have dozed off, because a voice woke him. He sat bolt upright and opened his eyes, and found he had a headache. Wonderful.

"I said," said the voice, "didn't you like your dinner?"

Daxen looked at him. A very tall, broad man with a wide face, completely bald, an Imperial, in plain light grey academic vestments; he had forearms like legs, and the gold signet ring of the Royal Clerical order. Daxen had never seen him before. He took a deep breath.

"You're going to be in so much trouble," he said.

The man smiled. "My name is Carrhasian," he said. "I'm the deputy chief clerk of the Observances office. You're Daxen."

Daxen grinned back at him. "No, I'm not. You've got the wrong man. Can I go now?"

Carrhasian nodded. "You queried the warrant," he said. "I've consulted the precedents, and I can confirm the warrant was in order and your arrest was entirely lawful."

"Like hell," Daxen snapped. "Clearly you don't understand. I'm the queen's authorised deputy; I answer only to her. As far as you're concerned, I *am* her. Now, you've got one minute to let me out of here, or your neck is on the block. Have you got that?"

But Carrhasian shook his head. "You were properly impeached *in absentia* on charges of treason," he said. "You no longer hold any office of any kind."

Daxen breathed in deeply. "I'd like to see some paperwork, please."

Carrhasian shrugged. "In due course, maybe. I'll see what I can do. Properly speaking, since you no longer hold office you don't have clearance to view restricted government papers. But I have a certain degree of discretion."

"What have you done with the queen? Is she still alive?"

A mighty eyebrow lifted. "Of course."

"You've got her locked up somewhere, then."

"Don't be ridiculous. We are loyal servants of the queen." He smiled gently. "You're the traitor."

Daxen had a shrewd suspicion that this man could break his arms like twigs if he wanted to. The thought helped him cool his temper a little. "That's not true," he said. "What am I supposed to have done?"

Carrhasian pursed his lips. "That's also restricted," he said.

"Really. You've charged me with something, but you're not allowed to tell me what because it's a secret."

"Yes, essentially. It's a problem in treason cases. I believe the Law Commission's preparing a consultation document on it right now."

Daxen sighed. He wanted to smash Carrhasian's face in, but without a weapon he knew he didn't have a chance, and the frustration was building up inside him, the way fatigue builds up in your arms and legs when you're doing exhausting work. The only option was to let it go, win by not fighting. (That always sounded good, but he wasn't quite sure what it meant; never mind, try it anyway.) "Fine," he said. "It seems to me that if you could simply get rid of me, you'd have done it already. Instead, I'm still alive, and banged up in a chapel instead of a dungeon. Therefore you want something or you need me for something, or else you're not nearly as sure of your position as you say you are." He made a vague gesture with his hands. "Oh, sit down, for crying out loud. Here, you can have the chair and I'll sit on the floor." He stood up and sat down again in the corner, his back to the wall. It worked; just for a moment, Carrhasian hesitated, then sat down, feeling (Daxen could see it) just a little bit foolish. "Now, then," he said, "it's just us, you and me. What the hell is all this about?"

Carrhasian looked at him for a while. It wasn't hatred exactly, or loathing, or contempt; it probably wasn't much higher in the intensity scale than distaste, but there was an awful lot of it. But you don't kill someone just because you dislike him. "All right," he said, "I'll be straight with you."

"Thank you so much."

Carrhasian took a moment to order his thoughts. "We—"

"Sorry, who's *we*? I don't know you."

"You wouldn't," Carrhasian said. "That's not important."

"It is to me. Who are you? You're not the government or the regular civil service. So either you're military, which I'm inclined to doubt, you don't strike me as a regular steelneck, or—" Suddenly he realised where he'd seen that same dislike before. "I'm guessing you might be the lodge," he said. "Well?"

Carrhasian's face didn't change at all. "We probably have the advantage of you, in that we know a certain amount about the desert people and the level of threat they represent. We also have intelligence about the activities of the insurgents which it would appear you do not. The threat is extremely serious." He paused, then went on. "In fact, it would be hard to exaggerate the danger the kingdom is in, now that the desert people have declared war. We simply don't have the resources, or the tactical expertise. All we can do is try and maintain the situation—hold the line, if you like—until a solution is found. In the meanwhile, it's vitally important that public morale is maintained, and that the people have confidence in the government and the army. Your antics in the desert—we've managed to keep it quiet for the time being, but everything comes out eventually. The people will need to be reassured that the incompetent first minister and the incompetent commander-in-chief—you, in other words—had been replaced with men they can believe in. Since the queen refused to listen to our advice and replace you herself, we had no option but to impeach you. Since the queen wouldn't hear of that either, we used the only resource open to us, which is treason."

Daxen felt numb, but he managed to nod his head gently. "So," he said, "how does that work, exactly?"

Carrhasian was very nearly smirking; clearly, he was proud of himself. "The queen is young, unmarried and female. We therefore have an overriding duty to protect her from undue influence of, let's say, a romantic nature; seduction, if you like. In such circumstances, where Her Majesty's judgement might be affected and compromised, we have a prerogative jurisdiction to override her wishes in her name, on her behalf, as we might do if she was suffering from disease or mental illness. Your relationship with the queen—"

Daxen stood up so sharply that, just for a moment, he could see that Carrhasian was intimidated. "No," he said, "I'm not having that. There was never anything like that. It's simply not true."

"Oh, come now." Carrhasian had recovered. "We have a substantial dossier; private conversations, clandestine meetings in a secluded cloister—"

"She's my friend," Daxen said. "Friends, that's all. Since we were kids."

"The Commission sees it differently," Carrhasian said. "We have found prima facie evidence of treason. Frankly, under normal circumstances, why the hell not? Queens have lovers, even unmarried ones. But, since you had to go, we're grateful to you for making it easy for us. You should be grateful, too. It spared us the necessity of killing you, which was the other option."

Daxen sat down again. There was a deadly casualness about the way he'd said it. "She'll have your heads," he said. "Unless you're going to kill her too. But if you could, you'd have done it already. You've got the proverbial wolf by the ears, if you ask me. You can't get rid of her, and as soon as she's figured out a way, she'll have you."

"It's a distinct possibility," Carrhasian said, and he was casual about that too. "But we have to protect the kingdom. If people have to suffer—you, or us—it really isn't important. You're smarter than I gave you credit for, so I'll tell you straight. You're alive because that's easier for us, as things stand. We have the situation under review, and we're exploring other possibilities. You would be advised to cooperate while things are as they are now. That'd be best for all concerned." Carrhasian took a deep breath, and then went on. "Let me see if I understand you. I think I do, but maybe I'm wrong. You became Grand Logothete because, more than anything else, you wanted to help your friend, the queen. Is that right?"

Daxen looked straight at him. "Yes."

"Good. Right now, the best way you can help her is to go quietly. If you kick up a fuss, it makes it harder for us to continue with her on the throne. Replacing her would be a serious headache, something we really don't need right now. We'd much rather she stayed where she is and you go away somewhere. But if we have to, we'll get rid of both of you. If it comes to that."

"You're the lodge, aren't you?" Daxen said. "But that's stupid. I met a lodge soldier in the desert, and he said you weren't taking sides. He said you and the savages—"

Carrhasian scowled at him. "I don't know what you mean by *lodge*," he said. "But I've got to tell you, you aren't even close. Our only concern is the wellbeing of Blemya. Anyway," he said, standing up, "here's what you do. You retire to your country estates, you kill animals and chase little peasant girls and do whatever it is people do in the country, and you take no further part in public life. You make no attempt to contact the queen. Or, if you prefer, we kill you. Take a few hours to think it over. Someone will be along eventually to let you out."

He was by the door. "Just one thing," Daxen said.

"What?"

"Let me have a pen and some ink."

"What for?"

"I think better when I write things down."

Carrhasian raised his eyebrows. "If you like," he said. "I really don't see what there is to think about, though."

He left, and about an hour later a footman arrived with a silver inkstand, a new goose quill, exquisitely sharpened (but no penknife, of course) and twelve sheets of best rag paper. After he'd gone, Daxen sat quite still for a while. Then, slowly and carefully, he inked in moustaches on all the angels in the Translation. He had to stand on the chair to reach Our Lady of the Penitent Spirit; in the circumstances, however, he felt he owed it to himself to make the extra effort.

Two of Spears

He was a big man, tall and broad-shouldered, bald, in a plain grey academic gown and expensive bespoke sandals, two angels a pair. He sat down on the stone ledge that ran along the cloister wall and folded his hands. "My name's Carrhasian," he said.

"No," Forza said gently. "It isn't."

"Quite right." A small, annoyed smile. "But for the purposes of this meeting, I am Director Carrhasian. Thank you for coming here, General Belot."

Forza leaned forward a little. "Purely out of interest—"

"He's indisposed."

Forza guessed he hadn't meant to snap like that; raw nerve. He made a note of it, for later. "Not to worry," he said. "You'll do, I'm sure. It's a shame, though, I'd liked to have met Carrhasian. He was a remarkable man."

"Yes." A little bit more tension; excellent. A bow is only useful when it's fully drawn. "Can we talk about the war now, please? We've got a lot to discuss."

"Of course." Forza spread his hands wide and pressed them palms down on his knees. "Though really I'm not sure why you want to talk to me about your war. It's none of my business. The Eastern empire's always had a good relationship with the desert nomads, thank God. They're not our problem."

"Quite," the man said, "but the fall of Blemya would be." He smiled; he had a mobile reserve. "Yours and your brother's, of course."

A position fortified in depth. "That goes without saying," Forza replied calmly. "You think it might come to that."

"If I didn't, I wouldn't have asked you here."

"All right," Forza said. "So why me, and not Senza? Or have you got him in a side room somewhere, waiting his turn?"

You can learn so much just by watching people. He saw the corner of the man's mouth move just a little, and remembered Fail Cross, where he'd seen an enemy cavalryman suddenly race away from his unit and gallop across the battlefield to the extreme left wing; from that he'd deduced Senza's entire battle plan, and had been able to turn a horrific defeat into a bloody stalemate in the nick of time. The recollection made him smile. *He's talked to Senza already,* he thought; and either Senza's agreed to the plan or he hasn't. Very well. Onwards.

"Anyway," he said briskly, "yes, I take your point. The question is, which would my lord the emperor prefer as a strategically crucial buffer state, Blemya or two million nomads with their heads full of holy war?" He grinned. "You've got me," he said. "I give in." He paused to let the last three words sink in, then added, "So what did Senza say? Is he on board too?"

A faint hiss of escaping breath, as though he'd trodden on a nail or something. "I don't know what you mean."

"Oh, come on," Forza said wearily. "Do you really think I'd be here if I didn't know you've already put the same offer to my darling brother? Here's the deal. If he's in, so am I. If not, it was a pleasure meeting you."

The man swallowed. He was breaking up. "He's in."

"Excellent." Forza clapped his hands. "The Belot boys, united at last for the good of humanity. Did he happen to mention whether he's cleared this escapade with his lords and masters, by the way, or doesn't he bother with things like that?"

"He has full discretion," the man said bitterly. "As do you."

"Indeed." In victory the essential thing to remember is not to follow up too far. "Well, in that case, we have a deal. Now then." He sat up straight, puppy-dog eager. If he'd had a tail, he'd have wagged it. "What's the position? Tell me all about it."

Three days' hard ride to get home; on a bloody schedule, as always.

He got rid of his escort at the Joy in Repentance; they stumbled into the taproom, too weary to argue when he said he was going on without them for a day or so. He left them drinking in grim silence, took out a fresh horse and followed the road, the last leg of the intolerable journey. Against regulations for the commander-in-chief to go wandering off without a half-company of cavalry at the very least, but he was sick to death of soldiers. Besides, if he brought them home with him, he'd have to feed them and find them beds, and that sort of thing quickly ran into money. He could picture her face as he told her that she had thirty men and thirty-six horses to cater for. He grinned. Screw regulations.

From the Joy to Chastel, four hours, or three if you thrash it. He made it in just over two. That was, after all, the Belot way—get there fast and unexpected, get in and do the job. Well, quite.

Just starting to get dark as he rode through the main gate. The hedges were badly overgrown, and there were clumps of shoulder-high nettles on either side of the drive. A few sheep in the park; the grass had been grazed away to nothing, but he wasn't sure if that was all right with sheep. He smiled. She wanted him to be a farmer when he was at home, and he'd tried, but it was no good, it just wouldn't stick. The rails beside the track needed patching up, he noticed. You turn your back for five minutes and the place goes all to hell.

There was a lamp in the stables, so he called out as he dismounted. The door opened and a groom he knew by sight came out and stared at him. "Flying visit," he said, handing over the reins. The groom looked at him as though God had manifested Himself in the stable yard and was expecting him to work overtime. He turned and walked across the yard to the back door, three days of ridiculously fast riding catching up with him in a matter of seconds. Damn, he thought, I'm going to creak about like an old man. How attractive is that?

The back door was unlocked, which annoyed him. He lifted the latch, taking care not to make any noise, swung the door slowly open and slid inside. Just the one oil lamp glowing in the kitchen passage, bless her economical heart. He walked on the sides of his feet, as if he was stalking deer in a forest. At this time of day, where would she be?

"Hello, Forza," she said. "Had a good time at the war?"

He spun round. She must've come out of the small pantry (but the door had been closed and there was no light showing under it). She was wearing one of those godawful tent-like nightdresses and carrying a candle in a plain pottery holder. "Hello, sweetheart," he said. "I'm home."

One brief, crisp kiss; that was the rule. She swept past him, down the passage and into the small parlour, where four of the sixteen candles were lit and a fire was burning in the hearth. He sat down in the larger of the two chairs, the ornate monstrosity his father had given them as a wedding present. It looked awful, but it was profoundly comfortable. She poured water from the kettle simmering on the hearth into a blue porcelain teapot, then turned to look at him. Her eyes were shining. "Well?" she said.

He allowed himself a pause, then a slow grin. "You'll never guess," he said.

With an incredibly swift movement—that knack she had of sort of flowing, like a liquid—she sat on his knees and kissed him till his head began to swim. Then she said, "*Well?*"

"Meet the new commander-in-chief of the Blemyan army," he said. "Well," he added, "one of them, anyway."

It was worth all of it just to see the look on her face. "You're joking."

"I'm not." He darted a kiss at her, but she was too quick for him. "It's all official," he said. "Me and one other."

He was looking at her mouth. Usually when he did that, she'd say "Stop it" with a mock scowl. "Not—"

"Oh yes." He loved it when he was able to surprise her. "It's going to be interesting," he said.

She slipped out of his lap, stood up, crossed to the fireplace and threw on another log. He didn't mind that; it gave him a chance to look at her properly. He loved that she was as tall as him and almost as strong. She'd distanced herself from him so she could think. "So it's that bad," she said.

"I think so," he said. "It's true, they've taken a major city. Grabbed hold of all the people and marched them off into the desert. Some clown of a politician went after them but never got anywhere near. If they want Blemya, as far as I can see, all they've got to do is take it."

She shivered. He was almost hot enough to sweat, but her idea of comfortably warm was somewhere just below the melting point of copper. "So it's the Belot brothers to the rescue," she said. "What does *he* think about that?"

Forza shrugged. "He's all right with it, presumably. I'd have heard if he wasn't."

"Don't you think you ought to make sure?"

Well, he'd been in two minds. "All right," he said. "I'll write to him in the morning. Is there any food?"

She frowned. "Probably," she said. "I've already had dinner. When do you go?"

"Day after tomorrow." He hesitated. "Can you come?"

She made him wait. "Oh, I think so," she said. "It might be warm there. I'm sick of being cold."

He tried not to grin, but failed miserably. "That's all right, then," he said. "It's a pretty godforsaken place, mind."

"Worse than Choris Seautou?"

He thought about that. "No."

"Then that's all right." She poured tea into two tiny bowls, handed him one. Jasmine and black pepper; delicious. "I'll pack a few things tonight."

And that was that; she was coming with him, and the horrible job facing him suddenly wasn't so bad after all. He wondered if she'd write and tell her parents, or let them find out from the official bulletins. They'd be furious; they always were. Ladies from fine old Imperial families shouldn't sleep in tents and shit in ditches. Exactly what they were supposed to do all day nobody had quite figured out yet; be put away in cupboards when not in use seemed to be the prevailing opinion. Raico wasn't like that; she loathed spinning and weaving, couldn't do embroidery to save her life, couldn't sit still and quiet for two minutes together. *Whatever possessed her to go and marry that soldier*—Something her mother could never hope to understand, that was for sure.

"You're doing it again," she said.

He laughed. "Sorry," he said. "I haven't seen you for—what, three months? I'm allowed."

"Husbands shouldn't ogle their wives," she said firmly. "It's not polite."

"I'm not ogling, I'm admiring."

She narrowed her eyes. "Admiring is what you do to old buildings," she said. "Go on. I'll be up as soon as I've seen to everything."

He stood up. "And anyway," he said, "I can't ogle worth a damn if you insist on wearing that tent thing. It's absolutely guaranteed ogle-proof."

"Forza, don't be annoying. Go and get cook to cut you some bread and cheese."

Much later, when she was asleep and he was lying on his back with his eyes open—when he was at home sleeping was such a waste—he thought about the day he'd first seen her, coming out of the fire temple; taller than her father and brothers, wearing one of those ridiculous golden mushroom hats that were in fashion back then; extraordinary rather than beautiful, but he'd known there and then what the purpose of his life had to be. Even now, after ten years of marriage, she fascinated him; his secret ambition was to spend a day just observing her, trying to predict what she was going to do or say—a good general is never taken by surprise, he anticipates every possibility, but she ambushed him all the time without even trying. He remembered the first time he managed to scrape an invitation to the family's town house; a whole afternoon of making small talk with her obnoxious mother and father; then, when the whole enterprise seemed lost, he'd launched his forlorn hope. I gather you play chess, he'd said, and she'd given him a look, later he'd realised it was fair warning; yes, she played chess. They had a magnificent coral and ivory set, worth a thousand acres of good arable land. He'd made a soft opening, the way you do when you're playing a girl, and suddenly he found himself staring defeat in the face—he'd never lost a game except three times, to Senza. Suddenly he realised he was playing for his life. The game lasted three hours, all the other guests had gone home, the servants wanted to lay for dinner and her parents went from vexed to embarrassed to livid; he knew he couldn't win, but there was just a faint hope of a stalemate, so he hung on, dug deep, *concentrated*, like he'd never done before off the battlefield; and finally she beat him, and as he sat there, numb with defeat and mental exhaustion, she'd smiled at him, and he knew—

Ah well. He'd beaten her twice since then: once on their honeymoon, though he still suspected her of throwing the game, and once on the day she lost the baby. And two out of eight hundred and six wasn't too bad, against such an opponent.

He turned round and prodded her in the back. She grunted. "Let's play chess," he said.

She made a noise like a pig. "Forza, it's the middle of the night."

"Hey, so it is. I'll be white."

She turned her head; fortunately it was dark, so he couldn't see the look on her face. "Forza."

"Please?"

The game lasted an hour. He very nearly made a draw of it, but she caught him when he least expected it.

The pillar was famous, apparently. Three hundred years ago a colony of holy men, sun-worshippers, had lived on top of it. They'd built a huge scaffolding tower, two hundred and seven feet tall, so as to be able to get themselves and their possessions up there. When the sixty stylites, their books and vestments and chickens and instruments of self-mortification had been safely offloaded on the pillar's flat top, the carpenters down below sawed through the legs of the tower, which came crashing down, leaving the colony alone with each other and God. According to the legend, each man had just enough room to sit cross-legged. There was one rope, for hauling up water and sacks of grain. There they stayed for thirty years until the last surviving stylite untied the rope and let it fall. It was the sun-worshippers' third holiest shrine, and a quarter of a million pilgrims crossed the desert every year to see it.

Senza had dismounted all the trebuchets, onagers, wall-pieces and heavy scorpions from the defensive batteries on the walls of the City and brought them to the base of the pillar, with two crews to each machine. Just getting such a vast quantity of equipment across the desert was a remarkable achievement. Doing it so fast and so quietly that the nomads didn't find out until the artillery crews had been pounding the top of the pillar non-stop for six days and nights was little short of a miracle. By the time the nomad army arrived, the pillar was only half the height it should have been, and there was no way of telling which of the countless boulders scattered across the sand at its base were fragments of the sacred rock and which were profane missiles launched by the enemy. As for Senza's expeditionary force, it had vanished without trace.

When he heard the news, Goiauz the prophet solemnly shaved off his hair, eyebrows and beard, buried himself in ashes and didn't speak or move for two days. Then he announced that he had been granted a vision of the Invincible Sun in glory. The Sun had told him that every non-believer in the world now belonged to Him, and that it was Goiauz' duty to go out and bring home the flocks and the herds.

The column that set out up the Great South road wasn't just an army. It was essential, Goiauz said, that the entire nation should join together in the sacrament. They would follow the enemy's road to the sea and take their capital city; then, embarking on the enemy's ships, they would sail to the Eastern capital, then march overland to the West. As he had already demonstrated beyond any possible doubt, the enemy were entirely incapable of withstanding the onslaught and arrow storm of the faithful. He was aware that the two brothers who led the armies of East and West were united against them, and that they were reckoned to be very fine generals. He wasn't particularly concerned about that. No living man, no matter how cunning, could withstand the wrath of the Invincible Sun, whose power was so great that all those who even looked at Him directly were struck blind. In six months' time—he, Goiauz the prophet, undertook it—the great work would be complete and the entire world would be filled with the glory of the holy truth.

"I had an idea it would be here," Forza said quietly.

Dead bodies don't stink in the desert the way they do in more temperate regions. Anywhere in the empire so many bodies would've attracted attention from miles away. As it was, they could easily have passed by without finding this place; you'd never find it if you didn't know it was there. The nomads had chosen a spot where the ground fell away sharply into a steep-sided bowl; quite possibly there had been an oasis there once, which would explain why someone had been to the trouble of dragging rocks into a circle. The wooden stakes—thirty thousand or so of them, a huge drain on the nomads' slender reserves of timber—were a new addition, though you could see them as a long-term investment. Wood doesn't rot in the desert; they could last hundreds of years, as could the sun-dried corpses nailed to them, unless some busybody came along and interfered. Forza made a mental note to do just that, at some point.

"Well," Forza said, "we've found the Erithryans. Though I guess *better late than never* doesn't really apply."

No way of knowing how long they'd been dead, though perhaps an expert on the desiccation of human tissue might have ventured an opinion. The absence of visible wounds on the bodies suggested that they'd been alive when they were nailed to the stakes. That made a sort of sense; they'd been given to the Sun god to do as He liked with, and He'd chosen to dry them out like raisins. Indeed. They'd keep better that way, practically indefinitely. Desert logic.

He was upsetting her, he could tell. She didn't much like gallows humour. His instinct, when faced with genuine horror, was to fight back instantly with a joke, like using archers and slingers in open order to slow up the advance of a pike formation. "What are you going to do?" she said.

He looked back over his shoulder to the top of the rise. "Nothing," he said. "We can't bury them; we don't have time. They'll keep. Also, I don't think we want to tell anyone about this. Men don't tend to do as they're told when they're angry."

She frowned at him. "I'd have thought—Well, motivation."

"Too much of a good thing," he said, with just a hint of what he felt. "We'd better get back; they'll be wondering what the hell we've been up to."

They rode back over the rim of the hollow. The adjutant gave him an enquiring look but he shook his head. "False alarm," he said. "Right, on we go."

The whole of the fifteenth book of Cartesuma's *Life of Forza Belot* is devoted to the campaign against the nomads, but the battle of the Twenty-third Oasis occupies a mere two pages. Understandably enough; all the imagination, vision, technical brilliance and élan was expended in luring the enemy out into the middle of the desert and then reaching the only oasis first and fortifying it against them. Cartesuma describes in loving detail the night marches and the remarkable skill of the navigators, the cunning measures taken to disguise the movements of the army, the triumphs of intelligence gathering and misinformation, and quite rightly makes the point that Forza Belot, in this campaign, completely revolutionised the science of desert warfare, with consequences for the history of the empires that cannot be overestimated. The battle itself, he points out, was practically an anticlimax; for the connoisseur of the Belot style, there's very little of interest. All Forza had to do was keep the enemy from reaching the water for two days, and this he achieved by the simple expedient of a strong natural defensive position quickly but effectively fortified and defended by an adequate number of archers supplied with a sufficiency of arrows. The genius of the Twenty-third Oasis lay in the preparations, not the fight itself; the battle had been won long before the first shot was loosed, and total victory was by that point inevitable. Having launched wave after wave of horsemen against the oasis, until all their arrows were spent, their horses exhausted, their casualties insupportable, their spirit utterly broken, the defeated nomads reeled away into the desert with what little water they had left and to date no trace of them has ever been found. The prophet Goiauz and a handful of companions were the only survivors, and for obvious reasons they chose not to dwell on the events of the Twenty-third Oasis, ascribing the defeat to the wrath of the

Invincible Sun over a catalogue of offences against doctrine committed by the prophet's political enemies some time earlier.

Fully a third of Cortesuma's account is taken up with a narrative of the remarkable way in which Raico Belot took command and held the line towards the end of the battle, while her husband was cut off from the army and wandering lost in the desert. For scholars interested in the so-called Raico Question, indeed, this incident provides the only point of real interest in the battle. Pro-Raico authors use the accounts of her conduct of the defence as telling evidence that she was indeed a major contributor to her husband's success and a considerable strategist and tactician in her own right; the anti-Raico school maintains that by that stage in the proceedings there was precious little that needed to be done except to encourage the men to keep shooting, and to conceal the fact that the general was missing, presumed dead; the accounts of her initiative and inspirational leadership were subsequently either grossly expanded or entirely fabricated by Senzaite historians expressly to detract from Forza's own achievements and, by giving credit to his wife, to belittle Forza himself. Clearly there is more than a kernel of truth in these allegations, and it is unlikely that, in such a politically charged and sensitive area of Imperial history, the actual course of events will ever be known.

Forza launched a wild diagonal swing at the tribesman's head; with a grin, he raised his right arm and blocked it easily. Splendid. As quickly as he could, Forza pulled down, drawing the concave cutting edge of the backsabre deep into the tribesman's forearm. For a moment there was an almost comical look of dismay on the poor fellow's face, as he realised he'd been taken for a fool; then Forza rammed the point into his stomach and twisted the hilt through ninety degrees. The tribesman's mouth opened but no words came out, only blood. He staggered a little, then stepped back, then fell over. Well. Served him right for not moving his feet.

Forza wiped the dead man out of his mind, straightened his back and looked round quickly. Five yards away, he saw the last man of his escort shot in the face at point-blank range; the arrow went in just to the left of his nose and the point poked through at the base of his skull. The archer swung round, searching for the next target, not looking down as he fumbled the next arrow from his quiver. There was no time. Forza threw the backsabre at him. Sheer luck, it hit him on the bow hand, side on, with just enough force to loosen his fingers and make him drop the bow. He stooped to pick it up. That meant his chin was at a wonderfully convenient height, a moment later, for Forza's boot. Forza felt the man's jaw crack, but that wasn't enough on its own. Luckily, the backsabre was just in reach, if he was quick. He grabbed it without stooping and swung, missed the neck, hit the side of the head, cutting off the top half of the ear. The man yelled, so still alive, but unlikely to be a problem. Forza looked back and saw a little gap between two rapidly converging tribesmen. I'm not that fast, he thought, I won't get there in time. Other possibilities, none.

Cursing himself for having no options, he ran at the gap. A tribesman had closed it; he'd drawn and was taking aim. Forza threw himself forward, landed on his elbows, heard the swish of the arrow passing over his head. He kicked at the sand, found his feet, shot up like a startled bird. A tribesman loomed into his field of view; Forza stretched out his right arm, holding the backsabre, and felt the edge run up against something as he passed. He heard a scream, so that was probably all right. He ran, waiting for the impact of the arrow in his back. He heard another swish, the flapping noise of the fletchings as they spun in flight, changing pitch as they went past him. He kept running.

As he ran, all he could think was: she'll be all right, the diversion worked, we drew them off. He had absolutely no way of knowing if that was true, because there were about a thousand tribesmen blocking his view. He tried to visualise—the breach in the barricade, the enemy surge, like floodwater; they'd closed it up a bit with dead bodies, shooting them as they nudged and elbowed through the gap, but not enough. He tried to remember how many reserves he'd had at that point in the line, but he couldn't. Nothing he could do about it now. Why hadn't they shot him yet?

He ran for a while, and then his chest hurt too much, nothing he could do got any air into his lungs. His throat was burning, he guessed it was a bit like drowning. His foot caught on something and then he was nose down in the sand. Ah well. He didn't bother trying to move. Enjoy breathing while you still can; won't be long now.

But he lay there, and nothing much happened. Gradually he started getting some air past the cramps and the burning sensation. He concentrated on breathing in deep, and his head began to clear. He wondered if there was an arrow sticking out of his back. Sometimes you don't feel it go in, apparently, or maybe the pain he'd taken as cramps was a puncture wound. He wriggled his back, felt no impediment. She'd be all right, wouldn't she? He tried not to think about it. The urge to get up and go back, to save her, while there was still time, was like a halter round his neck, dragging at him, choking him. He tried blocking it with logic. What could you possibly do, on your own? They'd kill you before you got anywhere near. You're in no fit state.

He raised himself on to his hands and knees, and a fit of coughing nearly split him in two. His knuckles brushed against something sharp; he looked at his hand, and saw he'd cut himself slightly on the edge of the backsabre. That made him want to laugh, but he couldn't spare the breath.

It took a bit of twisting and wriggling, but he turned himself round and sat up. All he could see was sand, with a double line of deep, scuffed footprints. Had he really run that far? He couldn't see anyone, standing or lying dead on the ground. Suddenly he felt the sun, like an extraordinary weight. His head swam, and he knew he wouldn't be able to do anything until it cleared. The sensible thing, surely, would be to close his eyes, just for two minutes.

When he came round, it was beginning to get dark. The temperature was dropping. He started to get up, but found he'd carelessly mislaid his strength. He remembered that there was something terribly important, but he had no idea what it might be.

The next time he woke up, he was shaking. That, it turned out, was because of the cold. It was pitch dark to start with, and then his eyes adjusted. A little faint moonlight became enough to see by. He tried to swallow but his throat was too dry. Oh hell, he thought, I'm going to die in the desert. He closed his eyes but he was too cold to sleep. He couldn't control the shivering, and there was nothing to crawl under or wrap himself in. He tried rubbing his legs, but his hands were numb, stupid useless things on the ends of his arms that wouldn't do as they were told. For some reason, when his eyes were closed, he could see the dead Erithryans, hanging off their posts like a lot of limp flags. Of course, if you die lying down, sooner or later drifting sand will cover you up. He thought, if I've been wrong all these years and there really is a fire god and an afterlife, it's going to be dreadfully embarrassing when I get there. Something in the order of a hundred thousand Easterners; oh, it's you, they'd all say, we want a word with you.

There was nothing he could do except crouch, his hands wrapped round his knees, and wait for the sun to rise. It took its own sweet time about it. At some point during the long wait he remembered—Raico, the attack, he had no idea if she was dead or alive. He could feel the panic, it was like an itch, or, rather, it was like being full of ferocious energy while also being unable to move; he couldn't sit still, but he could barely lift his arm. For God's sake, he thought. He strained his eyes staring at the sky, willing it to change colour.

When at last the dawn came, he stood up. For a while he didn't dare move; he was like someone standing on a very narrow bridge or a ledge, one slight misstep and he'd be gone. Somehow he managed to get his legs swinging, short steps to begin with; it didn't matter, because it couldn't be very far and he'd be at the oasis. Ridiculous, really; he'd been there all night in the vicious cold, and the oasis and the army couldn't be more than a few hundred yards away. He could do that crawling on his hands and knees, if needs be.

Think of something else. So he tried to order up images of home, of his house, the park, the barn where they laid up the store apples, wrapped in straw, on shelves; of her. He realised after a while that he was making up fake images and fake memories, because the real ones didn't seem to be there any more. Even her face was becoming indistinct, obscured, turned away, in shadow. He stopped. He'd come a long way, he was sure of it. He shot a glance upwards at the sun and saw it was high in the sky. He looked round. Then it slowly dawned on him that he'd been walking in the wrong direction.

Here lies Forza Belot, who died of stupidity. He sank to his knees, outraged at the sheer bitter unfairness of it. He tried to swallow and found he couldn't. The heat was like lead ingots strapped to his arms and legs. Of all the bloody ridiculous things, he thought, and a shadow fell across him.

Where they'd come from, he had no idea; he'd looked round a moment ago and seen nobody. But there they were: four tribesmen, on horses. They were looking at him. Then one of them leaned down and took his bow from the case that hung beside his leg. It wasn't strung; he watched the tribesman string it one-handed, very neatly done, with the elegant grace of long practice. He watched him choose an arrow. The distance was no more than twenty yards. The other three were watching him, as if they were going to mark him out of ten on his performance.

The backsabre was long gone, of course, lying forgotten in the sand somewhere. Made no difference; he knew he wouldn't have had the strength. He realised he felt nothing at all, no fear, no sudden spurt of survival instinct; he felt as if he was a long way off, watching something unimportant happening to someone else. The tribesman nocked his arrow, fixed his eyes on the target, pushed out with his bow hand, pulled back with the arrow hand, looking at Forza over the arrow tip. When his left arm was nearly straight, the power of the bow would drag the string out past his bent fingers and launch the arrow, it was a simple matter of geometry, a certain point on a straight line. The tribesman closed one eye, concentrated, approached the critical point; then he fell sideways off his horse and hit the sand face first.

His three companions had absolutely no idea what was happening. They leaned forward to peer, saw the arrow in their dead friend's back, swung round in their saddles; another one toppled backwards over his horse's arse. One of the remaining two dug his heels into his horse's flanks and yelled; he got about five yards, then slowly drooped sideways and toppled off. The last man just sat there, until an arrow hit him in the ear.

Unbelievable, Forza thought. Absolutely fucking mad.

That said, there were now three horses there for the taking. He tried to get to his feet, but it was as though his feet were caught in something. The hell with that; the horses were about to spook, any moment now they'd be off and that'd be that, the last ludicrous twist of the farce. No sudden movements, he told himself, rather superfluously. He stared at the nearest horse, trying to catch its eye, then remembered: horses don't like eye contact, it scares them. Let's all keep perfectly calm and still, and—

Quite suddenly, the horses put their ears back and sprang into a gallop. Forza tried to yell, but he couldn't make a sound. He watched them sprint away, no catching them now, not without twenty riders with ropes. Just so, so unfair. He closed his eyes, and then thought: so who shot the four arrows?

The answer was riding straight at him at a brisk trot: a dozen men in flowing white robes, so presumably they were angels or something. As they got closer, he realised they actually were angels, because they were too big to be ordinary humans, stupidly tall and absurdly broad across the shoulders, though it struck him as faintly ludicrous that angels should choose to ride stocky little black cobs; the angels' feet were so low they were practically trailing on the ground. But no matter; he'd reached the stage where he was seeing angels, and he knew perfectly well what that meant. He wondered if he'd hallucinated the four tribesmen, too. No, he decided, they looked pretty real, dead on the ground with arrows in them, lying in the unique carelessly dropped postures that are impossible for living men ever to fake. Four real men, and they'd been shot. By imaginary angels? In a way he was glad he was nearly out of it all. Trying to make sense of it would've been so very tiresome.

Two of the angels dismounted and came towards him. They cast shadows, which angels aren't supposed to do. They had scarves over their faces, but there was a little window around the eyes, and he noticed that one of the angels was an Imperial. One, but not the other. Fancy that.

"He's alive all right," said the Imperial angel. Forza opened his mouth; he wanted to say, no, I can't be, or I wouldn't be able to see you. On the other hand, could an angel be wrong about a question of life and death? He had to say, they weren't making a very good impression. "Fetch the water."

The other angel had blue eyes, like a Northerner. He nodded, went away, came back with a water bottle. The Imperial took it and pulled out the stopper. "Can you hear me?"

Forza mouthed yes, then nodded.

"Two mouthfuls, then count to twenty, then two more, got that? If you drink it all at once, it'll kill you."

Now he came to think of it, the Imperial angel was a head and a half shorter than the blue-eyed angel. Suddenly he thought, they aren't angels at all, they're big, tall Northerners commanded by an Imperial officer; in which case, he wasn't dead—

He grabbed the water bottle out of the Northerner's hand and gulped at it. He'd managed four huge swallows before the Imperial snatched it out of his hand. "No," the Imperial said. "Oh, why doesn't anybody ever listen? *Two* mouthfuls, then count twenty, then *two* more. What the hell's so difficult about that?"

"You're incredibly lucky," the Imperial said. "I mean it. Somebody up there must love you very, very much."

They'd caught one of the dead tribesmen's horses and put him on it, and they were riding back along a line of hoofprints, presumably in the right direction, though Forza had no idea. Nobody had asked his name or what he'd been doing or how he'd come to be there, which was probably just as well; for all he knew, they could be Senza's men, or bandits who'd hold him to ransom if they found out he was valuable. At least he'd found out why they wore the white robes: white reflects the light, like a mirror, so you don't get quite so hot. He made a mental note of that.

"Everybody in the desert knows that," the Imperial said. His name was Duzi, and he'd long since got on Forza's nerves. "When you've been in the desert as long as I have—"

"How long would that be?" His voice was still horribly croaky. He wondered if it'd ever be right again.

"Eight years," Duzi said. "Not a lot of people last that long out here, unless they're born to it. That's why they send me out the greenhorns, see, so I can show them the ropes, nursemaid them. They come here without a bloody clue, they go back hard as millstones or not at all . . ." He lowered his voice. "I reckon I've got my work cut out with this lot, though. Bloody Northerners, soft as butter, all they do is whine about the heat. That said, it's pretty cold up there, or so they tell me. Must be a bit of a shock, if you're used to breaking out in a sweat every time the ice starts to melt."

I must not ask questions, Forza repeated to himself. If he asked questions, he'd put Duzi on his guard and he'd clam up, though that would have the valuable collateral advantage of stopping him talking. But if he let him ramble on, he could easily learn something. "It must be difficult for you," he said.

"You're telling me. Though, to be fair—" Duzi wiped sweat out of his eyes with the underside of his wrist. There was probably a reason for that; he had reasons for every damn thing. "To be fair, a couple of these lads show a bit of promise. Rhesea, that's the one on the end, he's a natural with the horses, he can do anything with them. And Teucer, that's the carrot-top, he's a hell of a shot. It was him knocked off those savages for you. Hundred and twenty yards, and quick as you like. He was some sort of a national champion back home, though you wouldn't think it to look at him. Looks like he's half asleep most of the time. Reckons he's never shot a man before, just targets and animals. I told him, it's no different. Think of it as a target, do everything the same as on the range, you'll be just fine. He's from some place called Rhus, never heard of it myself, only been out here a week or so. He's handling the heat well, say that for him, or at least he doesn't moan all the time like the others. They're like a lot of bloody women."

Forza moistened his lips with his tongue. They felt like oyster shells. "Rhus to Blemya. That's about as far as you can get."

"You do see the world in this game," Duzi said, "that's one thing you've got to say for it. Of course, I'm from Torus originally, you know, on the south-east coast. Know it?"

Know it? Burned it. "I've heard of it," Forza said. "Wasn't there a really bad siege there a few years ago?"

"Not a siege, no. What happened was, the Belot boys had one of their scraps, and Torus happened to be right in the middle. No great loss, though. Miserable bloody place."

"Oh, come on," Forza said. "Your home—"

"If I'd liked it, I wouldn't have left," Duzi said firmly. "Fourteen when I went to the Academy, never been back since, and too late now, of course. Never look back, that's always been my rule."

"What about your family?"

"Oh, them." Duzi shrugged. "No, the Order's been my real family. Yes, I know it's a cliché, but it happens to be true. They looked after me when I was a stupid kid, they taught me everything I know, gave me everything I've ever had, and that's why I'm doing the same thing for these kids here. You've got to put something back, I always say, or what's the point of us being here at all?"

Which reminded him. "I don't think I've thanked you properly," Forza said, "for saving my life. If you hadn't shown up when you did—"

"Actually—" Duzi gave him a slightly guilty grin "—we'd been following your trail for a while, and then we saw those buggers and we held back. We're not supposed to fight the tribesmen, see, not unless it's absolutely unavoidable. So I told my lads, leave it to the very last minute. Didn't reckon on them taking it quite so literally. I saw that bastard stringing his bow and I said to the lads, what the hell are you waiting for? And Rhesea looked at me, you said leave it, and I said, for crying out loud; and then fortunately Teucer there, up with his bow, *ping, ping, ping*. Like I said, you're incredibly lucky. Almost like it was meant, if you believe in that stuff; can't say I do myself, but there you are."

The sun was high and Forza felt its weight; it was wonderful to be carried on a horse instead of having to make the intolerable effort of walking. There was a full water-skin hanging from his saddle, but he didn't like to drink too much in case his saviours needed it. For a dead man, though, he was feeling really quite well. He let Duzi's gentle flow of speech sweep round and over him, soothing now rather than annoying, now he'd got used to it and it was evident that he wasn't required to contribute. He was just starting to doze when Duzi reined in his horse and pointed at the skyline.

"See that rise over there?" he said. "Your oasis is just the other side, about eighty yards. Your lot's still there; we'd have seen the dust if they'd moved out."

Forza waited for a moment, and then it sank in. The army, his people, Raiso, and he didn't know if she was alive or dead. He'd *forgotten.* He said something, some trite expression of gratitude, and kicked the horse hard. It shot away, nearly toppling him off. He grabbed a fistful of mane with his left hand and gripped hard with his knees. He heard Duzi shout after him, but couldn't make out the words. He didn't dare look back, for fear of falling off the horse.

"So who were they?" she asked.

The lamp was burning low, but neither of them wanted to get out of bed to top it up. The flame was flaring and stretching, throwing strange extended shadows on the tent wall. "I have no idea," he said. "I mean, the leader was an Eastern Imperial, and his men were Northerners. I could tell you large parts of the leader's life story, if you need help getting to sleep."

"Large parts."

"Very large parts." Forza grinned. "Everything except what I wanted to know. They were following us, and their job seems to be rescuing survivors from battles, which is very nice of them. Why they do it, or what side they're on—" He shrugged. "They're an order, but that could mean anything. Anybody can be an order if they're prepared to spend five angels on a few badges."

"They were following us."

He looked at her. If I was as clever as that, he thought, I'd make damn sure people knew it. Or maybe that was the whole point. "Quite," he said. "Forza Belot, the military genius, unparalleled in all of history for his ability to move quickly and *unobserved.*" He looked at her, but she shrugged. "I don't believe they just happened to be in the middle of the desert, saw us and thought, wonder where they're headed, let's follow them. They *knew.*"

"Senza?"

"He doesn't know where I am, or at least I really, really hope he doesn't know. After all, the joint enterprise has been brought to a successful conclusion, so—" He didn't say any more. She didn't like it when he talked about Senza. "The only outfit I can think of that seems to know every damn thing is the lodge, but—"

"Daxen Maniaces met some lodge people in the desert," she said. "It was in his statement. Their job was trailing round rescuing survivors."

"Specifically craftsmen," Forza said, "but, yes, that's right. But Daxen said they had a truce with the nomads and wouldn't interfere. This lot shot first, they didn't try and bargain or anything."

"You said they told you they only shot at the last minute. They weren't supposed to fight the nomads unless absolutely necessary."

"You're right, he did say that." Forza smiled at her. "There you are, then, problem solved. I'm still not sure I'm madly excited at the idea of the lodge knowing all my top-level military secrets, but I guess I owe them. If it hadn't been for—"

"Quite," she said briskly. "Anyway, that's that. What next?"

He put his hands behind his head and lay back on the bed. "Seek out and destroy the enemy," he said.

"Oh," she said. "That."

That night he dreamed about the war. It had gone on for so long that there were only forty-six men and thirty women left in the world, and they lined up to fight. The men charged; the women kept formation right up until the last moment, when they realised they had no weapons. They were all killed, and so were all but six of the men. It doesn't matter, the six survivors said; we'll build a new heaven and a new earth. Then Raico pointed out that there weren't any women left, so the human race was bound to die out. That made Senza laugh out loud, so Forza shot him with an arrow in the back of the head; he pulled it out and looked at it, then threw it away. Then Forza and Senza and Raico were in bed together, because it was only right that he should share the last surviving woman with his brother. Senza was fast asleep and snoring, so Forza gently dug his fingers into Raico's back to wake her up. But his fingers went straight through her skin, which was as thin as paper; he took hold of her shoulder and pulled her towards him, and he saw that she was dead; the sun had dried her out, she was thin crisp skin overlaid on bone but no flesh, and her hair was brittle and snapped off when his arm brushed against it, and her fingernails were long and curled inwards, like claws. Then Senza opened his eyes and grinned at him, and said, Well, what did you expect?

Senza wouldn't be hard to find. All he had to do was look at a map and ask himself where he'd least want to fight a battle.

"That's easy," she said. "There."

He smiled. "That's what I thought at first," he said. "He's got his back to the oasis, rough ground there for his light infantry, and the rock formations; he'd know I'd worry myself sick, has he hidden his reserve cavalry there or hasn't he? But—" He sipped his tea, which had gone cold. "Then he'll have asked his local knowledge people, and they'll have told him there's a big field of sand dunes, here to here. I could come up through and be right into him and he'd never see me coming. So, not there."

She scowled at him. "You said just from the map. That's cheating."

"Yes," he replied. "It's what we do. Now here—" He rested a finger on the map. "That's more like it."

For a moment she didn't see it. Then she gave him a horrified look. "Oh, come on," she said.

He sighed. "I know," he said. "But he's my brother. I'd hate to disappoint him."

As usual, they met before the battle. Senza rode up with six of his beloved fish-men: Imperial regulars, covered head to foot in small steel scales. Forza took seven of his Parrhasian horse archers. It had been proved, many times, that their short bows could shoot through the fish scales. They drew up ten yards from each other. It was as close as they ever got.

"One question," Senza called out. "How did you know?"

Forza lifted his helmet on to the back of his head so he could hear. "I've got spies in your senior staff. Four of them. Want their names?"

Senza only grinned. "I only need one spy," he said. "The one who's fucking your wife."

Forza nodded. "Here we go, then. The usual," he said. "I've got you stitched up like a baby in a blanket and I know exactly what you're going to do. You're screwed, because I got here first. There's no earthly point in fighting. If you give a shit about your men, surrender now and let the poor buggers live." He paused, counted three under his breath. "Thought not," he said. "Ah well. You always were a heartless bastard, Senza."

He expected his brother to make a rude gesture and go. This time, however, he seemed inclined to linger. Forza shortened his reins to ride away.

"Nice bit of work, back there," Senza said.

"What, you mean—?"

Senza nodded. "We picked up a few of their survivors," he said. "But I gather you nearly got yourself killed."

"Nearly," Forza said. "Not quite."

"You want to be a bit more careful," Senza said. "Dashing off being brave, leaving your wife. You shouldn't drag her round with you all the time, a fine lady like that. It's not safe."

Forza sighed. "Maybe if you'd kept Lysao a bit closer she wouldn't have run off. Oh, I know where she is, by the way. Want me to tell you?"

"You're a real mine of information today, aren't you?" Just a tiny flicker; then Senza raised the grin again. "Sometimes I think to myself, this is stupid. He's my brother, for God's sake; we ought to be able to sort things out, at the very least we ought to be able to coexist without trying to kill each other all the damn time. And then I see you again and I realise, no, we can't, he's got to go." He lifted one hand in a courteous salute. "This time," he said.

Forza returned a formal nod. "This time," he replied, and rode away.

It was the perfect place, a slaughterhouse, a killing bottle. Senza had only two choices. He could attack uphill, his cavalry slowed to a walk by the gradient and the rocks and the shale, or he could stand his ground, receive Forza's furious charge and be driven back into the marshes, which had in their time swallowed up whole armies. Both flanks were closed; the left flank by the river, which was in spate, the right flank by the sheer cliff wall of the Hammerhead. The road he'd come in by was now blocked by two thousand of Forza's regular pikemen, who held the only bridge over the river. The trap was perfect, because Senza had designed it himself. His only mistake, if you could call it that, was getting there five hours after Forza; and it would've been asking a lot of him to have expected him to know about the hidden pass over the Hammerhead, because it wasn't on any map drawn in the last three hundred years. As Forza made a few final adjustments to his order of battle, he was sick with worry. Too perfect; he'd missed something. Or maybe it really would be this time, and that—

Over and over again, he kept asking himself, *What would I do if I was him?* So far, he'd come up with six answers, all of them brilliant; but he'd countered them all. His Northern archers were marking the fish-men, so Senza wouldn't try the sudden unexpected hook on the left wing. The false retreat, the feigned central collapse, the bull's head, the lobster and the threshing floor were all safely accounted for and taken care of. It was like playing chess against himself.

He went back to his tent to put on his armour. He hated wearing it. He'd had it made by the best armourer in the world—an

Easterner, as it happened; he'd had the man and his family abducted, and the entire contents of his workshop packed up and brought to him; then, when the work was done, he sent him back with a thousand angels and a plausible story—but putting it on always demoralised him. She had it all ready, laid out on the bed.

"Have I got to?" he asked.

She looked at him. "Baby," she said.

"Fine." He sat down and extended his left leg for the greave. She knelt and bent back the silver clips, then slid the greave over his shin. He winced as the clips tightened. He consoled himself by admiring the rounded muscles of her shoulders, which never failed to delight him. "Other one," she said. He stretched out his leg.

"It's too perfect," he said. "I'm worried."

"So you should be." She kissed his knee, then slid the greave into place. "I'd be worried if you weren't worried. Stand up."

The fish-scale skirt clanked as she lifted it. "Any ideas?"

Her arms encircled his waist as she tightened the buckle. "You've put on weight," she said.

"Impossible. I was starving in the desert."

"You've made up for it since. Remind me; I'll have to punch another hole. Right, arms."

Obediently, he held his arms straight out in front so she could lace up the manicae and vambraces. "Not too tight," he pleaded.

"Any looser and they'll slide off. There, how's that?"

He flexed his hands. "All right," he said grudgingly. "Well? Any ideas what he'll do?"

She laced the clamshells over the backs of his hands. "Probably something you couldn't possibly hope to anticipate," she said. "So you'll just have to make it up as you go along."

She grunted as she lifted the brigantine. It weighed eighteen pounds. "Head," she said; he lowered his head, and she draped the neck-strap over him. He supported the weight while she did up the buckles. "There, can you breathe?"

"Barely."

"You'll do. Oh, hold on." She took a little swab of wool she'd tucked up inside her sleeve, and wound it round the neck-strap so it wouldn't chafe the back of his neck. "Nearly done," she said.

"This could be the last time," he said. "Really, I think it could. I—I don't—"

She looked at him. "You've been having that dream again."

"Have I?"

"Arm. Other arm." He raised his left arm, and she dropped the pauldron over it, then teased the laces through the holes and tied them in a graceful bow. "Yes," she said, tightening the buckles. "You shouted, and then told me to wake up. But you were fast asleep."

"Sorry."

"*Other* arm. It's all right, it's not your fault. There." She stood back and examined her work. "How does it feel?"

"Horrible."

She rolled her eyes. "Can you move, or is anything binding anywhere?"

He experimented. "Fine," he conceded. "I'll just carry the helmet."

"No, you won't."

He hated the helmet most of all. The liner was still damp with sweat, from when he'd worn it earlier. "I'll get a headache."

"Tough."

It felt like cold, wet fingers pawing at his head as it pushed down. He took a couple of steps. "I clink," he said. "It's undignified."

"Everybody clinks. It's what soldiers do."

"Couldn't you get them to stick little pads of felt on the insides of the scales? It'd muffle the noise."

"And everyone will think you're a pansy. Stay there and I'll get your sword."

He'd have forgotten it. "Thanks."

She stood on tiptoe to get the strap over his head. "There's my brave soldier," she said. "Right, off you go."

He opened his mouth to say something, then closed it again. He never did say anything on these occasions. "Go *on*," she said. "You'll be late, and the other boys will tease you."

He turned his back on her—it was better that way—and strode out of the tent. *Clink, clink, clink.* As soon as he was out in the light, he made a stupendous effort and emptied his mind. For a moment he was blank. Then, methodically, he assembled the thoughts and concerns of General Forza Belot, with a battle to fight. He pictured the chessboard, superimposed it on what he saw in front of him. She'd told him once, it's the way you can suddenly concentrate, like closing a fist. Of course, Senza could do it too. Better.

The general staff was waiting for him, and the groom, with the damned horse. He realised he couldn't face it, not just yet. "Thanks, we'll walk," he said. "Well? Has he moved?"

Tavassa, colonel of the Seventh, shook his head. "Just stood there," he said.

"Won't be able to keep that up for long, in this heat," someone said, he didn't notice who. "We're fine, we're in the shade. It must be like an oven out there in the open."

"That won't bother him," Forza said. "Not even the bloody fish people."

As usual, he found the sight of the army disturbing. They covered the hillside like some strange crop, a composite of thousands of individual heads forming a single commodity. It had always bothered him to think that he was the head to this body; it seemed so improbable, somehow. He looked past them into the distance, where he could make out blocks of colour. *Concentrate.* Now then, what's the most unlikely thing I could possibly do?

He half-closed his left eye; for some reason, that always seemed to help. Almost at once, he saw it; such a little thing, a tiny part of a larger gap between two enemy units. He saw it in both space and time: an opening through which a fast-moving cavalry unit could break through, and two and a half minutes before Senza's mobile reserve could reach them. At times like this what he saw wasn't the present but a liquid stream of the future, as though he was remembering something he'd seen in the past, something that had already happened. Yes, that was the key point where the Third Auxiliary split the left front—do you remember that?—and then Senza made a desperate effort to plug the hole, and *that's* when the Tirsen horse archers suddenly darted in and caught his reserve in flank, and then the whole damn thing started to come apart. He watched it all happen; it was like one of those complicated town clocks, where there's a huge whirring, crawling mechanism to make a model of a man in armour come out through a doorway and hit a bell. His mind was full of cams and levers—pressure at this point to draw that unit that much to the side, so that this unit here could mask the advance, bringing this unit forward until it was close enough to make the dash across the gap; all mechanical, all self-activating, automatic once the lever's been pressed and the sear's been tripped, all starting with one set of orders, given by one man, in about thirty seconds—

The adjutant couldn't see it, of course. The orders made no sense. But he listened gravely and carefully, because this was Forza Belot, the greatest living general. He waited till Forza had finished, repeated the orders back to him word for word, jumped on his horse and thundered away, and men scampered to get out of the way before he rode them down.

It worked, of course. The slight shift in the position of the main front, made to look like a slight error of judgement, induced Senza to wheel his Fourth Guards just the precise amount to the left to open the gap; masked by the two concurrent infantry movements, the auxiliary cavalry edged their way forward and suddenly broke out, racing across the open ground between the two fronts and wedging themselves into the gap with a crash Forza could hear half a mile away. Forza counted to ten under his breath; off went Senza's reserve, straight into the curved line which only he could see represented the trajectory of the Tirsen horsemen. The reserve stopped dead, wheeled left in perfect order to receive cavalry; that meant their right flank was just in range of the five hundred Northern longbowmen Forza had seeded into the front rows of his heavy guards. The first volley arched across the open ground like a black rainbow. Now the Fifth—

"Sir." A voice somewhere off to the left. "They're behind us."

Made no sense. They were out there, getting shot and cut up and trampled. He dragged his mind out of the machinery. "What?"

"Behind us, sir. They're coming over the Hammerhead."

Forza spun round. "*What?*"

It was a young captain he couldn't remember having seen before. "The enemy, sir. Thousands of them, coming down the pass we came in by. Sir, what do we do?"

In that moment, he realised how a fly must feel when it hits the gossamer. He forced himself to understand. Somehow, God only knew how, Senza had got men round the back of the mountains and through the Hammerhead pass, and now, *right now*, they were pouring down into the camp, which was undefended, where *she* was— "Mobile reserve," he shouted; fatuous, they were six minutes away. Where the hell was Colonel Tacres? Someone had to take charge while he—He realised he'd stopped breathing and now his lungs seemed to have seized up. "Find Tacres," he yelled at the captain, and started to run.

You've been having those dreams again.

Her voice was in his head as he sprinted up the slope. Men were staring at him—the general, running; the general never ran—and he knew he was making a mistake, possibly a fatal one, but he was in the wrong place. He needed to get there *fast* (Forza Belot, who always got there first, who was the greatest general in history because he was always in the right place at the right time, except for now) and there was too much stupid distance in the way—Ahead of him, he could see frantic movement among the tents, unnatural movement, all wrong. *Concentrate.* He forced his mind to show him a plan of the camp, and the disposition of his resources. Nobody back here, nobody at all—except for the Second Pioneers, and they weren't even proper soldiers—

A man appeared, running like a deer, straight at him, but he was looking back over his shoulder. They collided with breathtaking force and collapsed in a tangled heap. Forza had had all the air knocked out of him, but at that moment air was a luxury. He dragged himself free, not caring that he trod on the man's face, and threw himself into a run. The Second Pioneers, for God's sake. Still—

And then it was like when you're trying to repair a smashed pot, but there's no way the pieces could ever have fitted together, and then you find one little bit you'd overlooked, and suddenly you have it. The gap in Senza's front, and the ease with which he'd been able to exploit it. It shouldn't have happened, because Senza should have read him like a book; but Senza hadn't, because *Senza wasn't there.* Oh no. Senza was somewhere else entirely, leading a party of picked men over the sheer, narrow trails of the Hammerhead. Everything down below—the two armies, the slaughter of whole regiments, was just bait, to set up the real thing, the story that would appear in the textbooks, which would happen up here: how Senza Belot won the war by killing Forza Belot's wife—

You'll just have to make it up as you go along. Yes, but with nothing to work with except the Second bloody Pioneers. Never mind. Concentrate. His chest was burning and his legs were weak and empty. He brought the plan of the camp into focus and thought: what would Senza least expect me to do?

Easy. Senza knows I hate getting my hands wet. So—

Five men were running towards him. For a moment he couldn't tell if they were friend or enemy; then he saw that they were wearing those stupid round felt hats, the sort that only the Pioneers wear, because they're not proper soldiers. The Second, led by Major, by Major, *what was the bloody man's name,* Major Harsena. They were within shouting distance. He stopped, swayed, called out, "Where's Harsena?" The words came out as a whisper.

Fortunately, one of the men was Harsena. "They're in the—" he started to say, but Forza put his hand over the poor man's mouth. "Listen," he said, and he was amazed at his own voice; calm, reasonable. "Rally your men, go round the side, in past the latrines, take them in flank. Have you got that?"

Harsena couldn't speak because Forza's hand was clamped over his mouth, so he nodded.

"Very good. Off you go."

Harsena and his friends turned and raced away, and Forza took a moment to breathe. No good to anyone if he passed out from exhaustion. Right, then; he'd set up the main show, what he needed now was the diversion. For which he needed at least eighty men. He looked round. Why are there never eighty soldiers around when you need them?

Then—later he went down on his knees and thanked the fire god, in whom he didn't really believe—he heard hooves behind him; he dragged himself round and saw, guess what, cavalrymen, the Parrhasians, his personal guard, who were never supposed to let him out of their sight once the unpleasantness started. There were forty-five of them. He did a quick calculation and decided they'd do. The captain, Jorteszon, drew up beside him. It was unfortunate that the man spoke no Imperial. To compensate, Forza shouted, "With me." Jortsezon looked at him. Oh, for crying out loud. Forza jumped up and pulled a rider out of his saddle, then hauled himself on to the man's horse. "Follow," he bellowed, then wrenched the horse's head round and gave it an unnecessarily brutal kick. It reared a little and Forza nearly fell off; then it shot away like an arrow from a bow, fortuitously in the right direction.

Forty yards later, it shied at something and this time he did fall off. Not to worry; it was a quick and efficient way of dismounting. He scrambled to his feet and ran for the camp gate, tugging at his sword, which had got itself jammed in the scabbard. He got it free just in time; it slid out, nearly slicing into the web of his hand. Dead ahead of him was one of Senza's horrible fish-men, dear God, why did it have to be them, but not to worry, this was far too important to let a little thing like virtual invulnerability get in his way. The fish-man raised his sword and assumed the orthodox iron-gate guard, the attitude of total defence, and then one of the Parrhasians shot him and he fell over.

In his mind he could hear his own voice, twenty years ago, to his father, after two hours' gruelling sword drill: *What have I got to learn this stupid stuff for, anyway? I'm never ever going to be a soldier.* Inside the camp, the fish-men were everywhere. He looked up the main street, towards his tent. He felt weak and sick. Then he heard a roar, and turned to face a fish-man, almost on top of him. He was taking a big stride forward, his sword raised over his head. Forza concentrated on the sword hand; as it came down, he stepped smartly backwards to take his head out of measure, and lifted his own sword, just so. The fish-man's wrist came down on Forza's edge, there was a grotesque spray of blood; Forza nudged past him, shouldering him out of the way, and ran up the main street.

His concentration was completely gone now; all the plans and diagrams. He could see nothing but the distance he still had to run. A fish-man lunged at him but the expensive brigandine turned the thrust; he ran past, not bothering to look back. An archer or two must've been keeping up with him, because three more fish-men folded up and collapsed as he approached; the Parrhasians adored him, though he had no idea why. Two more fish-men; he killed them, or let them kill themselves on his sword; he was furious with them for holding him up. "Get out of the way," he yelled at the second one, then sidestepped his lunge and let him run on to his sword point; he pulled the blade clear without looking round. It was a wicked thing to do, to end a man's life and not pay him the simple courtesy of witnessing his death, but there simply wasn't time.

He could see his tent, and there was a man standing outside it, relaxed but on guard. Just for a moment he took him for one of his own officers, but then, as he got closer—One brother doesn't need to see another brother's face to recognise him; he knows him from a long way off just by the way he stands, the slight and subtle details of proportion that come from total familiarity. He slowed to a walk, then, ten yards away, he stopped. It was as close as they ever got, these days.

"Shoot him!" he yelled; then he looked round. No Parrhasians behind him, they'd been slowed up or killed. Senza lifted his helmet on to the back of his head and laughed at him.

"Boys," he said.

Five fish-men came out of the tent. Well, of course; get there first, and with superior forces, and Senza knew him so well, knew how much he loathed fighting. One against two maybe, just possibly one against three and sheer rage might be enough, rage and anger and thirty years of motivation. One against five, though; simple mathematics. Four would almost certainly have done, but Senza loved his margins.

Then his father's voice again, the time he'd burst into the hall and pulled Forza off the fencing master, a split second before Forza could smash his skull with a broken chair: *What the hell's got into you, boy?* And then, after he'd seen the look on his son's face: *All right, you've made your point*. Because, at that moment, his father had understood why his eldest son didn't like to fight; because deep down, in a place neither of them ever wanted to go again, Forza liked hurting people a little bit too much.

But what the hell.

The first fish-man was a full stride ahead of the rest. Forza barged straight into him, trusting to the best armour in the world, took a savage thrust in the stomach, which the brigandine turned; because he wasn't dead, as he should have been, he was able to reach over the fish-man's arms and flick his sword under his chin, a light but firm scoring motion. While the man was dying, Forza kicked him straight at the man behind, then saw a tiny chance and cut off the hand of the fish-man on the extreme right. As he doubled up with pain (pain debilitates, said the fencing master, use it whenever you can) Forza skirted him, using him to block the remaining three—just for a second, but that was long enough to stretch out (he got hit on the head in doing so, but the fish-men didn't know how much he'd paid for that helmet) and slid his edge purposefully over the unprotected tendons on the back of an outstretched leg. He drew his arm back smartly enough that the ferocious cut that landed on it wasn't quite well enough placed to break the bone; the manica turned the edge, of course, and he was able to place a neat little jab into the gap between the bottom of the fish-man's helmet and the roped neck-guard of his cuirass. All he'd achieved, of course, was to clear away the hindrance and clutter obstructing his last opponent and give him room to swing and move his feet. No matter; Forza was just nicely warmed up now, totally confident and enjoying himself more than he'd done for twenty years, and this time his father wasn't there to stop him. He opened himself right up so the fish-man couldn't help but be drawn in; the fish-man obligingly took his swing, and Forza winced as the blow hammered down on his pauldron. It should've smashed his collarbone, but the best armourer in the world understood the art of padding as well as the heat treatment of steel. Then Forza grabbed the sword hand before he could snatch it away and held it just long enough while he cut the fish-man's throat.

Then he looked up.

Senza was staring at him, and he recognised that expression; so like the one his father had worn that time, but, then, Senza definitely had a look of the old man about him, especially as he'd got older. The same blend of horror and disgust; and, once again, it made Forza want to laugh. "Now if it'd been ten," he said, and Senza slashed at his head.

He felt it this time; he felt his brain move. But he'd learned this sequence, and how to counter it, from the same teacher as his brother; he gave ground, pivoting on his back foot, and gave himself a clear cut at the back of Senza's neck, remembering as he launched the blow just why he'd chosen that specific armourer and no other; because he'd made a suit for Senza, and it was just as good. At least Senza staggered; his head was probably spinning, too, and he was probably seeing double. Forza cut low, Senza anticipated and stepped back, giving himself measure for the stop thrust; it slid off Forza's double-proof chest-plates and exposed Senza's right side, whose armour shrugged off his counter-thrust. But he'd felt something give, a rib maybe; he could read pain in Senza's movements as he wound up for a cut to Forza's exposed neck, then aborted and gave ground. A good move, and he knew exactly what Senza had in mind. In particular, Senza would know he wouldn't risk a rising backhand cut to the chin, since, if Senza trusted his helmet and let the blow go home, it'd expose the unarmoured patch under Forza's armpit. So he did just that; taken off guard, Senza's head flew back, giving Forza just enough time to step in and grab for the sword arm—except that it wasn't there, it was low, stabbing the sword point up into the tiny crack between the cuirass and the scale skirt. He felt a searing pain and immediately gave ground (*how the hell did he do that, I never expected—*) and Senza, stepping forward, kicked his exposed left knee sideways and dropped him neatly on the ground; and, as he fell, Forza glimpsed out of the corner of his eye a Parrhasian archer bending his bow, taking aim—

"No!" he yelled, because Senza was directly in front of the tent, and the archer might miss or the arrow might glance off, and she was inside. He tried to push himself up off the ground, but all his strength had gone off somewhere; he pushed, and it was like arm-wrestling, the ground was pushing back and it won. "Don't shoot," he tried to say, but his voice didn't work, and all he could see was the deep black hole he was falling into.

Two of Arrows

Senza saw the archers and realised he'd lost. It was a shame, a great shame, but there'd be another day. He backed into the tent and turned, and then the pain hit him. Nothing he'd ever experienced had hurt that much. He reached round and felt the small of his back for an arrow, but there was nothing there, so it had to be from when Forza hit him. Broken rib, he guessed. He gasped, and looked round. Needless to say, the tent didn't have a back door. They'd be in after him any second. He blundered across the floor, bumped into a small table, knocked it over, maps and papers everywhere. He heard a faint whimpering noise, like a dog; but it was a dark-skinned woman curled up in a ball next to the bed—tried to crawl under it, he guessed, but it was too low. That must be the famous Raico. She lifted her head and stared at him. He heard the tent flap rustle behind him.

His mind filled up with geometry: lines, angles, the shortest distances between points. The trouble was, she was in the way. The geometrical diagrams became a chessboard; he decided he was a knight. "'Scuse me," he said politely, then jumped over the woman's legs, hit the tent canvas, stabbed his sword into it and ripped upwards. The hole was almost big enough; his head and body got through, but his foot caught and he tripped and toppled forward into daylight. As he fell, an arrow swished past; if he hadn't tripped, it'd have hit him. He twitched his feet free, scrambled up and ran like a hare.

The pain stopped him about fifteen yards later, but by then it was all right; a dozen of his guards were running toward him, and they got between him and the archers. A sergeant helped him up. The pain in his chest and back made him feel like a log with wedges driven in it, just before the last blow of the hammer. He grabbed the sergeant's shoulder to steady himself. "Where's Dets?" he said.

The sergeant shook his head. Damn, Senza thought. "Jortis? Major Asta?"

"Major's over there, sir." The sergeant pointed. There was a battle going on, his guards against too many men with axes, and he hadn't even noticed. "Hell," Senza said. "Where did they come from?"

The sergeant plainly didn't know, and why should he? Once again, Forza had conjured armed men up out of thin air; he really shouldn't be surprised any more. He didn't need to look twice to know his men were losing. He detached himself from the sergeant. "Get as many of them as you can out of there," he said. "Then back the way we came."

One of the men of his personal screen was down; why hadn't he brought archers, instead of heavy infantry? "Leave it," he called out and the guardsmen backed away, not before another one dropped, twitching. "Move!" he yelled; the guardsmen turned and ran. He hesitated; what the hell, he thought. Then he darted forward and knelt down beside the man who'd just fallen. He'd been shot in the stomach but was still alive. Senza managed to get his arm under the man's armpit and hoist him up; as he did so, the pain from his rib flared up like a barrel of oil catching fire. Bloody fool, he thought. He took a long stride, wrenching the guardsman with him, like pulling a tooth; the weight across his shoulders was going to split him in half any moment. The man's cheek, next to his, was wet with sweat and tears. "Oh come *on*," he said, and moved them another five yards or so. That was it; he was all done. *Idiot*, he thought; and then two guardsmen appeared out of nowhere, grabbed them both and hustled them away. He stumbled, the guardsman helping him barged into his side, and he screamed. More hands grabbed him, lifted him off the ground; he felt his feet dangling and swinging as they carried him along, and for some reason he thought of when he was a little boy. He tried to call up the maps and diagrams, but they wouldn't come into focus; there was a mist between them and him, and he couldn't see through it.

A bump and a jostle; agony like he'd never known before. "What the hell do you think you're playing at?" he roared, then noticed that one of the men carrying him had been shot; the arrow was through his elbow and into his flank, pinning his arm to his body. The man's face was screwed up tight; he hadn't said a word, and he was still keeping step. At least the man hadn't apologised for jostling him; he wasn't sure he could've handled that.

They were climbing now, so they must be on the narrow path. He remembered he was a general. "Stop," he said. They lowered him a little so he could stand, but didn't let go, which was just as well. "Help me round." The view below him came into focus, and he superimposed a chessboard. Then he looked round for someone to give orders to. There was a sergeant, face vaguely familiar; his name was, what, for crying out loud?

"Sergeant," he said. "Sergeant Lonous. Take ten men, hold this point. Don't let them through. Got that?"

The sergeant nodded. Maybe he wasn't bright enough to realise he'd just been condemned to death, but Senza doubted that. Just a nod. "Right," Senza said. "Onwards." It was his pet phrase. The men liked it, did impressions: *onwards*, and an exaggerated flick of the head, like a nervous horse.

A hundred and fifty yards up the path; had he remembered right, or just imagined it? No, there it was: no more than a goat track, for particularly small, agile goats. "Fifty men," Senza said, hoping very much that he still had fifty men, "down that track.

You'll go out of sight over the rise, then come back on this track thirty yards below where we left Lonous and his lads. By the time you get there, there should be a whole bunch of bastards. Take it nice and quiet, they won't see you coming. Then back up here along the main path, quick as you like."

They hurried off and were soon out of sight. Onwards. If Forza was leading the pursuit personally, they were all dead, naturally. But chances were that Forza would be back down below, comforting his wife or wiping out the main army. In which case, it wasn't over yet. "Get a move on, lads," he said. "We haven't got all day."

On the top of the Hammerhead he let them stop and get their breath while he looked down at the main action below. As he expected; Forza's men were right into his centre, tearing it apart, while the cavalry were sweeping round to take the Sixteenth and Twenty-Fifth in rear. Senza grinned. Forza definitely wasn't down there attending to business. "Come on," he said, "chop-chop."

It took rather longer than he'd have liked for them to reach the other path, the one that went straight down the east face of the Hammerhead. He glanced at it and knew there was no way he'd get down that, so he called over Sergeant Velsa, who he'd known for years. "Listen very carefully," he said, and told him exactly what had to be done. Then he added, "Tell Colonel Pauga we're running a bit late—my fault—so he'll need to get a wiggle on. He's got to get the auxiliary archers in place before Forza's lot smash through the centre. That's very important." He paused. It was a lot for anyone to remember. "Got that?"

"Sir." The fate of the world hung on Sergeant Velsa's memory, but Senza didn't tell him that. "Good man," he said, "off you go." Then he gestured for his porters to let him sit down. His backside hit the heather and he squealed like a pig. For a moment he couldn't see for the blur. Then his vision cleared and he got his breath back. He looked round for someone. "That man I brought in," he said. "Is he all right?"

They looked at him; someone shook his head. Oh.

"Take me a bit closer to the edge," he said. "I want to watch this."

Never watch a battle from an elevated position, General Moisa had told him once; you start getting delusions of godhead. Fair enough; but he reckoned the pain in his chest was a sufficient antidote. Another of Moisa's pet sayings was that when a battle's going well, it's like a symphony made visible. Here are the main themes, the variations; the theme passes from one group of instruments to another, but the melody is unmistakable. A bit fanciful, he'd always thought—Moisa said some fine, resonant things in his time but he'd never been much of a general; on this occasion, however, he could see what the old boy had been getting at. A ripple on the strings as the auxiliary cavalry swept down out of nowhere; lots of noise from the brass as the archers came out of the dead ground, stopped and loosed three volleys that more or less disintegrated Forza's mobile reserve. Then the big theme rolling out right across the orchestra, as Forza's men turn and discover they've been caught like fish in a net.

Well, maybe not. Too many fish, too small a net. Reluctantly he conceded to himself that it wasn't going to be today; another bloody stalemate, withdraw, regroup, try again later. He tried not to think about how close he'd been, closer than since they were kids, practically. If only one of his hits had gone home—Senza shook his head. Dad had always said Forza had a mean streak, under that sweet surface. Don't ever get in a fight with him, son, he doesn't know when to stop.

He'd lost interest in the battle now he knew how it was going to come out. He had to stay and watch, there was still so much he needed to take care of, but he let his mind drift a little. Did Forza really know where Lysao was, or was that just him being spiteful? Forza's wife seemed like a nice woman. The thought suddenly struck him: the archers didn't shoot because Forza knew she was in the tent. *Hell.* If he'd realised that, he could have had ten more seconds; maybe just possibly long enough—

Too late now, no point beating himself up about it. A man like Forza didn't deserve a nice wife like that. Probably he'd only married her for politics, and the legendary grand romance was all just publicity. She'd find out about him soon enough. They all did eventually, poor devils. Not for the first time, he cursed the wretched fact of his destiny—yes, someone's got to deal with Forza, otherwise the world's not safe, but why did it have to be *him*?

Suddenly he remembered Lysao, that exquisite image of her combing her hair; clever Forza, to have put it into his mind, knowing it'd be there for days, spoiling everything. She always gave the impression of being overwhelmed by her hair, as if it was some monster that lived on top of her head and needed to be contained, lest it escape and cause havoc among the civilian population. He remembered how it got in the way—ouch, you're pulling my hair—at the most inconvenient moments possible, how she loved and hated it, a glory and a burden and a dreadful tiresome responsibility, as though she was doomed to lug around a life-size statue by Teromachus everywhere she went. Once she'd threatened to give it to the nation, so it'd be up to the government, not her, to maintain it. And the combing ritual—dear God, every night, an hour and a quarter, like some religious ceremony. It's my duty, she'd say, and he'd think, yes, and Forza's mine. My duty and my fault.

He watched the last stages of the battle, but it was like reading a book you've read six times before. When he'd had as much as he could take, he called over a guardsman and sent him down with a message: that's enough, fall back, give them room to withdraw; and get a sedan chair or something up here, quick as you like.

The chair came quite quickly, and they were helping him into it when he glanced back one last time at the battle and saw something. "Just a second," he said and looked again. Something wasn't quite right about the way Forza's men were drawing out. He leaned on a guardsman's shoulder and superimposed the chessboard. Two, maybe three opportunities; if he'd been down there with a full staff of messengers, he could've had a world of fun with them, but up here he might as well be on the moon. Forza would never have left him openings like that, so evidently Forza wasn't down there running things; in which case, where was he? After all that, had Forza outplayed him with some brilliant long-reaching mechanism, a hidden reserve or a really wide outflank? The thought made him shiver all over. He called a runner and sent him down with a message: get out of there *fast*. Then he looked again, to see if any of Forza's capital assets were unaccounted for. No, but that didn't signify; Forza could summon up armies out of thin air. Where the hell was he? He's up to something, or else he's—

Surely not. I didn't hit him that hard. Did I?

The world stopped. *What if he's dead?* What if I killed him?

It was that empty feeling again; he knew it so well—the day his father died, the day Lysao went away, those dreams he had sometimes. He couldn't be, surely; I bashed him on the head a couple of times, but those helmets just shrug it off; he was certainly alive and full of beans when I left—Concussion? Fractured skull, internal bleeding? I couldn't have, could I?

"Well, don't just stand there," he shouted at the porters. "Get me down there, quick."

There's always so much mess after a battle: so many bodies, so many damaged men, so much ruined property scattered about. All things being equal (which they rarely are) the priorities are to see to your side's wounded, then the enemy's; strip and bury your dead, pile up and count the opposition; retrieve as much equipment as you can, though usually time, supplies and patience run out long before then, and the job is left to the private sector—first on the scene, the locals (if any), until they're chased off by the professionals, who follow the wars at a safe distance and bring their own carts. Ideally, by the time they've finished up and set off back to the nearest town big enough to host an auction, there should be nothing left but graves, ashes, trampled crops and the hoof marks of the cavalry.

When both sides are in a hurry to get away, it's not like that. A quick skirmish for the wounded, leave the dead; it takes an hour for the crows to figure it's safe, they're canny birds with a highly developed system of reconnaissance, more than capable of recognising live humans from half a mile off. To start with, they come in singly, gliding in on the wind, banking and turning into it to brake, dropping with wings outstretched, touching down and waddling; then twos and threes, then by the dozen; they circle, for choice pitch in nearby trees to make a leisurely assessment before committing themselves; when at last they settle, they cover the field like black snow, and you can hear them a thousand yards away. Then the first human scavengers show up, and the crows rise like angry smoke, yelling abuse at the interlopers. It takes a minute or so for the last reluctant stragglers to lift up and flap away—they know their place in the pecking order, but they don't feel obliged to be gracious about it.

If there are no humans, of course, they can take their time. They don't do much of a job. Too much meat is inaccessible under steel and leather, mostly they only get faces and hands—hair is useful, of course, during nesting season—and they're comparatively slow feeders. They don't get much help from other birds, foxes, the lesser vermin, nor do they do much to keep the flies off. Generally speaking, they leave a worse mess than they find. In those parts where jackals, kites and vultures are the predominant carrion species, it's a different story, but they're not often seen north of the Seventy-third Oasis.

Eight days after the battle, Senza came back. He left his escort on the far side of the Hammerhead and climbed the narrow path alone; he knew what he wanted to see, and the picture would be delicate, fragile; one ill-judged movement would spoil it. From the top of the rock he looked down and read the view below him like a book.

From the distribution and feeding patterns of the crows, which he'd taken great pains not to disturb, and from the smell, he gathered that nobody had been there for at least five days. The black stains the crows made on the brown and green would have told him the narrative of the battle as clearly as any despatch, if he hadn't known it already; the places where men had fallen thickest, the paths traced by stragglers and fugitives cut down by pursuers, the windrows of dead men shot by archers as they charged, or enfiladed as they advanced and retreated—dogs can read the past by smell, Senza could do the same thing by reading crows. It came from long practice.

When he'd seen all he needed, he walked down towards the place where he'd fought his brother. The tents, he saw with surprise, were still there; Forza's men must have left in a tearing hurry, and it seemed reasonable to assume that nobody had been in charge. Forza would never have left the tents behind unless he'd been driven forcibly from the field, which Senza knew for a fact hadn't been the case. He retraced his own movements, stepping over the guardsmen who'd died to save him (eyeless now, cheekbones showing through lacerated skin) and poked about in Forza's tent for a while. The maps and papers had gone, but the table, chair and bed were still there. Under the pillow, where he knew it would be, he found three small painted wooden panels, hinged with leather straps to make a triptych. He unfolded them, and saw for the first time in fifteen years the fire god in glory, attended by the greater and lesser seraphim. It had always stood on a shelf above the hearth; his mother nodded to it every time she passed, the reflexive dip of the head you accord to neighbours you meet in the street. He stood and stared at it for a very long time; fancy meeting you here. Then he took off the scarf he wore to keep his armour from chafing his neck and wound it six times round the boards; then he turfed junk out of his coat pocket until the bundle fitted snug and safe. A voice in his head told him that the battle had been worth it, just for this. He knew that was terribly wrong, but he couldn't deny his own belief.

She'd left her trunk behind; he went out, picked up a sword from the ground and used it to lever open the lid—the hasp was mighty strong and he bent the sword blade before the hinge pin finally gave way. His sister-in-law had good but expensive taste. At the bottom of the trunk he found a small bundle of letters, in his brother's handwriting. He grinned and pocketed them, for later.

Now, then. If Forza had been badly hurt, wouldn't they bring him in here and lay him down on the bed until someone found the doctor? He examined the blanket for traces of blood, but there weren't any. Likewise, the first thing you'd do for a wounded man would be peel off all that armour—yes, but they'd take that away with them regardless of the outcome, just as they'd taken the maps, though not her trunk; true, but they'd have stripped off the arming coat as well, probably other bits of clothing too, and there was nothing of the sort lying on the ground or on the bed. A dead body, though, you'd just load that up as it was and cart it away, once you were sure there was nothing that could be done. Or maybe he was jumping to conclusions. Maybe he was thinking too much like Forza—organised, efficient, intelligent. Suppose you were some captain or lieutenant, horribly stuck with command as your general lies at your feet groaning and bleeding, and (not being a military genius) you have no idea at all what the military genius leading the opposition has in mind; you'd get the chief and his wife out of there as soon as possible; maybe you'd have the residual trace of wit to grab the maps and papers, but not the personal stuff. You most definitely wouldn't know what was under the chief's pillow. All you'd be able to hear would be the voice in your head screaming *get out of there*, which you would obey implicitly, without hesitation.

Ambiguous, therefore; maybe he's dead, maybe he isn't. Fairly safe to assume that, at the moment of the army's departure, Forza wasn't in command; potentially fatal to assume that he wasn't in command now, and racking his brains to figure out what his kid brother would do next. If I was him, he thought, I'd send back a half-squadron, at the very least; tell them to hold off still and quiet so as not to disturb the crows; as soon as the crows get up, go in there fast. Would Forza guess that he'd be here? Yes, because he *was* here, and Forza knew him so well. In which case—

He ran out of the tent and looked round; half a squadron would kick up dust, unless Forza had ordered them to go on foot for that very reason. He couldn't see movement of any sort, anywhere. Which proved nothing. Time he wasn't there.

As he ran back up the path, he realised: come what may, if Forza was alive, he'd have sent someone for the painting, and probably his wife's letters, if he knew about them (he'd know). The absolute certainty of it hit him like a hammer; he stopped dead, unable to take a single step. Dead, or just possibly in a coma—no, because *she'd* know what he kept under his pillow, *she'd* know it had to be retrieved at all costs; no reason to believe she was dead too. He felt utterly weak and helpless, as though he'd just had a stroke. Forza—

Suddenly into his mind came an image of the Basilica at Vetusta, the biggest and most magnificent man-made structure in the world. Four generations of labourers had worked on it, he'd read somewhere; great-grandfather, grandfather, father, son, their whole lives spent on that one extraordinary piece of work—masons, carters, carpenters, smiths, brickmakers, plasterers, architects, painters, sculptors, all of them trades that traditionally run in families, like soldiering or ruling empires—until one day, one clearly defined, absolutely different day, someone took a step back, looked up, down again at the plans; nodded his head, probably, and declared that it was finished, and everyone could go home. A moment of triumph—the greatest achievement of the human race, brought to a magnificently successful conclusion—but also, for the fourth-generations achievers, the end of the world, everything they'd ever known over, done with and gone, their purpose fulfilled, their experiences obsolete; a frontier post on the border between present and past. A week later, they'd all have scattered far and wide, building cowsheds. Hereditary trades; family businesses. Like, say, the Belot brothers, purveyors of fine carrion to discerning crows everywhere.

Self-pity; because if a job's worth doing, do it yourself.

No confirmation, of course. He led the army back across the border, expecting to find messengers waiting, but there weren't any. He hadn't said anything to the men, but he had an idea that the shrewder ones were guessing pretty close to the truth. There was a buzz of excitement on the march and around the camp; we're going all the way this time, it'll all be over by midsummer—as though something was about to begin, rather than everything had just ended. The senior staff kept quiet, waiting for an announcement.

They stopped for three days at the old fort at Stroumena, ostensibly to wait for supplies. On the third day, when Senza had given up and was getting ready to move on, a breathless young lieutenant told him five horsemen were approaching the camp, escorting a covered chaise. He didn't actually use the words Imperial courier service, but he didn't need to. He was grinning.

Senza watched them from the top of the observation tower. He saw a big man in a blue hooded cloak get out of the chaise; there was something familiar about him, though Senza could only see the top of his head. There was a woman with him; she got out, handed him a satchel with the ends of a couple of brass despatch rolls sticking out, then got back into the chaise. Two of the riders started to follow the blue-cloaked man, but he sent them back and set off across the courtyard. Definitely something familiar about the way he walked; an aggressively long stride, impatient, a man very much aware of the value of his time. So much to do, and only me capable of doing it. He disappeared through a gateway, and Senza drew back from the window. Ridiculous, he thought. What on earth would he be doing here, middle of nowhere, in a war zone?

He heard footsteps running up the spiral stairs, and then there was a guardsman in the doorway, with a look on his face like someone who's just seen God coming out of the drapers' on the corner. "It's him, sir. Oida. Wants to see you."

"I'll come down," Senza said.

Oida was in the small courtyard, sitting on a mounting block. He'd taken off the cloak and draped it over his knees, like an old lady with a carriage rug. He was examining a scuff on the side of his boot. He looked up and smiled. "Hello, Senza," he said.

Senza felt his left hand clench tight; he relaxed it before it was noticed. "Oida," he said. "What are you doing here?"

"I've come to entertain the troops," he said.

Senza managed not to say the first words that sprang to mind. "It was very clever of you to find us," he said, "seeing as how we didn't tell anyone we were coming this way till we reached the border."

"Pure serendipity." Oida beamed at him. "I just happened to be in the neighbourhood, and someone told me you'd shown up out of the blue. As luck would have it I don't have to be anywhere special for a day or so; I thought, why not? Do my good deed for the week and see my old friend Senza. Any chance of a drink, by the way? I'm gasping."

Senza didn't say anything for four seconds. Then: "Of course," and he turned and started to walk. He went fast, trying to make Oida break into a trot, but with those great long legs Oida could keep up with him at a stroll. Senza didn't like tall people. By some cruel quirk of fate, he'd been surrounded by them all his life; he was exactly average height, but he'd always *felt* short, and bitterly resented it. Oida was a head taller than Forza had been. There was simply no excuse for something like that.

Four or five hundred years ago, when the fort had been a monastery, the monks had made a walled herb garden. Somehow it had survived, though now it produced fresh salad for the officers' mess. There was a small free-standing stone building in the north-eastern corner, where the cellarers had once dried and cured medicinal herbs; it was cool even when the sun was high and still smelt faintly of rosemary and cumin, though these days it was mostly used for storing eggs. There were three carved oak chairs, a cupboard and a massive table scored with knife cuts, and a door you could lock from the inside.

Senza opened the cupboard and took out a brown glass bottle and one horn cup, which he filled three-quarters full. Oida took it and drank about half. Senza pulled a face. "I don't know how you can drink that stuff," he said.

Oida laughed. "Your loss," he said. "They try and make it in the West," he said, "but it's a poor imitation. Someone told me it's the wrong sort of bees."

Senza shrugged. "Bees are bees, surely."

"You'd have thought so, but apparently not." He reached across the table for the bottle. "They make a passable imitation in Charattis," he said, "but it's a sort of browny treacly colour and rather too sweet for my taste. Cheers."

Senza watched him drink in silence. He'd never seen Oida drunk, never. Alcohol just made him a more intense version of himself: cunning, ambiguous and so very, very annoying. "So," he said, "what are you going to give them?"

Oida yawned. "Oh, the usual," he said. "A fine blend of sentiment and smut, with a few big, loud patriotic numbers at the end so they can all have a good roar. I like singing for soldiers, they're appreciative and easily pleased."

Senza remembered some of the reasons why he'd never liked Oida. "Who's the female?" he asked.

Oida pulled a face. "Political officer," he said.

"Ah. Ours or theirs?"

"Oh, yours. I'm not allowed to blow my nose without her reporting in triplicate to the Secretary General. If I didn't know better, I'd swear someone in your government doesn't trust me. Still, that's what you get for being neutral, I suppose."

Senza grinned. "I've always meant to ask you about that." He paused to rub his side; getting better, but it still ached all the damn time. "Later, maybe. Very kind of you to make time for us. Shouldn't you be somewhere else, earning money?"

"Yes," Oida said. "But what the hell." He drained what was left in his cup, looked at the bottle but didn't move. "To be honest with you, I'm dying of curiosity. There's this rumour going round."

"Oh yes?"

Oida nodded. "They say you've killed Forza."

"Do they now."

"Indeed." Oida was looking straight at him, and Senza realised he'd be a hard man to lie to. "Anything to it?"

"You know, I'm not sure." Senza waited; he didn't actually know why. "I may have killed him, but I can't confirm it. Actually, when you showed up, I was hoping it was Imperial couriers with something in the way of hard news."

"Sorry," Oida said. "They say it was you and him, hand to hand."

"Well, wouldn't that make a lovely story," Senza replied. "But, yes, there was a bit of a scrap, my guards and his. It's possible that he may have been killed. I nearly was. Complete balls-up, as a matter of fact, everything got completely out of hand. So, in answer to your question, I really don't know."

Oida nodded slowly. "That's interesting," he said. "Presumably you'd know if he's out of action from the way his troops are moving."

"If I knew where they were, quite probably, yes."

A truly irritating grin. "I might be able to help you there," Oida said, and from his pocket he took a map, stiff parchment, folded longwise. He laid it on the table and smoothed it out with the heel of his hand. "Some people I know reckon they saw a large body of men here—" He was pointing at a blank space in the middle of the map. "Not your lot, obviously, not the tribesmen or the Blemyans, because we know where they are. So, logically, it's got to be Forza's army. Headed north in a great hurry, my friends said." He pushed the map across the table. "I don't know if it's any use to you, but there it is."

Senza realised he'd stopped breathing. "These friends of yours."

"Ah." Oida looked away. "Strictly neutral," he said, "just like me. But reliable. Obviously, you can't take my word for it, but you can send some of your people up that way to have a look, if you want to. Here." He stretched out his arm, rested his index finger on the map and scored a faint line with his fingernail. "There or thereabouts," he said. "About five days ago, so you should be able to pick up the trail."

Senza stared at the map. He could see the faint furrow of Oida's nail. "It's terribly kind of you to tell me this," he said, "but it's not very—"

"Neutral?" Oida beamed at him.

"Not very, no."

"Mphm." Oida leaned back in his chair. "My old mother used to say, there's a time and a place for everything. Neutrality is wonderful when you don't know which side is going to win. But if Forza's dead—"

Senza had picked up the map without knowing it. "He may not be, I just said."

"Indeed." Oida massaged the side of his head with the tips of two fingers. "But—I'm no strategist, God knows, it's a closed book to me, I'm just an entertainer. But if Forza's alive, what the hell is he doing over there? I don't actually know the region, but surely the only reason you'd be over that way would be if you were trying to get back home as quickly as possible; and I can't see why Forza would want to do that."

"If he's alive."

"Quite."

"These friends of yours," Senza said.

"I'm a very lucky man. I have all sorts of friends."

"Talkative ones."

"Total bloody chatterboxes, some of them."

"If I knew where Forza's men are," Senza said slowly, "you're right, I could tell a lot from the way they behave. Generally speaking, I can read my brother's movements like a book. Actually, it's more like looking in a mirror. Or I could simply throw two squadrons of good fast cavalry at them and see what happens."

Oida raised a hand. "You're the soldier," he said. "I only came here to sing and play the mandolin. Thanks for the drink, by the way. If by some bizarre chance there happened to be a case of this stuff lying around, just gathering dust—"

Senza laughed. "You're a cheap date."

"My one redeeming quality," Oida said, standing up. "Oh, by the way, I nearly forgot. I ran into an old friend of yours the other day. Charming girl, name's on the tip of my tongue. Asked me, if I happened to bump into you, to give you her love." He paused, looking Senza straight in the eye. "Name beginning with L."

No point in trying to play chess. "Lysao."

"That's it, yes. She said, if ever you're in Araf, to look her up."

"Araf."

"Small town just south-east of Lath Escatoy. Right," Oida said, "this is all very nice but I'm sure you're busy. I was thinking of using the main courtyard, unless we'd be in the way."

"You go right ahead and do whatever you like," Senza said.

"I hoped you'd say that," Oida replied. "After all, nothing's too good for the men, is it?"

Senza smiled. "Not even you. Your friends." He was between Oida and the door. "Do you think they could be my friends too?"

Oida stayed exactly where he was. "You know what they say," he said. "With friends like them—" With a move as yet unknown to the science of fencing, Oida slipped past him to the door and shot the bolt. "I'll get them to save you a seat near the front," he said. "Thanks again for the drink."

Araf wasn't on any of the maps in Senza's enormous collection, but after an exhaustive search they found Lath Escatoy. Eventually, after he'd stared at the map for a long time, Senza said, "Well, that's that, then."

Colonel Avelro, the new commander of the guards, said quietly, "It's possible. It could be done."

Senza sighed. "It's three hundred and seventy miles behind enemy lines. Also, for all we know, he's lying through his teeth."

"Possible, I suppose."

"No." Senza closed his eyes and opened them again. Maybe he'd hoped that the two words might have miraculously disappeared from the parchment while he wasn't looking. "Two hundred and fifty miles, I might just have considered it. Three-seventy is too far."

"But if Forza—"

Senza looked at him, and he fell silent. Avelro rolled the map up and put it back in its brass tube. Senza poured himself a drink of water. Then he said, "But only eighty miles from the northern border. Now there's a thought."

Avelro knew him too well. "It's a pity we can't go there," he said firmly. "But you know what they're like in those parts. If we tried to take an army through their territory, there'd be hell to pay. It'd be far easier to cut our way through from this side. Far easier."

Senza laughed. "You should see your face," he said. "Oh come on, even I'm not that crazy. I'm not suggesting *we* should go there. God, no."

"Ah." Avelro looked wonderfully relieved. Then he said, "Someone else?"

Senza nodded. "Friend of a friend, you might say." He pointed to one of the folding chairs, and sat in the other one. "Changing the subject entirely, what do you make of Citizen Oida?"

Avelro hesitated for a moment. "Wonderful diction," he said. "I think maybe a bit suspect on the really high notes."

"Do you trust him?"

"If he told me I had ten fingers, I'd count my fingers."

Senza pointed to the rosewood box on the table. Avelro opened it, took out a silver flask and two small silver cups. Senza shook his head, and Avelro poured himself a drink. "What do we actually know about him? Well," he went on, before Avelro could say anything, "he's the most famous civilian in the two empires, fine. About a million people who've never even seen him think he's wonderful, and, to be strictly fair, he writes a good tune."

"Agreed."

Senza took his little silver box from his sleeve, opened it and put one of the tiny ivory counters down on the table. "All right, that's point one. Point two." He slid another counter out of the box. "He's something quite high up in the lodge."

"Is he?"

"Oh, I reckon so. Must be, don't you think?"

Avelro pulled a face. "He doesn't strike me as a very spiritual man, somehow."

Senza laughed. "Quite. But he makes friends easily, which is quite an achievement for someone so bloody annoying. Lots and lots of friends, and the most unlikely people." He laid down the second counter. "That's got to be because of the lodge. Well?"

"I guess," Avelro said. "Not that I know very much about that stuff."

"You never joined," Senza said. "Why's that?"

Avelro's face darkened just for a moment. "Against my religion," he said briskly, and Senza lifted his hand in a brief gesture of apology. "Sorry," he said, "I forgot."

"That's all right. Actually, it's good; it says a lot about the service. I mean, where else in the empire would you be able to forget something like that?"

Senza nodded. "Though I wouldn't count on it lasting," he said. "With this business in Blemya, I have an idea that sun-worshippers are going to be in for a hard time. Not in my army," he added quickly, "but you take my point, I'm sure."

"Noted."

"Very good. Now, where were we? Oh yes." He took out a third counter. "He's neutral."

"Is he now?"

"Told me so himself." Senza laid down the third counter. "So neutral, he gives me the location of Forza's army, free, gratis and for nothing."

"We haven't confirmed—"

Senza waved a hand. "It'll check out, you'll see. Actually, a part of me's hoping it won't, but it will. So, what's all that about?"

Avelro stirred uncomfortably. "Maybe he knows something we don't," he said.

"Confirmation that Forza's dead? Possible. I'm assuming that was the impression he was trying to give. Well, impression, he actually said as much in so many words; if Forza's dead, he wants to make friends with the winning side as soon as possible."

"Or he wants us to go racing off into the blue and get ambushed."

"Or that, yes. If Forza's alive, obviously he'd like to make me believe he's dead, so I'll go rushing off to wipe out what's left of his army and walk into a nice trap."

"And Oida—"

"Would be best friends with the winning side, quite." Senza picked up a counter and looked at it; slight chip on one edge. "On the third, no, make that the *fourth* hand, if Forza were to set such an obvious trap, I'd be delighted to play ball, on the grounds that I can predict what form Forza's traps will take with ninety-nine per cent accuracy. Put it another way, I think Oida's far too smart to put himself in the middle between me and my dear brother when we're having a row. Hence my previous statement, it'll check out."

"And the other business?"

"Ah." Senza stood up and walked a step or two. "Now there's a thing. Practically the last words my brother said to me were, he knew where she was. Want me to tell you, he said, and I know how his mind works; he wouldn't have said that if he hadn't known. So, if Forza knew—"

Avelro reached across and moved one counter to his side of the table. "If Oida knows," he said, "who told him?"

"Very good," Senza said, "you got there in the end. Who the bloody hell told him? That's the bit of broken pot that won't fit. Forza? His good friend Forza? I can't see that somehow."

"Other way round, maybe. Who told Forza?"

Senza nodded. "Quite," he said. "His very good friend Oida, or so we're expected to assume. Dear God, this sort of thing makes my head hurt. Because if that's the case, and Oida was extending the sticky paw of friendship, what reason would he have had to believe that Forza was going to be the winning side, and therefore worth cuddling up to? Doesn't bloody *fit*, does it?" He slid the counters into his hand and dropped them back in the box. "All right, here we go again. Forza tells Oida, so that Oida can tell me, so that I can go to this Araf place and get killed. A bit crude, but Forza knows I'm not entirely rational where a certain person is concerned. If she's really there, he reckons, I'll go, and screw the risk. Now *that* fits."

"But not if Forza's dead," Avelro said.

"No, and that's the buggery of it. Unless Oida wants us *both* out of the way." He stopped dead, and his eyes were wide open. "Now there's a thought," he said.

Avelro shook his head. "And then the war just goes on and on for ever," he said. "Nobody wins, and nobody is Oida's very good friend. No, there's nothing in that for anybody, except the crows."

Senza frowned, then shrugged. "Maybe," he said. "It all depends on who Oida's very best friend is, and that we don't know." He paused. "Do we?"

"Don't ask me, I'm just a cavalryman."

Senza sighed and sat down again. "At times like this I wish I drank," he said. "I'd love to pour myself a big stiff drink and go and hide in it until everything had gone away. That's what my father used to do. Not a good idea, but I can see why he did it. And he was only marginally less stupid when he was sober, so why not?"

Avelro grinned. "You, on the other hand—"

"Quite. Being stupid's a luxury I can't afford. Look, what *are* we going to do?"

"What we always do," Avelro said. "Send cavalry."

"Attack their army and find out if it's Forza leading it?"

"Absolutely. Even if we get a bloody nose, who gives a damn? We'll find out if Forza's alive and still in business. What could be more important than that?"

Senza nodded firmly. "Yes," he said, "let's do that. Have a safe trip, and I'll see you when you get back."

One of the disadvantages of being a general is that you almost never get to see the look on your enemy's face at the exact moment when he realises he's been comprehensively outflanked. "Me," Avelro said, but by then it was far too late.

"Of course," Senza said. "There's nobody I trust more to do a good job. Your speciality, I think: long-range cavalry raiding. Cast your mind back."

Twelve years earlier, when Avelro had been a captain and Senza his lieutenant, Avelro had made his name with a particularly daring surgical strike deep into enemy territory. *Never again,* he'd confided, just before he walked up to General Moisa to collect his medal. *No more heroics for me, Senza my boy. You only get so much luck this side of the Very Bad Place.* But he was a first-rate cavalry commander.

He was also a realist. "Fine," he said, and Senza couldn't help admire the grace with which he accepted defeat, though in his view grace was somewhat overrated as a military virtue. "Leave it to me."

"Thank you," Senza said with feeling. "And when you've done that—"

It's axiomatic in the torture industry that fear of pain, anticipation of pain, is far more powerful, therefore far more effective, than pain itself. Ninety-five subjects out of a hundred, they say, when shown the instruments of torture, will break down and start talking, if properly handled.

She looked at the machine and sniffed. "You do know," she said, "you've got that bit in upside down."

Five out of a hundred had to be different, of course. "And there's a camshaft missing there," she went on, "without which the stupid thing just doesn't work. When they sold it to you, wasn't there a manual or something?"

Senza decided he liked her. "We didn't buy it," he said. "We found it in with a lot of other junk we took from the enemy at Beal Ritor."

"Ah," she said. "That figures. The word *decommissioned* springs to mind. Your brother didn't approve of torture."

Note the choice of tense. "Is that right?"

"I believe so. For the same reason you don't drink. Sensible people tend to steer away from things they may end up liking too much."

She had his attention. "You know Forza, then."

"I've never met him, if that's what you mean. But the service likes to know about important people, naturally."

Senza allowed the broad grin to spread across his face. "The service," he said. "I meant to ask you about that."

She looked at him, then lifted her hands. "Could you please take these off now?" she said. "They're hurting my wrists."

"Not really," he replied. "For that, we'd need a blacksmith, or at least a file or a cold chisel to cut the rivets. Besides, I haven't finished with you yet."

"You're not going to torture me, though. Are you?"

"No," Senza admitted. "Not with this lot, anyway." He craned his neck to peer through the dungeon's tiny window. "Nearly midday," he said. "How about an early lunch?"

Ten minutes later they were sitting on the terrace under the North tower. The garrison commander's wife had had a lawn laid out and flowerbeds planted, and there was a table and two benches. Senza had ordered cold chicken and salad. "I'm waiting," she said.

"Sorry?"

"For my apology." She paused. He didn't say anything. She went on: "An apology for abducting and falsely imprisoning a government officer. I know, you're General Senza, you can do no wrong, but the least you can do is say you're sorry."

He inclined his head a little. "No apology," he said. "You're not a government officer, I checked. They've never heard of you. It interests me why Oida should pretend you're one. If you tell me that, we can dispense with the ironmongery."

She looked at him. "You checked."

"I check everything," he said. "Particularly where Oida's concerned, particularly right now. Pretty much everything else he told me appears to have been true—well, I'm waiting for confirmation on one point, but that may take a while. But I did catch him out in one lie. You're not a political officer assigned to spy on him, but he said you were. On the off chance that it was significant, I had you pulled in and brought here. Answer my question and you can go."

She looked down at the manacles. There were red weals where they'd chafed her skin. "Fine," she said. "I'm not a political officer. I'm Oida's personal assistant. All right?"

"How personal?"

She gave him a tired look. He held up his hand. "All right, fine," he said. "For that you do get an apology. Though, given his reputation—"

She gave him a sweet smile. "Oh, that," she said. "You know what they're saying about him in Bohec? They say that while she's asleep, he plucks two hairs from the bush of each successive conquest. His long-term aim, they say, is to stuff a mattress. Not true, of course."

"No?"

She shook her head. "Two medium-sized cushions, if that. As for me," she went on, "one good thing I'll say about him, he understands that no means no, and he doesn't bear grudges. Plenty more fish in the vast, unlimited ocean, is his view. So, no, that's not what I'm there for."

Senza ate a scrap of lettuce. "So what do you do?"

"Take notes," she replied. "Find things out. Carry messages, talk to people, keep my eyes and ears open. Political officer's a good cover because everyone knows what a pain in the bum they can be, spying on your every move. People who don't like him tell me things to get him in trouble, so he knows what his enemies are thinking."

Senza smiled. "Oida has enemies."

"Of course he does." She hesitated, as if afraid she may have said something she shouldn't. The hesitation was just a little bit too long, maybe. "You do know—"

He broadened the smile. "Know what?"

"Oh God." She closed her eyes for a moment. "Obviously you don't, and I assumed— *Hell*," she said. "He's going to be so angry."

"Know what?"

She let out a long, sad sigh. "Oida is the go-between," she said. "Between the two empires. There aren't any official lines of communication, no recognised diplomatic channels beyond the absolute bare minimum, but from time to time there are some things they've simply got to talk about; but obviously nobody can know about it. Oida's more or less the only man alive who's free to come and go, loved and respected in both empires, known to be completely impartial, never takes sides, he's the obvious choice. He spends his life shuttling backwards and forwards delivering messages, conducting negotiations, that sort of thing. He's got a permanent staff of ten assistants, and I'm one of them. Oh, come on, you *must* have known. You know everything, everyone says so."

Senza pursed his lips. "Apparently not."

"Oh." She frowned. "Why the hell not? I mean, I'd have thought that you— Oh, the hell with it." She paused, then added: "Forza knew."

"You're not eating your salad."

"I'm not hungry."

"But it's your favourite."

She shot him a startled look. He went on: "Cold roast chicken, lettuce, cucumber, dill pickle, red and green peppers, honey, white wine and vinegar dressing. Your favourite. At least, it's what you always have when you eat alone at the Two Stars at Bohec, so I'm assuming you like it. Or maybe there's some special ingredient we've missed out. In which case, I apologise. No excuse for sloppy intelligence work, after all."

She gave him a long look. "You do know," she said. "About Oida."

Senza sighed. "Now that," he said, "is a very good question. Yes, I know a lot of things about Oida. Ever such a lot of things, many of them true. Just not enough, that's all."

She'd changed. She even looked quite different. He wondered if, this time next week, he'd recognise her again if he met her in the street. Quite possibly not. "It's really true that he's the go-between," she said. "And you did know that already."

Senza nodded. "I have full access to government intelligence," he said. "Which means I know what's in the dossier, about him and you. I know you killed a man at Beloisa just for a place on a boat—well, I say a man, a political officer, so no harm done. But, yes, I know a little bit about both of you. I know what you really went to Blemya for." She winced just a little when he said that. "Which is why we're keeping the chains on for now, given that we're alone and there's sharp objects handy. No offence."

"None taken," she replied. "Fine, so what do you want me for?"

He smiled; then he grabbed her by the throat, his thumb pressing on a particular vein. It was just as well he knew his own strength. "Tell me who Oida is," he said. "Please."

She opened her mouth but couldn't speak. He kept the pressure up for another three seconds, then let go. She fell back, gasping for air. He counted to twelve, then repeated: "Please."

"Since you ask so nicely."

He shook his head. "You're a clever, attractive woman and you make me laugh," he said. "In fact, you remind me quite a bit of someone I used to know. I'd hate to have to hurt you, but this is *important*." He turned round and made a sign; two soldiers hurried over, carrying a box. They put it down on the table and Senza lifted off the lid. "Go on," he said.

She looked at him, then into the box. "Oh," she said.

"Quite. That's the missing camshaft, and that's the pinion for the worm drive. You missed that."

"So I did," she said quietly.

"And, yes," Senza went on, "we do have the manual." He nodded, and the soldiers closed the box and took it away. "Please," he said, "I'm serious. I really do need to know about Oida. I've just sent off one of my oldest friends on a cavalry raid, based on what Oida told me, I'm scared stiff he won't come back and I'm being led into a trap. The lives of my men are at stake, and that means more to me than anything in the world. So you can see—"

"Anything?" she asked quietly.

He didn't smile. "You're quite right," he said. "Killing my brother is the most important thing, assuming he's not dead already. To that end I've sent tens, *hundreds*, of thousands of good men to their deaths, and I did it because it had to be done. But every single death was one too many, and I'm damned if there's going to be any more, if I can possibly help it. Compared to them, I'm afraid you just don't signify. I'm sorry," he added, "really. But that's how it is."

She looked at him. "All right," she said. "I believe you. You're cruel and nasty and you're prepared to hurt me. So, what do you want to know?"

He breathed in slow and deep, out again the same way. "Oida isn't just the go-between," he said. "He works for the lodge. Is that right?"

"Yes." He noticed her hands were quite still and relaxed under the table. "Yes, Oida's first loyalty is to the lodge. As is mine."

"What does he do for them?"

"What he's told," she replied. "It's what we all do."

Senza nodded. "Who does the telling?"

"I don't know." She lifted her head and looked at him. "That's the truth, and if you know anything about the lodge, you'll know it is. The lodge has a long and complicated chain of command, and at the top end you only know your immediate superior. You don't know who's above that, or who the real leaders are. Oida answers to someone, I honestly don't know who. That someone answers to someone else. Maybe there's a level above that, I really couldn't say. It's how we run things."

"All right," Senza said. "I don't suppose it matters all that much, in real terms. What's more important is, what does the lodge *want*? What's it trying to do?"

He watched her face, but could see nothing he recognised. "I don't know," she said. "It's the lodge. We have faith. We do as we're told."

"I really am very sorry," he said. Then he clapped his hands, and the soldiers came back. He nodded, and they took her by the arms and raised her to her feet. "I'm inclined to believe you," he said, "but that's not good enough, I have to *know.* All right," he said to the soldiers, and they led her away. He didn't watch to see if she turned back to look at him.

Later, he went to see her in the cells under the guardhouse. It was bright sunlight outside and dark in the cell, and it took his eyes a while to get used to the contrast.

"They broke your arm," he said.

"Yes." She was sitting on the floor with her back to the wall, cradling it in her lap.

"I'm sorry."

"Of course you are."

He didn't want to look at her, but he felt he had to. "You didn't tell them anything."

"No."

His mouth felt dry. "The chief examiner says he can't be sure you're not holding something back. He's very experienced in these matters."

"I'd sort of gathered that."

"He thinks he should try again, just in case. Better safe than sorry, was what he said."

She closed her eyes. "I can see his point," she said quietly. "After all, it's his reputation at stake."

He swallowed. It wasn't easy to do. "Are you sure there's nothing you can tell me?"

Just the ghost of a grin. "I wish there was, believe me. But unfortunately there isn't."

He nodded. "There's a very good surgeon here," he said. "He'll be able to save the arm, I'm sure of it. He patched me up once when I was in a hell of a mess."

"That's a comfort," she said.

"I'm sorry." He turned away and spoke to the wall. "I just wanted you to know, I understand what it's like."

She looked at him as though he was stupid. "No, you don't."

"I had a broken leg once. My men took it in turns to carry me. It was four days before we got to the outpost. It hurt like hell and by the time we got there I was hoarse from screaming." He looked back at her. For some reason, he was angry. "Does that count?"

"No," she said. "No, it doesn't."

Of course it didn't. Now she'd made him feel ridiculous. All wrong; he was supposed to be torturing her, not the other way round. "You knew the risks," he said. "When you joined."

"What the hell has that got to do with anything?"

Nothing at all. "I'll send the surgeon to set your arm."

"You can if you like. A bit pointless, though, don't you think? If they're going to break the other one tomorrow. Or will it be tonight? Or were you going to do a leg next?"

"Please yourself," he said.

"Am I being ungrateful?" she said. "Stupid ungrateful bitch. Not a very attractive quality in a woman. Mind you, neither is an arm the wrong way round." And then she laughed. "You look so stupid when you're embarrassed," she said. "Practically half-witted. Please go away now, it hurts when I laugh."

He banged on the door. The jailer took a long time, and for just a moment he was afraid he'd be stuck there, locked in, with her, indefinitely. The bright light outside hurt his eyes. He went and found the chief examiner. "Are you sure?" he said.

The examiner was eating bread and cheese; he'd worked through and missed lunch. "It's not a precise business," he said mildly. "In my professional opinion—"

"Yes?"

He pursed his lips. "Probably she's not got anything to tell us, but it could be she's really strong and clever, it's still too early for me to say. That's why I recommended—"

"I think we'll leave it at that," Senza said.

The examiner shrugged a little. "As you wish," he said. "It's your decision, after all."

Then he went and found the surgeon. "Please do the best you can," he said.

The surgeon gave him a mild glare. *You mean, as opposed to the careless, couldn't-give-a-damn job I usually do,* he didn't say. "Of course," he said. "Have they finished with her, by the way? Only if she's got more coming, I'll need to brace the splint pretty damn tight. The convulsions—"

"All finished," Senza said quickly. "And get her moved somewhere decent."

He climbed the tower and sat alone on the watchman's seat for a while, but this time it didn't help. All wrong. He couldn't help wondering what Forza would have done if he'd got his hands on Lysao—cradling a broken arm in the dark, but she'd never have fought back, and she too would have nothing to buy her release with. Not that Forza would have minded too much about that—

Could he really be dead? If so, that would change everything. Everything, and it'd be *over.* No need for any more of this. No more anything.

That summer in the country; before—well, *before.* Forza on the white pony, his legs so long his feet trailed furrows in the tall, wet grass. They'd shot—Forza had shot—a hare, sixty yards (they'd paced it out), and they took it home, and Father laughed and let them both have a quarter of a glass of wine, even though they were far too young; it had tasted foul, but he'd swallowed it because it was a reward, it was actually drinking victory (and how bad it had tasted, and how it had burned inside him), and how Father had told Forza that since he'd shot the hare it was up to him to gut and skin it; but Forza was squeamish, he hated that sort of thing, so when Father wasn't looking, Senza did it for him; and later, when they were alone, Forza had actually said, Thanks (out loud); and he remembered thinking: come what may, for as long as we live, I know Forza will always be on my side, and I on his, right or wrong, no matter what, and isn't it a great thing to have the most wonderful brother in the world?

"You again," she said.

He sat down on the bed. "How are you feeling?"

"You really want to know?"

Pain is not becoming. It had made her face thin, and she had a washed-out look that brought out the pallor of her complexion; she looked like parchment, you could write on her— "No. No, I don't think so."

She nodded. "So now you believe me."

He looked at her. You have to be able to read people if you intend to command armies. "No," he said.

Not what she'd been expecting to hear. "Is that right."

"Indeed. You may congratulate yourself. You beat Senza Belot." He reached into the leather satchel he'd brought with him and took out a small wicker basket. He lifted the lid. "Honeycakes," he said, "with almonds. Your favourite."

She looked at them as though she'd never seen anything quite like them before. "I'm surprised she left you," she said.

Not what he'd been expecting to hear. "What?"

"Your Lysao," she said. "A man who's considerate, who finds out what you like. Women go for that sort of thing, you know."

He laughed. "That's just attention to detail," he said. "Which wins wars, but—"

"And who's prepared to admit he was wrong."

He shook his head. "I wasn't wrong, though. At least, the chief examiner wasn't, and I trust his judgement. And anyway, she wasn't like that."

"Oh?"

He frowned. "She hated it when I pulled stunts like that," he said. "She said I only knew what her favourite cakes and flowers were because I had spies watching her every minute of the day, snooping round asking questions; she said it was horrible, creepy." He made a very slight gesture with his fingertips. "I can see her point."

"And who considers the woman's point of view," she said. "Why *did* she leave you, out of interest? Come on, I've told you things. Now it's your turn."

He looked at her. "Sorry," he said. "You'll have to break my arm first."

She looked right back. "Some day, maybe. Was it something you did?"

He shifted a little. "Several times you referred to Forza in the past tense," he said. "I tried not to react, because I assumed you were doing it on purpose to see how I took it." He paused for a moment; it was almost as if he was trying to decide something. "Do you know if he's alive or dead? Please," he added.

"I don't think I like it when you say please," she said. "Bad things tend to follow. But, yes, I know."

He nodded. "All right," he said. "How about a trade? You answer my question, and I'll answer yours." She opened her mouth, but didn't speak. He went on: "Someone once told me the key to negotiating is to give the other fellow something he actually wants—something you don't want, preferably, but, like everything, it's a question of proportion. Is my answer worth enough to you to buy your answer? Well?"

She smiled at him. "You're a clever man," she said. "If you'd used your brains earlier, you might have spared me all this." She lifted the splinted arm just a little. "By the way, no, it isn't."

"Ah."

"Because you'd be getting two answers for the price of one," she said.

He touched his forehead with his middle finger, then lifted it off with a slight flourish; the fencer's acknowledgement of a true hit. "You're slightly too old and not quite pretty enough," he said, "for which I am profoundly grateful."

"Ah." She gave him a grave stare. "My grandmother had an expression: she's prettier than she looks. That's me. Also, you're not exactly catching me at my best."

He shook his head. "I couldn't ever love a woman who was stronger than me," he said. "That's why she was perfect, of course. I don't know how much you know about these things—quite a lot, I should imagine—but there's a type of armour that's actually designed to crumple when it gets hit; it absorbs the strength of the blow and stops it churning your insides into dog food. In other words, it succeeds by failing, it's strong through weakness. That's her. You'd never think of hitting her, because if you did, she'd have *won*. So, we never fought." He stopped. "Well done," he said. "You got that for free."

She shrugged. "You gave it away as bait," she said. "Show an opening, invite an attack."

"Indeed." He smiled. "Would you like to come and work for me? I'll give you command of a regiment."

With her good hand she moved a few strands of hair away from her face. "The hell with it," she said, "you're too sweet to lie to. I'm sorry, I don't know if Forza is still alive or not. Nobody seems to know, not even Oida and his friends. So I can't play, because I haven't got any stake money. There," she went on, "you got that for nothing, so we're even."

He leaned back a little and folded his hands; it was a little-boy gesture, which he usually avoided. "She left me for another man," he said. "I think. I don't actually know. And who he is I have no idea."

Her eyes widened a little. "I don't know this game," she said. "How do you play?"

"Easy. We give each other something for nothing. Whoever gets what he or she wants is the winner. I think," he said gently, "it's your turn."

She was looking at him as though he was a badly written letter; she could make out some of the words, but not quite enough. "What I told you about the lodge is basically true," she said. "Oida answers to someone, I don't know who. That someone has a superior, but Oida doesn't know who he is, or whether he's the top man or not."

Senza frowned. "You already gave me that."

"Yes, but this time it's true."

That made him laugh. "All right," he said. "My other question is, what does the lodge *want*?" He paused, then went on: "How much will that cost me?"

She shook her head. "Sorry," she said. "You can't afford it." She was reading his face again. "Does that mean I get my toes crushed in a vice or something?"

The thought had just crossed his mind. "No," he said, "that counts as cheating." Suddenly, without quite knowing why, he stood up. "I fold," he said. "You win. And now it's your moral duty to have grandchildren, so you can tell them: I made Senza Belot admit defeat, twice. Thank you for your time."

"My pleasure," she said. "Do stop by again if you have a moment. We could play chess."

Senza smiled at her. "Not bloody likely," he said.

*

Later, he thought about the celebrated battle of Cereinto, the largest and bloodiest engagement of the Third Solantine War. The Federalists, under Marshal Aistu, were determined to stop the Loyalists, under General Lios, from reaching Astapaloeia. The Loyalists were desperate to get past Aistu's army and reach the port of Pesymon before the autumn storms cut off all further supplies from home. After a slogging match that lasted from just after dawn until mid-afternoon, General Lios' heavy dragoons finally burst through Aistu's pikemen and opened a gap through which nearly the whole of his surviving army was able to pass. The result was that Cereinto was saved and the Loyalists entered Pesymon just as the supply ships were sighted in the bay. Both sides, quite justifiably, claimed a glorious victory, and Cereinto was taught in military academies right across the empire as a classic example of a battle won by both sides, until Acobius, in his commentaries on Aistu's *History of the War*, pointed out that Cereinto only happened because both commanders had completely misread the other's intentions, and the same results would have been achieved, and without the loss of eleven thousand lives, had the battle never taken place at all.

So, Senza told himself as he walked up the steep spiral staircase to the top of the gatehouse tower, the best battle is the one that doesn't happen; instead, we negotiate, we trade, we give and take. Unfortunately, in the real world, certain formalities tend to supervene: abductions, broken arms. Only when all the clutter is out of the way can the real business be done.

Bullshit, he thought. But Forza would have stayed and watched.

Alone on the turret, he watched the sun set. He tried to project the tactical grid into the blue darkness, but he couldn't see the lines. It was almost impossible to avoid the conclusion that Oida, Oida's friends, the lodge, wanted him to win; whether or not Forza was dead, they had more or less given him Forza's apparently leaderless and shambling army, wandering lost in the wilderness, trying to limp home like a wounded animal. Furthermore, they'd sought to *bribe* him to accept this amazingly generous gift by telling him where Lysao was.

All right; take it at face value, just for a moment. Why now? Because of Blemya and the mad prophet; a million fanatical nomads unleashed on the civilised world, and only the best soldier alive can stop them, save countless lives, preserve the true Faith from extinction. Forza is dead; or Forza is, in the opinion of the competent experts of the lodge, not quite as good as his brother. It was plausible. You'd probably forgive a young second lieutenant on his first tour of duty for believing it.

Oida answers to *someone.* That someone answers to someone else. Above that, nobody knows, and that's how it works. That he was prepared to believe; practically an antidote to politics, a magnificent idea, where applicable. But what did the lodge *want*? Either she didn't know or, more likely, she was prepared to risk the torture chamber rather than tell him. But that was crazy. The lodge wasn't just half a dozen old men in a chapter house; it was huge, vast, the biggest open secret in history. You can't have an organisation to which ten per cent of the population of the empire belongs, and where only three or four men know what it's actually *for.*

He caught his breath. He was suddenly aware of all the soft, ambiguous noises of the twilight: animals, birds, the wind slapping the stays of the flag against the flagpole. Couldn't you, though; couldn't that be exactly what the lodge really was? Imagine—purely for argument's sake—that in a thousand years' time the empire has fallen and sun-worshipping savages pasture their sheep on what was once the Forum of the Tribunes. Look east from the Forum, and you'll see the ruins of the Great Baths. Go inside, and there you'll see shepherds watering their flocks from the natural mineral springs. Ask them about this place, these twelve-foot-thick walls, the shattered shell of the Great Dome; probably they'll tell you that once upon a time there were giants, and that they built it to water their sheep, which stood fifteen feet high at the shoulder and drank a hundred gallons each a day. That was why the arches were so high and the floors were paved with slabs of basalt, because otherwise the sheer weight of the sheep would have cracked the paving.

Precisely. They'd use the Baths for their own purposes, enjoying the convenience and the readily appreciable benefits, and never need to know what it had really been built for; and the mere size and splendour and glory of it would make them need to believe in the existence of giants, who once lived and knew better than the little people of today—but never mind, no matter, not to worry, because the water here is clean and it's nice and cool at midday, dry when it rains.

Now suppose that there really were giants, and they built the Baths for some other purpose beside a place for senators to wash their feet, and the senators were as gullible as the shepherds who came after them—

Now suppose that the President of the Senate reports directly to the Master of the Rolls, and the Master reports to the Lord Chamberlain, who reports to an emperor that *nobody knows about except him*—

A moment later, he'd snapped out of it because, when all was said and done, who *were* the lodge, anyway? What could they actually do? Most of all, how many divisions could they put in the field? Answer, none. No army? Screw them. Likewise, screw the two Masters of the Rolls, east and west, the Lords Chamberlain, and their majesties the emperors. All power—all *real* power—in the two empires was actually vested in the army, therefore in the hands of the two Belot boys, who'd been using it for as long as anyone could remember to try and kill each other—

Two empires, two armies. Two brothers—

Oh, he thought. Now that's *clever*.

It took two weeks to get the army back to Bohec. Unexpected late rain flooded the estuary and washed away all three bridges north of the mountains, turned the south road into a slow-moving river of mud and made the short cut through the marshes impassable. For the first time in years, Senza Belot was reduced to trudging, a long, weary, sticky trek round three sides of a square, just to get home.

When he got there, having been out of contact for ten days, there was no news; nothing had happened while he'd been isolated from the rest of the world, and, in particular, there was no word as to whether Forza was alive or dead. He sat impatiently through the usual debriefings, was rather ungracious about receiving the Order of the Headless Spear for his part in defeating the nomad threat, and went to the chariot racing at the Hippodrome, where he bet seventy angels on a rank outsider at thirty-three to one. It won, needless to say. He gave the money to the orphans' fund.

Then a summons; an audience with the emperor. For crying out loud, Senza thought, and sent for his dress uniform.

The New Palace had taken three hundred and eighty-four years to build. Originally planned as a modest ninety-acre site, scheduled for completion in a mere seventy-six years, it had grown in size, scope and ambition with each successive emperor of the Fourth and Fifth dynasties; the civil wars, military coups and foreign occupations that followed the collapse of the Fifth dynasty did little to interrupt the trend, as each new ruler sought to legitimise himself by adding his own personal touch to the palace complex; very few of them lived to see ground broken on their contribution, but, once an addition had been entered on the architects' Supreme Overall Plan, there appeared to be no official mechanism for removing it. As a result, usurpers and dictators spent fortunes they couldn't afford building monuments to the glory of the men they had betrayed, assassinated or driven out, while large parts of the original core design, such as the outer walls and gatehouses, remained in abeyance while the newer projects were given priority. Because the outer perimeter was therefore not defined and restricted, it was easy for the next new emperor to decree a further extension, wing or colonnade, often involving the clearance of several blocks of valuable City real estate, and the demolition of other parts of the palace complex already completed or still under construction. Only when Rheo III achieved the throne and decreed that no alteration to the design would be considered until the walls and gates were completely finished did the palace take on its final shape; which proved to be a rambling, ugly and wildly inconvenient assembly of hopelessly heterogeneous styles and forms, in which a man could walk for three hours, climb well over a thousand stairs, and only cover half a mile. Tapheon IV loathed the palace so much that he decided to abandon Bohec completely and relocate the seat of empire to a new site on the southern shores of the Mare's Head, and it was only his untimely death that prevented the move. Eventually, after nearly four centuries of scaffolding and hoardings, the palace was declared finished by Eucreon II, and there was a magnificent, if slightly ridiculous, opening ceremony. It's one of history's prettiest ironies that Eucreon's death led directly to the civil war, the partition of the empire and the establishment of another capital city, with another New Palace, on the other side of the Gulf of Sinoa.

Legend has it that it was among the blacksmiths employed for generations on the manufacture of hinges, nails, railings and the like for the New Palace project that the Order first came into being. As thousands of decorative-ironwork specialists from all over the empire travelled or were drafted to Bohec, they formed a trade guild—necessarily clandestine, since guilds were outlawed on government works—to protect their interests and safeguard the trade secrets on which their value to the project depended. As senior guildsmen evolved from mere artisans into artists and project managers, so the guild increasingly extended its interests and activities into areas rather more refined and socially acceptable than the shaping of hot iron; in particular (inevitably, during the successive waves of religious fervour that accompanied and followed the troubled Interregnum after the fall of the Fifth dynasty), guild members found themselves attracted to spiritual and philosophical issues, the pursuit of esoteric learning and religious arcana. At this point it became fashionable in Society to be a craftsman, and the lodge achieved the unique place in the established order which it enjoys to this day.

All the guards on the Sixth level knew Senza by sight. They should do; they were all distinguished veterans of his campaigns, assigned to the palace guards on his personal recommendation. Accordingly, there was a bizarre class reunion feel about walking from the Lion Gate to the foot of the Barbican tower. Every face he passed was familiar, someone he'd once known well and not seen for ages; instead of grinning, shaking hands and asking after wives, sons and old comrades, however, he had to march briskly across the endless marble floor (that rather nauseating shade of sunburn pink) without catching any eyes or saying a single word to his old friends, for fear of breaching the most sacred laws of protocol. The guards themselves knew the score, of course. By now, they were masters of silent communication and perfectly capable of conveying, *Hello, sir, how are you, great to see you again, best of luck*, without making a sound or moving a muscle.

Once he was past the threshold of the Dice Chamber, however, it was all quite different. Beyond that was the territory of the Household, recruited exclusively from the Northern and Eastern savages, whose only loyalty was to the emperor who paid them such a very large amount of money. Even if he'd been allowed to talk to them, it wouldn't have done him any good, since they wouldn't have understood a word. It was treason punishable by death to learn their languages or possess a relevant dictionary or grammar book, unless you were a linguistics officer accredited to the Chamberlain, on the grounds that it's hard to conspire with someone you can't talk to.

No guards, not even Household, north of the Pearl Chamber; from there on, security was the responsibility of the Gentlemen Doorkeepers, an order of chivalry founded in the Seventh dynasty and confined to twelve ancient families whose loyalty to the emperor was proverbially fanatical. That was the paradox. If you could somehow slip or fight your way past them, get to the emperor, cut his throat and cram the diadem on to your head, you were then the emperor and they would defend you to the death. The only known exception had been the pretender Phormia, who had managed to grab the crown before the Gentlemen reached him, but who, in his haste, put it on back to front. This was deemed to be procedurally incorrect, and he was cut to pieces on the spot.

The Captain of the Gentlemen knew Senza Belot, of course. He opened the Blue Chamber door without a word, and Senza walked in.

"Senza." The voice, high and frail, came from somewhere in the blinding gold light, but the echo effect made it hard to place. "Dear boy. Thank you so much for coming. Do sit down. What'll you have to drink?"

The Blue Chamber was so called because Eita II had had it painted blue; to be precise, a perfect reproduction of the night sky over his home town of Gumis on the night he was born, the constellations picked out in diamonds and freshwater pearls. Five years later Eita was stabbed to death hiding in a latrine in the Guards barracks, and Lanceor IV had had the Chamber redone in gold mosaic, hence the bewildering glare when you first walked in; the Blue Chamber, however, it had remained. Although the mosaics were by Perperis and one of the ten finest artistic achievements of the human race, their purpose was coldly tactical. Dazzle an assassin for five seconds, and you have a much better chance of summoning the Gentlemen in time.

During his previous visits Senza had mapped the Chamber in his mind. He could've walked to where the chairs and table were with his eyes shut; not that having them open made much difference. His one fear was that he'd blunder into the old man along the way. If the emperor was in a bad mood, colliding with him would be treason, the noose or the block. If he was in a good mood, it'd be, *My dear fellow, how clumsy of me.*

"Tea, please," Senza called out into the blaze. It would already be there, of course. There'd be slightly too much jasmine in it for his taste; which would please him, because it would prove that Imperial intelligence didn't know absolutely everything about him.

He found the back of the chair by feel, waited until his eyes were accustomed to the glare (treason, on a bad day, to sit down while the emperor was still standing). He could make out a golden glow reflected in the smooth top of a bald man's head. It was all right to sit down.

"Thank you so much for the Paleostrate didrachm," the old man said. For a split second, Senza hadn't the faintest idea what he was talking about. Then he guessed it must be the old coin he'd sent him. The emperor collected ancient coins, among many, many other things. "Do you know, there's only five of them in existence? And your one's got to be the best specimen yet. You can make out nearly all of the obverse inscription."

"My pleasure," Senza replied. The chair was like being eaten by a monster with no teeth. He wriggled as he went in, but the back cushions got him all the same. He could barely move for softness and give. "There's a what's-its-name, provenance, that goes with it. I'll have it sent round."

"Thank you." True gratitude: far more so than if he'd just

added a new province to the empire. "As you know, provenance is everything with antiquities. It's criminal the way some dealers blindly ignore it. They're destroying the past. It's as bad as burning books."

There the old man was exaggerating. In his view, nothing was as bad as burning books. Well, almost nothing. With great effort and difficulty, Senza leaned forward, found the little blue and white tea bowl and sipped. Perfect; just right. The thought made him shudder.

"And the same goes for so-called restoration," the old man went on. "Criminal. Worse than murder. If I had my way, anyone who restores old paintings or cleans the patina off genuine old bronzes would be strung up. Sheer vandalism, but they keep on doing it."

If I had my way. But he did; that was the point . . . A good forty per cent of what the emperor said was curses and bloodcurdling promises concerning curators, art dealers, historians and musicians, but he'd never issued a single decree or arrest warrant for the sins he professed to detest so much. Plenty of decrees, ever so many death warrants, but none for offences against aesthetics. That was what he considered being a civilised man. "You wanted to see me, sir," Senza prompted.

The emperor was a tall man, though these days a slight stoop made him look shorter; but his shoulders were still broad, and there wasn't an ounce of fat on him. He'd been a mighty wrestler in his youth, so they said—classical wrestling, of course, strictly in accordance with the rules set down by the Academicians nearly a thousand years ago. His high cheekbones and long, straight nose looked very well on the backs of coins, though in real life his eyes were small and just a bit too close together. But you wouldn't know that if all you'd seen was his gold and silver profiles. Still, it was impossible to deny that he was a fine-looking man, very dignified and intellectual. It was hard to believe, just looking at him, that he'd murdered all four of his brothers.

"Now, then." The old man put down his wine glass. "What's all this about young Forza? Is he dead or isn't he?"

The little glow of hope in Senza's heart sputtered out and died. "Ah," he said. "I'd been hoping you could tell me."

Slight frown. "You don't know."

"I'm afraid not, sir, no."

A grunt of disappointment. "Well, we don't know either. Been trying our damnedest to find out, of course, but none of the usual sources can tell us a damned thing. Mardesian reckons they don't know themselves, which I suppose is possible." He paused, and peered at Senza with those sky-blue eyes. "I'd have thought you'd have known. First report that came in had it that you'd killed him yourself, single combat."

Senza took a moment to reply. "That may quite possibly be true," he said. "I hit him pretty hard at one point, though he was still very much alive when I ran for it. If he's dead, it's my guess that that's what he died of."

The old man considered that for a moment—you could almost see his intellect and his instincts in conclave—then nodded briskly. "Quite likely," he said. "Blunt force trauma to the head, entirely possible for death to follow sometime later. Ursinian, third book of the *Medical Commentaries*. Sulpicius disagrees, of course, but he was two centuries earlier. Blunt force trauma leading to internal bleeding inside the skull. You could be quite dead and still walking around. Question is, though, is he or isn't he? Until we know *that*—"

"Quite," Senza said quickly, hoping to forestall any further scholarship. "Meanwhile, acting on information received, I've sent cavalry to where what's left of his army might be. If it's where it's supposed to be, we'll soon find out if Forza's alive and in charge of them. If he is, he'll have our boys for breakfast, and then we'll know."

The old man grinned at that; thought it was funny. "Good idea," he said. "What information, exactly?"

"I was hoping you weren't going to ask me that."

"Ah." The old man thought about it. Good day or bad day? "Well, we'll forget about the source, then, for now. How about the quality?"

Good day, evidently. "To be honest with you, sir, I have no idea. That's why I sent the cavalry." He paused. More was required. "My best guess is that it's good information. I could so easily be wrong."

His Serene Highness Glauca III was a clown but definitely no fool. "You'll know soon enough, I imagine. It's the same in my business, of course; intelligence and scholarship, it's the source that matters. If your source is reliable and sound, you have facts." He paused to nod approval, as though he was also the audience. "On the other hand, even a doubtful source is still *information*. If a man's lying to you, you can learn ever so much from his lie. Why's he lying, what for, is he lying so as to mislead you or because he doesn't know? And lies, of course—It's like astronomy, I always say. Clever fellows, the astronomers, they can tell ever such a lot about something they can't see by the shadow it casts over something they can. Same with lies. The shape of a lie will often give you the truth." He stopped for a moment, thinking about something else. "In that case," he said, "what are you going to do next?"

"Good question," Senza replied. "In fact, I'd welcome a suggestion."

He'd said the right thing. The old man went all still and quiet for a while—the Pillar of the Earth, deep in thought—then leaned back a little in his chair. "Here's how I see it," he said. "There's this new trouble in Blemya."

Senza nodded.

"Blemyans can't cope. You and Forza go in and save their skins, but they're still damned weak. Forza, alive or dead? We don't know. Without Forza—" He made a falling-over gesture with his hand. "Invade Blemya," he said. "Reclaim the province for the empire, crucial strategic position and rich as fig sauce, so I gather. Men and money. Just what we need for a final push. The nomads—" He closed his eyes, then opened them again. "They're the problem, aren't they? Phraxantius, seventh book of the *Universal Geography*—two hundred years ago, but I don't imagine anything's changed very much out there. Fascinating people, very much a force to be reckoned with, underestimate them at your peril. The question is, if we ignore them and spend all our resources taking back the empire, will they pounce on us while we're weak and overwhelm us? That's it, isn't it? Herulius and the Sashan, fall of the Twelfth dynasty. Fifteen years of bitter war wiping out the Sashan so they'd never be a threat ever again, and then realises that it was only the Sashan standing between him and the entire Auzida confederacy. Savages overrun the empire. Result, a dark age lasting ninety years. All there in Phraxantius, and pray God it doesn't happen again. Well?"

"Quite," Senza said. "I'm glad you see the problem so clearly."

The old man grinned. "Not such a fool as they say I am," he said cheerfully. "I've had them all in here, you know, last couple of weeks. Do this, do that, annexe Blemya immediately, ripe for the picking and all that. Half of the damned fools have never opened a book in their lives. No, all they're interested in is the copper mines and the linen trade and the spot market in charcoal and palm oil futures and God knows what. And then there's your lot, any excuse for a fight, killing my soldiers and spending my money. For two pins, it'd be the galleys for the lot of 'em. Present company excepted," he added graciously, "of course."

"Thank you," Senza replied. "So, what you're saying is, we don't invade Blemya."

"I don't know," Glauca said, rather disarmingly. "On the other hand, you see, what if Forza isn't dead, and *he* invades Blemya? Worst of both worlds. Same ghastly mess, only we don't even have the initiative. Or even if he is dead, if you see what I mean.

If my bloody fool of a nephew takes it into his head to invade, by way of showing he's still a force to be reckoned with even without your damned brother—And so he blunders in there, stirs up the nomads, them at our throats, war on two fronts, exactly what we don't want. Answer: get in there first. If the bloody stupid thing's going to be done by one of us, better it's you than my imbecile nephew. Better still if it's not done at all, but do we have that option? You can see the problem, I'm sure."

Senza's head was beginning to hurt. "Precisely," he said, and waited. Not for long.

"I think the best thing," the old man said, "would be for us to agree a diplomatic rapprochement with the nomads, leaving us free to annex Blemya and then take the fight to my nephew. Not sure that's possible, mind you; the nomads aren't fools, last thing they want is a united enemy instead of a divided one. Still, you've just given them a bloody nose, so they wouldn't mind a bit of breathing space, and that prophet fellow's got his own position to think of, major military defeat and the insult to the god still unavenged. Don't suppose he'd object to a little peace and quiet so he can sort out his domestic enemies. Question is, do we *want* to give him that? Wouldn't it be better to make his life as miserable as possible, so that one of his own people cuts his throat for us and saves us all a lot of bother? Plenty of parallels for that in history, and you don't need to go very far back. You know," he went on with a sad sigh, "I never could understand why so many people want my job. Hell on earth, sometimes, trying to figure out what to do. What I wouldn't give for it all to go away, so I could have some peace and concentrate on my work."

That, from the cause and author of the civil war. But Senza had heard it many times before. "People just don't understand," he said sympathetically. "So, going back a bit, we don't invade Blemya."

"Not at this time, no." The old man frowned. "No, I don't think so. Really, we need to know about your goddamned brother before we can do any damned thing. That's what it comes down to, isn't it?"

Out of the mouths of emperors. "I guess you're right, sir. When you put it like that."

One of these days he'd go too far; and it'd be a bad day, and that would be the end of Senza Belot. Not today, though. "Stands to reason, really," the old man said. "Oh, I know what they say about me behind my back, nose always stuck in a book, armchair tactician, doesn't know a damn thing. Truth is, though, it's all there in the books, if only you can be bothered to look. Atriovanus of Pila, eight hundred years ago; he said, the ideal form of government is the rule of the king who is also a scholar, a poet and a philosopher. Read that first when I was six years old, always stayed with me. Of course, back then it never occurred to me that one day I'd be in a position to put it into practice, not with three healthy brothers all older than me. Wish it hadn't been that way, of course. Still, you never know, maybe it was all for the best. When I stop and think what might've happened if one of those boneheads had had the running of things, it makes me shiver. Utter disaster, no other word for it."

As opposed to, say, the civil war. Well. The sad, dreadful thing was that he was probably right, at that. Senza didn't dare get up, not until given a clear sign to do so, but he did his best to look like a man who was just about to stand up, in case the emperor was inclined to take the hint. Apparently not.

"My didrachm," the old man said. "You mentioned there was a provenance. Good God, man, you've hardly touched your tea, it'll be stone cold. I'll send for another pot."

"Please don't trouble, sir," Senza said. "Really."

"No trouble to *me*," the old man said accurately, and rang the little silver bell. "So, where exactly did you come across it?"

Senza told him, and what he couldn't remember he made up. Then, as flippantly as he could, he added, "Talking of coins."

"Yes."

"I'd rather like some. Modern ones. For my men."

Puzzled frown; then a click of the tongue and a grin. Amazing what you could get out of the old man if you could make him laugh. "Pay for the troops, well, of course you must have that. Tricky, though, money's damned tight. Those idiots troop in here, morning, noon and night; the Treasury is empty, the people won't stand for more taxation, the money simply isn't there. Don't be so stupid, I tell them, go and read Varian on economic theory. All you need is a slight adjustment of the gold-to-silver ratio, suddenly you've made two million angels out of thin air. Can't overdo it, of course. You can only go so far, playing about with the coinage. Take Euthyphro V, for example. Old Coppernose. They called him that because he drank like a fish, but also because he added so much copper to the silver coins, quite soon it wore through, and the nose on his portrait was the first bit to show up red. Cost him his throne, and all because of a nickname. Still, we've a fair way to go before we reach that point. Don't you worry about money, I'll find it for you. Thank God nobody reads Varian these days except me, so they don't know what I get up to."

"I read the copy you sent me," Senza said, remembering just in time. If the old man sent you a book, God help you if you didn't read it. "Mind you, I'm not sure I quite follow all the stuff about money of account. I got a bit lost somewhere around Ezentius' reform of the gold standard."

The old man's eyes shone. "Oh, it's perfectly simple," he said, and launched into an explanation that (to do him credit) almost made sense, at times. "Basically, it's just the old, old rule," he concluded: "bad money drives out good. Really, so long as you remember that, economic theory is child's play."

So that was all right. "Thank you, sir," Senza said, "I'll bear that in mind. So, if I send a requisition to the Treasury—"

The old man shook his head. "Better let me have it," he said, just as Senza had hoped. "Can't trust those idiots with anything important; if they don't lose it they'll quibble over it for months while the soldiers starve. Pay them first, find the money later. That's what Herulius did, during the insolvency crisis. I mean to say, that's the whole point of having an emperor, it means things can actually get *done.*"

Sadly true, Senza thought. At least with an emperor things get done, even if they're catastrophically bad. Last time, or was it last time but one, he'd had one of these summit conferences in the Blue Chamber, the old man had told him all about the rise and fall of the Blue Sky Republic. Much to his regret, he'd had to take the point: autocratic rule by a succession of incompetents and lunatics was bad enough, but government of the people by and for the people had been a disaster, from which only a handful had been lucky enough to escape alive. Moral (the old man had said), government of any sort is the art of putting out fires with lamp oil; the less you do it, the less you make things worse. All there in the books, as His Majesty hadn't failed to point out—

Senza tried not to relax, now that he'd achieved the one thing he wanted out of the meeting. Victory is, after all, a rose; hard to acquire without getting pricked, harder still to preserve once achieved. Time, therefore, to attack. "There was one other thing."

The emperor blinked at him. "Oh yes?"

"The savages on the northern frontier," Senza said. "The Jazygites and the Hus and the Tel Semplan, out in the badlands beyond Beal Escatoy. Doesn't it strike you that they've been quiet for an awfully long time?"

The Imperial hand stroked the Imperial chin, rasping on the Imperial bristles. Glauca was a martyr to razor rash. "They've been quiet, certainly. Ever since you gave them that thrashing five years ago."

"Five years is a long time," Senza said. "To be honest with you, I'm a bit concerned. You see, if I was Forza, right now I'd be looking round for something extra, some new piece to bring in to the game. Actually, if *I* was Forza, I'd have brought in the nomads, on my side, nine months ago; luckily, he's not quite as smart as me in some areas. But the Northerners—well, they're just sitting there, of no real use to anyone. If I was Forza, I'd think that was a real waste."

The old man nodded slowly. "Like Meshel and the Bechanecs," he said.

Who? What the hell. "Exactly. Classic case in point. Now I'm guessing that Forza hasn't just overlooked them, that's not him at all. Nor, up till now, did he want to go to all the bother of sweet-talking them on to his side. He was happy for them just to be there, worrying me to death, interfering with my long-term plans. Now, though, with the nomads suddenly involved on *nobody's* side, and Blemya the obvious logical next big thing, what better time to open a second, sorry, third front, up there where it's a real bitch doing *anything*, just to make my life truly wretched? So—"

"Forestall him," the old man said.

"Exactly."

"If he's still alive."

Senza nodded swiftly. "And even if he's dead. After all, what's it going to cost us, compared with war on three fronts, to see if we can't patch up some sort of deal, neutralise them if we can't bring them in on our side? Get there first with more resources; that's the only way I know of doing business."

The old man nodded. "Meshel and the Bechanecs," he repeated. "Seventy years of peace. I couldn't agree more." He paused and thought of something. "So why haven't you done it?"

"Ah." Senza did his owl impression. "Because they're not stupid," he said, "they don't dare be seen negotiating openly with us or them. If we sent an officially accredited embassy, more likely than not they'd cut their throats and stick their heads up on poles along the frontier."

"That would be awkward."

"Wouldn't it ever. Which means," Senza went on, "we have to find an intermediary, someone who isn't us, but will do what we want him to."

The old man looked at him blankly. "I see," he said. "Who did you have in mind?"

Senza paused and checked the grid he'd superimposed on the old man's face. "I was thinking," he said, "of Oida."

17

The Scholar

When the boy had gone, Glauca rose stiffly to his feet, stopped for a moment until the stabbing pain in his knees had subsided a little, and hobbled slowly across the tessellated gold floor until he reached the wall. In front of him a great bank of cabinets, gilded to match the walls and floor, stretched away in either direction until they were swallowed up in the blaze. Glauca didn't need to look for the number stencilled on the door. He could have found cabinet thirty-seven blindfold.

From inside his plain cotton shirt he drew a bunch of keys nearly the size of a man's fist, hung on a stout steel chain; these days they bruised his chest, but he didn't feel safe unless he was constantly aware of them pressing against his skin. He peered at them through the rock-crystal magnifying lens that was always folded inside his clenched left hand—it was unique, and the sum he'd spent on it was more than Senza would need to pay his army—until he saw the number 37 on the barrel of a slim brass key. He scrabbled it into the cabinet's lock (his hands shook badly these days), turned it, pulled it out again and let the bunch go. It swung against his chest like some piece of siege equipment.

> Most reliable sources state that the first pack was designed and executed by the silversmith Ebbo, to the orders of Tandulias of Pyrrho. As is well known, the first pack and the imitations made of it for the next ninety years were not wood or planed bark but silver, each card being made in two parts: the generic back, embossed with a generic stylised abstract design, and the face, on which was embossed the image specific to that card. The two parts were then soldered together and carefully fettled so that, when placed face down, they appeared identical.
>
> Fortune-telling as it is practised today was never a part of Tandulias' intention. In his writings, now lost, he stated that although the dealer should not be able to see the faces of the cards as he laid them out, it was both inevitable and desirable that the fingers of an experienced dealer would come to recognise—not consciously, perhaps, but on a subconscious level—the feel of the embossed designs of each card. His idea was that the dealer would be guided by what Tandulias called his inner eye to select the cards appropriate for the sitter; most certainly, he never believed that some directed chance or supernatural agency operated to pull the right cards seemingly at random from the pack. Later, however, as the pack became more widely known outside the inner arcana of the Order and the demand for affordable packs for private owners grew, painted copies began to be made, and naturally these could not be read with the fingers in the same way as the silver embossed versions. Tandulias' original intentions were ignored or forgotten, and the practice of fortune-telling, which all right-thinking men so properly despise, became widespread among the ignorant and profane . . .

Thus Felician, in the introduction to the *Mirror of True Wisdom.* These days, only twenty-seven genuine silver packs survived; nineteen of them were secured in cabinet thirty-seven, the other eight were in the Western empire, in the hands of rich individuals; that hateful boy his nephew had decreed that any attempt to offer them for sale would be construed as treason. All of the nineteen were unspeakably precious, but it was always the Five Oak Leaves Pack that his fingers reached for; supposedly (the provenance was good but not unshakeable) the fourth pack ever made, by Ebbo's apprentice Vecla, and briefly owned by Tandulias' son-in-law Panchion, the worthy, prosaic dentist of Lauf Barauna who founded the first ever lodge.

Glauca shuffled back to his seat and laid the pack on the table. The cards scared him; not just the usual proper awe, but a definite, palpable feeling of disquiet, the sort of thing he used to feel when he hunted boar with his father in the woods, and they'd dismounted and started to walk up through dense undergrowth; the same feeling that something close by was waiting for him, and when it burst out of cover and headed straight at him he simply wouldn't have the time or the presence of mind. Silly old fool, he thought; he closed his eyes and walked his fingers up the table until one fingertip encountered the cold silver.

Damn idiots nowadays, fortune-tellers and frauds and cheats, smooth cards and pretending there was a precise, fixed meaning to every card and every sequence and combination of cards. He slid his thumb between the top card and the one underneath, then hinged the top card sideways until it fell into the palm of his hand. In Rhaxantius' day they favoured blind men as dealers, because a blind man couldn't see to cheat; idiots, because a blind man can read with his fingertips far better than a sighted one. He let the pad of his middle finger drift across the metal, following the contours of the embossed relief. Eight of Arrows. He supported its weight as he spread it on to the table, like laying down a woman who's fainted in your arms. Done that once or twice over the years, of course. Ah well.

Next card, Victory. Of course, Victory doesn't mean *victory,* just as Death doesn't mean death. He laid it down and slid it until its edge met that of the Eight of Arrows. The Two of Spears, which always made him shiver. Poverty; he let his fingertip dwell on her face before he turned the card and put it next to the others. She always reminded him of his second wife—a remarkably inappropriate similarity, but he'd been in love with the little silver face since he was twelve years old, and even now the feel of her made him smile. A pattern, or at the very least a faint obscure shape, was beginning to emerge. He dealt the Nine of Spears, which made no sense at first, followed by the Angel, and then he understood.

Tandulias maintained that a brief pause for reflection after dealing six cards allowed impressions to seep through from the unconscious mind, and avoided the dangerous tendency to leap to conclusions. Well, the Two was almost certainly young Senza Belot, couldn't really be anything else. The Nine must be a reverse of some sort; impossible to say at this stage whether the Angel was figurative or personal. Trump, number, trump was nearly always a transition, but trump, number, trump and then a Nine was a problem; it all depended on how you read that disputed passage in Vexantian, and whether the verb was to be construed as indicative or subjunctive. Damn nuisance, and if there really was an afterlife he eagerly anticipated meeting the unknown copyist in it, so he could kick his arse for being so wickedly careless. Until then, all he could really do was go by context and the overall mood of the cards.

Onwards, as young Senza would say. Next he turned up the Five of Stars, which of course made everything much clearer; personal, had to be, in which case the Angel was presumably some savage chieftain—the nomad prophet, perhaps, or some headman of the Hus or the Tel Semplan. The feeling of tension slackened off just a little—odd, that, but somehow he felt he could cope better with people than with abstract ideas, laws of nature and war and economics. He turned up the Blind Woman, who presumably was someone he hadn't met yet.

Four of Spears—three Spears in one deal, for pity's sake. The Blind Woman and Senza Belot; he frowned. He assumed that young Senza liked girls—yes, there'd been that one he'd been particularly keen on, though wasn't there some story about what had happened there? Slipped his mind, but presumably there'd be someone about the place who knew it, a damned gossip factory like the palace. Then it occurred to him that three of the same suit meant that the last three cards must be subjective—yes, fine, but who was the subject? Four of Spears, Senza Belot. Fine. He turned up a new card to find out who Senza would encounter next.

Two of Arrows.

Oh, he thought. Well, at least now we know. Not dead after all.

Two cards to go. The first was the Sun, followed by the Seven of Shields. That made him sit back in his chair. Personal and subjective, he reminded himself; the end of the world for Senza Belot wasn't necessarily the same thing as the end of the world, although the two could so easily amount to the same thing—He felt a spasm of pity for the boy, the only one of the damned lot of them he had any time for, but then he reminded himself that he was the emperor, and the interests of the empire had to come first. Besides, if Forza was dead, Senza was no longer indispensable. There were other generals. Bound to be.

He counted slowly to twenty, and passed his fingertips over the cards once more, just to be sure. No mistake. Such a damned shame. He'd miss the boy, for one thing; someone he could trust, always a pleasure to talk to, very bright, clearly interested in art and history, with a genuine appreciation of the finer things. But all men, even scholars and aesthetes, are bloody fools where women are concerned. It occurred to him to wonder who she was, what she was like; had to be something special, he decided, to bring down young Senza. Damned shame. But if it was in the cards, there was nothing he or anyone else could do about it.

Well, he'd still have the pack, the Five Oak Leaves. All his life he'd been aware that things mattered more to him than people. He loved things, material objects, in a way he could never love a human being; they could be perfect, the way no human being ever was, they could resist change, they could be relied on. Things had been his friends when everyone else had turned against him, his own flesh and blood, and the Five Oak Leaves was his oldest and dearest friend; never let him down, never once lied to him. Without realising he was doing it, he turned his thoughts to the other packs, the eight trapped on the other side of the border—the Theugistes, the Chipped Star, the Third. Damn that bloody nephew of his, spiteful, hateful boy. Damn fool had written to him once, offering to trade, the Chipped Star for the frontier castle at Deura Adrabati. He'd refused, of course, he had to; sent the messenger back with his tongue cut out for delivering such an insult. But the Chipped Star; if it had been up to him—But it wasn't, of course. That was the cruel irony. The emperor, and, really, there was so little he was allowed to do.

He sighed with pain as he stood up. He never got up for anyone these days, but he stood up and took the pack to cabinet thirty-seven and lodged it securely in its proper place, found the key, turned it in the lock, then paused for a moment to recover himself after the exertion. Damn fool of a doctor said it was his heart; clearly hadn't read Mnesimno—what earthly bloody use is a doctor who doesn't read the books? Glauca knew precisely what was wrong with him, a complex and eventually fatal imbalance between the Marine and Aerial humours, brought on by his quarrels with his family, exacerbated by the wicked defiance of his nephew; even if the war ended tomorrow, the empire reunited, his nephew's head on a pike in the palace yard, he knew that too much damage had already been done. He had nine years, two months and seventeen days left, so much still to do and so much irritating nonsense getting in the way—No, mustn't allow himself to fret about it. Fretting, Mnesimno said, accentuated the imbalance by polluting the Terrestrial humour with green bile. Nine years was a maximum, not a guarantee.

The fire in the brazier was burning low. He was cold so much of the time these days, but he daren't have the room any warmer because of drying out the textiles and the bindings of the books. He picked up the bell and rang it; when the boy came, he ordered rugs and his goose-down coverlet. Then he sat for a while and listened to his own breathing; sounded all right, but of course you never can tell.

That night, according to Seuinto's Perpetual Calendar, the White Swan ought to be visible in the skirts of the Great Ship. Glauca hated climbing stairs more than anything else in the world, but a comet—Well.

The Observatory was the highest point on the west side of the palace. Quite unreasonably—since it was only logical that its principal users would be scholars, wise men, therefore of necessity *old* men—the only way up there was a narrow spiral staircase, its treads bowed and slippery with wear. Glauca had ordained a rope handrail, which helped a little. What he really needed was someone behind him to push, but his dignity forbade it. The only thing worse than climbing the Observatory stair was coming back down it, but he tried very hard not to think about that.

Instead he thought about the comet. Primitives believed the appearance of a comet was an omen, usually a herald of disaster, not knowing that science and observation had made such appearances entirely predictable. It followed that, since men had free will to choose their path, and the comet's course through the heavens was strictly predetermined, a comet could not be a portent. Instead—rather more significant and fascinating—a comet marked an interval, like a bar line on a sheet of music. In a sense, it was a fixed place by which one could gauge the movement of those astral entities that were capable of change and flux. Accordingly, it was necessary to drag oneself up these intolerable stairs, not to observe the comet, but, rather, everything else.

Gajanus had wanted two guards to go up with him, but he wasn't having that; no room on the damn stair, and the last thing he needed when he got up there was a pair of kettlehats breathing down his neck while he was trying to concentrate. Idiotic, the very idea. Nobody was going to climb the sheer outer face of the tower with a knife between his teeth. Gajanus had pulled his on-your-own-head-be-it face but he'd ignored it. Bloody mother hen.

He stopped four times on the stairs to catch his breath, but even so, by the time he scrabbled his way through the trapdoor at the top on to the leads of the turret, he was exhausted and gasping for air. No pain in his chest or arm, though, which proved what he'd always suspected about those damned fools of doctors. Heart be damned; misaligned humours, just as he'd—

Something was wrong.

Not for the first time, he cursed his own frailty. Because he was puzzling and wheezing so loudly, he couldn't hear a damn thing except his own sad noises, and naturally it was too dark to see, but something was very wrong indeed. He tried to keep still—pretty poor fist of it—and concentrate. Something—yes, damn it, of course. Taranice's Garland, a constellation of nine stars low down in the south-eastern quadrant, first identified by Nuammes in auc 176. It wasn't there.

But it was a clear night, and there were the Three Brothers, and Causica, and the curling tail of the Wyvern. But, in the gap between the Brothers and the endmost star of the tail, nothing but a dark patch—

It was sixteen years since Glauca had been called upon to fight, but there are some things you don't forget. Clear as a bell in his mind, the words of his old drill instructor: *full measure or right up close; it's half-measure that gets you killed*. He took a long step forward, aiming himself straight at the last star of the Tail. He had no idea if he was still strong—had been once, strong as a bear—but he knew he had no option but to find out. At the last moment he bent his knees, unable to stifle the whimper of pain, and shot his arms out. As he'd anticipated, they encountered legs, the legs of a man. He wrapped his arms around them, hugged them to his chest and stood up.

It didn't work quite as well as it should have. As the unseen enemy fell back over the parapet, one of his feet lashed out wildly and hit Glauca on the side of the head, pinching his ear against his skull. The pain was so fierce he nearly lost his concentration, but he knew that wouldn't do, wouldn't do at all. He'd only seen one enemy, but there could, *should*, be another, and until he was entirely sure he couldn't allow himself the luxury of acknowledging pain. In that category fell the terrified howl of the falling man; it tore into him like a knife but he knew he had to ignore it, until he could be sure—

Something like a cloud moved very fast, briefly obscuring Junonis and the Garter. Glauca knew what to do—long stride forward, grapple, hook and throw; Figure Six in Ultapian's *True Mirror of Defence*—but this time his body refused; he had no strength left. Miraculously, though, the enemy didn't close with him. He'd gone the other way. Damn it, the fellow was trying to *escape*—

Over the roar of his own breath, he heard a thump, then a series of bumps. If he'd had breath to do it with, he'd have laughed. Damned fool had stepped through the trapdoor and fallen down the stairs.

It was over. As soon as he decided that it was safe to arrive at that conclusion, all his control left him and he felt his back slam against the parapet, his feet slide out from under him, his backside jarring painfully on the leaded floor. All his scholarship now was centred on the art of breathing, which for some time proved difficult to master.

Even so: *Not bad,* he heard a voice inside him say, *not bad for an old man,* and he wanted to laugh. Sixty years a student of classical wrestling, but always in books; his first bout, then, and a victory. All things considered, an opportune moment to retire.

It took five kettlehats to get him down again, damned clumsy fools. The doctors wanted him put straight to bed, like a naughty child, but he wasn't having that. He made them carry him back to the Blue Chamber, where his collections were. They would heal him far better than any damned medicine.

He ordered an hour of complete peace. An hour and two seconds later, there was a knock at the door and in came Colonel Gajanus.

"Oh, it's you," Glauca said. "I ought to have you hanged."

But the look on his face—The poor fellow looked completely drained, as if his soul had been sucked out. "Yes, sir," he said. "Yes, you should."

Glauca scowled at him. "Don't be so damned stupid," he said. "Not your fault. You told me, take two guards with you, and I didn't listen. My own damned silly fault. What you should've done, of course, was send someone up there first, to make sure it was clear."

"Actually, sir, I did. I went myself. I thought there was no one there."

Glauca felt a pang of sympathy. Gajanus was, what, five years younger than he was; poor devil, dragging all the way up those awful stairs just because the old fool takes it into his head to go star-gazing. He was aware that at times he could be inconsiderate to the people around him, who by and large did their best. "It was dark," he said, "and those fellows knew what they were doing. Only noticed them myself because I was looking at the stars." He paused, aware that his last statement hadn't come out the way he'd wanted. Never mind. "You're a useless bloody fool, Colonel, but it's all right. Just make damned sure it never happens again."

The look of relief on Gajanus' face he found mildly disturbing, because it reminded him of the incredible, unconscionable power his words carried; he could just as easily have said, "Guilty, take him away," and that would have been that—a life ended, no more Colonel Gajanus, and what possible sense did that make? He remembered the yell of the falling man, the terror; far too much death and destruction around as it was without adding to it because of a temper tantrum. "Sit down, man, for God's sake," he said. "Pour yourself a drink and stop gawping at me like that."

No, Gajanus was a good fellow, fundamentally. When he'd had his drink and pulled himself together, he said that the second man was alive and that they'd caught him.

"After falling down all those damned stairs?" Glauca said. "Must've broken every bone in his body."

"His left arm, sir," Gajanus said, "and a nasty cut over one eye. Otherwise in one piece."

"Remarkable. Fellow must really know how to fall. It's something you can learn, you know, it's in Furminia, *Art of Wrestling*. Oh well, if he's alive we've got something to go on. That's a real stroke of luck."

Gajanus nodded gratefully. "I've sent for the examiners—"

"Oh no you don't," Glauca snorted. "Damned fools, they'll kill him and we won't find out a bloody thing. No, I want him looked after, and then I'm going to talk to him myself."

They were taking no chances. The prisoner had a chain attached to the wrist of his broken arm. He was lying down, of course, but even so it was obvious how tall he was; well over six foot—tall as me in my prime, Glauca thought, maybe even an inch or so on top of that, and broad, too; just like me. He felt a great surge of pity for the boy—what was he, nineteen, twenty? And after all, Glauca told himself, I won, didn't I? The other bloody fool was nothing but a bag of broken bones by now. Everything was death and killing these days. No need for it, no real need at all.

"It's all right," Glauca said. "He isn't going to kill me; he's not an assassin."

Gajanus rolled his eyes. The guards carried on staring dead ahead. "With respect," Gajanus said.

"Yes, yes, I know." Glauca slapped him on the shoulder. "Indulge me. You can peer through the keyhole if you like."

Gajanus opened his mouth to speak, but clearly words had failed him; he executed a smart about-turn and stalked out of the cell without a word. The guards hesitated. "Out," Glauca said. They went.

Glauca looked round for something to sit on. There was the bed, but the boy covered all of it; or there was a little low three-legged stool. With a great and terrible effort, Glauca bent down and sat on it. He felt a stabbing pain in his knees, which he managed not to show. The boy was watching him.

"It's all right," Glauca said. "I'm not going to bite you."

The boy looked as if he wasn't so sure. Glauca grabbed his right knee and forced his leg straight; then the other one. "Never get old," he said, "it's not worth it." He stopped; an unfortunate thing to say, in the context. The boy was still staring at him, and it suddenly occurred to Glauca that maybe he didn't speak Imperial. "You," he said, slowly and loudly. "Can you understand what I'm saying?"

The boy looked startled, but nodded. That was all right, then. "Say yes, sir."

"Yes, sir."

Curious accent; Glauca hadn't heard it for a very long time, but he recognised it. Rhus; the half-savages up north somewhere. Damned if he could remember whose side they were on.

"Now, then," he said. "I told Colonel Gajanus you're not an assassin. I'm right, aren't I?"

The boy opened his mouth, but it was a moment or so before he spoke. "Yes, sir."

"Well, you would say that, wouldn't you? But you could've killed me easy as anything up on the tower there, but you didn't. You held still, hoping I wouldn't see you. You're not a killer, are you? You're a thief."

"Yes, sir."

It wasn't dumb insolence, but it sounded annoyingly like it. "Now, listen to me, you damned young fool," Glauca said. "There's two thousand, six hundred and forty-eight people in this palace, and two thousand, six hundred and forty-seven of them want to string you up. The only one who doesn't want to is me." He hesitated. Impossible. But— "Do you know who I am?"

"No, sir."

"Dear God." Glauca shook his head slowly. "I believe you," he said. "You'd have to be the best actor since Lamachus. Fine. My name is Glauca Seusan-Catona. I'm the emperor."

It was worth it just for the look on the boy's face. "It's true," Glauca said. "Call in Colonel Gajanus and the kettlehats if you don't believe me. Well?"

"I believe you, sir."

"Damn it, boy, don't you ever look at your money? That's my face on the coins, don't you know."

"We don't have a lot of money where I come from, sir."

A smart answer, maybe just a little bit too glib. Glauca thought for a moment, then swung his fist at the boy's jaw. The impact jarred his arm right down to the elbow, and he discovered he'd cut the skin on his knuckles. Stupid thing to do. Should've quit while he was ahead, where fighting was concerned. "Don't be funny with me, boy," he said—it didn't come out quite right because the pain made his voice a little shaky. Still, it was pleasant to know he hadn't entirely lost his punch; the boy was shaking and plainly terrified. "Get it into your thick skull. The people out there want to hang you. If you annoy me, I'll let them do it. Do you understand?"

The boy nodded. It occurred to Glauca that maybe he'd broken the boy's jaw, in which case he wouldn't be able to tell him anything for weeks. "Answer me when I talk to you," he shouted.

"Sir."

Glauca waited, then realised he hadn't actually asked any questions yet. "So you admit it. You're a thief."

"Yes, sir."

"What did you come here to steal?"

"A map, sir. There's a special map in one of the rooms directly under that tower."

The cartulary, in other words. Yes, plenty of special maps in there: the coastal defences, the supply lines, the map Senza had filed with him showing his anticipated movements for the next three months—not that it was worth the parchment it was drawn on, the way that boy kept changing his mind. Directly under the observatory tower, perfectly true. If you were in the cartulary and heard someone coming, you'd leg it up into the tower till they'd gone, because nobody ever went up there. "You're sure about that."

"Yes, sir. Perfectly sure."

Glauca scrabbled for a moment in the pocket of his robe. Other things—a handkerchief, a small book, a bronze miniature by Calopa he always carried with him, because he couldn't bear to be parted from it. Ah. He found it. "So what was this for?"

He thrust the pack of cards under the boy's nose. "You recognise them, yes?"

"Oh yes, sir. They're mine." A slight pause; the boy could tell Glauca didn't believe him. "Really, sir, they're mine. I made them."

For a moment, Glauca's head swam, as though he'd been the one who'd just been punched. "You did what?"

"Made them, sir. I cut the boards out of a thin bit of wood from a packing case, and I painted them."

He's lying, Glauca thought; he must be. But, if so, he was a superb actor. "You can't have."

"I did, sir. Really."

"Nonsense, boy. Rubbish. Whoever sent you here gave them to you, so you'd know which pack from my collection to steal. Well? Isn't that the truth?"

"No, sir." The boy was looking straight at him. "I painted them myself."

Glauca had to make an effort to breathe. "Who told you what to paint?"

"I copied the pack the brothers showed me, back home, in our village. They've got a pack like that one, only it's not made of wood, it's thin sheets of silver. I remembered the pictures, and I painted them as close as I could."

"Silver," Glauca repeated.

"Oh yes, sir. They're all black because they're never cleaned, but the raised bits on the figures, the silver's rubbed through and they shine, where the brothers put their fingers when they deal. And that's what I copied."

Glauca didn't know what to do. Part of him wanted to smash the boy's face in, for telling such a cruel, tantalising lie. The rest of him was afraid he'd shatter, like a porcelain plate that can never really be mended so it doesn't show. "You're lying."

"No, sir, really. I promise."

Glauca took a deep breath. His heart was pounding. Hell of a good way to assassinate him, he thought: tell him this particular lie and let his own heart do the rest. "What brothers?"

"The brothers," the boy said. "Usually there's five or six of them, and they go round the villages with a donkey cart. People give them food and let them sleep in their barns. Sometimes, if you ask them just right, they'll tell you about—well, all sorts of stuff."

"These brothers have a pack of silver cards." The boy nodded. "And they let you copy them."

"Not really." The boy hesitated, as if wondering if he'd done something wrong he shouldn't admit to. "The brothers showed them to me, and I liked them so much I made my own pack, like I just said. I didn't think it'd do any harm."

Glauca could feel his heart pounding. "All right," he said. "Describe them. In detail."

"Well," the boy said. "The Ace of Arrows—"

"Forget about that. Describe Poverty."

The boy nodded. He cleared his throat and began to recite. "She's standing under an apple tree, wearing a crown of bay leaves—"

"Which way's her head turned? Right or left?"

Trick question. "She's sort of looking straight at you," the boy said. "And in her left hand there's an empty bowl, and in her right hand there's a pair of tongs."

"How many apples on the tree?"

"Five," the boy replied without hesitating. "And there's two birds in the tree, crows I *think*, and under the tree on her left there's a thin dog with its ribs showing, and on the right there's a fire altar with a loaf of bread on it and something else, I couldn't figure out what it was meant to be because it was so worn, on the card the brothers showed me, I mean. Oh yes, and in the background there's three men and a cart."

Three men and a cart. Glauca held back a smile; a fine way to describe Photeus and his brothers on their way to found the New City. "You're sure the dog's on the left."

"Oh yes."

"And two crows in the tree, not three."

"I'm sure of it, yes."

"Anything else? Think."

The boy frowned, then relaxed. "Sorry," he said. "Yes, there's a jug next to the dog. It's broken in three pieces."

Glauca's knees had gone soft; he couldn't have stood up if he'd wanted to. The two crows might be a coincidence, and maybe the something else on the altar might not be the globus cruciger. But the crows, the second object on the altar, the tongs, Poverty full-face *and* the broken jug—And the tongs were only recorded in a footnote to the commentary on Abbianus, which only he and maybe three other scholars in the world were aware of, and they were right here, in the City. The Sleeping Dog. It had to be. Every detail he'd looked for had been there. His hand shook as he took out his writing set and opened the lid. "Draw it," he said. "Now."

The boy lifted his chained left hand. "That'd be awkward," he said. "I'm right-handed."

"*Do it.*" He made himself calm down. "Do the best you can. It doesn't have to be perfect."

It came out quite ludicrous; a shaky, smudgy Poverty under a lopsided tree, and the dog looked like a goat. But Glauca could tell even so; the boy had drawn the pack, the style was definitely the same. He was telling the truth, Glauca was sure of it. In which case, this boy, this clown, terrified incompetent thief, had seen the Sleeping Dog Pack itself—seen it, maybe even touched it. *It existed.* It was somewhere out in the world, at large, obtainable.

He wasn't sure he could cope with that.

"Listen very carefully." His voice was shrill and unsteady. "I want you to go and get that pack for me. If you get it and bring it here to me, I'll give you twenty thousand gold angels. Do you understand?"

The boy was staring at him. Of course he didn't understand. "I don't think the brothers would want to sell it," he said.

"So what? You're a thief."

Glauca had been reading human beings even longer than he'd been reading books. He told himself he was good at it, and the fact that he was still alive after so many years on the throne suggested he was right. And if he'd read the boy anything like accurately, he'd just shocked him so deeply that his next words would be a refusal. There might not be a way back from that. "They'll sell it," he said. "For thirty thousand."

"Thirty—"

"And twenty for yourself," Glauca said. "When you put the pack in my hand, twenty thousand angels, new gold coins. And an estate, a thousand acres. You could be anything you wanted."

"I don't know." The pain in the boy's voice was far worse than anything the examiners could generate. Even Tencuilo, author of the *True Dialogue of Tortures,* couldn't hurt anyone that much. "I couldn't steal from the brothers, sir," he said, "I couldn't." He paused, and his eyes were enough to break Glauca's heart. "I'll try and make them sell it," he said. "But I couldn't steal it."

"Good lad. Very good." Glauca started to get up, but cramp stopped him. He had to wait, regroup, concentrate before he was able to stand. "I'll get you out of here and into the hospital, and they'll fix you up in no time. Good men, my doctors, even if they do fuss all the damn time." Senza's army, he realised as he spoke; the fifty thousand would have to come out of the money for paying the soldiers, and Senza wouldn't be happy about that. "I'll see to it that all the arrangements are made. Of course," he went on, just a bit too casually, "if the brothers do agree to sell, I'll need to see the pack before I hand over the money, but I'm sure they'll understand." He stopped. "What did you say your name was?"

"Musen, sir."

"Musen anything, or just Musen?"

"Just Musen, sir."

"Who sent you, Musen?"

The boy looked at him. "Do I have to say, sir? Only, they said if I told on them, they'd kill my mother."

What was it the boy had come to steal? Some map. Spy stuff. The hell with maps. "You can tell me when you get back," he said. "You'll be a rich man then, they won't be able to touch you. I'll see to that. I promise."

He could tell the boy was relieved, as though he'd put down a heavy sack he'd been just about to drop. "Thank you, sir."

"Perfectly all right, my dear fellow. Don't you worry about anything. You'll have your money and your land, and you and your mother will never have to worry about anything ever again. You have my word on that."

"You can trust me, sir," the boy said. "Really you can."

Attention to detail—the scholar's mentality—had always been Glauca's weakness, and his strength. Weakness, in all its connotations, was very much in his mind when he finally made it back to the Blue Chamber, having personally seen to the boy's transfer to the hospital, then driven to the Exchequer to see about the money. As he subsided painfully into his chair he realised that he was completely exhausted. He had no strength left; it'd be several hours before he'd be able to stand up again, and his hands were shaking uncontrollably. Hard to believe that only hours before he'd fought and killed a man. But he had. The pride he felt in that accomplishment shocked him rather, but he couldn't deny it. From his father, he supposed; Father had always valued men directly according to their ability to fight—*let the best man win* was, to him, a meaningless exhortation, since the winner was always the better man, by definition— He had a vague idea that someone really ought to give him a medal, or a trophy of some sort; who, though, he had no idea.

Attention to detail, then; he'd known he wouldn't be able to sit still and be peaceful until he was sure the boy was safely in a hospital bed, and the fifty thousand angels were irrevocably earmarked and written up as such in the books. That done, he could relax—

No, he couldn't. *The Sleeping Dog Pack*. He desperately wanted to get to his feet, but he knew he couldn't, so he rang the bell. It took for ever—nine or ten seconds—for that damned fool Crinuo to get there. As soon as the door opened, he snapped, "The scholiast on Abbianus, quick as you like. And Dasenna, and the *Universal Concordat*, and Nurisetta on miracles, and the sixth book of Nardanes' *War Chronicles*. And get me my rug," he added, "before I freeze to death."

Two hours later, he was sure. The books had proved it. The pack the boy had seen was either the genuine Sleeping Dog, lost for two hundred years and possibly the oldest silver pack still in existence, or a forgery perpetrated by scholars of the highest possible calibre. He examined the second hypothesis first.

Naturally, he knew every academician working in the field; a few by repute only, most of them personally. It was possible that one of them might have been tempted or suborned; anything's possible, including winged serpents and the men with no heads and eyes in their stomachs recorded in Essynias, but he wasn't inclined to believe in them. No; there were five men, apart from himself, with the necessary knowledge. Four of them would be there in an hour if he sent for them; the fifth, Carytta, must be ninety if he was a day, nearly blind last time he'd heard, living in a monastery on top of some godforsaken mountain in the Mesogaea. Further or in the alternative; why would anybody go to the trouble of tempting or suborning a first-rate scholar to make a forgery of the Sleeping Dog, and then give it to some band of wandering hedge-priests in the barren wilderness of Rhus? He'd seen enough forgeries over the years, God only knew; superb, some of them, true works of art in their own right, created by the finest craftsmen, at staggering expense. The motive was obvious.

Two or three times a year someone would come to him with the Sleeping Dog or the Broken Bow—always with a story of course, a cast-iron provenance. It had been captured by pirates or raiders from such and such an irreproachably documented previous owner, and the robbers had buried their loot and then been killed, but the great-grandson of one of the robbers had come across a map; or it was looted from such and such a temple by an ignorant soldier, and his widow had sold it to someone who had no idea what he'd bought, and then the buyer's great-grandson had overheard a chance remark; or it had passed into the collection of such and such a great family, and so-and-so, a junior footman, had pocketed it and then panicked and hidden it; they told wonderful stories when they came to see him, dressed up with real people and genuine facts, like almonds on a fruit cake, and it was always just to get money, and when you saw the silverware, if you knew what to look for, it was always so obvious—Not this time, though. In the end it came down to the feel of it, the man's eyes, the tone of his voice. The boy believed he was telling the truth; of that, Glauca was certain. Of course, that was no reason to assume that what the boy had been told was actually true. It would be an ingenious way of planting a fake provenance. Take an ordinary farm boy, stupid but a genuinely talented thief; send him to steal a map from the cartulary, on the one night when a properly learned astronomer would know that the emperor was guaranteed to be climbing the observation tower. The boy is caught; in his pocket is found a pack of craftsman's cards, cunningly wrought to snag the attention of the greatest living authority on the silver packs; the boy has been skilfully coached so as to be able to pretend quite plausibly—

Glauca shook his head. Too much. For one thing, he'd believed the boy, and he wasn't wrong about that sort of thing. For another—a leading expert on the silver packs, a top-ranking astronomer; practically the whole senior faculty of a major university would have had to be in on the scheme. And the risks; it was sheer chance that he'd thrown the other thief off the battlements, not the boy Musen; sheer chance that either of them had survived to be interrogated; sheer chance that Glauca himself had been sufficiently intrigued by the presence of a pack in a thief's pocket to take a closer look. Weigh the investment required against the remoteness of the possibility of a return, and it simply wasn't a business proposition. Besides which, anyone in the forgery business would know the histories of the previous attempts to sell to the emperor; no matter how gloriously unimpeachable the provenance might be, the pack itself would still have to pass inspection by the greatest expert in the world, the man who owned nineteen of the things—No, it simply wasn't credible. By the time you'd been to all that work and expense, you'd need to get fifty thousand just to break even. There were easier ways of making money, and without the exceptional degree of risk.

The other alternative, then: that up in the wild north, where people were so primitive they barely counted as human, a tiny college of priests or craftsmen had preserved a silver pack, intact and unknown. Well, such things happened. Take the Cossudis Bowl, for example, or the Red Victory Icons, found in a hayloft; or the Three Noble Chalices, used by an ignorant country squire to feed his dogs. Silver is a precious metal, but not so precious or rare that it'd be broken up and melted down on sight. A particularly rich or unusually discerning savage might take a fancy to a pack of silver cards, just because he liked the look of them, and decide to keep them as a treasure; or there were genuine documented cases of wandering scholars and vagrant colleges and mendicant orders of monks and friars; the craft had lodges everywhere, even among the barbarians, and it was just possible that a great scholar, say the abbot of a monastery who'd played at politics and lost, might be exiled there, or need to go where nobody would ever think to look for him—He laughed because it sounded so very like the false provenances he'd come to know so very well. But they faked them like that because *such things had happened*, really and truly, and surprisingly often over the years.

The world is full of lies, his father used to say, but sometimes, just occasionally, people tell the truth.

"Of course I don't trust him."

Pleda didn't say anything, just sat there methodically chewing. Porridge again. Pleda hated porridge.

"But I've got no choice," Glauca went on. "Yes, obviously, nine chances out of ten the boy's no good. Either he's a liar or he's been lied to. Likelihood of the Sleeping Dog still existing, and suddenly turning up after all this time in the frozen north, practically nil. It's almost certainly just another damn masquerade. But—" He shrugged. Pleda understood. "Well?" he went on. "You dead yet?"

Pleda, who'd been asked that question at least three times a day for twenty years, shook his head. "Not yet," he mumbled, with his mouth full.

"Probably all right, then."

Pleda nodded. "Unless it's aconite."

"I'd taste that, surely."

"Be too late then."

Pleda was one of those slow eaters. Some people bolt their food; there's a blur, and then there's an empty plate. Pleda ate slowly, steadily, like a cow. Not a problem most of the time, but right now Glauca was *hungry*. "I'll risk it."

"Your funeral."

The finest, most discriminating palate in the empire; there had been a grand competition, with cooks from the great noble houses preparing special dishes crammed with the rarest and most abstruse ingredients, prepared in such a way as to mask or subtly alter the flavours. Pleda had identified ninety-seven out of ninety-nine; his nearest rival had only managed seventy-six. In a somewhat grimmer trial, he'd also identified forty-two of the forty-seven known poisons, from samples served to him on the tip of a pin. The job paid exceptionally well, but Pleda maintained (and Glauca believed him) that he wasn't interested in money. So why do you do it? Glauca had asked a thousand times, and Pleda just shrugged.

"Give it here," Glauca said, and snatched the bowl from his hands. Then he hesitated. "Aconite?"

"Can take up to twenty minutes," Pleda said, through a gag of porridge. "Quite a strong taste, fairly distinctive. But you will insist on salt on your porridge, and that might just mask it. Probably not, but—" The trademark shrug.

"I like salt on my porridge."

Pleda didn't need words to express what he thought about that. Glauca put the bowl down on the table. "I'll get them to warm it up for me," he said.

"Ah." Pleda grinned at him. "Morsupeto."

"You what?"

"Morsupeto," Pleda repeated. "It's a fourth-degree distillate of your basic Archer's Root. Clever old stuff. Completely inert and harmless raw, lethal when cooked. So, you bung the stuff raw in a thick soup, say, or a stew. I taste it, nothing happens, but we wait twenty minutes anyway. Then they heat it up again, that cooks the morsupeto, it turns to poison, you eat it, two minutes later you're rolling on the floor screaming. Bloody clever."

Glauca stared at him. "Morsupeto, you say."

"That's right. Blemyan for Sudden Death."

"Never heard of it."

"Ah," Pleda said. "That's because it's new; it's not in your old books. Only been two cases so far. That we know about, I mean."

"Dear God." Glauca looked at the bowl. "I can't be doing with cold porridge," he said.

"What you want," Pleda said, "is a nice fried egg."

Translated: what *Pleda* wanted was a nice fried egg. Also, eggs are notoriously hard to poison while the shell remains unbroken—it can be done, but the shell is distinctively stained—so if the egg is prepared in your presence, while you watch the cook's every move like a hawk, you're probably all right. "A boiled egg would be all right," Glauca said, but without much hope—a certain white crystal, dissolved in the boiling water, penetrates the shell without staining and kills in thirty seconds. As anticipated, Pleda shrugged. Glauca sighed and rang the bell.

"Three fried eggs," he told the footman.

There was a little spirit stove in the corner, next to the window. Glauca hated fried eggs.

"You do it on purpose," he told Pleda, as he cringed at the feel of runny yolk on his lips. "Everything I like, there's some damned new poison. You take pleasure in torturing me."

Shrug.

"I know what it is," Glauca went on. "It's the power. You enjoy bullying your emperor."

"It's for your own good," Pleda replied placidly, and Glauca noted the absence of denial or contradiction. "Anyway," he went on, "you were saying. About this Rhus lad."

"Oh, him." Glauca had to make an effort to redirect his mind. "I don't trust him."

"So you said."

"But I believe him."

"There's a difference?"

Glauca nodded. Yes, there was a difference. Talking to Pleda often cleared his mind, though rarely because of any astounding flash of insight on Pleda's part. Amiable enough fellow, and he quite enjoyed his rudeness. There has to be someone who's allowed to be rude to you, or what would become of you? An intellectual, though, Pleda definitely wasn't. "Well," he said, "what's the worst that can happen? Fellow goes off and we never see him again. On the other hand, he might just come back with the goods."

"Which are probably fakes."

"Oh, almost certain to be. In which case, this lad Musen doesn't get any money."

"And the army gets paid, quite. And if it's not a fake? If it's real?"

Glauca closed his eyes for a moment. "Let's not tempt providence," he said.

Pleda did the shrug. "The eggs are fine," he said. "You have my word."

Glauca stared down at the plate the footman had put in front of him. He didn't feel nearly as hungry as he had a while ago. "Splendid," he said, without enthusiasm. He picked up his spoon. "Meant to ask you, by the way. That young fellow Raxivas."

"Raxival," Pleda amended.

"Yes, anyway, him. How's he coming along?"

"Very well indeed," Pleda said. He was picking his teeth with a little ivory and silver toothpick. Tooth-picking in the presence of the emperor was quite definitely treason, but Pleda had never quite grasped that. "I'd go so far as to say he's got the makings. In five or so years, if anything happens to me, you'll have nothing to worry about."

"Five or so years."

Pleda frowned. "Are you thinking of getting rid of me or something?"

"My dear fellow, no, of course not. My fault, didn't think what I was saying. No, absolutely no question of that. No, what I was wondering was, do you think he's up to covering for you? Just for a month or so. No longer than that."

"Why would anyone need to cover for me?"

Glauca turned himself round in his chair so he could look Pleda in the eye. "I want you to do something for me," he said.

"Of course." No hesitation whatsoever. "Such as what?"

Glauca took a deep breath. But it'll be fine, he told himself. After all, old Pleda's from those parts originally, he won't mind. Might actually be pleased at the chance. "I want you to keep an eye on this boy Musen," he said.

Pleda frowned. "What, you mean taste his food?"

"Not that specifically," Glauca said. "I meant, when he goes home to get the silver pack for me, go with him. Find out what's going on, that sort of thing. Because something *is* going on," Glauca continued, unable to stop his voice getting louder and higher. "Damned sight more to this than meets the eye, I'm sure of it."

"You think so."

"There has to be," Glauca said. "I mean to say, even if it's all just the usual thing, trying to cheat me out of money. That means there's a scholar out there, someone I've never heard of, who knows as much about the silver packs as I do. That's not possible."

"I see what you mean," Pleda said quietly. "Yes, that's a thought."

"You see what I'm getting at? It'd be like saying there's a top-flight university out there somewhere that nobody knows anything about. And that's mad. Makes no sense. But if there's this mysterious scholar, he must have books, rare books, special books; so there's got to be a library, and who'd have a library like that that I'm not aware of? I don't mind telling you, it's bothering me to death. Makes no sense at all. A secret university. Completely insane."

"Who has universities?" Pleda said.

"Exactly, my dear fellow, exactly. Have you any idea what the Academy costs to run? An absolute fortune, bleeds me white. Who's got that sort of money? And if you've got your own private university—well, the question arises, what else would you be likely to have? You answer me that."

Pleda was nodding slowly. He looked like a clown. "So you want me—"

"Yes," Glauca said. He made an effort, and added: "You're the only one I really trust."

Silence. Pleda was embarrassed. Well, he would be.

"Well?"

"Of course," Pleda said. "If that's what you want."

When he'd gone, Glauca unstoppered his ink bottle and started to write out warrants. *To any into whose hands this warrant might come*, and so forth. Yes, but it was true; nobody else in the world he trusted half as much. He had to. It was all in Exinas; eleven of the forty-seven poisons—if you took a tiny dose of them every day for a long time, you became immune; so that, if you then swallowed a full, lethal dose, it wouldn't hurt you at all. A food taster held the power of life and death over his master. Three times a day he had means and opportunity. After all, why had all the emperors since Azalo worn beards? Because nobody could be trusted to hold a sharp edge to the emperor's throat.

. . . afford to the said Pleda any and all goods, monies, service, assistance and facilitation whatsoever that he may require of you notwithstanding any contrary orders and provisions, express, statutory or customary . . .

His hand ached from writing—clerk's job, but he couldn't trust those damned fools to get it right; the wording had to be exact. If a thing's worth doing, do it yourself. Everyone had always agreed, even his enemies, even his father, that he had exceptionally good, clear handwriting. Should've been a clerk, they sneered, more use in the scriveners' office than on the throne. Well; they had a point.

Pleda dropped in to say goodbye. He was a sad sight. He'd wrapped himself up in coats and scarves and mittens until only his eyes and nose were visible (it was an unusually warm day, as it happened). He looked like a child's toy.

"Look after yourself," Glauca said. "I need you back here in one piece, understood?"

"Same to you," came a voice from deep inside the insulation. "I told Raxival, you take bloody good care, and don't listen to him if he says it's all right, he'll chance it. Let him know who's the boss, I told him."

Glauca laughed. "That I believe," he said. He dug in the pocket of his gown and pulled out a purse. Fifty angels. "Buy yourself a few decent meals," he said. "Keep out the cold."

Pleda took the purse, glanced at it and shoved it away in a pocket. "I don't like foreign food," he said. "Doesn't agree with me."

Eight of Swords

A nice inconspicuous four-wheeled cart, chipped paintwork, the sort of thing nobody notices; an elderly, massive black mare, just the right side of dead, and a stocky piebald gelding. "You'll be fine," the groom had assured them both. "They know what to do, even if you don't."

"You're not a horseman, then," Musen said as they rolled slowly down Foregate towards the Land Gates.

"Me? God, no." Pleda shifted uncomfortably on the driver's bench. "My dad kept horses, but I never got to drive. Fuller, he was. Him and me, we used to go round the City first thing and empty all the piss-pots. Dad drove, I did all the running around. Filthy bloody job." He looked at the boy, then added, "You don't know what I'm talking about, do you?"

"Sorry."

Pleda shrugged. "Don't suppose they have fullers where you come from. How do you bleach your fine cloth, then?"

"We don't."

Pleda nodded. "Figures," he said. "Anyway, it's a foul job, that's all you need to know about it."

"We had horses on the farm," Musen said. "I steered clear of them, as much as I could. Got kicked in the head when I was six. Been scared of them ever since."

Not true, Pleda thought. At least, not true about being

frightened of horses, he could tell by the way the horses had reacted to him, right from when they were led out of the stable. Horses know, and the black mare had recognised a horseman. Odd lie to tell, though he could think of half a dozen perfectly good reasons. "Still," he said, "beats walking. I hate walking. Tires you out and makes your feet hurt."

Foregate was busy today. Tomorrow was the first day of the Old and New Fair, and the country people had come to town. They were setting up stalls and pens for livestock—at one point the cart had to negotiate its way through a couple of hundred geese, waddling like a tired army, filling the street like floodwater. It was a long forced march from the poultry-keeping villages that straggled alongside the South road, so every single goose had been shod—wooden pattens with leather straps; Pleda remembered that job from his youth, struggles and feathers and goose shit everywhere, the smell got into your hair and stayed with you for days. The marching geese made him think of Senza's army, herded efficiently along other roads to a slightly different kind of fair. And as well as geese there were escaped rams, too fast and nimble to catch, too terrified to bribe, and the sticking-out back ends of carts, and sudden unexpected lengths of scaffolding pole, thrust out into the carriageway like pikes by men not thinking about what they were doing. Busy, stupid, thoughtless people, with work to do and a small but entrancing possibility of getting their hands on some real money, just for once; five donkeys loaded till their legs buckled with rolls of good coarse hemp matting; an old, thin man carefully arranging two dozen blue duck eggs on a mat of straw in the middle of a very big trestle table; two cheerful women tipping the last of last year's store apples out of buckets into a sawn-in-half barrel, not giving a damn if the apples got bruised; a splendidly dressed fat man and his splendidly dressed fat wife, laying out a huge stall of the shabbiest second-hand clothes Pleda had ever seen. Two men, so dark they might almost have been Imperials, dragging a long wooden crate overflowing with nails, that grey and purple colour that tells you they're fire salvage, no good, soft, bend double at the gentlest tap. A very big stall of kettles and fire pots made out of soldiers' helmets; and, a few yards further down, hundreds of faggots comprised of suspiciously straight, planed inch-and-a-half round poles, broken spear shafts, only the best five-year-seasoned cornel wood. They'll sell quick, Pleda told himself, and plenty more where they came from; someone had got hold of a good thing there, assuming the carriage costs were manageable. Boots, of course, one thing the war had done for the common man was ensure a plentiful supply of good, cheap footwear. And gilded bronze finger-rings, the sort the Southerners wore, you couldn't give those away; some optimist had set out two great big tar barrels full of them, at a stuiver each or six for a quarter, but mostly they went straight into the melt and came out as candlesticks or buttons for the military, and each ring represented a dead soldier's hand; not so good if you had a tendency to mental arithmetic. All in all, it was a good day to leave the City. The noise would be intolerable, and the smell, for a man with a delicate palate—

The boy, he noticed, was fascinated by it all; first sight of the big City doing what it does best. So many *things*, so much property—cities do things very well, never quite got the hang of people; where the boy came from, no doubt, a man could probably list all the man-made things in his village—an easily estimated quantity of ploughs, axes, spades, knives, spoons, ladles, pairs of boots, straw bonnets, work shirts and best shirts, you'd be able to compile a tolerably accurate inventory. He must think we're rich, Pleda thought; stupidly rich, with all this stuff. Then he remembered the boy was a thief, a profession which gives you a slightly different perspective on material objects, especially the readily portable kind. Actually, more like a vocation; classified along with priest, artist, philosopher, actor, it's something you do because you're made that way, and, no matter how hard you try, that's what you are, and always will be. A different way of seeing the world, he guessed. Add soldier to that list? Maybe. But thief, definitely.

A country thief, seeing his first City market. Definitely a spiritual experience. "Bit different from what you're used to," he said.

"What? Oh, God, yes. It's amazing."

Pleda tried straightening his back, stretching it a little. Didn't help. "Can't have been easy for you, back home."

"What makes you say that?"

"Stands to reason," Pleda said. "In a small place, something goes missing, people notice."

The boy didn't like that. "You learn to be careful," he said.

"Must cramp your style, though. I mean, how do you get rid of the stuff? Nobody's going to buy something off you if the moment the real owner sees it, he yells out, hey, that's mine, what're you doing with it?"

For a moment he was sure the boy was going to get angry with him. Then a sudden grin, and the boy relaxed. "Like I said," he replied, "you learn to be careful. Like, if I stole your billhook, I'd knock the handle off and whittle a new one. Or, more likely, I'd wait a couple of weeks, then give it back to you and tell you I found it in a hedge somewhere. You'd be so pleased you'd give me something, or do something for me. That's better than money, where I used to live."

Pleda nodded. "And no harm done," he said, "and everybody's happy."

"Exactly."

Not just a liar, Pleda thought, a special kind of liar—like the actors who prepare for a role by pretending to be the man they're going to portray on stage; don't think, just *be*. That's why he lies all the time, even when he doesn't need to. He likes to practise. That was why it was so hard to tell the boy's lies from the truth. They were jumbled in together, like beans and peas in a casserole, and because he lied for no reason it was almost impossible to catch him out. Someone who lies with no immediate intent to deceive, who steals not for money or gain but because he wants to, needs to; oh yes, they'd been quite right about this one. A collector's item, like the Sleeping Dog.

Even so. He waited until they'd passed through the Land Gate, and the traffic had evaporated, and they were to all intents and purposes alone on the road. Then, as casually as he could, he said, "Hold on a minute, I need to take a leak." He slid off the bench and handed the boy the reins to hold. Under cover of a roadside thorn bush, he took the pack of cards from the inside pocket sewn into his robe, palmed the three top cards, put the rest away. Then, as he scrambled back up and took back the reins, he slipped the cards into Musen's hand.

It was a moment or so before the boy realised what he'd done; he noticed something in his hand, looked down to see what it was. Pleda made a point of not looking at him. He got the horses moving. Not a word from the boy. All right, then.

"Four of Spears," he said. "Victory. Ace of Arrows."

The boy said, "What's all this about?"

"Four of Spears," Pleda repeated. "Victory. Ace of Arrows. Well?"

Just for a moment Pleda felt a little pang of apprehension. He had a padded jack under his topcoat, proof against a casual knife thrust but that was about all. The boy could quite easily have hidden a knife or a blade of some kind in the sling that supported his broken arm. Then: "Nine of Coins, the Angel, Ten of Spears."

"And?"

"What? Oh, God, sorry, Eight of Swords."

"Say again."

"Eight of Swords."

There is, of course, no suit of Swords. Not in a normal pack.

So that was all right, then. With a sigh, Pleda shifted the reins from his right hand to his left, then balled his right fist and, without looking, swung it sideways. He hit the boy on the elbow of his broken arm. As he'd expected, the boy howled with pain. Quickly, Pleda stuffed the reins under his left thigh and clamped both hands on the collar of the boy's coat, twisting it, almost but not quite tight enough to throttle him. "You bloody fool," he said.

The boy was staring at him; sheer terror, no lies there. Very hard to keep straight who you're pretending to be when you're in agony. He'll have to learn better than that, Pleda thought, but that's not my problem. He maintained the pressure while he counted to four under his breath, then slowly let go. "Idiot," he repeated. "Clown. What the hell did they send you for, anyway? You're not fit to be out without a nursemaid."

"I'm sorry," the boy said. "What did I do wrong?"

"Acting up." Pleda fought down the anger. "Bloody acting up, is what. Making up a lot of nonsense just for the hell of it, when you didn't have to. Nine times you've contradicted yourself, did you know that? Nine times. If anyone with half a brain had been listening to you, they'd have been on to you like a weasel. Bloody acting up. And don't say you can't help it, of course you can. You just need to bloody well think what you're doing."

He'd got through to him all right; scared, guilty, resentful. "I'm sorry," Musen said, "I didn't realise I was doing it. It's more a sort of a habit, really."

"That's no excuse. That just makes it worse. First rule is, concentrate. Think about what you're doing. It's not just your neck now, it's mine. You want to remember that."

He'd done enough. Any more and the boy would turn against him; padded jack or no padded jack, he'd rather that didn't happen. "Anyway," he said. "Allow me to introduce myself. I'm Pleda."

Pause. "Are you—?"

Pleda took back the reins. "You know better than that. There you go again, overdoing it. I'm the Eight of Swords, that's all." He settled himself firmly against the bench; it was digging into the small of his back. Six hundred miles, he thought to himself. What I do for philosophy. "So," he said, in a very slightly more conciliatory voice, "what exactly happened on the tower?"

"I don't really know," Musen admitted. "We heard footsteps. We froze. The old man came up. I'll swear we didn't move or make a sound, really. I couldn't see a thing, it was so dark. Then I guess the old man moved. I heard this horrible yell. I guessed Par—"

"No names."

"I guessed Six of Arrows had gone over the side, so I ran for it. Tripped over something, and then it felt like I was being trampled by horses or something, and then I was in a prison cell. That's it."

Pleda nodded slowly. "What was supposed to happen?"

"The old man was meant to come up on to the tower. Soon as we could, we'd slip past him and go back down the stairs and get caught by the guards. Or the guards would've come up first and caught us. But they told me that wasn't so likely, because the old man likes to be on his own up the tower. Can't concentrate on his star-gazing if there's people with him."

Pleda frowned. "That's a bloody stupid plan."

Musen grinned. "That's what we thought. We said so, and they told us, yes, it is, so why don't you think of a better one? So, we did as we were told." He hesitated. "Nobody was meant to get killed."

Quite. If they'd asked me first—But they couldn't, of course, could they? "Things like that happen," he said. "Play with knives, get cut. I don't know. Whoever picked you for this job's got a lot to answer for."

"I don't see what else I could've done," Musen said. "And it worked, didn't it?"

"More by luck than judgement."

The boy could have argued the toss, but he didn't. Time for a unilateral declaration of victory, Pleda decided, and then let's move on. "When we get there," he said. "It's all laid on at that end, is it?"

"So they told me."

God help us, Pleda thought. You go through life thinking the Wild Cards know it all; they're wise and cunning, and their carefully distilled plans run the world. Then you actually get involved in one, and you find out the bastards are basically just making it up as they go along. His fault, he supposed; he'd let things get too lax in his own parish, too busy nursemaiding the old man—but if anything happened to him, God only knew what'd happen, so they couldn't blame him for that. Trying to run half the world from a cubbyhole in the East Wing, no staff, no support, if he needed to write a letter it was a day's work, and then all the misery of finding someone to carry it. It's an honour, they'd told him; you must be very proud. Bastards.

"We'd better get one thing straight," Pleda said. "We're going to be months on this job, and it's a lot of travelling and I hate travelling, and there's so many things that could go wrong before we even get there, it makes me want to scream just thinking about it. If you make any difficulties, even one tiny step out of line, then so help me I'll make you wish you'd got gangrene out on the moors and died. Is that clear?"

The boy gave him a wounded look. I didn't ask to get caught up in this, it said; it's not my fault, don't blame me. Quite, he thought. It was time to crack a big, friendly grin. "We'll be all right," he said in his special everyone's-favourite-uncle voice that always worked so well with young idiots. "You do as I tell you and we'll be just fine."

A long, long ride to the coast, where they sold the cart to pay for passage on a ship to Beloisa—they'd started making the run again, though there was nothing there but rain-soaked ash and a few blocks of black stone. "Don't know why we bother," the captain told them, "force of habit, mainly. We go out empty and bring back maybe five dozen bales of wool and a bit of firewood.

The passenger business has gone right down the drain, not that that's any surprise. What do you boys want to go there for, anyhow?"

Pleda told him they were going home, to visit family and friends. That seemed to be an acceptable answer, though Pleda was quite sure the captain didn't believe it. Of course, as Pleda knew perfectly well, the government was subsiding the shipowners to keep the north–south crossings going, so the captain wasn't quite as hard done by as he was pleased to suggest.

"Ten years since I was last in Beloisa," Pleda observed as the ship dawdled through choppy water on the second day.

Musen didn't feel much like chatting. He appeared to be working on the assumption (unfounded, as Pleda knew only too well) that if you keep perfectly still, eventually it gets better. "It's all changed now, I expect."

"Bound to be, since some bastard burned it to the ground. It wasn't a bad old place when I knew it. A bit something-and-nothing, but I've seen worse." He turned his back on the sea and rested his elbows on the rail. He'd forgotten, but actually he quite liked sailing. "I'm from Arad Sefny originally. Know it?"

Musen shook his head. A mistake. He closed his eyes and swallowed a couple of times.

"About a day and a half's walk up from Burnt Chapel. Between Bray Downs and the Greenwater valley."

"Sorry," Musen said. "No idea where that is."

Pleda shrugged. "We had a nice little farm, forty acres on the flat, grazed three dozen sheep on the downs. My mother bred geese, we used to drive them down into Burnt Chapel for the autumn fair. Three brothers, I was the youngest, and a sister; she married a man from Corroway. I used to go over there sometimes to help him with the peat-digging."

Musen turned his head. "You said your father was a fuller."

Pleda nodded. "Happy days," he said. "Haven't been home for, what, thirty years. Don't suppose they'd recognise me if I walked through the door."

"In a town."

"Burnt Chapel. Smallish place. Used to be a chapel there, but it burned down."

Musen was grinning. "One contradiction."

"Good boy. I made it easy for you, mind."

Musen turned back so that his mouth was directly above the sea. "Where are you really from?" he asked.

"Here and there. The lodge has always been my home. You go where you're told. I like that."

The boy thought for a while before he spoke again. "I can see where it saves you a lot of fretting," he said. "Lots of choices you don't have to make."

Pleda frowned. "Oh, there's choices," he said. "All the bloody time, and the higher up you get, the more of them you've got to make. Don't get any easier, either, and nobody thanks you for anything, nobody ever says well done, bloody good job." He spread his elbows wider along the rail; it helped his back, a little. "I think that's probably why the lodge works so well," he said. "It's not like anything else I know; not like governments or armies or Temple or any of that lot. Everywhere else, you always get people who want to get on, people with ambition. When the choices come along, they choose because they want to get to the top, because of the money and the power and all that rubbish. In the lodge, now, the higher up you get, the worse it is. No, don't pull faces at me; it's true. You don't get paid, you live where you're put, and if they send you to a tannery or a slaughterhouse, cleaning out the stalls, that's where you go and that's where you damn well stay. You don't get fame and glory because there's only a handful of people know who you are, and they're lodge, not easily impressed. Just when you've got yourself settled in somewhere and your life feels like it's starting to make sense, the bastards *promote* you, and it's off somewhere else and start all over again, whether you like it or not. You can be Grand Vizier to the Sultan of Dog's Armpit, and if you get promoted and the job means digging ore fifteen hours a day down an iron mine, that's that, off you go, you don't argue. Take me, for instance. Before I was put on this food-tasting thing, I was a chief clerk in a treasury office in the home provinces. Big house, nice bit of garden, servants, a bunch of little clerks to do all my work for me. And before that I was an assistant harbour master, and you can take it from me, there's no better dodge going if you want to make a bit on the side. I could've raked it in, if I'd been that way inclined. Now I'm here doing this, glorified footman, with a good chance of getting myself killed any day of the week. That's promotion in the lodge, my boy, and don't you forget it. Nothing but trouble and sorrow. Like I said, I guess that's why it works so well."

Musen was looking at him with a mildly startled expression. "I don't want to be anything special," he said. "I just want to serve the lodge, that's all. It's the only thing I ever wanted."

"Sure. That, and a load of stuff that doesn't belong to you. Just as well the lodge can use you, then, isn't it? Mind, that's the other reason the lodge is so successful. We can use *everybody*." And then the grin. "Even you."

Maybe the grin wasn't working today. He could tell Musen didn't like what he'd said—not the stuff about promotion and all, the other thing. "Fact is," he said, "we're all the same. We wouldn't do it otherwise. We serve the lodge because we believe in it. And if you're a believer—well, the rest all sort of goes without saying. I don't think it's something you choose. It's inside you, right from the start." Like stealing, he didn't say. "Some people are like that, they were born to be just the one thing. That's us. That's why we don't need money and flash clothes and big houses." He paused for a moment, then added: "You're one of us, sunshine, I can tell. Don't expect praise. After all, it's none of your doing."

He'd said the right thing, at last. "That's it," Musen said.

"That's exactly how I've always thought about it. It's why—well, when I was growing up, in Merebarton. That's my village. I was the only craftsman there."

Pleda frowned. "Now that's hard," he said. "When you're the only one. Different for me; there were always at least half a dozen of us, we always had someone to talk to. We felt special, you know, strong. Just you on your own, that must've been tough."

Musen's eyes were wide and bright. "It was," he said eagerly. "You know, I think that's why I started taking things. I always felt, you know, different, shut out. Actually, it was more than that. I felt like they were all blind and I was the only one that could see. But somehow that wasn't an advantage, if you get what I mean."

Sooner or later, Pleda thought, sooner or later. There's always a certain combination of words that gets through, and then you've got them; like those amazing locks they have in Sond Amorcy, the ones with no keys, and you turn three little dials to line up the tumblers. Work people a click at a time, you'll get there eventually. He let the boy talk. There was a whole lifetime waiting to come out, like a blocked drain.

Beloisa was just depressing. There was a structure calling itself an inn, on the quay, where the customs house used to be. It was mostly made of doors, charred on the outside, but military-spec crossply is too dense to burn right through; someone had been all round the site and gathered up about a hundred charred and scorched doors, nailed them to scaffold poles and lengths of rafter; oiled sailcloth for a roof, which sagged where rainwater had pooled—any day now, the cloth would give way and some poor devil would wake up drenched. Meanwhile, the weight of the rainwater had bowed the walls inwards. They'd tried to draw them straight again with guy ropes, but the pegs had already started to pull out. Sorry, the innkeeper said, we're full up; try again next week, or the week after that.

The plan had been to buy a cart. No problem there; country people desperate to get across the sea had plenty of carts for sale, but horses to pull them were a different matter. The military paid cash—about three stuivers in the mark, but cash—for anything with four legs and a faint spark of life. So the country people had mostly turned their carts on their sides and added a lean-to of sooty planks, and there they sat, nothing to do but wait, observing the new arrivals off the boats, like sheep at market watching the butchers.

"Looks like we're going to have to walk," Pleda said. "I hate bloody walking."

But Musen had other ideas. "I've got a letter," he said.

"What sort of a letter?"

Musen reached inside his shirt and produced a thin tube. It looked like brass, but there are other yellow metals. "Put it away, for God's sake," Pleda hissed. "You want to get our throats cut?"

Musen hadn't thought of that. "It's signed by the emperor," he said, pulling his shirt down so the tube wouldn't show. "It says we can have anything we want. I don't know if that actually means anything."

Dear God, a plenipotentiary warrant. A real one, not a fake. "It means something," Pleda muttered. "Means we don't have to walk, for one thing. Right, we need the prefect's office."

The Beloisa prefecture was a genuine stone, brick and tile building, one of the five still standing. The prefect, a pale, thin man Pleda had never heard of, took the tube as though he'd just been handed a sleeping cobra. "What's this?" he said.

"You might like to read it," Pleda suggested.

The prefect had difficulty getting the parchment out of the tube. First he tried to pinch hold of the end with his fingernails, but they were too short. Then he tried prodding with his forefinger, but somehow he managed to get the base of the parchment crumpled so that it jammed. Then he got up, crossed the room to a big rosewood chest on a stand, opened the chest, rummaged around for a while until he found a foot-long piece of ebony dowel, the sort of thing people who need to draw lines on maps use as a ruler. He tried that, but it was too wide to fit in the tube.

"Let me," Pleda said. He poked the uncrumpled end of the tube with his little finger, and the roll of parchment slid out on to the prefect's desk. The prefect gave him a baffled look, unrolled the parchment and started to read. Then he lifted his head and stared. "Sorry," he said. "What can I do for you gentlemen?"

Not nearly as much, it turned out, as they'd hoped. Horses, yes, not a problem. They could go to the stables and help themselves from a wide selection of military-spec thoroughbreds. Only trouble was, they were cavalry horses—first class for charging the enemy, no good at all for pulling carts. All the draught horses in the place had been requisitioned, day before yesterday, and loaded on transports and whisked away over the sea. Not best pleased, as you gentlemen can imagine, since there was now no way of moving supply carts, hauling firewood or emptying the latrines. Sorry about that.

Pleda replied that that wasn't good enough. He had a warrant in the emperor's own handwriting promising him whatever he needed. It would not go well with the prefect, he suggested, if he was responsible for making the emperor break his promise. The prefect gave him a smile of pure hate and fear and said he'd see what he could do.

An hour later, by some miracle, two carthorses were suddenly available. Sheer coincidence, the prefect told them, some farmer just wandered in off the moor and offered to sell them. They weren't bad animals, as it happened: shaggy, short-legged, nearly as broad as they were tall. Pleda gave the prefect a list of the emperor's other promises, and the prefect assured him everything would be loaded on the cart in an hour. Until then, perhaps they would care for a bite to eat in the officers' mess.

"Why the hell didn't you tell me you'd got a warrant?" Pleda said, with his mouth full. Roast pork with chestnut stuffing.

"We didn't need anything."

Farm boy, he thought. No matter. "Well, it's nice to know it's there if we need it. Don't suppose it'll be much help once we're out of here, not unless we run into soldiers. Still, you'd better let me keep it."

Musen looked at him, then nodded. Pleda mopped up gravy with his bread. It would be interesting to find out, he told himself, just how good a thief the boy was. The first thing, of course, would be to remove the warrant from the tube; a fair bet that it was the tube he'd be after, since it was shiny and pretty. "You know the way, I take it."

"Me? God, no."

Oh joy, Pleda thought. "Fine," he said. "They're bound to have a map."

"Their maps are all wrong."

Naturally. "Well, in that case, what do you suggest?"

Musen thought about it for a while. "I may be able to remember enough," he said. "But we didn't come straight here, last time. We got lost and wandered about a lot."

"We?"

"Me and someone else from my village. Don't know what happened to him."

Pleda sighed. "Not to worry," he said. "I'll ask the prefect nicely for the good map. There's always one."

No, there wasn't. Instead, there was the military survey, seventeenth edition, which still showed Norsuby as the regional capital, or the prefect's own heavily revised and annotated version, copied for them in rather too much of a rush by a sullen clerk with questionable eyesight and poor handwriting. They chose the survey. After all, Pleda said, where they were going there weren't any villages or other man-made features, not any more, and the hills and rivers were probably in the same place as they were a hundred years ago; and, anyway, who needs a map when you've got the stars to guide you?

"We just keep going north till we can see the Greenstock mountains, then we turn left along the Blackwater till we reach the Powder Hill pass, then due south and we're there. Adds a couple of days to the journey, but we simply can't go wrong."

Musen looked at him. "If you say so."

"Trust me," Pleda said. "Geography's a bit of a hobby of mine. Soon as I get my bearings, I won't need any stupid maps."

The main thing was, they still had plenty of food and water; not to mention beer, cider and tea, which Pleda took great pleasure in brewing up on the tiny portable charcoal stove the prefect had given them. "Charcoal," he explained, as he fried pancakes in a dear little tinned-copper pan, "because there's no smoke. No smoke, people can't see you."

"We're lost, aren't we?"

"I don't know how you can say that," Pleda replied, wounded. "We're going north, like I said we should. Any day now we'll see the Greenstocks." He paused to flip the pancake. It landed with a delicate *plop*. "True, I can't actually point to a place on a map and say, this is where we are. But *lost*—"

"Well," Musen said, sitting down on the rock beside him. "I don't know about you, but I'm lost. I have no idea where we are."

"You can't be lost," Pleda said. "You're with me."

The important thing to bear in mind was, they still had plenty of water. The flour would last another two days, three if they were careful. By then, they were sure to reach the Greenstocks, at which point they would have the river dead ahead of them, and Pleda was an expert angler. "Used to spend hours on the riverbank when I was a boy," he said, wiping grit out of his eyes. "Give me a bit of string and a bent pin, I can feed us indefinitely."

"Have we got a bit of string and a bent pin?"

Secretly, however, Pleda was somewhat concerned. There should have been a road. He remembered it clearly from the last time he was here—a long time ago, admittedly, but roads don't just vanish. Instead, they were creaking slowly over heather, stopping occasionally to lever, drag, lift, worry and prise the cart out of the boggy patches that you simply didn't see till you were in them. They'd brought two changes of clothes each, but every garment they had was now caked with black, stinking bog mud, which never seemed to dry out and wouldn't brush or wash off. It was ingrained so deep into their hands that they might as well be Imperials. Even the rain didn't wash it off, even though it soaked right through to the skin and trickled down their bodies and legs, when the wind was behind it. Water, though; not a problem. Wring out a shirt, you had enough for a week.

"This moor's so flat," Musen was saying, "you must be able to see for, what, thirty miles?"

And the horizon was still flat. Quite. Pleda had been wondering about that. Was it possible that the mountains simply weren't there any more—commandeered for the war effort, stolen by profiteers to make ballast for the fleet, demolished by the Belot brothers in a supreme moment of collateral damage? He doubted it. Even the war couldn't level mountain ranges, or so he'd always been led to believe.

"It can't be thirty miles," he said firmly. "Here." He reached down inside his shirt and pulled out the map. There wasn't much left of it. Rain had washed off all the coloured ink, and a lot of the black had rubbed off against his chest; the parchment was soft and squishy, and smelt like newly boiled rawhide. "Look for yourself. There's no open space three hundred and sixty square miles big. Too many hills and mountains. It must just be a trick of the contours."

That was his latest phrase. He'd come to believe in it, the way a dying man believes in the gods. He wasn't entirely sure it meant anything. Musen handed the map back without looking at it. "If you say so," he said.

"Sod this," Pleda said. "We might as well stop for the night, get under cover before that lot over there sets in."

Musen glanced at the skyful of thick, black low cloud dead ahead of them. "It's an hour away," he said. "And there isn't any cover."

"Shut your face."

They slept under the cart, their backs in pooled bog water. When he woke up, Pleda could see a brilliant blue sky, and three pairs of boots.

Oh, he thought.

One thing they hadn't brought was weapons. Asking for trouble, he'd told the prefect. Anybody catches us with weapons in the middle of a war zone, they'll think we're spies or saboteurs. Ah well.

He nudged Musen in the ribs. The boy groaned. Not a morning person. "Wake up," he said quietly. "We're in trouble."

Musen lifted his head, opened his eyes and saw the boots. To his credit—Pleda was genuinely impressed—he didn't panic or anything like that. He rolled over on to his face and crawled out from under the cart. Pleda did the same.

Five men. Three of them were sitting on chairs, the other two standing behind them like footmen in a great house; they might have been sitting for a portrait. Certainly they were dressed for it. The left- and right-hand chairs were regulation military folding, but the middle one was a deluxe model, gilded, delicately curved and tapered legs, arm rests carved into lions' heads. On it sat the most handsome man Pleda had ever seen in his life. Not particularly tall (it's so hard to tell when someone's sitting down); strongly built but perfectly proportioned; beautiful hands with long fingers;

dark hair just shy of shoulder length; high cheek bones, quite a long face ending in a square chin, straight nose, clean-shaven, clear grey eyes, a strong mouth, a smile of mild amusement. He was wearing an ornate, heavily embroidered robe with a fur collar, the sort affected by merchants with three times as much money as taste, but on him it wasn't the least bit flashy or vulgar; he had dark green boots, and a broad-brimmed leather travelling hat rested on his right knee. The men on either side and behind him wore armour, regulation, an eclectic and informed blend of the best of East and West. They sat and watched like the audience in a theatre, waiting for the actors to come on stage.

Pleda scrambled to his feet; Musen stayed kneeling, in the wet. Pleda felt sure he had a reason, though he couldn't see what it might be. The handsome man smiled. "Good morning," he said. His voice was soft, deep and accentless.

Five men, three chairs, no horses. "Hello," Pleda said. "What can I do for you gentlemen?"

He'd said something amusing. "You know, I can't think of anything," the handsome man said. "The cart's loaded, and you'll see we've already tacked up the horses. No, I don't think we need you for anything at all."

Well, hardly a surprise. "Are you going to kill us?"

The handsome man shrugged. "I haven't decided," he said. "What do you think?"

"I wouldn't bother," Pleda said.

The handsome man rested his chin on his beautiful right hand. "That's what I thought," he said. "My colleagues here reckon it'd be tidier to get rid of you. I took the view that with no food and no transport, it's a moot point anyway." He inclined his head just a little toward the cart. "Is that really all you've got in the way of supplies?"

"We're lost," Musen said. "We've been wandering about for days."

"That'd explain it," the handsome man said. "Well? Haven't you got anything to say for yourselves?"

Pleda looked at him, and then at the four men in armour. The handsome man was clean, well-groomed, his gown untorn, his boots unscuffed; the other four looked like soldiers on active service with a good outfit, kit clearly well used but properly looked after. The standing man on the left held a strung longbow, though there was no arrow on the string. "Where's your horses, then?"

"No horses," the handsome man said, "we walked. We owe you our lives. I'm sorry we can't be properly grateful."

"You're lost," Pleda said.

The handsome man considered him for a moment, as if translating him from some abstruse dead language. "True," he said. "So are you."

"You don't want to listen to the boy," Pleda said. "We're not lost. We've got a map."

"Is that right?" The soldier on the left leaned across and muttered something in the handsome man's ear. "I'd like to see it please."

"I bet."

"I can take it from your dead body if you'd rather."

"Fine." Pleda reached slowly inside his shirt and took out the map. He lifted it so it could be plainly seen, then threw it on the ground. Nicely pitched; about halfway between him and the men. The soldier on the right sighed, got up, retrieved it and gave it to the handsome man.

"This is no good," he said. "It's ruined; I can't read it."

Pleda smiled. "No, you can't," he said. "But I can remember what was on it."

The handsome man nodded slowly, as if in approval. "Of course you can," he said. "And there's only enough flour in your jar to last us a day or two, so if we kill you we're killing ourselves. But you know where the nearest village is. You're not the least bit lost, and your friend there's talking nonsense. Well?"

Pleda was still smiling. "If you're lost in the wilderness," he said, "why bother lugging those chairs around with you? Why not dump them?"

"I like to sit down in a civilised manner. They carry them because I tell them to. Well?"

"I know where the nearest village is," Pleda said. "He only said we're lost because it's his village. He doesn't want to lead the likes of you there. He'd rather die than betray his family and friends. Me—" Pleda shrugged. "Screw them."

The handsome man looked at Musen, who was still kneeling; he's got a knife or something, Pleda realised, something he can throw; he's doing mental geometry. The man on the handsome man's left said, "We don't need both of them, do we?"

"Yes," Pleda said, "you do."

"I don't think so," the handsome man said. "Gatho, shoot the boy."

The archer took an arrow from the quiver at his waist. Musen stood up and threw. It was a knife—he'd had it hidden in the bandages of his sling, though Pleda had looked for it when the boy was asleep and hadn't found it—and it didn't fly true. Rather a lot to ask at that range. Instead, it hit the archer's cheek side on, cutting him deeply and making him drop his bow. Oh for God's sake, Pleda thought. Here we go.

As he bounded forward, Pleda cast his mind back to the course he'd been on, five years ago, at the Institute. The secret of the Belot brothers' success, they'd told him, was their ability to see the battlefield as a schematic, a diagram. Senza Belot had once described it as superimposing an imaginary grid on to the battlefield, turning real life into a chess game. Now you try it, the instructor had said. And Pleda had tried, ever so hard, but he simply couldn't do it. Wrong sort of mind, they'd told him. Not everyone can do it. Not to worry.

Maybe, back at the Institute, all he'd lacked was motivation. The lines of the grid formed instantly, each square representing a quantity of both space and time. Another thing they'd told him was that a fight is a fluid, rather than a collection of colliding solids; a fight *flows*, it has tides and currents, and it's vital not to let yourself get swept away. That probably meant something too, but he still didn't get it.

The handsome man was standing up; the soldier on his right hadn't quite realised what was happening. The other standing man was out of it for now, and so was the archer. Pleda made for the soldier on the left, who was standing up and drawing his sword at the same time. He got to him just as the tip of the sword cleared the scabbard; he grabbed his wrist and continued the draw for him, sliding the cutting edge under the point of his chin. The soldier stumbled backward, tripped on his chair and went sprawling, leaving the sword in Pleda's hand. The archer was so close he could have cut him straight away, but he wasn't an immediate threat; Pleda swung round, but the handsome man wasn't there. Instead, the right-hand soldier was on his feet, backing up to give himself a bit of room. He was dangerous. Pleda jabbed at his face, just enough to keep him at a distance, then pivoted on his back foot to bring himself face to face with the standing soldier on the right. He'd just drawn; his sword hand was raised at shoulder height, and he was wide open. All that bloody armour; Pleda tried a fast, light jab at his head and hit him in the mouth; the sword point jarred on his teeth, drifted up and sliced into his top lip.

That'll do, Pleda decided; he had his back to the boy and couldn't see what was happening to him, but the absence of the handsome man spoke for itself. He took three long steps back and made a half-turn. Sure enough, the handsome man was standing behind Musen, one arm round the boy's throat, the other pressing a short knife to his neck.

"I think we've got off on the wrong foot," the handsome man

said, catching his breath. "Let's start again. Allow me to introduce myself. My name's Axio. Who are you?"

Well, now. "Axio," Pleda said. "You're—"

"Yes," the handsome man snapped. "That's me. And, no, I don't look much like him. He takes after his father, and I'm the spit and image of our mother, or so people tell me. All right?"

Pleda grinned. "Actually, there is a resemblance, now I think of it. Same neck and shoulders. Of course, he's that much taller."

"Absolutely." Axio didn't seem to like talking about it. "Now you know my name, let's have yours."

"I didn't know you'd turned to crime."

"It's not something he wants people to know, oddly enough. But, yes, in the proclamations you see nailed up on doors I'm described as a robber and a thief. Not through choice. Personally, I prefer to think of myself as the last line of defence."

Pleda wasn't sure he understood that, but never mind. "I'm Pleda. He's Musen."

Axio frowned. "Hang on, I know that name. Pleda Lanxifor. You're the food-taster. Good Lord. Suddenly, everybody's famous."

"It's a small world," Pleda agreed. "Would you mind letting my friend go now, please?"

Axio glanced at his companions, who were still preoccupied with trying to stop the bleeding. "Put that sword down."

"No chance."

"Fine." Axio relaxed his grip and drew his hand away from Musen's throat. Then he stopped. "Hello, what's this?" he said, and pulled the gold tube out of Musen's shirt. Musen took his chance and scrambled away. Axio was entirely preoccupied with the tube.

"Let me get this straight," he said, turning the tube round with the tips of his fingers. "The emperor's food-taster, in a farm cart, with a load of government-issue camping gear and a gold despatch tube. Empty," he added. Then he looked at Pleda. "A food-taster, but no food," he said. "And a message tube with no message."

Pleda sighed. "The boy steals things," he said. "He can't help it."

"That makes two of us," Axio said, tucking the tube in the pocket of his robe. "Would you mind telling me what you two are doing out here in the middle of nowhere?"

"Visiting family," Pleda said. "His family, in the village."

"Of course. You?"

"I'm going to marry his sister."

Axio raised an eyebrow. "Is that right?"

"I bloody well hope so. I paid twenty angels."

Axio nodded slowly. "I get you. Sight unseen?"

"Looks aren't everything."

Carefully, Axio put the knife away in a fold of his robe. "In that case, let me be the first to congratulate you. I love weddings. Particularly," he added, "weddings with lots and lots of food."

Pleda glanced quickly at the soldiers. They were watching him, and he read them easily—we can take him, but we'll get cut up some more, and one of us might not make it; do we really have to? The decision clearly rested with Axio, which made Pleda think over what he knew about bandits and their tendency towards democracy. *The last line of defence*; curious way for a professional criminal to describe himself. "I don't suppose you've got any food," he said.

Axio smiled. "Not enough to share."

"Not if you're walking," Pleda said. "But if you were lucky enough to get a ride in a nice cart—"

All sorts of issues there, needless to say. From Pleda's perspective, the essential question was, could Musen drive a team of horses? Inevitably, Axio would be addressing the matter from a different angle. Not impossible, even so, that both parties could arrive at the same conclusion.

"Indeed," Axio said abruptly. "The hell with all this fighting, anyway. If I'd wanted to fight, I'd have stayed in the army. Isn't that right, boys?"

They might be fiercely and unthinkingly loyal to Axio; that didn't mean they liked him. The looks on their faces suggested that, at that moment, they didn't like him at all. That couldn't have been lost on him, but he didn't seem worried by it. Curious people, Pleda thought, can't wait to be rid of them. But that wasn't going to happen any time soon.

The arrangements were fairly straightforward. The four soldiers, Axio and Pleda rode in the back of the cart—they had to dump some of the gear, but no great loss; the soldiers and Axio at the far end, Pleda with his back to the driver's bench and the sword across his knees. Musen and the soldiers' weapons sat on the driver's bench. Axio cheerfully handed over his knife, which Pleda took as definitive proof that he had another one. Still, wedged in between two of his friends in a cart that jolted horribly all the time, his capacity for sudden movement was somewhat diminished. Musen proved to be a competent driver, which was just as well.

"You're sure you know the way," Axio asked, as they set off.

"Oh yes," Pleda replied cheerfully. "I know this country like the back of my hand."

Not long after midday, they saw the Greenstocks.

They'd been going steadily uphill for a long time; the gradient was so gentle they'd hardly noticed it until, quite suddenly, the ground seemed to fall away at their feet, and they were looking down a steep slope, on the other side of which was a river and, beyond that, mountains.

"We can't get the cart down that," said the archer.

"Don't have to," Pleda replied. "We follow the top of this ridge for a bit, parallel with the river until we see a gap in the hills on our right. Then we turn left. There's a road," Pleda added hopefully. "Takes us straight there."

As a boy, Pleda had always loved the story about the boy who rescued an old woman from a lion, and the old woman turned out to be a witch, who gave him a magic something-or-other, whose special power was that everything he said thereafter turned out to be true. It was a ring, or a five-sided coin, or a walrus-ivory comb, or a pebble with a hole in it; something ordinary, anyway, something you might well pick up and forget about, and never realise you had. An hour before sunset, Pleda surreptitiously searched his pockets. He narrowed it down to the bit of old rag and the horn-handled penknife; could be either of those, or maybe, just possibly, it was luck or coincidence and not magic at all.

"There's the road, look," he said, pointing. "Bang opposite the Powder Hill pass, just like I said it would be."

Axio tried to stand up to get a better view, but a jolt sat him down again; he landed hard on the knee of the man next to him, who winced. "That's all right, then," he said. "Tell you what. Let's stop here for the night and then carry on in the morning. Don't know about you, but I'm starving."

They sat warily round a fire—Pleda wasn't keen, because of the smoke, but Axio insisted; they smashed up the cart's tool box for firewood—and ate the last of the biscuits and some rock-hard dried sausage from the archer's pack. Nobody seemed to be in any hurry to go to sleep. It was going to be a long night.

"Anybody fancy a game of cards?" Pleda said.

He'd got their attention. "Why not?" Axio said, and reached in his pocket, from which he produced a beautiful ivory box with gilded hinges. "Should be enough light to see by for a little while."

Pleda hadn't expected that. Still, it wasn't unreasonable for a thief to have a luxury item like a pack of cards, especially if it came in a valuable box. "Let's play Bust," he said. "Eastern rules?"

"Of course." Axio smiled. "We're all patriots here, aren't we?"

He opened the box and took out the pack. "Here we go," he said. "Three cards, face upwards."

He dealt a card and suddenly Pleda couldn't breathe. He clenched his hands very tight and concentrated all his efforts on keeping his face straight and not staring. Axio dealt quickly and with the easy fluency of long practice. Even in broad daylight, it would've been next to impossible, for anybody else, to see how he cheated.

"And three covered," Axio went on, dealing the face-down cards. "All right, here we go. Stuiver in and a penny raise."

"Oh," Musen said. "Are we playing for money?"

"Bless the child," Axio said.

"I don't have any."

Pleda dug in his pocket, found his purse, picked at the tie, pinched out the knot, emptied the purse on the ground, picked out a dozen quarters and flung them at him. Then, trying really hard not to let his hand shake, he took up his cards.

Seven of Arrows. Two of Spears. Poverty. His mouth was dry as a bone. "I'm in," muttered the soldier to his left, and Pleda heard a coin chink. His turn. "Just a second," he said. Two crows in the tree, and a jug, broken in three pieces.

"Come on," Axio said. "Before it gets too dark to see."

"I'm thinking," Pleda snapped. He forced himself to consider the cards tactically. With the open three, he had a pride in Arrows, Poverty and the Angel. "In and up twopence," he said.

"Your turn." Axio was talking to Musen.

"I'm in." The boy was frowning. "And raise a penny."

The Angel's crown had four fleurets. No question about it. The archer shook his head and folded. "In and up a penny," Axio said. "Right, I dealt, so you start."

The soldier to Pleda's left bought a card, threw away the Five of Arrows. Pleda snapped it up, dumped his two and raised two-pence. Musen passed. Axio bought two and threw them away again. The soldier passed. "Buy one," Pleda said. Axio handed him the Star-Crossed Lovers, which he dumped. Musen passed. "Right," Axio said. "Here's a quarter says it's my lucky day. Let's meld."

Pleda scrabbled on the ground, located a quarter by feel and flipped it into the middle. They all laid out. Axio won; a run in Spears and the Ship. He was grinning. "Go again?"

Two of the soldiers were scowling at him. "Yes, why not?" Pleda said. Musen nodded. The archer shrugged and said, "Go on, then." Axio gathered the cards. "I won, so I deal," he said. "Let's make it interesting. Stuiver in and raises are a quarter."

Pleda didn't watch him shuffle. For his open cards, he got the Three, Four and Five of Shields, an open run. Covered, Seven of Shields, Hope and the Ten of Swords.

There is no suit of Swords. Not in a normal pack.

"Tens are wild," Axio said. "Right, who's in?"

The soldiers and Musen looked at Pleda's open cards and decided not to bother. Axio threw a stuiver into the middle, then another one. His open cards were rubbish. "Well?"

"Tens are wild, did you say?" Musen picked up three stuivers from the pile in the grass beside him. A week's money where he came from. "I'm in."

Axio beamed at him. "Right," he said. "Since it's just you and me, your two stuivers and double it."

Another week's pay. "Meld," he said. He turned over his cards. "Three to Seven of Shields, plus the trump."

Axio picked one card out of his hand and turned it face outwards. It was the Ace of Swords. "Sorry," he said, and scooped up the money.

Musen frowned. "Just a second, that's not—"

"Eastern rules," Pleda said quickly. Musen stared at him, then shrugged.

"Aces high in the East, remember?" Axio said. "You know

what, I'm enjoying this. How about another? Or we could play Cats and Buckets."

Pleda stayed awake all night—he couldn't have slept if he'd wanted to—but Axio made no attempt to talk to him privately; he rolled himself up in a thick blue blanket, with the archer's pack for a pillow, and went straight to sleep. Pleda toyed with the idea of sending Musen to steal the ivory box from his pocket, but decided against it. He'd seen enough, anyway.

Ace of Swords. The Ace, for crying out loud.

Just before first light, he hauled himself up and shuffled a few yards the other side of the cart for a pee. When he got back, under his blanket, he found the ivory box. He covered it up and looked at Musen, who appeared to be fast asleep. He crawled under the blanket and opened the box by feel. It was empty.

If Axio missed his treasure the next morning, he gave no sign of it. They resumed their places in the cart and set off down the miraculous road. Thirty miles, maybe less, to Merebarton.

"Another good game," Axio was saying, "is Blind Chopper. Do you know that one? We used to play it a lot in the army. It goes like this. Dealer deals five cards face down, you're not allowed to look at them—"

Pleda was having second thoughts about Axio's men. At first he'd assumed they were deserters, with Axio as their officer; it was common enough, a platoon or half-platoon deciding it had had enough of the war, or finding itself in trouble on account of some breach of military law, or simply unable to resist the commercial opportunities of the total breakdown of civilisation. That might in some part explain the unswerving obedience, and the way Axio took them so completely for granted. Pleda was still fairly sure that the four silent men were soldiers—the way they walked, talked and moved, they couldn't be anything else—but unless there were provinces of the Eastern empire he knew nothing about, which was rather unlikely, they most definitely weren't Easterners. Possibly they were the other lot, which would make sense of Axio's remark about all being patriots, and there was a degree of logic in a group of Western deserters moving east, where the ferociously keen military proctors couldn't follow them. It was the loyalty thing that bothered him most; more than loyalty, it was rather a sort of involuntary devotion. It reminded Pleda of a shepherd he'd known; horrible man, who used to take his bad temper out on his dog, but the more he kicked the dog for no reason, the more it worshipped him. That and the business with the cards—Well. Axio had cheated on the deal, he'd seen it quite plainly. To win, of course, to make money. But the hands he'd dealt; oh, he was a clever man, sure enough. And the pack (yes, but it had been Pleda who'd suggested a game of cards), and the Ace of bloody Swords. He made a quick interpretation of the two hands; inconclusive. Pleda didn't really believe in fortune-telling, because with a bit of skill and sophistry you could make a deal of cards mean anything you wanted it to. The cards Axio had chosen for him could have meant he'd reached the end of his journey and now it was time to hand his burden on to a better, stronger man; even that would be a bit too vague and convenient to base a decision on. Of course, he had no way of knowing that the handsome man really was Axio, though if you were going to assume someone's identity, there were a lot of better ones you could choose. One thing he was sure of. No way in hell could Axio be the Ace of Swords—

Could he?

He glanced at him, then looked away quickly. The good looks, of course, the easy manner, commanding personality; you could add the honest and sincere conviction that he was the centre and sole purpose of the universe. And smart, too, almost as smart as he thought he was. And it would explain a number of otherwise inexplicable mysteries—why the war was dragging on, why both empires were going to hell, why nobody seemed to be *doing* anything. But no. Pleda didn't believe it, *couldn't* believe it, just as he could never bring himself to believe it if someone told him the fire god created the heavens and the earth for a bet, and that plagues, wars, earthquake and famines were his idea of livening up a tedious afternoon. That's the whole essence of faith. You wouldn't believe something like that, even if it was true.

All that day, oddly enough, Pleda had trouble staying awake. He yawned all the time, and only the ferocious bumps and jolts kept him from nodding off. That, he knew, would be a bad idea. Now that they'd found the road, his usefulness was at an end, whereas the cart was still every bit as valuable as it had been. Just because you've played cards with someone doesn't mean they wouldn't cut your throat in an instant, with something as precious and rare as a cart at stake.

The soldiers had scabbed up nicely, no immediate prospect of infection, which suggested that the man he'd taken the sword from had kept it scrupulously cleaned and polished; not like an old soldier, who knows that rust and blood poisoning can make a valuable contribution to the war effort. From time to time he caught them looking at him; a hungry sort of look, like a dog watching a joint of meat just out of reach on the kitchen table. He hoped they were good dogs.

He wanted to ask Musen if the countryside was starting to look familiar, but anything he said would be plainly heard by Axio and his men, so he couldn't. All he could see of Musen was his back. When Axio made noises about stopping to stretch their legs and eat something, he put him off with a vague nearly there; the sun gave the lie to that as it lifted overhead and headed west, and still nothing to see except heather and gorse. Hell of a place to make a living, Pleda thought; don't suppose the war's helped much, either. At the very least there should be sheep at this time of year—summer grazing—and the shepherds living out at the shielings. But the only living things he'd seen had been larks and crows.

"Your boots," he said.

Axio had been gazing vacantly up at the sky. He sat up a little. "Sorry, are you talking to me?"

"Yes. Your boots."

"What about them?"

Pleda made him wait for a moment or so. "There you were, the five of you, miles from anywhere with no horses. So, wherever you came from, you must've walked."

"Correct."

"Not in those boots you didn't. Soles are barely marked."

"Oh, I see." Axio beamed at him. "You're quite right." He lowered his voice, mock-furtive. "Entirely between you and me, strictly speaking, these aren't my boots. Well, they are now, of course. Their previous owner had no further use for them."

Pleda studied him, as if learning him for an audition. A plausible enough explanation for a bandit to give. But, the night before they'd encountered Axio and his gang, he'd looked all round to see if there was anyone, anyone at all, out on the moors with them, and he was absolutely sure he'd seen nothing and nobody. Impossible that anyone could have walked, particularly in the dark, from the horizon to where they'd stopped the cart in the space of one night. But when he'd woken up and found them sitting there on those idiotic chairs, there were definitely no horses. And boot soles that clean and unscuffed had barely touched heather at all.

"Right," he said. "That explains that, then."

"Glad to have set your mind at rest. I won't go into details, if you don't mind."

"No, that's fine."

The cart stopped with a jolt. "What's the matter now?" Axio said. "We're not stuck in the mud again, are we?"

It meant taking his eyes off Axio and his men, but Pleda twisted himself round. "What've you stopped for?" he said. Musen didn't answer. The horses were still, their ears back, their heads up. Something's wrong, Pleda thought; there's something the horses don't like, and they've stopped.

"Drive on," he said.

Musen didn't turn round. "Look," he said.

The cart shifted as Axio stood up. "Where did they come from?" he said.

"Who?" Pleda demanded; then Axio dropped to his knees, not caring who or what he landed on. There was a yelp of pain from the man next to him. "Get down, you bloody fool," he shouted. Who to? Then Pleda heard a sound he recognised, a sort of swish, followed by a solid noise. *Missed,* said a voice inside him, because nothing appeared to have happened. Then Musen fell sideways off the bench.

He landed on his bad arm, but he didn't make a sound. That wasn't good.

"Sod this," Axio said suddenly. He jumped up, snatched the sword from Pleda's hand and vaulted out of the cart. His men followed as though tied to him by a rope. Another swish, this time so close that Pleda felt the slipstream as the arrow—he'd caught just a glimpse of it out of the corner of his eye, a shapeless blur going so fast he couldn't really track it—passed by the left side of his head. He threw himself face down into the bed of the cart.

The boy, he thought. He tried to get up, but fear was like a hand pressing him down, so instead he crawled down the cart and fiddled with the tailgate bolts; they were stiff and he couldn't get them free. He used the heel of his hand as a hammer, and got cut. He tried again with his other hand, the bolts shifted and the tailgate dropped down with a bang. He slithered out over the back edge and landed on the heather with a thump that winded him.

Musen was lying on his side, quite still. Beyond him, Pleda could see Axio and his men, fighting—wrong word, it was too one-sided for a fight. They were outnumbered three to one at least, but the harvester faces far greater odds, one scythe against a hundred thousand stalks; it was like watching a skilled man cutting wheat, the same momentum, small, efficient movements, controlled deployment of strength, footwork, concentration and, above all, experience. Pleda thought, they weren't anything like that when they were fighting *me*. He left them to it and crawled over to where Musen lay.

He turned him over; he was breathing, which was good, but the arrow was through him and out the other side, the shoulder side of the collarbone. There was also a big smear of blood and an ugly graze on the side of his head—he must have bashed it falling off the cart, and that was what had put him out. Pleda realised he had no idea what he was supposed to do. Damaging people he'd learned about, but fixing them once damaged hadn't been covered on the course he went on.

He looked up. Axio and two of his men were standing very still, their hands empty. Men with bows were walking towards them. Apparently they'd lost, after all.

Pleda glanced over his shoulder; clear behind the cart, as far as he could tell. He could run, maybe get out of bowshot before he was noticed. Then what? Down the road to Merebarton—assuming the archers hadn't come from there. He had no idea if Musen could be left, or if he needed urgent help, or if he was as good as dead already. The archers could've shot down Axio and his two surviving men where they stood, but they hadn't. He seemed to remember that you don't pull an arrow out of a wound, you push it through, because of the barbs. The simple fact was, he was out of his depth. One of the archers had seen him; he was pointing, and now a couple of the others had seen him as well. Two seconds in which to run, and then the window of opportunity would be closed. He let them pass. Hell, he thought.

*

Axio was furious. "Bloody fools," he was shouting. "You didn't call out or anything, you just started shooting. And now two of my people are dead, and one's got an arrow in him, and all because you can't control your own men."

Difficult to gauge the reaction of the man he was shouting at, a big, stocky type in a grey hood, which covered a lot of his face. "Be fair," he was saying; "you killed eight of mine."

"Yes, and whose fault is that? Only makes it worse. That's ten men dead, thanks to your incompetence. There's no excuse for it, do you hear? You're an idiot."

"I was told not to take any chances."

"Oh, right. So, at the first possible opportunity, you pick a totally unnecessary fight and lose eight men."

It wasn't, Pleda thought, the way prisoners usually speak to their captors. Two young men, very tall (like Musen, who seemed to have disappeared), stood behind him. They'd unstrung their bows and looked bored and sad.

Axio had calmed down a little. He'd stopped shouting, which made it harder for Pleda to eavesdrop; he heard, "Yes, I see that, but even so," and, "Well, yes, of course you must, but you should've—" and the man Axio was talking to had stopped backing away. Just as well. Pleda couldn't wait any longer. He went forward—his two shadows stayed where they were—and coughed loudly. Axio and the hooded man turned and looked at him.

"My friend," Pleda said. "Where is he? Is he all right?"

"He'll be fine," Axio said. "They got the arrow out and they've stopped the bleeding. They took him on to the village. There's a doctor there."

In Merebarton? That didn't seem likely. Pleda looked at the hooded man, who nodded. "He was lucky," he said. "And our doctors know what they're doing."

At any other time he'd have been on to the plural like a dog on a rabbit. "I want to see him, now."

"Of course." The hooded man was obviously pleased to be talking to someone who wasn't Axio. "That won't be a problem. You can ride back with us if you like, or you can follow on in your cart."

Pleda looked at Axio. "Fine," Axio said. "We'll follow you. But I haven't finished with you yet."

They walked back to the cart. Axio's two men were nowhere to be seen. "That man," Axio said, "is a halfwit."

"Who are they? Come to that, who the hell are you?"

Axio jumped up on to the bench and gathered the reins. "Untie the horses, there's a good fellow."

"Do you mind? That's my cart."

"Oh." Axio frowned slightly. "Did you particularly want to drive?"

"Well, no."

"Fine. Untie the horses and we'll be off."

Pleda did as he was told, then hauled himself up on to the bench, as Axio moved the horses on. "You didn't answer my question."

"You know all that. I'm Axio, and I'm a thief. Well, actually, I rather like *highwayman*, it's got a bit of tone to it."

"You're lodge," Pleda said.

"Well, yes, of course. I mean, we're all lodge here, that's pretty obvious. Isn't it?"

Pleda's turn to be angry. "You were going to kill us. Craftsmen are supposed to help each other."

"Of course we weren't going to kill you. Just wanted to scare the boy a bit, that's all. Not entirely sure whose side he's on, to be honest. Of course, you'd know more about that."

If he hadn't seen the way Axio had laid into the archers, Pleda would've punched him off the cart. "It wasn't a coincidence, was it? And you did have horses."

"Well, of course." Axio frowned at him reproachfully. "I must say, I don't know what you could've been thinking of, carrying on about my boots like that. The boy must have heard; what was he supposed to think? I assumed you were in the loop, and I thought the card game made it perfectly obvious. I don't know, maybe you're just not very quick on the uptake."

Maybe it'd be worth getting killed or beaten to a pulp, just for the sheer joy of breaking that beautiful straight nose. "You know. About what we're here for."

Axio shook his head. "The specifics, no. All I heard was, watch out for an Eight of Swords and some hick boy; they're running an errand up your way. They neglected to mention whether the boy was secure, so I thought I'd play it safe and act the big, bad bandit. Gave me the shock of my life when you started carving up my men. That's taking being in character too far, I thought."

"Who are you?"

Axio smiled at him. "Sorry," he said. "You'd need clearance for that. For all I know you've got it, but that's the point, I don't *know*, do I? Any more," he added, "than I know who these clowns are. Except that they're lodge; high cards, no trumps. At least, none I've been shown yet." He broadened his smile into a grin. "I never did see the point of everyone being face down. I mean, I know the fundamental reasoning behind it, but it makes life so damned difficult sometimes. As witness this latest balls-up."

The last line of defence. Defending what? Presumably that was face down as well. "You knew we were coming."

"I got a notification, yes, as a matter of courtesy. Also," he added, "we genuinely were out of food. Mostly because of traipsing about after you in the wilderness. I don't know where you got your map from, but it can't be any good." He shifted the reins into his left hand, so he could scratch the tip of his nose. "Out of curiosity, where are you going?"

"Don't you know?"

Axio sighed. "I'll say it again. I was told to look out for two craftsmen, keep an eye on them, make contact if necessary. As it happened, it was necessary, because we'd run out of food and we hoped you'd have some. I don't know the purpose of your mission, and I'm not really interested. Right now, my priority is finding out who these lunatics with the big coach are. I mean, obviously they're lodge, but nobody said anything about them to me. I should know that sort of thing, I'm responsible."

"Big coach."

Axio nodded. "That's right. They're escorting a big coach to this Merebarton place." He gave Pleda one of the big smiles. "You said that's where you're headed, but I'm assuming that's not true."

"Really."

"Well, it can't be, can it? Not unless you're meeting up with whoever's in the coach. And you seemed as genuinely surprised as I was."

Pleda thought for a moment. "Do they really have doctors with them?"

"Oh, I should imagine so. Your boy will be fine, you'll see. I saw far worse than that in the army, believe you me. Men like human porcupines, and they were up and about again in no time."

A thought struck Pleda; as hard as the arrow had hit Musen, but in a more awkward place. "Your brother," he said. "Is he lodge?"

Axio stared at him then burst out laughing. "Are you joking? Of course he is. You don't think he got to be rich and famous on pure musical ability."

"I assumed—" Pleda shook his head. "It can't have been easy."

"It never has been." Axio said it as though it was nothing—time of day, what a lot of weather we've been having lately—but Pleda guessed that that was how you knew he was being truthful. Of course, Axio probably knew that, too. Very like the boy in so many ways, with the obvious exception of intelligence.

"There we are." Axio pointed with his free hand. "At last."

Pleda followed the line indicated, but he couldn't see anything. Then something caught his eye, a square, too regular for anything in nature. He looked carefully and could just make out a drystone wall enclosing a patch of heather. At the far end was a low hill that was too straight and level. It brought back memories. An archery range.

"Good spot," Axio was saying. "Almost completely hidden by the contours of the combe; you could ride past here with an army and not know it was there, if they'd got the wit not to light fires. And then they go and build their butts on a hilltop, so they're visible for miles around." He shook his head sadly. "Soon as we've got five minutes we'll grub out that wall."

Not long after, they rode up a lane that followed the course of a broad stream which wound along the bottom of the fold between the sides of the combe. Pleda had some idea what to expect; *mere* meant marshy ground, where the run-off from the steep combe pooled on the flat—they'd have drained that centuries ago, of course—and *barton* meant land good and flat enough to grow barley, which you'd get in strips along the combe floor where the water had washed down silt from the hillsides. The houses were close together—there would have been a stockade once, for defence—which told him the villagers had originally been tenants rather than freeholders, though all that would have changed long ago, when all the great families were wiped out by wars and taxes. Sheep, he guessed, barley for bread, animal feed, thatch and beer; small gardens for beans and cabbages; they'd have to cart a long way for lumber and firewood, now that all the big copses that used to grow in these parts had been cut for charcoal for the war effort. But they'd have wool to sell, and there'd be pigs and poultry. People could live quite effectively in a place like this, if allowed to do so by their betters. He remembered that he hadn't seen a sheep since they left Beloisa.

"Had our eye on this place for a while now," Axio was saying. "Passes, like this one, either end of the village, only real way in or out. You could block them off with a series of thick, low walls with narrow gates and still not be visible from the road. Vulnerable from above, of course, you always are in valleys, but the slopes are pretty steep, too steep for cavalry, and you'd have a really good field of fire, so you could make them pay through the nose for coming at you that way. The main problem would be if they dammed the stream, but we're pretty sure there's water not far down, half a dozen wells would be enough for an army. Plenty of good local stone. Timber's a problem. We could plant on the far side of the hill, but a new plantation in the middle of all this garbage would be a bit of a giveaway. Other than that, though, it's ideal, and, best of all, nobody knows it's here."

"Except the people who live here, of course."

Axio looked at him as though he'd said something stupid.

The street was empty, but there was a carriage drawn up outside a large house at the far end. In the City, particularly the district between the palace and the Wall, where the best people lived, it'd have been so normal as to be invisible. Here, it was absurd.

"We'll level all this, of course," Axio said. "We can reuse most of the stone from the cottages, and it's cutting and shipping materials that takes the time and costs the money. For now, though, they're just camping out as best they can." He drew up behind the gorgeous carriage. "I'll drop you off here," he said. "I imagine your boy's in there, but, if not, just keep asking people till you find someone who knows what's going on. I'll drop the cart round to the stables when I've finished with it."

Pleda could see why they'd chosen that cottage; it was either the forge or the granary, because a long single-storey building jutted out from it at right angles, which made it the biggest covered space in town. He watched his cart jingle away, then walked to the door and gave it a gentle push. It swung open and he went inside.

"Hello, Musen," he said.

The boy was lying in one of five beds in the middle of the main room. Three of the other four were occupied, no doubt with casualties from the unintended battle. Musen was sitting up. There was a pack of cards on the blanket, but not laid out in any recognised pattern. The boy was holding one; he'd been gazing at it with a faraway look on his face.

Pleda came closer. "You all right?"

"I think so," Musen said. He was swathed in clean bandages, and his broken arm was in a clean, neat new sling. "I thought I'd had it back there, but they say I'm going to be all right." He lowered his voice. "It's the brothers," he said. "The ones who used to come here. I recognised two of them straight away, and they remembered me."

On the far wall was a tall cabinet with long shelves, lined with jars and bottles, and a long oak table, with straps halfway down and at the end. On a rack on the wall next to it were surgeons' tools. The floor was gleaming oak boards, not a trace of dirt anywhere. A tall barrel stood in the corner, and next to it a large copper cauldron, with a charcoal stove under it. Whoever ran this place knew what he was doing.

"Where is everybody?" Pleda asked quietly.

Musen smiled. "This used to be the forge," he said. "So it's fitting, really. Everybody's gone. I asked them where, but nobody seems to know."

Best of all, nobody knows it's here. Not any more, at any rate. "What about your family?"

"Oh, they lived out of town a way, down the street and up the hill." Lived, he'd said, and didn't seem particularly concerned. "They've been telling me what they're going to do here. It's amazing. It'll be a stronghold of the lodge, right here in Merebarton."

The lodge is my family, always has been. Pleda decided to remember that he was here to do a job. "The brothers," he said. "They're the ones who—"

Musen nodded. "I haven't said anything about why we're here. But—well, it must be going to cost them a fortune, building a castle and a library and a school and everything." He paused and frowned. "That big coach outside," he said. "Do you know what all that's about?"

Pleda shook his head. "That flash bastard knows, but he wouldn't tell me."

"This bit here's the hospital," Musen said, "but there's more out back, where the smithy used to be. Of course, I haven't seen in there. I think there must be another way in." He grinned. "The smith who used to be here wasn't a craftsman," he said. "Can you believe that? It's so stupid. Mind you, he was an idiot; you couldn't have made him understand in a million years."

Pleda looked at him for a while. The thing was, Musen was happy; you could see it all over his face. "Do you want me to try and find out where your family's gone? Someone here must know. I could take a message."

Musen shook his head. "I never liked them anyway." He lowered his voice. "For a start, I don't think my father was actually my father, if you know what I mean. He and I were always so different. I think—" He paused. "I think one of them, the brothers, was my real father. Maybe that's why my dad never had any time for the lodge or anything like that. Dead set against it, always. And I think that's why he killed my mother."

Pleda hadn't expected anything like this. "Your father—"

"Oh, nobody ever said anything. She died when I was a baby, and nobody ever talked about her. I'm sure he killed her, because of me. So you see, really they're not my family, the lodge is."

Difficult to find words. "Have you got any proof for any of this?"

Musen shrugged. "Not really. I don't need any. I mean, I'm not going to *do* anything about it. I can't be bothered, to be honest. Anyway, they're probably all dead by now. It really doesn't matter."

Probably all dead. No sheep. Where would several hundred refugees go, in this country? It really doesn't matter, said the son of the lodge. Cut their throats or turn them out on the moor, it'd come to the same thing in the end. They'd have died anyway, because of the war. Meanwhile, a choice piece of real estate, just right for the purpose—

"I don't suppose anyone's said anything," Pleda said quietly. "But do you know why they're doing this?"

Musen frowned. "Doing what?"

"Building a fortress. Here in the middle of the wilderness."

"Oh, I see. Well, it's for the war, I guess."

That made no sense. "Don't be stupid. The lodge isn't in the war. We're neutral."

"Oh, not this war. This war doesn't matter. They're doing this for the next war. The important one. Us against them. *The* war." Musen frowned at him. "You know that," he said. "You must do."

Pleda made a huge effort and kept his voice low and steady. "Where did you hear all this?"

"At the college, of course. You know, where I went to be trained. They told us about it. Not very much, obviously, we're not secure, but just the basics, so we'd know. You know," he added, with a touch of impatience. "*The* war. The one that this one's clearing the way for. And I'm going to be in it," he added, with a hint of wonder in his voice. "Me and all the other wild cards, it's what they've been collecting us for." He stopped, and looked closely at Pleda's face. "You don't know, do you?"

"What? No, of course, of course I know. I'm an Eight of Swords, remember?"

"You don't know." An accusation. "You don't know anything about it at all. But I thought—getting you here, I mean. I thought that was what it was all *for,* to get you here. The emperor's cards, I mean, and all that rubbish. To get money for the building, and to bring you here. I thought—" He stopped again. "I thought you were important. But you're not, are you? They just wanted the money."

Pleda took a deep breath. "What war?" he said. "Tell me."

But Musen shook his head. "You don't know," he said. "So I can't tell you. Don't ask me any more. In fact, you'd better go away. I don't know what I'm allowed to tell you, or anything."

"Eight of bloody Swords," Pleda said, in a low, harsh voice. "You'll tell me what I ask, understood? *What war?*"

There was nothing on Musen's face but contempt. "You don't matter," he said. "I'm home now; you can't touch me. You're not allowed to ask me questions. You might as well go and do what you're here for, get those stupid cards. I don't want to see you again, do you hear me?"

Pleda found the strength to smile at him. "Screw you, then," he said. "And get well soon."

He headed for the door, half expecting someone to stop him. What war? What war, and who against, for crying out loud? Clearing the way? There were the desert nomads, yes, the idiot Blemyans had stirred up a hornets' nest there, and it would take the combined efforts of both empires to deal with them once and for all. Glauca knew that, and Senza Belot must realise it, too; and he imagined they weren't stupid in the West, either. But *the* war, the one that this one's clearing the way for— This war was certainly clearing the way; it had cleared sheep and men off every hillside from here to Beloisa, and from what he understood things weren't much better anywhere else. But *the* war; for a war, you had to have armies. The way this war was going, it wouldn't be long before there was nobody left. The Blemyans? That'd be a campaign, not a war, a paragraph in the official history. *What war?*

You don't matter, the boy had said. You're not important. Now there was a thought. Eight of Swords, and not important enough, a card you throw away when you've bought something better.

The light outside was painfully bright after the cool shade of the hospital. The fancy carriage, he noted, wasn't there any more. In his pocket was the plenipotentiary warrant. He needed to talk to someone in authority.

(Because a run of low cards, two, three, four, will beat a pride of tens; if you're holding three and four, two is *important*, two *matters*. You'd run through the whole damned pack to get a two if you needed one, and dump your eight, nine, ten without hesitation. The wild cards, the boy had said, it's what they've been collecting us for. Thief School? Were there other schools like it—covered cards, face down—he didn't even know about?

Anything that's face down you have to pay to see. Fine, so long as you can afford it.)

A man stepped out of a doorway. He wore a robe that looked vaguely ecclesiastical but belonged to no order Pleda had ever heard of over a regulation Western scale cuirass, and Eastern issue boots. Of course, you could buy anything you wanted from the battlefield clearance contractors. "You're Pleda," he said.

"That's right."

"Do you think you could possibly spare a moment? They'd like to talk to you."

"Why? I'm not important."

"Please?"

Well, he'd always been a sucker for politeness, especially when it wore armour. "Go on, then," he said, and followed him round the side of the hospital. There was a paved yard, probably left over from the smithy, and there was the long building that had once been the forge. The armoured man led him to a door, then stood aside to let him pass.

It was dark inside, and he recognised the smell as damp plaster. He heard the scratch of a tinderbox; a little red glow, as someone blew on smouldering moss, followed by a bigger yellow one, as whoever it was lit an oil lamp. Before that, he supposed, he'd been sitting there in the dark.

Correction: they. Three men, and a woman in a long black veil. The men wore the same robes as the man who'd brought him here, but no armour. One was bald and middle-aged, one had a bushy head of grey hair, and the third was very old indeed, with little white wisps, like sheep's wool caught in brambles. There was nothing in the room except for five plain wooden stools and a small round table, on which lay a tarnished silver box. The walls and ceiling were off-white; freshly applied plaster, still wet.

"Pleda," said the old man. "Please, sit down."

You paint frescoes—masterpieces of religious and esoteric art—on wet plaster. He sat. The old man smiled.

"Glauca sent you," the old man said.

Not *the emperor.* "That's right."

The old man laid a finger on the lid of the box. "Thank you for coming. I trust the journey wasn't too arduous."

Pleda shrugged. "I'm here now."

The old man nodded and lifted the lid. "The asking price," he said, "is one hundred and fifty thousand angels."

One million angels paid for the war for a year. "No," Pleda said. "It's too much. The emperor hasn't got that sort of money."

"Then you've had a wasted journey," the old man said. "But in any case, I don't agree. In your pocket you have a plenipotentiary warrant. Do you know what that means?"

"Yes."

"It means," the old man said, "you can do *anything*. Including," he went on, lifting something out of the box, "endorsing the back of the warrant with an order to pay the bearer one hundred and fifty thousand angels. I happen to know that exactly that sum of money will arrive at Beloisa in twelve days' time, to cover arrears of pay and finance the rebuilding and fortification of the city. So you see, the emperor does have the money."

"Yes, but he can't afford—"

The old man lifted his other hand, a gentle but categorical gesture. "So let's see what happens. You go back to Glauca and tell him you refused our offer. Glauca is furious. He sends you straight back again. Next time, the price will be two hundred thousand angels. He can well afford not to fortify Beloisa. He can afford for the troops who will shortly arrive here to mutiny because they won't get their back pay. He can afford for them to defect to the enemy and hand Beloisa over to them. He has other provinces, and this one isn't much use to him in its present deplorable state. The Westerners will occupy it; sooner or later Senza Belot will come and take it from them, and Glauca will be back where he started. And he'll have these." He put down what he was holding on the table, a block wrapped in red silk. It clinked. "And you will have lost his favour and trust, which you've worked so hard to gain, and the lodge will have lost a highly placed observer at a key point in the chain of command. Now, we'll start again. The asking price is one hundred and fifty thousand angels."

Pleda breathed in slowly, then out again. It was supposed to calm him down, but all it achieved was to fill his lungs with the wet plaster smell, and make him want to cough. "What do you want the money for?"

The old man laughed. "To decorate this room," he said.

Pleda looked at him. He was serious. "That's a lot of money," he heard himself say.

"Loxida of Blemya, the greatest living painter of religious subjects, has agreed to paint this room with scenes of the Transfiguration of the Host. We've negotiated a fee of one hundred and twenty-five thousand angels, which we feel is entirely reasonable, given that his work will quite possibly be the supreme achievement of the human race. It will most certainly still be here, admired and valued and a source of immeasurable spiritual strength and energy, in a thousand years' time. Or the money could be spent on building a set of walls, which siege engines will have battered into rubble within five years. Oh, in case you were wondering, the balance of twenty-five thousand angels will pay for the materials. Loxida has specified ninety-nine-pure gold from the mines in the Aradian desert; apparently, the colour is very subtly different. We're exceptionally fortunate to be in a position to give him this commission."

Loxida of Blemya; never heard of him. "I'll need to see them first."

"Really? What for? Only Glauca and three other men alive—I'm one of them, incidentally—know enough to be able to tell whether these are the genuine Sleeping Dog or an extraordinary skilful copy, made by either Praxidas or Tariunno of Licynna. Please don't be offended, but you're completely incapable of forming any sort of valid judgement." He smiled. He had six teeth. "You're just going to have to trust me, I'm afraid."

Pleda could feel his brain melting and dripping down his throat. Even so; he needed to *think*. "Here's the deal," he said. "I'll endorse the warrant in escrow. The paymasters at Beloisa will release the money once they hear from the emperor that the pack is genuine."

"Unacceptable." The old man didn't sound upset or anything. "Glauca will say that the cards are fakes. He'll keep them, and refuse to pay over the money. He can't be trusted. You, however, can trust us, because we're all fellow craftsmen. This is the Sleeping Dog Pack. You have my word on it."

Pleda wanted to laugh. He also wanted, very badly indeed, to ask who the toothless old man was. But there'd be no point. Even if he got an answer, a true one, it'd be meaningless to him. Instead, he said, "Tell me about the war."

The old man's face didn't change. "Excuse me?"

"Not this one," Pleda said, "the next one. The one this one's clearing the way for."

"Now why should I do that?"

To see a covered card, you have to pay. My entire life, Pleda thought, and raise you a stuiver. "Because if you don't, there's no deal. I'll go home and tell Glauca that the cards were fakes. Such obvious fakes that even I could tell. The colour of the silver was all wrong. Too pure for the period. There were no copper tones on the raised areas."

The old man frowned. "Would you please wait outside?" he said. "I'd just like a private word with my associates."

Feeling slightly dizzy and light-headed, as though he'd been drinking, Pleda got up and walked to the door. It seemed a long way. The man in the cuirass was there to open the door for him. Outside, the air was dry and fresh. He rested his back against the wall. If his legs weren't so weak, he'd have run away. The lodge, he thought; that man is a fellow craftsman. He's supposed to be on the same side as me. He's supposed to be my brother.

Brothers, like Senza and Forza Belot.

On the roof of a nearby house he saw two crows, the first living things apart from men and horses he'd noticed for days. He watched them for a while. Senza Belot reckoned you could learn a lot from watching crows, so he'd been told. His hands were beginning to get cold; he put them in his pockets and found his deck of cards. The temptation to lay out his fortune, there on the paving slabs, was almost too strong to resist. Nine of Shields; you will meet an influential stranger. Four of Spears; you will learn something to your advantage. Poverty, reversed; you will achieve your heart's desire.

Sometime later the guard called him back in. There were three men and a heavily veiled woman. Different men.

"Please sit down." The speaker was an elderly man, with a full head of short grey hair and a neat, pointed beard. "We're sorry to have kept you."

Pleda sat down. "That's fine," he said. "I needed a breath of air."

"The asking price," said the neat man, "is one hundred and seventy-five thousand angels. We have considered your request for information, but we have to refuse. The information is sensitive and you are not secure."

He felt as if his strength was draining slowly away, like oil from a cracked bottle. "The extra twenty-five thousand," he said. "There's no more money."

The neat man shook his head. "The garrison commander at Beloisa holds a thirty-thousand-angel contingency fund," he said. "Our best information is that he still has nineteen thousand of it left. The balance will have to be raised by means of a forced loan from the soldiers of the garrison." He held up his hand before Pleda could interrupt. "We appreciate that that will likely precipitate a mutiny," he said. "But that's going to happen anyway, so it really doesn't matter. Meanwhile, we would encourage you to contemplate the repercussions of your actions." He paused, and looked meaningfully at the little round table. On it, beside the silver box, was a small silver-gilt inkwell and a goose-quill pen. "It would probably be best if I dictated the wording of the endorsement," he said. "These legal formulae have to be exactly right, you know."

Pleda took out the warrant, leaned forward and got hold of the pen. He wrote the words he was given, resting the parchment rather awkwardly on his knee. "Now sign it, please," the neat man said. "One of my associates will witness your signature."

He handed the parchment to the neat man, who glanced at it briefly and gave it to the man on his left, a short, broad-shouldered Imperial. He had his own pen. Then he put the warrant down on the table, as if it no longer mattered.

"And this," the neat man said, "is yours."

His left hand rested for a moment on the silver box. Pleda looked at it, but stayed where he was. The neat man waited for a moment or so, then said gently, "You can examine it, if you wish."

"No thanks," Pleda said. "I trust you."

The neat man smiled at the joke. "Well," he said, "I think that concludes the formal business of the meeting. Now, perhaps you'd care for a cup of tea. Or something stronger, maybe."

Pleda nodded. "Something a lot stronger, please," he said.

The man on the neat man's right laughed. "I think we can

manage that," he said, and clapped his hands. From nowhere, apparently, someone in the same cut of gown appeared; he leaned forward so the Imperial could whisper in his ear. Then he nodded and went away. "Bearing in mind the fact that we're playing host to possibly the most discerning palate in the East," the Imperial went on, "I've had the cellarer find us something rather special. I'd like your opinion."

The servant was back again, with a silver tray. On it stood a dusty brown pottery pint bottle, its mouth stopped with beeswax, and four tiny, exquisite horn and silver cups. The servant produced a dear little silver knife, with which he cut and chipped away the wax; then he filled the cups. One each for the men; the lady in the veil wasn't getting any. Pleda looked down at the overgrown thimble in his hand; an inch of a clear yellow liquid, very slightly paler than urine. "Your very good health," the Imperial said, and didn't move.

Well, Pleda thought; and he nibbled a drop of the yellow stuff. It was without doubt the most delicious thing he'd ever put in his mouth, and it kicked like a mule. Oh, and none of the known poisons. "Not bad," he said, and swilled down the rest of it. There was a brief war in his intestines. Like the other war, nobody won, but there was considerable damage.

"Cheers," the Imperial said; he took a sip, and then the other three followed suit. Pleda smiled and looked pointedly at his empty cup. "Care for another?" the Imperial asked.

"Oh, go on, then," Pleda said.

The really good stuff, of course, gets better and better the more of it you drink. After the third cup (the others were still on their second) Pleda felt like he was briefly floating on a lake of burning honey, just before going down for the last time. "You know what," Pleda said. "I wouldn't mind a barrel of this."

The Imperial grinned at him. "No doubt," he said. "Regrettably, that was the last known bottle in existence."

"Really."

"Oh yes. It's a hundred and twenty-five years old."

"Keeps well, I'll say that for it." The Imperial laughed and leaned forward to top up his cup.

"Sort of mead, I'm guessing."

"Sort of."

Pleda applied his wealth of technical knowledge, then gave up. "Beats me," he said. "Basically mead but—well, different."

"Exactly."

"Ah well." He smiled. "Another secret. And I'm not secure."

"Alas." The Imperial pulled a sad face. "A lost secret, I'm afraid. A warning to us all, I think. Secrets too closely guarded can die of confinement." He glanced at the other three, then added, "There's a difference, of course, between telling a secret and giving a hint."

Quite suddenly, Pleda was stone cold sober again. He tried his very best not to let it show. "That's right," he said. "A little hint never hurt anybody." He mimed slow, painful thought for a moment. "Tell you what," he said. "Gamble you for it. If I win, you give me a little hint."

The Imperial had another quick telepathic conference with his colleagues. "And if we win?"

"Oh, I don't know. My head on a pike?"

Next to the neat man, on his left, was a big man with red hair and a beard. "We could've had that already, if we'd wanted it."

Pleda shrugged. "That'd have been cheating," he said. "Difference between fleecing a man at the tables and mugging him in the alleyway outside. Anyhow, it's all I've got. Take it or leave it."

The Imperial nodded briskly and opened the silver box. Then he hesitated. "I forgot, these don't belong to us any more. With your permission?"

"Go ahead," Pleda said.

The Imperial took out the cards and shuffled them. "Let's make it strictly chance," he said. "Fairer that way. You cut, then we cut. Highest card wins all. Agreed?"

Pleda waved vaguely. "You're the doctor."

The Imperial fanned out the cards. Pleda leaned forward. He knew, better than anyone, how to force a card on somebody. He took his time, and picked from the left-hand edge of the fan. He looked at the card. Eight of Swords. He felt suddenly cold. Oh, he thought.

"No, don't show me yet," the Imperial said; then he offered the fan to the veiled woman, who took a card and covered it with her other hand. The Imperial put the cards down carefully on the table and looked at Pleda. "Now," he said. "You first."

Pleda turned over his card and held it up. "Ah," the Imperial said. Then he nodded to the woman, who revealed the Nine of Arrows.

There was a moment of dead silence. Then the Imperial said, "Congratulations."

I'm a dead man, Pleda thought. "You what?"

"Northern rules," the Imperial said. "Swords are trumps. You win," he explained.

Pleda opened his mouth, but no words came. He closed it and tried again. "Oh," he said.

The Imperial leaned forward and gently pulled the card out of his hand. "So you get your hint," he said, returning the card to the pack. "Try not to look so sad about it." He shuffled the pack and laid out nine cards, face upwards."Well, now," he said.

Pleda leaned forward. The Hero. The Thief. Poverty. Virtue. The Two of Spears. The Two of Arrows. The Scholar. The Eight of Swords. The Cherry Tree.

"Hint," the Imperial said.

"Personal," Pleda said. The Imperial shrugged. "I don't tell fortunes," he said.

Now, then. Two of Spears and Two of Arrows back to back had

to be the Belot brothers. The Thief was presumably meant to be Musen, though the identification struck him as facile. By the same token, the Scholar had to be Glauca. Eight of Swords; now who could they possibly mean by that?

"Who's the Cherry Tree?" he said.

The woman drew back her veil. He saw a pale, thin, sharp face with light blue eyes; twenty-seven or -eight, though he was a poor judge of women's ages. Not pretty, not beautiful, but if she walked into a room it wouldn't be long before every man there noticed her. "That's me," she said. "I'm Lysao Pandocytria."

Pleda caught his breath. Senza Belot's Lysao; except she wasn't, that was the point. He remembered someone using the expression *collector's item*, and two things Musen had said: something about wild cards, and *it's what they've been collecting us for.* He decided he'd changed his mind about what the lodge were planning to do here. Not a fortress or a temple, a museum. "That was your coach outside," he said, for something to say.

"Yes. I've just arrived. I'll be safe here."

The Cherry Tree. He wasn't quite sure he got it, but that was probably because he was being rather slow. He looked at the Imperial. "Does this mean I can't go home?"

The Imperial smiled at him. "Don't be silly," he said. "We trust you. After all, you're a craftsman. We know what side you're on."

Glad somebody does. "I'd better be going, then. Thanks for the hint."

"I trust everything is now perfectly clear."

"As mud, thank you. I don't suppose you'd tell me who the Hero is."

The Imperial shrugged. "I could tell you his name," he said, "but it wouldn't mean anything to you."

"Shouldn't the Scholar be reversed?"

"No, I don't think so."

Well, that was something. He was actually quite fond of Glauca. "What about the Two of Spears?"

The Imperial hesitated, then reached out and turned the Two of Spears face down. "We think," he added. "If you find out for sure, please let us know."

Liar, Pleda thought. He collected the cards—they clinked, because his hands were shaking—and put them in the box, and put the box in his pocket. "We must do this again sometime," he said.

"No," the Imperial said. "We shouldn't."

The big red-headed man stood up and opened the door for him. "Thank you for the game," he said.

"My pleasure," Pleda replied, and stood up to go. "Who won, by the way?"

The Imperial beamed at him. "We're craftsmen," he said. "We all won. Have a safe journey home."

Pleda reached out, grabbed the bottle by the neck and walked out quickly. He didn't look back until he heard the door slam shut. He shook the bottle gently. Empty, of course. He put it down on the ground; as he let go of it, he discovered that his hand wasn't empty. He turned it palm upwards and opened his fingers. Squashed into his palm was a card, from a cheap, throwaway pack, like the sort soldiers have. It was the Ace of Swords.

He grinned. There is no suit of Swords. He crunched the card into a ball and stuffed it into his pocket.

The Raise

Two days later, Senza Belot won a crushing victory over the main Western army at Cenufrac. The Westerners, under the veteran General Gamda, seem to have had no idea that the Eastern Fifth Army was ahead of them; either that, or they assumed that the Fifth would avoid contact, since they were outnumbered six to one. Accounts of the battle are frustratingly vague and inconclusive; the entire Western staff was wiped out, and therefore no official report of the battle was filed, since there was no one left alive to file it; for reasons unknown, Senza Belot's despatches were uncharacteristically terse and elliptical, simply stating when and where the battle took place and the numbers of combatants and casualties. All that is known for certain, therefore, is that the main battle took place on both sides of the Ilden brook, which flows out of the mountains to join the Bosen estuary, that the Westerners fielded over sixty thousand men against Belot's twelve thousand, and that twenty-seven thousand Western soldiers died there, as against nine hundred Easterners.

One can only speculate as to Senza Belot's reasons for not leaving a detailed account of one of his most conclusive victories. Anecdotal evidence gathered some time later suggests that he did not regard the battle as particularly interesting from a tactical point of view, or that he was somehow ashamed of the ease and scale of his triumph. One much later account has him in tears on the battlefield, as the dead of both sides were collected up; however, the source is a dubious one, embroidered and romanticised and with an unhappy tendency to adapt facts to fit its explicitly pacifist agenda. The likeliest explanation would seem to be that General Belot, aware that he was operating deep inside enemy territory and that communications with the East might well be intercepted, was reluctant to commit to paper any details that might prove useful to the enemy; later, it is argued, he lacked the time and the motivation to write the battle up, or assumed that someone else would do so. Whatever the reason, it is to be regretted that so little is known about one of the great man's finest achievements.

It is ironic that what should have been a decisive moment in the war turned out to have little or no lasting effect, coming as it did a few weeks before the mutiny of the Beloisa garrison and their defection to the West. The Western losses at Cenufrac were more than made up for by the unexpected acquisition of thirty-one thousand seasoned Eastern veterans, who were immediately transferred to the Northern theatre to block any advance Senza Belot may have contemplated making in the aftermath of the battle. A smaller army, some nine thousand men, was sent to fortify and hold Beloisa and its dependent territories against the expected Eastern counter-attack; this, however, did not materialise, and the Westerners were able to rebuild and garrison Beloisa at their leisure. They were given the opportunity to do so because Glauca II had quite literally run out of money. He could afford to hold what he still possessed, and maintain Senza Belot and the Fifth Army in the field to discourage aggression from the West, but any kind of offensive operations were, for the time being at least, entirely beyond his means until the hole in his exchequer had been replenished. To achieve this, he was compelled to embark on a programme of retrenchment and austerity, combined with increased taxes and the further sale of crown and government assets, all of which weakened the Eastern economy and severely hampered his ability to wage war. The West, which could reasonably have expected to face an all-out assault in both the Northern and Southern sectors following the defeat at Cenufrac, found that it had been granted an unexpected reprieve. Bearing in mind the crisis that was soon to break, this was undoubtedly just as well.

Merebarton. 3 a K Mersilia, auc 1095.

Lysao Pandocytria to General Senza Belot, greetings.

I am being held here against my will.

I can't actually complain about how they're treating me. They brought me here in a grand carriage, and this place I'm locked up in is quite comfortable, and the food's nice and the people are quite kind. But I don't want to be here. You know what I'm like about being cooped up. I feel like I've been buried alive or something. I can't stand it. I just want to howl and scream.

I know that after what I've done and what's happened between us, I have no right to expect you to help me. But there's nobody else who can help me. I can't trust anyone. Obviously they're doing this to get to you. I know they are, they're not exactly making a secret of it. They're going to keep me as a hostage to control you, which means they can control the war. They're up to something very big and very dangerous. I'm scared to death of them. I'm pretending to be on their side so they won't just kill me out of hand, but I don't suppose I can keep it up for very long. You know what a terrible liar I am.

If you get this letter, please give the messenger a lot of money. He'll have earned it.

You will come, won't you?

The story continues in...

The Two of Swords

Volume 2

extras

meet the author

K. J. PARKER is the pseudonym of Tom Holt, a full-time writer living in the south-west of England. When not writing, Holt is a barely competent stockman, carpenter and metalworker, a two-left-footed fencer, an accomplished textile worker and a crack shot. He is married to a professional cake decorator and has one daughter.

Find out more about K. J. Parker and other Orbit authors by registering for the free newsletter at www.orbitbooks.net.

if you enjoyed

THE TWO OF SWORDS: VOLUME 1

look out for

THE TWO OF SWORDS: VOLUME 2

by

K. J. Parker

Declaration

When it comes to processing the dead, there is no more respected name than Siama Ocnisant. For thirty years, Ocnisant's Emerald Caravan has followed closely in the wake of every major war, performing such vital services as burying the fallen, treating and repatriating the wounded, clearing up and making good the mess, liaising with and reassuring local farmers and landowners—all without costing the combatants' hard-pressed taxpayers a single stuiver. Strictly neutral and impartial, the Emerald Caravan finances its entire operation (without compromising in any way on quality of service) by retrieving and selling abandoned military equipment, which would otherwise go to waste or fall into the hands of undesirables. By reselling war materiel at sensible prices, Ocnisant also helps keep military spending down and make war affordable—a vital consideration in an age of protracted multi-theatre conflicts. "I simply don't know how he does it for the money," the Eastern emperor is reported to have told his close advisers. "Without exaggeration, we simply couldn't have kept the war going this long without him."

Poverty

"The good news," he said, "is that they found you not guilty of witchcraft." He smiled. "All the evidence was circumstantial, no positive identification, therefore no case to answer."

He paused.

"And?" she said.

"The bad news is," he said, "they convicted you on three of the five counts of spying, and they're going to hang you in the morning. I tried to lodge an appeal, but it appears there is no right of appeal in espionage cases, so there's not a lot I can do." He hesitated again. "I've asked the ambassador to petition the court for clemency, but—"

"He's a busy man?"

"Very. And in any case, clemency would mean forty years minimum in the slate quarries, and nobody lasts more than three years down there, so it's as broad as it's long, really. I'm very sorry," he said. "But there you are. Is there anything I can do for you?"

Outside it was raining again. She thought for a moment. "Apparently not."

He frowned slightly. "It goes without saying," he said, "that the Department will look after your children and dependent relatives—"

"I haven't got any."

"No? Well, that's something, isn't it? Now, you can nominate who gets your back pay, death-in-service gratuity, any money you may have paid in to a funeral club, your share of plunder, spoil and prizes, if any—" He waited for a moment. "Or, if you don't nominate, it all goes to the Benevolence. It's a good cause, they do splendid work."

"That's all right, then."

His frown deepened, but he persevered. "Now, if you haven't made a will, you can dictate one to me now and I can get the dispensation from proper procedure. I strongly advise you to, you don't want to leave your family a mess to clear up."

She smiled at him. "I haven't got anything to leave."

"Really? Ah well." From his sleeve he produced three rolls of parchment, a quill pen and a brass ink bottle. "In that case, I just need you to sign these forms, and that's pretty much everything covered."

He handed her the rolls of parchment. She unrolled them, glanced at them and tore them up. He sighed. "Any last message you'd like me to pass on?"

"Actually, yes."

He nodded briskly. "Fire away."

She told him. He looked at her. "I'm sorry you feel that way," he said. "But, after all, you knew the risks when you—"

"Yes."

"Well, then. I know this is a very difficult moment for you, but I would remind you that even in the final extremity, you still represent the Service, and what you say and do reflects on us all. It'd be a great shame to tarnish an otherwise exemplary record at the last moment, so to speak." She looked at him, and he got up and banged on the cell door with his fist. "I'm sorry," he said.

"Why? It's not your fault."

"The duty chaplain—"

"Goodbye."

A key turned in the lock and the door swung open. He

looked at her, opened his mouth, closed it again and left. The door closed and the lock turned. She breathed out slowly.

Five hours later, she started banging on the door. "Keep it down, will you?" she heard the jailer say on the other side. "You'll start them all off."

"I want to see the chaplain."

A pause; then, "Yes, all right," in a resigned voice. She sat down on the bed and waited. Some time later, the door opened and the chaplain came in. He was a tall man, thin, bald, somewhere between sixty and seventy; he wore nothing but a tunic, for security reasons.

"I want to confess," she said.

He hadn't shaved recently, and there were crumbs in the folds of his tunic. "Of course," he said, and perched on the end of the bed.

She looked at him for a moment, then said, "I have committed murder, theft and arson. I have lied and carried false witness. I have wounded and practised torture, both physical and mental. I have forged documents, including sacred and liturgical records."

His face didn't change. He nodded.

"I have blasphemed and ridiculed the articles of the faith. I have preached heretical doctrines. I have neglected to assist fellow craftsmen in their time of trial."

He closed his eyes, just for a moment. Then he opened them again. "I understand," he said. "Your sins are forgiven." He stood up and knocked three times. The door opened. The guard stood aside to let him pass; as he did so, he drew the sword from the guard's scabbard and stabbed him in the throat, at the junction of the collarbones. The guard dropped to the floor; the chaplain stuck his head out of the door, then came back into the cell. "All clear," he said.

She nodded. "Thanks," she said.

He gave her a filthy look. "You'd better take me with you," he said. "I don't know what to do."

"That's fine," she assured him. "I do. Stick with me, you'll be all right." She took the sword from his hand. "Where does this corridor lead to?"

"How should I know? I only ever come down the stairs."

She breathed out through her nose. "Fine," she said. "We'll go *up* the stairs."

"You can't. There's a guard."

"Of course there is." She grabbed his ear with her left hand, pulled his head back and rested the edge of the sword against his neck. "Just in case anyone sees us," she said.

The stairs he'd talked about proved to be a narrow spiral staircase, without even a rope to hold on to, so she let go of him while they climbed. As soon as they reached the top, she grabbed him again. There was no guard.

"I thought you said—"

"There should be. There is usually."

They were in a long gallery, with arrow slits every five yards. She stopped and peered out through one of them, but it was pitch dark and she couldn't see anything. After a while, they came to a small door—more of a hatch, really—in the wall. "What's that?"

"It's a garderobe. Where they empty the chamber pots."

"Splendid." She let go of him, dumped the sword on the floor and pulled open the door.

"You can't go that way. It's a hundred-foot drop."

She smiled at him. "Thanks for everything," she said. "I hope you don't get in any trouble."

"Don't be bloody stupid. If you aren't smashed to bits, you'll drown."

"My risk," she said. "Now, go and tell them I got loose and took you hostage."

The door slammed behind her before he could answer. He stood for a while staring at the closed door, then turned and headed back down the gallery. After about ten paces it occurred to him to break into a run and start shouting.

The guards who found him sent for the castellan, who ordered two men to go down the garderobe shaft on ropes. They came back up after a while, white-faced and foul-smelling; no sign of anyone down there, they said, but it's got to be ten feet deep and no handholds; if she fell into that, she drowned, no question about it. Hell of a way to go, one of them added, though if she was lucky she hit her head on the wall on the way down. The castellan asked them; are you sure? Oh yes, they told him. Positive.

She heard most of their conversation, since the tunnel amplified sound quite wonderfully. She was still climbing. It was desperate work, with her back arched against the opposite wall, her fingers and toes crammed into mortar cracks between the stones—fortunately the builders had lined the garderobe with undressed stone, which gave slightly more purchase. Halfway between floors she came to the conclusion that she'd made a dreadful mistake and she wasn't going to make it, but she kept going nevertheless. She found the door on the upper storey by resting her back against it, thinking it was solid wall; it swung open, she lost her grip, actually slid down the best part of a yard before finding a crack with one wildly scrabbling foot. For a moment her weight was too much for four toes to bear, but she found a handhold just in time, and then another, and then got the tips of three fingers over the sill of the door. It was pure luck that the upper gallery was empty, at a time of day when there should have been a sentry there; but he'd gone down the stairs when the alarm was sounded on the floor below.

Well; she was officially dead and nobody was actively looking for her, but it still wasn't wonderful. Fortunately, she had a resource that most escaping prisoners are denied: she was female and women carrying baskets of washing don't attract attention in the inhabited parts of castles, particularly if they're supposed to be dead. She searched until she found the cupboard where the dirty linen lived, grabbed a big armful that covered most of her face and staggered along the gallery looking for the backstairs. Three guards took no notice of her whatsoever, and then she was trotting down a proper square-section stairway, bare-walled and imperfectly whitewashed, which could only lead to the kitchens, laundry and other tactically negligible facilities where fighting men rarely go.

She came out eventually into a lantern-lit courtyard. A quick glance upwards told her that she was now in the very centre of the castle, surrounded on all four sides by impenetrably thick stone walls, at the junction of all routes of communication and access used by the garrison and the castle servants. Best-quality Mezentine armour wouldn't have saved her, but the armful of washing made her invisible. The difficulty was that a laundry maid had no lawful excuse for leaving the castle, even by daylight; in the middle of the night, forget it. Nor could she spend the rest of her life wandering around with an armful of dirty sheets.

A castle is a fair-sized community, larger than many villages, almost the size of a small town. Even in a small town, of course, everybody knows everybody else, unless their faces are obscured by washing. But she was exhausted, bone-weary and finding it increasingly difficult to think about anything except finding somewhere to sit down and rest. It was only later, in hindsight, that she realised that the exhaustion and the indifference almost certainly saved her life – it made her impersonation of a laundry maid in the last quarter of the night shift far more convincing than mere acting could ever have done. If she'd had to walk past the sentry on the gate between the middle and outer courtyards, almost inevitably she'd have given herself away, if she'd been acting natural. Instead, she caught her foot on the lintel out of sheer weariness, stumbled into the guard, scraped the back of her hand on the stonework, squealed at the pain, mumbled an apology and trudged away, unchallenged, sworn at for clumsiness and completely accepted as genuine.

The outer courtyard was another world entirely, and as soon as she emerged into it she realised she'd made a mistake. A laundry maid could believably carry dirty washing from the outer yard to the middle, but not the other way round. She calculated that she had five, maybe ten seconds to deal with the error before someone noticed. She made her mind up in three.

There were two sentries posted outside the doors to the Great Hall. She headed straight for them, well aware that they'd noticed her. "Excuse me," she said, "but I'm new here and I'm lost. Which way to the laundry, please?" They laughed and told her. That posed another problem. The route she'd been given to the laundry meant going back the way she'd just come, past the guard she'd bumped into. Here the bone-weariness was unquestionably her salvation. She left the guard thinking she was mad or drunk or probably both, but that was fine. Even with her back to him as she walked away, she could tell he wasn't looking at her.

Well, she thought; and what would a worn-out laundry maid do next, if she was as tired as me? The answer was perfectly obvious; she'd caught her own maid doing it once, about a thousand years ago in another life, and given her a tongue-lashing for being lazy. She found a dark corner under some stairs, crawled into it, pulled the shirts and sheets up round her until she looked from a distance like a pile of discarded laundry and closed her eyes. Just for two minutes, that's all.

When she woke up, bright light was streaming in from a window high up on the stairs. She made herself stay perfectly still, and listened, and tried to think. At this time of day, in a well-run castle, where would everybody be? The chambermaids would be in the bedchambers, the kitchen staff would be fixing the midday meal, the laundry maids would be doing yesterday's washing before the chambermaids brought down today's. None of them would be using the backstairs. If anyone came and saw her, they'd know at once that she was an anomaly. But why would anyone come? They all had work to do somewhere else.

If there was an alternative, she couldn't think of it. From the pile of washing she pulled out a plain off-white linen smock, property of some ladies' maid from the third or fourth floor—now there was a group she hadn't taken account of; too late now, she was naked on the stairs, one foot in the smock. She hauled it up round her and knotted the belt, then clawed at her hair in the vain hope of getting it into some sort of order; realised that she'd just made another serious mistake; caught sight of a white mob cap in the pile of discarded washing, thanked God for saving her from her own stupidity, pulled the cap on, settled it firmly and tucked stray hair under the headband. The rest of the laundry she kicked into the shadows under the stairs; didn't matter if it was found and commented on; the laundry maid who'd left it there no longer existed. She noticed her filthy, grimy hands and skinned knuckles, tucked them into her sleeves. The hem of her smock covered her feet. Saved again.

The wonderful thing about ladies' maids is that they can be strangers, in service to guests. They can also go almost anywhere, because their mistresses can order them to do all manner of improbable things at inappropriate times—get me a drink of water, an apple, six yards of fine green silk, scissors (no, you stupid girl, *sharp* scissors, the *other* scissors), sixteen cheese scones, a half-bottle of the '06 Pirigouna, something to help me sleep, I want to see the doctor, my coachman, my dressmaker, the castellan, go and find where my useless lump of a husband's got to, quickly, *now*. More freedom than any other category of servant; more freedom than the fine lady herself, come to that. Being a ladies' maid is next best thing to being a man.

But not enough freedom to get her across the yard, through the gate and out the other side. For that she was going to have to spill blood, or be very clever, or athletic, or all three. She chose a doorway at random, climbed the stairs to the very top and barged open a long-closed door out on to the roof.

Having caught her breath, and making sure she kept her head down below the level of the parapet, she turned her mind to contemplation of the principles of military architecture. The aim of castle building is primarily to keep people out; but the same principles and functions do a very good job of keeping people in, which is why castles make such good prisons. Theoretically, she could spend the rest of the day getting hold of a rope and then, once night had fallen, lower herself down off the tower, swim the moat and run for it, if she still had the energy.

Alternatively—her mind went back to lectures at the Tactical Institute at Beal; fat, one-eyed General Tirza. The weakest part of any defensive structure is the man standing in front of it. There were two guards on the main gate, she could just see the tops of their helmets. The first one would be easy – walk up to him, say, "Excuse me," in a little-girl voice, then stab him in the eye as he bent forward to listen to her. But the second one was stationed on the other side of the gateway (fifteen feet? There or thereabouts). Lesson one: space is time. Even if she was wonderfully quick about killing the first guard, she had no guarantee of getting to his colleague before he had time to realise what had just happened, lift his shield and level his spear. True, she didn't actually want to fight him, she wanted to get past him and away, but—She did the mental geometry, and three times out of seven the numbers came out badly. And besides, stab the guard in the eye with what? She'd grown so used to having a knife up her sleeve that she'd forgotten it wasn't there any more. No, too many conditions precedent. Think of something else.

Then, in the distance (no, be precise; in the Great Hall, on the other side of the yard) someone started to play the violin. Her eyes opened wide, and then she laughed.

if you enjoyed
THE TWO OF SWORDS: VOLUME 1

look out for

SOUL OF THE WORLD

The Ascension Cycle

by

David Mealing

Three heroes must rise in a world on the brink of destruction in the first book of this epic fantasy trilogy that RT Book Reviews *called "an impressive fantasy debut with... a unique magic system sure to capture a fantasy readers attention"!*

It is a time of revolution. In the cities, food shortages stir citizens to riots against the crown. In the wilds, new magic threatens the dominance of the tribes. And on the battlefields, even the most brilliant commanders struggle in the shadow of total war. Three lines of magic must be mastered in order to usher in a new age, and three heroes must emerge.

***Sarine** is an artist on the streets of New Sarresant whose secret familiar helps her uncover bloodlust and madness where she expected only revolutionary fervor.*

***Arak'Jur** wields the power of beasts to keep his people safe, but his strength cannot protect them from war among themselves.*

***Erris** is a brilliant cavalry officer trying to defend New Sarresant from an enemy general armed with magic she barely understands.*

Each must learn the secrets of their power in time to guide their people through ruin. But a greater evil may be trying to stop them.

1

Sarine

Fontcadeu Green
The Royal Palace, Rasailles

"Throw!" came the command from the green.

A bushel of fresh-cut blossoms sailed into the air, chased by darts and the tittering laughter of lookers-on throughout the gardens.

It took quick work with her charcoals to capture the flowing lines as they moved, all feathers and flares. Ostentatious dress was the fashion this spring; her drab grays and browns would have stood out as quite peculiar had the young nobles taken notice of her as she worked.

Just as well they didn't. Her leyline connection to a source of *Faith* beneath the palace chapel saw to that.

Sarine smirked, imagining the commotion were she to sever her bindings, to appear plain as day sitting in the middle of the green. Rasailles was a short journey southwest of New Sarresant but may as well have been half a world apart. A public park, but no mistaking for whom among the public the green was intended. The guardsmen ringing the receiving ground made clear the requirement for a certain pedigree, or at least a certain display of wealth, and she fell far short of either.

She gave her leyline tethers a quick mental check, pleased to find them holding strong. No sense being careless. It was a risk coming here, but Zi seemed to relish these trips, and sketches of the nobles were among the easiest to sell. Zi had only just materialized in front of her, stretching like a cat. He made a show of it, arching his back, blue and purple iridescent scales glittering as he twisted in the sun.

She paused midway through reaching into her pack for a fresh sheet of paper, offering him a slow clap. Zi snorted and cozied up to her feet.

It's cold. Zi's voice sounded in her head. *I'll take all the sunlight I can get.*

"Yes, but still, quite a show," she said in a hushed voice, satisfied none of the nobles were close enough to hear.

What game is it today?

"The new one. With the flowers and darts. Difficult to follow, but I believe Lord Revellion is winning."

Mmm.

A warm glow radiated through her mind. Zi was pleased. And so for that matter were the young ladies watching Lord Revellion saunter up to take his turn at the line. She returned to a cross-legged pose, beginning a quick sketch of the nobles' repartee, aiming to capture Lord Revellion's simple confidence as he charmed the ladies on the green. He was the picture of an eligible Sarresant noble: crisp-fitting blue cavalry uniform, free-flowing coal-black hair, and neatly chiseled features, enough to remind her that life was not fair. Not that a child raised on the streets of the Maw needed reminding on that point.

He called to a group of young men nearby, the ones holding the flowers. They gathered their baskets, preparing to heave, and Revellion turned, flourishing the darts he held in each hand, earning himself titters and giggles from the fops on the green. She worked to capture the moment, her charcoal pen tracing the lines of his coat as he stepped forward, ready to throw. Quick strokes for his hair, pushed back by the breeze. One simple line to suggest the concentrated poise in his face.

The crowd gasped and cheered as the flowers were tossed. Lord Revellion sprang like a cat, snapping his darts one by one in quick succession. *Thunk. Thunk. Thunk. Thunk.* More cheering. Even at this distance it was clear he had hit more than he missed, a rare enough feat for this game.

You like this one, the voice in her head sounded. Zi uncoiled, his scales flashing a burnished gold before returning to blue and purple. He cocked his head up toward her with an inquisitive look. *You could help him win, you know.*

"Hush. He does fine without my help."

She darted glances back and forth between her sketch paper

and the green, trying to include as much detail as she could. The patterns of the blankets spread for the ladies as they reclined on the grass, the carefree way they laughed. Their practiced movements as they sampled fruits and cheeses, and the bowed heads of servants holding the trays on bended knees. The black charcoal medium wouldn't capture the vibrant colors of the flowers, but she could do their forms justice, soft petals scattering to the wind as they were tossed into the air.

It was more detail than was required to sell her sketches. But details made it real, for her as much as her customers. If she hadn't seen and drawn them from life, she might never have believed such abundance possible: dances in the grass, food and wine at a snap of their fingers, a practiced poise in every movement. She gave a bitter laugh, imagining the absurdity of practicing sipping your wine just so, the better to project the perfect image of a highborn lady.

Zi nibbled her toe, startling her. *They live the only lives they know,* he thought to her. His scales had taken on a deep green hue.

She frowned. She was never quite sure whether he could actually read her thoughts.

"Maybe," she said after a moment. "But it wouldn't kill them to share some of those grapes and cheeses once in a while."

She gave the sketch a last look. A decent likeness; it might fetch a half mark, perhaps, from the right buyer. She reached into her pack for a jar of sediment, applying the yellow flakes with care to avoid smudging her work. When it was done she set the paper on the grass, reclining on her hands to watch another round of darts. The next thrower fared poorly, landing only a single *thunk*. Groans from some of the onlookers, but just as many whoops and cheers. It appeared Revellion had won. The young lord pranced forward to take a deep bow, earning polite applause from across the green as servants dashed out to collect the darts and flowers for another round.

She retrieved the sketch, sliding it into her pack and withdrawing a fresh sheet. This time she'd sketch the ladies, perhaps, a show of the latest fashions for—

She froze.

Across the green a trio of men made way toward her, drawing curious eyes from the nobles as they crossed the gardens. The three of them stood out among the nobles' finery as sure as she would have done: two men in the blue and gold leather of the palace guard, one in simple brown robes. A priest.

Not all among the priesthood could touch the leylines, but she wouldn't have wagered a copper against this one having the talent, even if she wasn't close enough to see the scars on the backs of his hands to confirm it. Binder's marks, the by-product of the test administered to every child the crown could get its hands on. If this priest had the gift, he could follow her tethers whether he could see her or no.

She scrambled to return the fresh page and stow her charcoals, slinging the pack on her shoulder and springing to her feet.

Time to go? Zi asked in her thoughts.

She didn't bother to answer. Zi would keep up. At the edge of the green, the guardsmen patrolling the outer gardens turned to watch the priest and his fellows closing in. Damn. Her *Faith* would hold long enough to get her over the wall, but there wouldn't be any stores to draw on once she left the green. She'd been hoping for another hour at least, time for half a dozen more sketches and another round of games. Instead there was a damned priest on watch. She'd be lucky to escape with no more than a chase through the woods, and thank the Gods they didn't seem to have hounds or horses in tow to investigate her errant binding.

Better to move quickly, no?

She slowed mid-stride. "Zi, you know I hate—"

Shh.

Zi appeared a few paces ahead of her, his scales flushed a deep, sour red, the color of bottled wine. Without further warning her heart leapt in her chest, a red haze coloring her vision. Blood seemed to pound in her ears. Her muscles surged with raw energy, carrying her forward with a springing step that left the priest and his guardsmen behind as if they were mired in tar.

Her stomach roiled, but she made for the wall as fast as her feet could carry her. Zi was right, even if his gifts made her want to sick up the bread she'd scrounged for breakfast. The sooner she could get over the wall, the sooner she could drop her *Faith* tether and stop the priest tracking her binding. Maybe he'd think it no more than a curiosity, an errant cloud of ley-energy mistaken for something more.

She reached the vines and propelled herself up the wall in a smooth motion, vaulting the top and landing with a cat's poise on the far side. *Faith* released as soon as she hit the ground, but she kept running until her heartbeat calmed, and the red haze faded from her sight.

The sounds and smells of the city reached her before the trees cleared enough to see it. A minor miracle for there to be trees at all; the northern and southern reaches had been cut to grassland, from the trade roads to the Great Barrier between the colonies and the wildlands beyond. But the Duc-Governor had ordered a wood maintained around the palace at Rasailles, and so the axes looked elsewhere for their fodder. It made for peaceful walks, when she wasn't waiting for priests and guards to swoop down looking for signs she'd been trespassing on the green.

She'd spent the better part of the way back in relative safety. Zi's gifts were strong, and thank the Gods they didn't seem to register on the leylines. The priest gave up the chase with time enough for her to ponder the morning's games: the decadence, a hidden world of wealth and beauty, all of it a stark contrast to the sullen eyes and sunken faces of the cityfolk. Her uncle would tell her it was part of the Gods' plan, all the usual Trithetic dogma. A hard story to swallow, watching the nobles eating, laughing, and playing at their games when half the city couldn't be certain where they'd find tomorrow's meals. This was supposed to be a land of promise, a land of freedom and purpose—a New World. Remembering the opulence of Rasailles palace, it looked a lot like the old one to her. Not that she'd ever been across the sea, or anywhere in the colonies but here in New Sarresant. Still.

There was a certain allure to it, though.

It kept her coming back, and kept her patrons buying sketches whenever she set up shop in the markets. The fashions, the finery, the dream of something otherworldly almost close enough to touch. And Lord Revellion. She had to admit he was handsome, even far away. He seemed so confident, so prepared for the life he lived. What would he think of her? One thing to use her gifts and skulk her way onto the green, but that was a pale shadow of a real invitation. And that was where she fell short. Her gifts set her apart, but underneath it all she was still *her*. Not for the first time she wondered if that was enough. Could it be? Could it be enough to end up somewhere like Rasailles, with someone like Lord Revellion?

Zi pecked at her neck as he settled onto her shoulder, giving her a start. She smiled when she recovered, flicking his head.

We approach.

"Yes. Though I'm not sure I should take you to the market after you shushed me back there."

Don't sulk. It was for your protection.

"Oh, of course," she said. "Still, Uncle could doubtless use my help in the chapel, and it *is* almost midday..."

Zi raised his head sharply, his eyes flaring like a pair of hot pokers, scales flushed to match.

"Okay, okay, the market it is."

Zi cocked his head as if to confirm she was serious, then nestled down for a nap as she walked. She kept a brisk pace, taking care to avoid prying eyes that might be wondering what a lone girl was doing coming in from the woods. Soon she was back among the crowds of Southgate district, making her way toward the markets at the center of the city. Zi flushed a deep blue as she walked past the bustle of city life, weaving through the press.

Back on the cobblestone streets of New Sarresant, the lush greens and floral brightness of the royal gardens seemed like another world, foreign and strange. This was home: the sullen grays, worn wooden and brick buildings, the downcast eyes of the cityfolk as they went about the day's business. Here a gilded coach drew eyes and whispers, and not always from a place as benign as envy. She knew better than to court the attention of that sort—the hot-eyed men who glared at the nobles' backs, so long as no city watch could see.

She held her pack close, shoving past a pair of rough-looking pedestrians who'd stopped in the middle of the crowd. They gave her a dark look, and Zi raised himself up on her shoulders, giving them a snort. She rolled her eyes, as much for his bravado as theirs. Sometimes it was a good thing she was the only one who could see Zi.

As she approached the city center, she had to shove her way past another pocket of lookers-on, then another. Finally the press became too heavy and she came to a halt just outside the central square. A low rumble of whispers rolled through the crowds ahead, enough for her to know what was going on.

An execution.

She retreated a few paces, listening to the exchanges in the crowd. Not just one execution—three. Deserters from the army, which made them traitors, given the crown had declared war on the Gandsmen two seasons past. A glorious affair, meant to check a tyrant's expansion, or so they'd proclaimed in the colonial papers. All it meant in her quarters of the city was food carts diverted southward, when the Gods knew there was little enough to spare.

Voices buzzed behind her as she ducked down an alley, with a glance up and down the street to ensure she was alone. Zi swelled up, his scales pulsing as his head darted about, eyes wide and hungering.

"What do you think?" she whispered to him. "Want to have a look?"

Yes. The thought dripped with anticipation.

Well, that settled that. But this time it was her choice to empower herself, and she'd do it without Zi making her heart beat in her throat.

She took a deep breath, sliding her eyes shut.

In the darkness behind her eyelids, lines of power emanated from the ground in all directions, a grid of interconnecting strands of light. Colors and shapes surrounded the lines, fed by energy from the shops, the houses, the people of the city. Overwhelmingly she saw the green pods of *Life*, abundant wherever people lived and worked. But at the edge of her vision she saw the red motes of *Body*, a relic of a bar fight or something of that sort. And, in the center of the city square, a shallow pool of *Faith.* Nothing like an execution to bring out belief and hope in the Gods and the unknown.

She opened herself to the leylines, binding strands of light between her body and the sources of the energy she needed.

Her eyes snapped open as *Body* energy surged through her. Her muscles became more responsive, her pack light as a feather. At the same time, she twisted a *Faith* tether around herself, fading from view.

By reflex she checked her stores. Plenty of *Faith.* Not much *Body.* She'd have to be quick. She took a step back, then bounded forward, leaping onto the side of the building. She twisted away as she kicked off the wall, spiraling out toward the roof's overhang. Grabbing hold of the edge, she vaulted herself up onto the top of the tavern in one smooth motion.

Very nice, Zi thought to her. She bowed her head in a flourish, ignoring his sarcasm.

Now, can we go?

Urgency flooded her mind. Best not to keep Zi waiting when he got like this. She let *Body* dissipate but maintained her shroud of *Faith* as she walked along the roof of the tavern. Reaching the edge, she lowered herself to have a seat atop a window's overhang as she looked down into the square. With luck she'd avoid catching the attention of any more priests or other binders in the area, and that meant she'd have the best seat in the house for these grisly proceedings.

She set her pack down beside her and pulled out her sketching materials. Might as well make a few silvers for her time.